EVERY INCH A LEAR

Some of the Company

Left to right: LeRoy Schultz, William Webster, Richard Monette, David Stein, Mervyn "Butch" Blake, Patrick Christopher, Sean T. O'Hara, Janice Greene, Michael Benoit, Francois-Regis Klanfer, Alicia Jeffery, William Hutt, Berthold Carriere, Frank Maraden, Lorne Kennedy, Gregory Wanless, Vincent Berns, Ann Stuart, Maurice Good, Barrie Wood, Rodger Barton, Peter Ustinov, Douglas Rain, Robin Phillips.

Maurice Good

EVERY INCH
A LEAR

*A Rehearsal Journal of
"King Lear" with Peter Ustinov
and the Stratford Festival Company
Directed by Robin Phillips*

1982
SONO NIS PRESS
Victoria, British Columbia

Copyright © 1982 by Maurice Good

Canadian Cataloguing in Publication Data

Good, Maurice, 1932-
   Every inch a Lear

   A backstage view of the Stratford Festival's
1979 production of King Lear starring Peter
Ustinov.

ISBN 0-919203-26-4
   1. Shakespeare, William, 1564-1616.   King Lear.
2. Shakespeare, William, 1564-1616 — Dramatic
production.   3. Ustinov, Peter, 1921-   4. Good,
Maurice, 1932-   5. Stratford Festival (1979)
I. Title.
PR2819.G66   822.3'3   c82-091253-0

This book has been published with the assistance of
the Canada Council Block Grant Program.

Published by
SONO NIS PRESS
1745 Blanshard Street
Victoria, British Columbia v8w 2j8

Designed and printed in Canada by
MORRISS PRINTING COMPANY LTD.
Victoria, British Columbia

CONTENTS

LIST OF ILLUSTRATIONS

INTRODUCTION
by Peter Ustinov

By definition, rehearsals are periods of trial and error. They are confidential, paradoxical, and secretly industrious, a time when excessive concentration can explode into illogical giggles or spontaneous tears. What is said is ephemeral, often of little consequence, even if what is done will bear ultimate fruit. Much like Watergate. The tapes are, on the whole, dull, diffuse, and quite desperately unenlightening. They sound like rehearsals, which is what they are. This does not, of course, take into account the national and personal gifts of Maurice Good. National because he has an Irish mind; personal because he has a fine Irish mind.

Also his memory is better than mine, whether he is telling me what King Lear was actually supposed to have said at any given time, or what I actually did say, either at rehearsal or in performance. He is more actor than critic, since his humility before the magnitude of the task confronting those setting out to explore a masterpiece is only matched by his enthusiasm when the tiniest thing is achieved in a moment of communal clairvoyance. The Stratford of Robin Phillips produced the ideal climate for the physical and mental enjoyment of hard work, and the evocative pen of Maurice Good, with all the necessary ingredients of charity, cunning and intellectual honesty, make this essential fact abundantly clear.

While discipline was rigid, it was also strangely voluntary. It had, for me, all the advantages of drama school, luxury of time and the possibilities of profound research, without the disadvantages — puppy love and acne. After the rough approximations of the commercial theatre, with its necessary short-cuts to excellence and the journalistic deadlines, here was the possibility of an ample voyage of discovery into one's own resources in an untroubled sylvan setting.

Shakespeare, who seemed so archaic in school, so remote and so unfriendly, gradually thawed to reveal himself yet again as the most modern of playwrights. The ultimate revelation is his ever-present irony, hidden by centuries of misplaced piety, as pictures were hidden by varnish or the added fig-leaves of high-minded prudes in epochs of modest enlightenment.

No edition of Shakespeare's works is complete without the copious footnotes of those who loved him at times unwisely if forever too well. One phrase in my edition remained as a monument to all this exquisite pedantry. After a lengthy illumination of a textual detail by some professor, the editor threw the particular question open to debate once more with the immortal phrase "Kirschbaum, however, disagrees with this." No actor attempting a role like Lear can afford to ignore the ponderings of Kirschbaum, or indeed of those he disagrees with, but their opinions dwindle in importance as the practical man of the theatre struggles to liberate the writer from the crushing weight of fellow-travellers who entwine him with the same loving caresses the serpents lavished on Lacöon.

However intimidating the laws laid down by the learned may seem, the actor is compelled to realize, after weeks of rehearsal, that whereas many may have read *King Lear*, few indeed are those who have played him, and that those who play him, and have contact with an audience playing him, find themselves in uncharted waters, alone with the author.

Throughout the ages, grand, magniloquent, and careless actors have added thin shreds of prejudice to the general impression of what King Lear should be; a windswept old man of granite, outshouting the hurricane, outbelching the storm, outspitting the rain. At times, in history, the pill has been sugared to the extent that Cordelia has been allowed to survive, and indeed, marry Edgar, for the greater serenity of Britain and her people. The intrinsic foolishness of the old king has been accepted as a necessary adjunct to the nobility and folly of kingship, going out in style.

There is absolutely nothing in the text to justify this simplistic concept of royal behaviour, nor will sheer vocal power successfully dramatize the old codger's jealousy of the elements.

The key which gives utter consistency to the seemingly wild inconsistencies of the text is senility. The sad aspect of senility is that it is, in itself, an inconsistent state. There are moments of lucidity, moments of control, among the catnaps and the rages, and the same man has to live with the decisions he made during lapses of concentration, and he is usually too stubborn by nature and by accident of birth to reverse those decisions. Second childhood is as subject to tantra as the first. Lear wants to give up his cake, and eat it. A relegation of power in unimportant matters to have more time for hunting, shooting and fishing, before the heights of enjoyment are snuffed out altogether. But you cannot create a vacuum without inviting others to fill it.

If Goneril, Regan, and indeed Cordelia, have never before shown certain sides of their characters, it is because they have never been given that opportunity. With an active despot in charge of an influential family, the others tend to lie low and bide their time, showing spirit perhaps at random moments, but never being at each other's throats.

The play starts at the moment of Lear's resignation, the creation of the vaccum, which the old man thinks he can still fill in an emergency. In fact, he attempts to legislate for such an eventuality, but an open oyster will never be quite the same as it was within the shell. There is no way back, however much he struggles, cajoles, threatens and weeps.

His death begins on the heath. He uses up vital stores of energy before the final sprint, not in order to make more noise than the elements, which is in any case an absurd ambition, but in order to conclude grand alliances, no longer with France or Burgundy, but with thunder and lightning, whose reactions can be imagined, just as the outcome of private games can be imagined by a playing child. Once the fever passes, the old king finds release in the general belief that he is mad. He is, of course, sane for the first time in the play; not merely sane, but wise; not merely wise, but visionary. And yet the pretence of sanity is such a burden on his slim resources that he can only enjoy the fruits of his sanity by relapsing into the negligence of lunacy.

One after another, he recognizes Gloucester, Cordelia and Kent, but does so discreetly, as though not wishing to reveal his sanity, and emerge irrevocably from his refuge. With Cordelia, he expresses tenderness and even a certain jocularity, which was always in his nature, and at the end, the stamina runs out. 'Had I your tongues and eyes, I'd use them so / That heaven's vault should crack.' He no longer has voice or sight. The last few notes, diminuendo from barely audible to silence, are the climax of the play, the high point of poignancy, prepared for by over four hours of every other kind of emotion.

As an illustration of Shakespeare's diabolical sense of irony, to which I made allusion before, I cannot quote a better example than Lear's contemplation of the naked Edgar on the heath. 'Consider him well . . . Thou ow'st the worm no silk, the beast no hide, the sheep no wool, the cat no perfume.' Obviously, as Lear approaches the unwashed fellow, the three visible attributes are expended first, leaving to the last the beastly natural aroma which comes within range of his nostrils, and causes him to recoil. The public reacts with laughter. If this were not the intention, the order would be different. The intention is as clear, the technique as perfect, as though the lines had been written by Noël Coward, even if the canvas on which the delicious details appear is cosmic, embracing the whole of humanity rather than a civilized drawing-room.

The sound of laughter in *Lear* strikes some critical opinion as being as irreverant as a guffaw in a cathedral, and it caused a rumour to spread that I had "played Lear for laughs." I submit that this is an impossibility, and would be a stupidity even were it possible. What is possible, and even necessary, is to play it truthfully, according to Shakespeare's clues and an observation of the quirks of old men. If the public laughs, so much the better; if it fails on a given night, it is no great loss. All depends on the temper of a particular audience. There is all the difference in the world between this and "playing for laughs."

Laughter humanizes tragedy, making it poignant. A tragedy which only impresses, but does not move, is as outdated as a pterodactyl. Today tears need laughter as never before. Absurdity permeates political and private initiations, and the public has attained a pitch of refinement to make the boldest uses of contrast both acceptable and even consistent. *Lear* is a contemporary play if ever there was one.

If I seem to be dogmatic, and even a little arrogant, it is due to the fact that I was privileged to marinate for a while in the juices so lyrically and wittily described by Maurice Good, and that I was privileged to play in this monumental yet intimate play, led by a director of genius and surrounded by actors and actresses whose generosity matched their inspiration, before an audience by now typical of Stratford, Ontario, at once sensitive and eager, pristine and intelligent. Every performance began as an initiation, and ended as a shared experience.

I have no right to suggest what others carried away from the theatre: I can only say that my visit to this secular temple was one of the great experiences of my life, one for which I will be ever grateful, more especially now that my memory is fed by the loving yet mordant comment which makes up this excellent book, which has the added virtue of making us all seem a little more Irish than most of us have any right to be.

PETER USTINOV, *1980*

AUTHOR'S PREFACE
AND ACKNOWLEDGEMENTS

I've often thought that an inside view of a major masterpiece in rehearsal by a major ensemble, free from indulgence of show-business chit-chat, is something that many people who love the theatre will welcome and share. There isn't much, or any, gossip here. It wasn't my intention, however tempting, to play Boswell to the Doctor Johnson of Peter Ustinov. As he is so well aware himself, there were a great many others at work on our play with talents sometimes as funny — almost — and often as wise as his own.

Most of this book is about the extraordinary collective achievement of our entire Stratford Company of *King Lear*, as actors, as technicians, working together in rehearsal. There's more, also, in these pages, about my thoughts on how they did it, on other *Lears* I've seen or in which I've acted, and even more about the story of *Lear* itself. The job of any company of actors doing *Lear* is to tell the story, and we certainly did that: and in doing it well, I'm sure, we did a great deal more.

Being an Irishman I've something of an inclination to write as I talk, and being also a member of the Stratford Acting Company I fell into the role of storyteller. A self-appointed chronicler though I was at the start of this work, in the course of writing it I was honoured (as recipient of a Tyrone Guthrie Award) in becoming an accredited one. After hoofing my way half-way round the globe on three continents, and, most recently, from coast-to-coast on one of them as actor-director, playing many of the ripest roles in classical drama (ancient and modern), I found myself faced, at Stratford, with the second understudy duty I've ever undertaken in my life. In this instance to be Stand-By for Peter Ustinov. It's been gloriously worth doing, for many reasons, not least of which was gaining a further external perspective on this play, and embracing the impulse which has forced me to tackle this work.

This book is meant to be a special gift, I hope, for actors. Also, it's intended for those who have seen our *Lear* and are curious, and want some record of how we did it. Also, it may be especially valued by those who saw our *Lear* and loved it, and even those who saw it and didn't. These were few, but they were there. Better still, it may be some consolation for those many who never managed to get in. But most of all this book is for those (and these are legion) who have seen some other *Lear* of the past, have some hope of watching a *Lear* of the future, or simply, those who prefer to stay at home and read the play. These last are the customers we, who work in theatre, woo most ardently. I'd like to think, some day, that my words may lure some listeners for *Lear* into our theatre, or any theatre. There might be a better way to spend an evening, especially a long one, but I can't think of any.

It's worthwhile pursuing Peter Ustinov's opening comment. Rehearsals are, indeed, however amusing and often exciting, no more than rehearsals. But my rehearsal journal strives neither to be too summary nor tiresomely off the main point — which is, in fact, all of the learnings, risks, feelings, explorations and retreats, certainties, hesitancies, and especially the frequent failures which lead our actors so often to success. I've aimed to open the doors fully at last, and let our customers in on this adventure. My objective has been Demonstration, rather than Explanation. My main task was compression.

The craft of those of us who work in theatre is intensely collaborative. And the raw material from which this book is fashioned, and without which it couldn't exist, was the day-by-day commitment of all of those who worked on our *Lear*. My acknowledgements of all their contribution is both a duty and a pleasure.

Very personal thanks are due to my friend Robin Skelton for his advice and most enthusiastic commentary on my text, guideline editing of earlier pages and final decisions on all of them; to Barry MacGregor for his invaluable practical help; and most of all to Susan Malley, my very gifted Editor for the entire book, on which she worked with such professional diligence.

The text used in our production of *King Lear* is *The Arden Shakespeare*, published in paperback by Methuen & Co. Ltd., London, U.K., edited by Kenneth Muir, and to which reference may be made by Act and Scene numbers given throughout my own text to indicate what part of the play is under work or discussion.

I am especially grateful to Peter Ustinov for his generous Introduction, and for the cartoons of the cast of *Lear* which he drew during their work together; for the rehearsal photographs I am grateful to Jane Edmunds, and for the production stills to Robert Ragsdale. Finally, I am deeply indebted to the tolerance, good-will and supportive approval of our Artistic Director, Robin Phillips, and the entire Stratford Company Cast, Stage Crew, Stage-Management and Production Staff for *King Lear*, to whom this work is collectively and most gratefully dedicated. This is their story, and I was proud to be with them during one of the most challenging times of my life.

MAURICE GOOD, 1980

ACKNOWLEDGEMENTS

King Lear by William Shakespeare

Directed by Robin Phillips
Designed by Daphne Dare
Music by Berthold Carriere
Lighting by Michael J. Whitfield

King Lear	PETER USTINOV
Goneril, his daughter	DONNA GOODHAND
Regan, his daughter	MARTI MARADEN
Cordelia, his daughter	INGRID BLEKYS
Earl of Kent	JIM MCQUEEN
Lear's Fool	WILLIAM HUTT
Earl of Gloucester	DOUGLAS RAIN
Edgar, his son	RODGER BARTON
Edmund, his bastard son	RICHARD MONETTE
King of France	EDWARD EVANKO
Duke of Burgundy	JOHN WOJDA
Duke of Cornwall	WILLIAM WEBSTER
Duke of Albany	FRANK MARADEN
Oswald, steward to Goneril	TOM WOOD
Old Man	MERVYN BLAKE
Doctor	ROD BEATTIE
Knight	REX SOUTHGATE
Servants to Cornwall	PATRICK CHRISTOPHER
	DAVID STEIN
	JOHN WOJDA
Gentleman	PATRICK CHRISTOPHER
Officer to Cordelia	GREGORY WANLESS
Captain, under Edmund's command	STEWART ARNOTT
French Messenger	GEORDIE JOHNSON
Herald	CHRISTOPHER BLAKE
Officer	LORNE KENNEDY

ATTENDANTS, KNIGHTS, OFFICERS, SERVANTS, SOLDIERS: Stewart Arnott, Christopher Blake, Patrick Christopher, William Copeland, Janice Greene, David Holmes, Alicia Jeffery, Geordie Johnson, Lorne Kennedy, John Lambert, William Merton Malmo, Sean T. O'Hara, Bob Ouelette, Pamela Redfern, LeRoy Schultz, David Stein, Barbara Stewart, Hank Stinson, Michael Totzke, Gregory Wanless, Colleen Winton, Barrie Wood.

UNDERSTUDIES: Stewart Arnott (Edgar); Christopher Blake (Duke of Cornwall); Patrick Christopher (Earl of Gloucester); Janice Greene (Goneril); Alicia Jeffery (Regan); Geordie Johnson (Duke of Albany), Lorne Kennedy (Edmund); Bob Ouelette (French Messenger); LeRoy Schultz (Knight to Lear); Rex Southgate (Earl of Kent); David Stein (Duke of Burgundy); Barbara Stewart (Cordelia); Michael Totzke (Herald); Gregory Wanless (Oswald, Doctor); John Wojda (Lear's Fool); Barrie Wood (King of France).

ORCHESTRA: Conductor, Berthold Carriere; Flute, Earl Riener; Oboe, Tony Toth; Clarinet, Shannon Purves-Smith; Trumpet I, James Spragg; Trumpet II, Alan Ridgway; French Horn, Randy Patterson; Trombone, Susan Trethewey; Keyboard, Berthold Carriere; Cello, David Hirschorn; Double Bass, Arthur Lang; Percussion, Robert Comber, Michael Wood.

Fights staged by Patrick Crean, Fencing Master; Voice Coach, Lloy Coutts; Movement Coach, Jeffrey Guyton; Stage Manager, Vincent Berns; Assistant Stage Manager, Michael Benoit; Personal Assistant to the Artistic Director, Ann Stewart; Assistant to the Director, François Regis-Klanfer; Literary Manager, Urjo Kareda; Researcher and Archivist for King Lear Production, Dan Ladell; Technical Director, Kent McKay.

Wardrobe and Wig Department Co-ordinator, Sue LePage. Costumes made in the Festival Workshops, and executed by: Cynthia MacLennan (Head Cutter); Renato La Selva, (Men's Tailoring); Enid Larson, Bruce Mallet-Paret, Wendy Wilkinson, assisted by: Lenabell Campbell, Vera Catania, Clara Eusebi, Theodora Gilliard, Marrianne La Selva. Buyer, Sharon McMorran; Wardrobe Mistress, Pauline Harrison; Wig Mistress, Doreen Freeman; Wig Master, Paul Elliot; Millinery by Jan Shipway; Jewellery by Gayle Tribick; Painting by Lisa Hughes; Dyeing by Buffy Bailey and Karen Matthews.

PROPERTIES made in the Festival Workshops under the direction of Roy Brown, assisted by: Frank Holte, Joy Allan, Beverly May Adam, Kenneth Dubblestyne, Georges Kamm, Stewart Robertson, Lorraine Senecal, Pauline Turner.

SCENERY constructed by: Allan Jones (Head Carpenter) with Neil Cheney, Ben Keller, Walter Sugden, Byron Williams. Draftsman and Assistant to the Technical Director, Graham Likeness. Assistant to the Lighting Designer, Harry Frehner; Stage Carpenter, Simon Palvetzian. Master Electrician, Bruno Hacquebard. Property Master, John Hoodless. Sound: Roger Gaskell. Stage Crew: Mark Fisher, Jeremy Lach, Martin Penner, Les Spits, Harry Van Keuren.

The Tyrone Guthrie Awards Committee: Secretary to The Foundation, Frances Tompkins; Colleen Stephenson, Vincent Berns, Eric Donkin, Lewis Gordon, Jim McQueen, Robin Phillips, William Needles. Assistant to the Artistic Director, Production and Casting, Margaret Ryerson.

FURTHER ACKNOWLDGEMENTS: Jack Hutt, Thomas Hooker, Harvey Chusid, Gerald Corner, Shelagh Hewitt, Peter Moss, Graham Newell, Gary Thomas, Polly Bohdanetzky, Michael Maher, Joanne Corrigan, John Pennoyer, Peter Roberts, Christopher Wheeler, Anne Selby, Leonard McHardy, Bryan Grimes, Elaine Jones, Betty Ross, Louise Swan, Larry Appel, Marguerite Pletsch, Louise Ellis, Mel Frazer, Phyllis DeVeulle, Laurie Freeman, Ed Doadt, Ron Davies, Sheldon Kasman, Carol Holland, Michael Bolubash, Alan Mann, Valerie Holland, Lesley Belland and Marion Isherwood.

FOUNDER: Tom Patterson. The late Sir Tyrone Guthrie, Artistic Director of the first Stratford Shakespeare Festival.

EVERY INCH A LEAR

For All the Actors of This Lear
Lears Past
and Lears to Come

A FIRST LITTLE LOOK

Stratford, Ontario, is a prosperous town of twenty-seven thousand people, with a lot of light industry. It's an attractive and tough town; people work hard here. Few work harder than the hundred or so members of the Stratford Festival Company. At the height of the season, with five to sometimes six performances at our three theatres (Festival, Avon, Third Stage), we play to a total audience of almost six thousand people in one day — who crowd into the parks and streets from noon to midnight.

A few days before rehearsals for *King Lear* began, with Peter Ustinov as Lear, and directed by Robin Phillips, a tornado slashed a swathe through townships and farmlands a mere twenty-five miles away. Three people were killed and one hundred and fifty injured.

The first morning of rehearsal is windy still, with an ominously clouded sky. A sense of Fall, prematurely and unmistakably a part of the mood, tends the first full Company call in the Festival rehearsal hall. The mood is reflected among the cast, assembled in a large tight square of chairs — tense, expectantly concentrated.

Robin Phillips, promptly at 11 a.m., quietly (he is always intrinsically quiet) turning to the first person on his right, instructs the company to name themselves and, in one sentence, suggest what the play means and then, as a bonus, relate its action. On completion of the exercise, by the time he hears last from Peter Ustinov on his left, he expects to have learned the entire story of *Lear*.

Younger company members blanch but steel their nerves to match the seeming nonchalance of their seniors. "My name is ——, I think the play is about human responsibility, and — the story starts in Lear's court." "My name is ——," (Phillips alertly leaning forward, watching, listening, with immense keenness as though he knew nobody). The cast responds, the plot emerges confusedly. "We've skipped an important bit, I *think*." "My name is —— I'm sorry, I'm completely lost." Fifty voices round and we've hardly ended the opening scene, though some have jumped ahead to the storm sequences, and some assert that they've read the play only the night before.

When the turn comes to Peter Ustinov: "My name is . . . (baffled pause), and the play is about senility." Under the laugh (there have been some other mild laughs already) the pulse of the Company is

3

beating out the certainty that he means just what he says. Then: "My name is Robin Phillips, and I don't know what the play is about." But we know that he already knows much, and that he is committed to knowing more, and that the Company and he will help each other in discovering more.

Bluntly, Phillips informs us that the play "happened here." Amassed on the table beside him are accumulated books of reference, including much of Thomas Hardy. He later quotes briefly from 'Tess', and 'The Mayor of Casterbridge', which he suggests as prime sources — "just the right *feeling*," for this *Lear* is to be mid-Victorian. He flicks out his initial ideas on the play, guidelines steel-spined enough to sound like orders. He has had a "lot of thought" on its construction. It will require, from everyone, "immense, extra-ordinary concentration." Phillips' productions, as all present know, always demand that. The play itself is merely the tip of the iceberg, indicating the size of the thoughts beneath. He finds the text "strange — very strange." (A pause.) "Not difficult, but simple," with amazing adjustments from verse to prose. We will do it with one interval, uphill all the way to the intermission, and then steadily downhill, with always "lots of thought and concentration."

Costume drawings by Daphne Dare, Head of Design, are passed round. We learn that the "nasties" are in black to red, or black to green, with sleek black for most and little other basic colour, but an occasional "gash in the raw flesh," which is "more dangerous, more passionate" than the obviously bloody colours. There will be few warmer tones other than some rare candlelit glows, as in Cordelia's costumes, "an attempt to shine a little in the slime." The slime, it seems, is to be quintessential, a green slime relieved only by some tentative blues at the opening, as in the costumes for the King of France and his retinue, which will envelop us with some comfort towards the conclusion. I can already feel the calm of that blue, of day and the light, a quattrocento dawning.

So, design throughout can be effectively caught in images of the Crimean War — Florence Nightingale. "Does anyone share my fascination with this period of ... confrontation?", asks Phillips. Many present do. Previously, similarly accoutred productions, this year's *Love's Labour's Lost*, last year's *Winter's Tale*, the earlier *Measure For Measure* have testified to that era, or a little later. We begin to understand why the Victorian period can be so right for *Lear*. He asks us to think beyond the heavily romanticised surface, beyond (yet always including) "the false eyelashes and hair just washed ... It's just when it starts to look a *bit* more raw *at times*."

4

Phillips is adroit at ironic understatement, and actors are sensitive to this.

He is passing round books with, one feels, very carefully selected illustrations, ("Don't change the page as you go round"): some classic idyllic poses, girls out of Ingres, incandescent, unearthly, beautiful; Disraeli — photographed — ("something terribly real about perspiration"); interspersed savage cartoons, the beggared and the crippled, satirizing mismanagement in the Crimean War: ("Of course, the *camera* helped a lot"). The images hurtle towards us. This isn't pretty. It's easier to smell what it was like.

His point is rigidly clear. Audiences since the beginnings of photography, even still photography as in Matthew Brady's masterpieces of the Civil War, could no longer, as they do even now with earlier periods, stand back sheltered, to be cosily awed by stately courtliness. The lens, even before the movies, hits us with the truth. (Is *that* what he means by "confrontation"?) We are to have Civil War style costumes for the "military chaps" which are "slightly more personal" than their British counterparts. And inescapably, the green slime will be in the costumes as well as trickling down the walls. Also: "We'll corset all the 'Fellahs'. Let 'em suffer with the girls. We'll see what happens to the ribcages, then, in those long speeches. It'll be interesting on the 'heath' when things begin to get — shrill."

One feels that the actors believe in him. (One might add that they have to.) The look of the show is to embrace the "prettyfied *and* the harrowed." We are regaled with references to Elizabeth Barrett and Robert Browning; claustrophobic images of walls *and* windows wall-papered over; the inner cruelty of family; the lace and lavender; the "*real* starchiness." Collars welded, grown into the shape of neck and face, soon limp with daily, ever-present sweat. Before the dawn of dry-cleaning. Very little air in the interiors: "Those candles and oil-lamps have taken it all." Small problems like measles, now taken in our stride, then lethal. One wonders how 'lethal' other things may prove. Marti Maraden's costume (as Regan) "if unbuttoned" — as Robin informed the costume cutters — steam would, indeed *should* rise."

And now: "Let's have a little read." The cast is cautioned that "what you think is more important than what you say." As the lines pass, Phillips' head is dipped into his text, the devouring brown eyes the crux of his curve of concentration. This first read-through runs uninterruptedly to the end of Act II, Scene IV. We've stopped just before the storm scene (Shakespeare's Act III) which, I suspect, he has already decided is to be the Intermission. A slight problem:

"I've a feeling the first half is, very probably, all at night, which will mean evening gear." His glance is to Daphne Dare.

There's some discussion then on equating the first scene in Lear's court (I.i) with Windsor party games. Desperate tales, from those not so well-placed in the hierarchy, are mixed with family charades. Amongst the casually sweatered, the occasional odd multi-million dollar heirloom. Princess Margaret on one of her 'with-it' kicks. Levity mixed with unease. Perhaps, someone suggests, a few farting corgies. The enforcement of the games: "We'll play, but with only half commitment." But, suddenly, Cordelia refuses to play. The cast will work towards this 'attempt' at an easy atmosphere. A younger cast member suggests that it's hard, now, to understand such absolute power in monarchy.

Then Ustinov, who has been heard from wryly already (calculatedly subdued), glintingly inserts some thoughts on Idi Amin. A ripple of alertness. He follows with an intrinsically British anecdote: his *style* is all for the moment, any description of it rash, the story apocryphal, an old military chap's two best dictates on life: "One was to thank God you're English." And the other was *"Everyone can help."* A pause, before Ustinov concludes, "Nobody was sure what *that* meant."

Through the laughter, there is the sense of getting into gear; the whole cast knows it is helping in this work on *Lear*. Phillips sticks to his point that to say "no" at Lear's court takes a lot of courage, to the point where "it is almost incomprehensible." Greg Wanless tells of a somewhat deaf Stanley Holloway at the Shaw Festival in a back-stage line-up responding to Her Majesty with "I beg your pardon," obliging Her Majesty to a reprise of her lengthy compliments. Ustinov contributes a story of "an early phase in that entente cordial," an encounter of his mother (who had designed a production at Covent Garden) with Queen Mary. He renders us an hilarious female dualogue of the Queen and a Courtly-companion, the sounds perfection yet totally incomprehensible, while his mother, silent, follows instructions not to seek the eye of royalty but to wait until the royal eye should seek out hers. The incomprehensible dialogue reaches her, stops. Very long pause — nothing uttered — and then sudden departure of royal party.

Phillips, in a seeming non-sequitur, but, in fact, tenacious to his theme, cements the argument. He speaks of the desperation of "non-wills", the "domestic idiocy of the court" with which *Lear* begins, and its growth beyond this limitation as it gains stature, beyond the merely domestic, to those final colossal images of rights and wrongs.

6

Tom Wood wonders how weird it is for Lear to "give away all." Ustinov says, "No — he isn't abdicating." The political question of inheritance is raised by others, and it is agreed that the crisis initially doesn't move beyond a struggle for power within a family, and that the two traditional "wicked two sisters" are motivated by concern about housekeeping logistics. Lear is giving up his job of state, passing the buck, yet hanging on to title and a hundred followers. With Cordelia discarded, his abrupt choice to sojourn 'by monthly course' with the two married daughters smells like big trouble. How long before you put the old man into a small apartment!

Ustinov tells of the aging, slow-expiring Franco, attached to his heart and lung machines, querulously asking of a daughter softfooting it by his bed, "What's that noise?" "It's the Spanish People, Father, come to say good-bye." "Oh! ... Where are they going?" Old age, especially powerful old age, won't let go. Nor will Phillips. Resuming his justification of Victorian rather than Saxon locale, he "*Can't* accept all that Bronze Age remoteness, of which we now know so little, those early Brits in blue, rushing round in woad." Head craning down into his script, he picks out phrases which even in Shakespeare's time were anachronistic: "Casement of my closet!" (an incredulous inflection in this), "Foppery of the ..." "... Bo-Peep!" For the play to move from domestic to enormous themes it can't all happen in some remote landscape. He reminds us: "We've just had a tornado," (apparently he was out somewhere quite near it) "and as it got darker, and darker, and darker, I thought — I thought — it was *clearly* the end of the world".

A long pause. Then, before we have "another little look," Phillips asks the actors to consider if there are any "*mental* clouds" passing over them during a lengthy speech. Or any speech. "Just check to see if you have a cloud." There is some general talk of that threat of change gradually building up to the second half. One can almost hear Phillips' mind jump around the whole perimeter of the play.

Turning to Ustinov he asks: "Any sense of history in Lear's first speech about crawling towards death?" "No," replies Ustinov promptly, "But lots of self-pity. He wants to be admired for making fun of age, striking the deliberate note of gloom to make people protest ... Oh — I'm a realist. ...!" Phillips is "amazed" at the number of references to eyesight and nature.

A short dialogue between them follows. A great deal to do with power, not only in kings, but also in immigration officers, lawyers, doctors, boy scout and girl scout leaders, and Artistic Directors. Phillips pulls the talk back to the Gloucester sub-plot. We're back in court, the Victorian court, and the terror of which way judgement will go. Cordelia was "desperately brave to say 'No'."

After lunch some courtly furniture is set into the readers' square. The first scene (I.i) is read again among the furniture so that Phillips can see as well as hear. It is loudly played, the actors demonstrating that they can at the very least be heard. He immediately asks for a second try. This time all he wants to see are "smiles — or the opposite", contained in "tight shot" stance. "If you waver, you're out of frame." Having been an actor himself, on stage and screen, he frequently uses technical film terms in acting or direction. One remembers, often, his other fascination with film, his ambitions for a Stage One studio development at Stratford and, ultimately, movies of the best Stratford productions, the first of which may be shot next year.

As the work starts again (I.i), muted, reduced, he watches, occasionally smiling a childlike smile, listening relentlessly. Then, as they finish, he goes forward and sits, perched typically on mid-thigh, his commentary inaudible except to those within touching distance. Some actors crane in to hear. Few can. It's a tight conspiratorial group. Some words float out: "*This* lot," (everyone *other* than Lear) "is telling me so much about *him*." A sudden shout: "Now *that's* shouting . . ." Muted again: "Give me the atmosphere of a room you've known for years". More actors move in closer. Ustinov, voice pitched in easy middle range, suddenly confusedly 'Ga-Ga': "What *day* is today?"

Phillips returns to his seat, brightly tossing a comment to those so long out of earshot: "We're only sniffing." They try again. Ustinov more and more confused (as Lear) as to which is Albany, which is Cornwall. Edward Evanko (King of France) wonders at the context of his role, and that of the Duke of Burgundy in 19th-century England. Is this a problem? Phillips suggests that the problem, if there is one, is solved. "Stonehenge doesn't make any sense at all." The rehearsal is over.

SNIFFING THINGS OUT

The larger part of the cast is working elsewhere today, as there are matinées at all three Stratford theatres, so it's a tiny group: Phillips with Douglas Rain (Gloucester), Bill Hutt (The Fool), and Ustinov, who arrives as the double cannon booms outside announcing the start of a show in the theatre downstairs. "Aaah — what's that?" It's a formidable explosion, especially when you hear it for the first time. "The Mounties get their man?" Ustinov makes even a cliché joke richly funny. Phillips gets straight to work, asks him "How much do I have to see eye to eye with you, Peter?" Ustinov demurs, relaxing into his first cigar, hands waving affably out from the large belly: "So far — merely sniffing things out. It's *difficult* — playing a very old man." They are already adopting each other's terms.

How "revolutionary" is Ustinov's "head," asks Phillips, about the play. "Not very." (One wonders at that.) It's agreed, however, that one shouldn't be afraid of *anything* "useful." Ustinov has recently seen Othello in Arabic, played to Tunesian soldiers. Iago let them in on the plot. Played it like Moliére — got a lot of laughs, as Othello did, also, in consequence. "Especially when he spots the handkerchief." There is basic agreement that Lear is dotty at the start, with judgment gone, and the play shows him regaining it. A heading in the Festival Brochure subtitles the production 'the Education of a King'. We're not to have the traditionally wicked two sisters. It's a "housekeeping problem." Physically not up to many challenges, this Lear; which is why, in the opening scene, Ustinov says he may well fall asleep. Phillips cites recent comment on the aging Diefenbaker, and Ustinov tells a story of the very elderly Churchill arriving late for a dull debate, catching a remark on him being ga-ga from twenty yards distance as he finally settles into his front bench seat: "Aaaaaaand — they say he's *deaf*, too!" Peter's Churchill is as Churchillian as Churchill himself.

Bill Hutt (the previous Lear at Stratford) thinks that the Fool also is "getting awfully old." Douglas Rain points out that Gloucester may easily be younger than himself, but they settle for sixty, for the time being. Is the Fool older than Lear? Hutt: "Very possibly — but we can't *both* be shaking all night." Ustinov: "Yes ... Boy ... do keep still!" Hutt: "It's only my little finger, Lad ... You're quivering all over."

9

Phillips, referring to Ustinov's ability to do any accent in the world, wonders about Voice, which "changes so much depending on who you are." True. During the morning we've heard at least twenty, including half the unit on a film-stage in Calcutta, a plaintive female Cockney pensioner, a calypso-singing revolutionary: "Yes — she's my girl — and she gets no fun — only my-ay Machine-gun." He also gives us Brando in his UNICEF appeal on Japanese TV. Significantly, Ustinov is himself very active on behalf of UNICEF, but he makes no mention of this, or his recent audience with the Pope to discuss fund-raising. I'd like to have been a fly on the papal ceiling for such an encounter.

Phillips is still insistent on the question of Voice, and Ustinov promises we'll "have a smell around that." Hutt, usually so rotund of voice and presence, is already looking "terribly thin." Audiences have extraordinary expectations about appearances (says Phillips); they run tapes in their minds of what they've already seen and heard. Ustinov speaks of Lear's probably "large stride," but Phillips pursues the sound of Lear. He tells us that when talking to Ustinov of Olivier (as Lear, apparently), "I remember there was something . . . your face was not 'up front'." The something extraordinary will be found, its look, its sound. We won't want to know what Ustinov is thinking, explains Phillips, "Just *do* it! Try *that*. Go *there* . . . You'll have colossal support from the Company." Douglas Rain says he thinks Lear almost a second father to Gloucester; Ustinov, agreeing, finds something "very touching in the credulity" of Gloucester, Kent, Cordelia. A long pause. Urjo Kareda, Director and Literary Manager of the Festival, sits silently in the background.

"Is Lear cruel? Is he cruel at all?" asks Phillips. "No," says Ustinov, "it's just a series of snap decisions. Like Churchill at Yalta — it wasn't Stalin did that, you know, it was Churchill — who said that Poland must take two steps to the left, placing countless people in misery." "But is he *aware*?" insists Phillips. Because, as Ustinov tells the story, it "reads as being aware." "No," responds Ustinov instantly, "It's just that as the King you have to shut your mind." There is a slight pause, and Phillips (it was something he was after) concludes: "I feel better now. I saw your face do something."

Turning to Hutt and Ustinov he then says we should find out something about "where *these two* are at." It's apparent very quickly that with these two actors, as Fool and Lear, no joke is ever really going to end (I.iv). Both achieve, sitting at the table, incredible physical alertness in the head. They read the scene slowly, each hanging on to the text, two old dogs worrying at the same bone. They emanate generations of word-game and crossword expertise. Even when the dialogue runs out they improvise on. Hutt: "You can't do *that* one again, we had 'Intransigence' *last* week!" Ustinov: (with a playful slapping gesture) "You're my portable Sphinx!"

They move on to the scenes of encounters of Gloucester and Lear (II.iv). 'Who put my man in the stocks?' Ustinov: "He keeps coming back to that — he's forgotten each time he asks it." Phillips suggests he may decide to sit absent-mindedly beside Kent in the stocks. "*On* him, if you like," rejoins Ustinov.

Suddenly, they return to the earlier Lear/Fool exchange in that pre-storm scene (I.iv). 'Dear Heaven, keep me in patience', (this tried as a quick aside to the Fool), 'let me not be mad'. Phillips thinks there is something "*very* extraordinary" here. Extraordinary

Mr. William Hutt: The Fool
"A Portable Sphinx"

is a word he often uses, the extraordinary thing being that he invariably uses it when something extraordinary is already or should be there. Ustinov, meanwhile, is concerned with that "sane terror of madness" that perhaps others (in *Lear*) may recognize though not himself. One importance of this Lear's Fool is that he's an assurance of sanity. But the Fool doesn't always succeed. 'Be my horses ready!': Ustinov, thinking himself forward in the play as Lear, sends him off at a gallop, momentarily eased by action. But as he feels the horse move familiarly under him, once again it is "something known, not reassuring — in his mind he is still in the pits."

WEDNESDAY, AUGUST 15TH *concluded*

THE STORM WITHIN

After the lunch break Phillips sends someone to find Ustinov, probably lost somewhere in the building. He dwells on the morning's discoveries. I assure him that I, also, felt a certain jolt when Ustinov spoke of the King as doing what he must do. Phillips states, "I didn't sleep much last night, I'll tell you." We know it's the truth; his energy level and commitment when working are unrelenting.

When Ustinov settles in with the small group a theme is quickly established. Self-pity, in Lear, is the point of surrender from which the play begins. Defeated, at the start, by his own weakness, Lear makes the journey outwards from it. He seeks the guts to have anger, which can release a capacity for action. As Phillips puts it: "The fight to make our mind get control of our heart." They are together now, linked in objectives. Ustinov explains how he will be looking for "another colour" to divide him in two, internally.

Lear provokes his own pain. There is always reality in the hurt, but he does it all to himself. Shakespeare manipulates us until we reach the point when we can at last admonish ourselves that we mustn't give in to self defeat. Phillips recalls one of Ustinov's imitations (we'd all seen it earlier) "when that woman had begun to *look* like a whine!" The storm outside is a measure of the storm within. The worst crimes are those committed against ourselves. Inhumanity comes back always to our special inhumanity to ourselves. Lear moves finally through threatened madness to a serenity of self-knowledge and self-forgiveness.

Phillips tells of encounters with people, seemingly sane (but he guesses better), who always approach him ("why me?") in raving trauma. Ustinov at a bullfight, watching a sorry sight of a bull "they just *couldn't* kill" inquired of a group of spectators clearly delighting in the spectacle: "Surely you can't *enjoy* this?" It turned out they were all Swiss, "and had always come together on their holidays — and they were all butchers. (Pause.) And *they* were sane?" asks Ustinov.

Suddenly, Phillips asks if anyone knows any ghost stories. One doubts if his intent is a simple distraction from the course of rehearsal. After a slow start (it's mid-afternoon, and sunshine at last is beginning to return through the rehearsal room windows) Hutt and Ustinov contribute a few they've garnered. The afternoon is waning; the tales, though curious, seem indulgence. Not so. Phillips leans forward in a short pause and asks us to mark the low scale of these narratives. His precisely delineated gesture of thumb and forefinger measures for us a two-inch space, beyond which range he asserts (he tirelessly asserts this) the voice need not go, should never, ideally, go in our work. It reminds me of Beckett's stage-direction on tonal containment, pushed even to that eventual tonelessness altogether for those inscapes of his *Endgame*, a play which, like all his others, shows the massive influence of Shakespeare's *King Lear*.

Overacting, especially in the voice, as this group knows, is not confined to actors; in fact most of our best actors don't do it at all. Not so with politicians, or others. How, wonders Ustinov, would Hitler or Mussolini have fared proposing their worst agressions on a TV fireside chat? He once heard a recording of Asquith — made in 1910 — who added "was that right?" on the tail of the last sonorous phrase, too late to be erased. Poets, too, doing their own stuff. Yeats. Hearing him hardly hurries anyone back to Inisfree. Or Browning (a recent find): "Very plodding." Or Tennyson: "Cannon to the leeeft — cannon to the riiight," a sepulchral growl. We're back to the Crimea. Where *Lear* can be. It's almost happening now.

Yeats wrote the line 'Both Hamlet and Lear were gay'. Happiness has to be earned, but that can be our destiny, too: it's even engraved in some constitutions, like Peter Ustinov's. Phillips, Rain, Hutt, Ustinov, all know they share something larger than talent. They share the privilege and responsibility of work in this play. They all possess what Kent recognizes in Lear. 'You have that in your countenence which I would fain call master'. 'What's that?' 'Authority'. You could count on that answer getting a good laugh from the Lear of this show, if he decides — as he so often does — that he wants one.

CIGARS AND CORONETS

Two days have drifted by. I hadn't intended to write any further, but now I've been tempted to try a journal of at least the first week or two of rehearsals because some friends who read the first few pages have urged me to continue. The collaborative growth on which our craft depends, as actors, spills out into the corridors of the theatre; talk and comment on hopes and expectations and objectives follow me with the chat into the green-room, dressing rooms, and actors' drinking places. But the core of the work still burns in the rehearsal room. Harking back to that first rehearsal of this Lear, and those other Lears I've witnessed; McMaster's, Wolfit's, Gielgud's, Michael Hordern's, Scofield's, and now Ustinov's, it seems to me that the play is about erosion. In time, everything, as well as every character in *Lear*, will be pared down to lean essentials.

Peter, working in low gear on this morning, in the Goneril Courtyard scene (I.iv) mutters to an as yet unselected follower to 'Call my Fool hither.' Several Knight-Followers budge uncertainly. "Yes — you, or you — or you, call my fool!" Several Knights offer to go. "*Yes*," ad-libs Ustinov, "that's it . . . Call *all* my Fools hither!" Soon after, lifting a raised booted foot to Kent (Jim McQueen, an actor with particular grave charm), 'What services can'st *thou* do?'; Ustinov plays the line in rude sotto-voce, lewdly ambiguous.

The laughter continues, intermittently, with firm pull-back always by Phillips to considerations of text. Ustinov, word by word, (not in spite of but, often, *because* of his humour), shows tenacious accuracy of meaning, but he hasn't yet satisfied Phillips, who is working towards a pent-up frustration in the later scene (II.iv) with that other daughter, Regan. They agree that there is a change of pace or tempo required: "There is a difficulty — technically — here."

Phillips seems to argue, subtly, for something larger theatrically. Ustinov is "Sorry I ran through it." The paring down goes on. Phillips asks for a check in the *Compact Edition of the Oxford English Dictionary* on the word 'patience'. He feels certain there may be "something special there." References to this fountainhead, in two huge tomes, copies accessible at strategic points in all theatres, is a frequent Company discipline. No mere guesswork will do. "It's interesting how much we now miss from all this," says Phillips, speaking of the Shakespearean density of connotation. Here, when we look it up, 'patient' is isolated as carrying with it some admonishment 'to accept suffering'. Soon afterwards, Ustinov as Lear picks out this resonance of 'patience': 'I can be *patient,* I and my hundred knights.' Before the play is over Lear will have used this word an amazing number of times, and Phillips, after much homework on the text, is taking note of this curiosity.

He is now pursuing Ustinov with the thought that he can play some elements "to sound like an adversary in Parliament," as a link into a following passage of higher rhetoric leading to: 'All the stor'd vengeances of Heaven fall / On her ingrateful top!' (II.iv). Is he, in fact, asking Ustinov to be bigger? Will he succeed? There are, inevitably, *some* operatic requirements for the role. And Ustinov loves opera enough to often direct it. For the moment, however, Ustinov assures him that he will "Kick that around . . . tenderly." They work on. 'I can be patient . . . ' One can hear him get the new thoughts as they come. In the 'curse' speech to Regan, it would seem (to me) that the *tune* is somehow inescapable — for everyone. Ustinov loses nothing of the intent, ad libbing, "What are you doing — you Gods," and he brings it down to an utterly believable, everyday familiarity.

As we rehearse towards the end of the first part, (our Intermission being at the end of Act II, Scene IV), up to the storm, Phillips works on, unrelentingly, building up the details and every nuance of frustration and unease in Regan and Goneril. All this upheaval is only a portion of what they've had to go through in the last fifteen years or so. Shutting Lear out will accelerate their guilt. The terror of the approaching, sudden, irrefutable acts of cruelty are probed with many analogies — Ustinov, especially, developing a nightmarish sequence of the Ayatollah Khomeini's more recent judgments. "Send someone like that to Eton — on top of all that Kipling tradition — and watch the results."

Phillips, meanwhile, dwells on the essentially domestic ingredients of our first act, in which the violence is confined to nothing more extreme than Edmund cutting his own hand. (I'm tempted to think of the violence as already unleashed in the words exchanged, those spoken — or worse — those unspoken.) But then, from the storm on, every horror awaits us: madness, feigned and real, treacheries, assassinations, the blinding of Gloucester. Bill Webster, as Cornwall, works technically, with unwavering commitment, learning the route to aggression.

Ustinov, delineating for us some extremes in behaviour, invokes an image of Strindberg in mid-winter leaving his cosy hearth for the sub-zero exterior, by morning "frozen solid in ice — to show his fourth wife how unhappy he was." Didn't hurt him a bit, it seems, "returned indoors and started work on a new play."

We learn from Phillips that a wonderful 'Storm' is being prepared, to build to just before, and maybe run right through, intermission. One wonders how big the 'Storm' will get, or how an old gent in nineteenth-century garb would fare in an Ontario blizzard. Despite the elements, only one day has ever been lost from production in recorded winter rehearsals. You can lose your way and perish by taking two wrong steps here, fifteen feet from your own front door, but a Stratford actor can, and is expected to get through anything. After seven Canadian winters I've learned that the blizzard, though deadly enough (I almost floundered in one in downtown Winnipeg) is often as deadly quiet. Assuming, however, that Ustinov will be contending (as will Hutt and McQueen) merely with thunder, lightning, wind and rain, one wonders again about Voice. Ustinov has a disconcertingly large range, highly flexible, including a rich elder-statesman resonance in the bass, but as yet he still elects to confine it to conversational cadences.

There is more talk of power, from that of kings to bank managers. This Lear, disclaiming his youngest daughter, Cordelia, erupts with astonishing mobility into the speech of severance (I:i). For me, the first surprise of the show is a visual one. Heaving his wheezing rotundity up from his chair of state, he moves with ferocious alacrity to the big desk down left, throughout his speech scrawling an edict of disinheritance, rubber-stamping it with repeated vehemence. How many Lears would consider leaving their chairs at such a moment? The effort is a painful display; irrational, petulant, resulting (most convincingly) in a near heart attack, the clever thing being that the seizure might be real or feigned. Returning with much difficulty to his chair he exhaustedly, absently, instructs Cornwall and Albany (getting their names right this time) to 'digest the third' of the inheritance, 'Which to confirm . . .' (he has great difficulty concluding, waving most eloquently confused, fluttering fingers) . . . 'this coronet — part — *between* you.' Cornwall and Albany (Frank Maraden) both reach for the bauble — what else can they do? —

extending the moment, before abandoning the absurdity of their combined gesture.

Donald Wolfit's Lear (which Ustinov greatly liked) is recalled. Sir Donald, who played it for generations to the histrionic hilt, in the same moment produced the two gleaming coronets from within his own ample crown; and by inference could easily have conjured up a third if Cordelia had been prepared to play ball. "Everywhere a coronet," remembers Ustinov affectionately; he himself will wear none, making do, as evidence of royalty, with the finest of after-dinner cigars. A cigar accompanies him in these opening rehearsals for most of the play, and he will assuredly be waving one abstractedly in that opening scene. Everywhere a cigar. Until he becomes abandoned, presumably, without his hundred Knights, in the rain and the cold and the night, and without even a cigar anywhere. Unless he produces in the storm scene — as well he may — a butt from a vest pocket.

But how long can this most impudent of actors, with that enormous head and inordinate intelligence, decide he can hold off the 'traditionally' considered climax. We are not, it seems, going to be presented with the passé postures of tragic bravura. I've already heard him comment casually that the real crisis point comes when you finally say you'd be better off dead. By inference I believe him to mean, when you've got past that nonsense and know you have to go on. It will be interesting to watch this Lear come to that. Maybe it's the jokers who know best how to live with and use the pain.

Work goes on quietly. Phillips, getting up, paces about, lingeringly considering options on the use of space by Richard Monette (Edmund) in his opening soliloquy. Monette, wisely accepting Phillips' pattern, then paces identically. He knows that Robin is, or was, also a fine actor. Phillips, concentratedly relaxed, hums an occasional guess at some incidental music, perhaps muted piano and applause as the after-dinner party offstage, following Lear's exit. Berthold Carriere, composer for most of Robin's productions, is already sitting in with us, scrawling an occasional flight of notes across his ever-ready staves. And Ustinov, a great talker, watches very absolutely, a perfect listener. There's a lot of laughter at some points of adroit bemusement in the work of Douglas Rain and Monette. We are laughing because the trusting naiveté of Gloucester is so painfully true, as Gloucester, accepting Edmund's blatant lies for truth, tidies up the disorders on that down-stage desk. It's very possible this is a very modern play.

A change in gear. They jump suddenly to a much later scene. An actor has become unexpectedly available from other work. Phillips goes into a long quiet chat. He's not trying to exclude anyone: it's a refining down of attention, the more intimate the stronger.

I'll be missing some rehearsals because of involvement in performances elsewhere, but no more than any other member of the cast. In fact, I'll still see and hear more than most of them. I wander off. Perhaps I'll go no further than the fitting rooms, where I may encounter Renato La Selva, Men's Tailor in the design department, whom I'd heard in full flight of voluble Italian with Ustinov during a fitting the day before.

There's one thing I'm sure of — I hope I'll never have to go on for Peter in *Lear*. There'd be some difficulty just with the costume; they'd have to envelop me first in the Falstaff padding. In the meantime, of course, I'll just have to learn all the lines. The actor's day and night, at Stratford, is a busy one.

SUNDAY, AUGUST 19TH

'WHO'S THERE, BESIDES FOUL WEATHER?'

We are still working in the rehearsal room at the Festival Theatre, and they are having a look at the opening scene yet again. Rehearsal keeps swinging back to that, and I'm reminded of Ustinov's remark (on that first day) that the opening scene was the most difficult in the play, and that we probably would not find out how to do it until quite late in rehearsals.

Some actors, including Ustinov, are beginning to offer up fuller, rounder sounds. Kent (Jim McQueen), especially, tries a burst of strength in that early attempt to resist Lear's abandonment of Cordelia. Phillips asks why. McQueen says that "as an exercise I felt I was obliged to try it." Phillips cautions that, as a director, he is "obliged to say that it isn't necessary." Jim explains his objective, that in reaching for the right age (for Kent), he's been increasing the vocal strength, but he accepts from Robin the comment that "In ten years from now — are you forty yet? — you'll have the same strength at fifty."

They continue with work on the storm scenes, the opening of our Part Two, 'Who's there — besides foul weather!' (III.i). It's the

18

physical impact of the wind Robin is considering. Jim as Kent, Patrick Christopher as the "Gentleman" will be encountering in a screeching gale.

Both actors are held by three or four others in the exercise, simulating the thrust and pressure of the wind. Words are wrenched away in the mere struggle to remain on their feet. Ustinov then has a try: 'Blow winds and crack your cheeks' (III.ii). I can already recognize much of that duality of which he spoke earlier. Lear, in this extremity is "So close — *so close*," insists Robin, to Gloucester's house, from which he has just been turned out, and in Peter's voice and face I can see the rapid changes of focus. He's so glad, for instance, to see Kent, tired as he is of looking up so long into the rain. Afterwards, Peter reminds himself (and us) how: "One gets an enormous sense of identity in a storm, especially at sea, to the point at which one is not even very frightened." Phillips, concluding the session, quietly reads an ominous, dank and chilly landscape sequence from *The Mayor of Casterbridge*.

EASIEST IS BEST

Monday, at Stratford, is the actor's day off, and Tuesday, after an initial work-through of some scenes, opens with a long chat from Phillips on the importance of restrained acting. He is working towards an exceptional containment in the scenes of Lear's expulsion from the homes of Goneril and Regan (I.iv and II.iv). One begins to feel and understand this family conflict from both sides. Mere noisy histrionics are least what is needed here (as Phillips sees and guides it); though voices get raised sometimes, they are as instantly lowered, pulled back, increasing the intensity of the frustration, the venom, the failure on both sides (Lear's and the two sisters') to find accord or compromise. Of course, if Lear could accept their earliest advice, or the better, more reasonable parts of it, there would be no play, and nobody would end up out on the heath.

So Ustinov offers us, as he puts it, "Not so much a sizeable curse, as an irrational outburst." Phillips continues to conduct this recurrent diminuendo, accepting only an occasional flash into forté, and Ustinov in the long speeches is "Quite willing to mutter" as some

19

of it is "awfully difficult to remember." "Save all the big stuff for the storm," says Phillips, and yet, we've already heard much that was restrained there also. All are encouraged to "keep crawling along there." Easy, isn't it?" comments Phillips. "Easiest is best."

We have another look at the opening scene. Ustinov, ad-libbing to Douglas Rain, "Do you have French, Gloucester? . . . There's a couple of those French fellahs back there" — a petulant jerk of his cigar over his shoulder. Then another little look at the arrival at Goneril's (I.iv). I should explain that a 'little look' means doing the scene rather than reading it. It's a hunting-riding entrance. Robin becomes the farmyard: roosters, a stray dog or two, a bleating of sheep. Lear, arriving, attended by his hundred knights. Phillips stops for a "little crowd-work." "Sixteen for a hundred, it's economy time." Indeed, Lear's entourage here is limited to sixteen actors. Some are Company members of considerable experience and long standing. There are only a few (too few) mature faces, but such are the exigencies of the budget. These are especially difficult roles in any Stratford production. There are no "Extras" in this Company, and the commitment by these mostly younger Company members is exacting, difficult, and absolute.

Phillips sketches a number of improvisations. They will enact a series of tableaux, in frozen stance, "frame by frame"; watching, participating, above all involved in action: "A horse-race," "A goal score in ice-hockey," "A cocktail party," "A ship arriving in New York harbour — and a bomb goes off." (Just to make it a bit more difficult.) The "improvs" are first done individually. Then, numbered 'One' to 'Sixteen', each actor joins the others in building the collaborative structure of the exercise. Sound is added, or excluded, as in a silent move. The tempo is built up (One to Sixteen, or all together), the "frames" of the action overlapping, coalescing. It's a typical example of a Phillips acting exercise. It's strenuous, demanding, often very funny (there's a great deal of laughter and enjoyment from those participating and those watching). And it's very real.

Conclusion: "When you *add* an idea, when you add an activity, in speech or movement, it fills the space more truly; it's simply much much richer than when you're merely thinking as a group." It's a fact. The sixteen seem, if not a crowd of one hundred, certainly a leading edge of it, which is all that can be accommodated on the Avon stage.

A little footnote: those sixteen should, in fact, have been seventeen, and Mr. Seventeen, LeRoy Schultz, one of the maturer

Knights, was absent-in-revolt for a couple of days respite, with Robin's blessing. It's tough work if you've already done it in a couple of previous productions. LeRoy (he tells me later) went shopping, had a pleasant walk, met Hélenè Ustinov, who accepted his invitation for drinks in the Queen's Hotel Bar. It's been an interesting day for all of us.

WEDNESDAY, AUGUST 22ND

FEN SUCK'D FOGS

As Ustinov settles in with us (he times his arrivals to the second) the two o'clock cannon booms twice for the start of the show downstairs. "How do those swans (there are many on the lake) ever give birth?" he wonders. Easing himself down into Lear's chair he then asks, "What page are we on, ancient, or modern?"

Robin is concerned, today, with establishing why the action is confined to this courtyard in the 'Arrival at Regans' Scene (II.iv). "Only anger could keep you outside." What brings Lear to the point where he'll beat upon the door "til it cries sleep to death!'? For there's been no talk of going inside, putting one's feet up, having a hot toddy. Phillips, again, seems looking for a device for getting Ustinov 'up', vocally. Ustinov suggests, referring to the speech 'Age is unnecessary, on my knees I beg . . .' that, "It's rather good to stay on my knees, until I get *very* unpleasant." A trumpet shrills from the theatre downstairs, a few lines before 'What trumpet's that?' in our text, and "too soon," interjects Peter, in the flight of his own speech. Robin is very frequently moving furniture to accommodate Peter's as frequently varying positions; now it is that ubiquitous bench with a hinged top-lid, which seems to accompany Lear (his personal luggage) everywhere. Ustinov, with his very small boy's inflection "Oh — it's *that* thing again." Later, he lifts the lid for a not incurious look inside on the line, 'I would divorce me from my mother's tomb, / Sepulchring an adult'ress!'

Phillips, off on a new tack, sensing something useful, asks Regan (Marti Maraden) "What do you think you've got *on*, Marti?" The new possibility is discussed and added: Regan, halfway undressed, putting on a hastily snatched shawl, coming out to the yard and the impatient Lear. Robin stops for an improvisation, leading it (as he often does) himself. "Can't you see what you're doing to my chest? . . . We're all going to catch our deaths of cold." The scene is built, slowly, detail on detail. "And don't forget, he's covered in all that horse-slobber, too." Ustinov, still in low scale, small steps, often backwards, finds words exactly. In the 'curse' speech, petulance is mixed with a growing desperation and a new venom, and he searches for its images; those 'fen-suck'd fogs, drawn by the powerful sun', are to — he finds the idea, slapping the skin on his arm repeatedly — 'Fall and — *blister* her !'

Robin wants Marti and Peter to highlight the embarrassing picture of Lear on his knees, as he pushes assistance aside from Regan, who is clutched and entwined in this grovelling and floundering on the ground with him: "A most embarrassing time for children, when real emotion is suddenly exposed in parents." As Ustinov sums it up: "Lear is scared that the two sisters may get together and infect each other; it's a problem of 'getting to Auntie first' to get his story in." Lear is so anxious that he overmakes his point, with attempts at sleezy jocularity to the husband, Cornwall, *hoping* he'll say the right thing, a hope continued until Regan turns to face him, and he sees the expression in her eyes. (Which, from Marti, is *not* encouraging.) Or trying tears: 'O Regan — I can scarce speak to thee.' As the old, like the young, try tears — and know they're doing it.

Peter interjects a quick personal story: a glimpse of his aunt sitting near him in a television interview, rigidly composed, imagining the TV picture to be that of the frozen frame of the daguerreotype, hissing to his mother, "You've a drop on the end of your nose!", and his mother replying, "Well . . . leave it alone." He continues his affectionate reminiscence of them both playing Scrabble, staunchly opposed and uncommunicative, leaving him like a child "to tell the other what the other said." (Could it be there's an idea or thought in his tale which may later feed the scene? I've a hunch there may be.)

They try again (II.iv). Lear complains of 'Sharp tooth'd unkindness' ("He keeps coming back to that"), and we have more of that desperately degrading grovelling on the ground: yet this is mixed with some traces of his former astuteness, glimpses of how the man *used* to be. One wants to slap him, and, yet, in the midst of all his domestic mess, some of the things he says are deeply touching.

It's joke time again as Peter has another go at that second curse with those 'Fen suck'd fogs', reversing those initial consonants in the traditional spoonerism to get the trap out of the way. "Whoops," he comments, hardly stopping in the speech, "a bit of that *older* English getting in there." And with Lear going off, out into that storm, Robin ad libs for those who've sent him there, "Then *stay* out, if that's what you *want*, and *get* fucking pneumonia!" Peter reminds us that Lear has been deliberately "playing it older than he is," all shaking hands and arms. "You can see I'm not *there* yet, I'm not *that* bad yet, daughters!" All of which makes the mess more terrible for them.

Again it's time out for a short Ustinov tale. This one is of an old man he'd visited in hospital who, after appropriate precautions for intimacy ("Shut the door there, Nurse!"), confided that he could now only achieve the sexual act once a month. Peter consoled him with: "That isn't *too* bad for eighty-three." "But my brother's eighty-five," added the old man, "and he says he can manage it every week." "Then there's no reason," suggested Peter, "why you shouldn't say the same."

SATURDAY, AUGUST 25TH

A HOVEL

Rehearsal has moved from the air-conditioned theatre to the humid interior of St. John's Church Hall. Leaded windows open to the sound of noisy birds and cicadas. The entire floor space is our acting area. There's a small group again due to matinées on all three stages: Ustinov, Rain, McQueen, Hutt and Rodger Barton (Edgar). We explore Shakespeare's (or, rather, our Arden Edition's) 'A Chamber in a Farmhouse' (III.vi), traditionally, and misleadingly, described as 'The Hovel Scene'.

Certainly the furnishings are scant. Phillips sets up a bench, an old table to the side. Dogs are barking, and the traffic soughs nearby. After a first try, Phillips asks "how dotty Lear is at this point?" "Not altogether raving," suggests Ustinov. Lear is more at that phase of thinking aloud; mixed in with all the exhaustion, he is free in his own thoughts. Half of the alarm of Kent, Edgar, and the Fool, is in seeing how much conviction Lear has in what and who he thinks he sees — the phantom dogs and daughters. The compulsion for a

23

trial is overpowering. It's there in Lear's second line of the scene: 'It shall be done; I will arraign them straight.' All feel that a good night's sleep would help a lot. Phillips wants a still stronger intention to create the atmosphere of a trial. Talking of tiredness in children (as with old men), Ustinov points out how even the most intractable of children, when sufficiently exhausted, are "Almost gracious in leaving — quite glad to see Nanny." Kent, thinks Jim McQueen, is watching for any sign of weakness, of Lear tiring down. Perhaps they are all using their concern for Lear's physical well-being to mask their greater fear, that something may fail to protect them against the imaginative forces unleashed by Lear. All three are very glad to get him finally settled down on the straw, until Gloucester returns to warn them and send them off on their wanderings once more.

After another quite tiring work-through of the scene, this Lear leads off again into the night and more journeyings, ad libbing to Douglas and the others, delightedly still in character, "We really should have booked *ahead*, you know!"

Then they have another go. We get the fantasy and terror of Lear's growing madness, Peter slapping at mosquitoes; for a moment I thought we had them in the room with us. But it's a bit late in the season for them now, and still getting colder outside. 'The foul fiend bites my back', screams Edgar (as Poor Tom); Rodger Barton has run all summer getting in shape for this great role. Ustinov slaps at his back, shaking away another mosquito. 'Sit thou here, most learned justicer!' Bill Hutt's Fool, husbanding his last few lines, and his last choices to move, in this, the Fool's last scene, is somewhat reluctant to sit. 'Thou, Sapient Sir, *sit here*'. Kent, also: 'You are o' th' commission, Sit you too'. A madman (feigning), an Earl (in the guise of 'the common man'), a Fool (not altogether Fool), and a King (not altogether mad); it's a weird quartet. 'I here take an oath before this honourable assembly, she kick'd the poor King, her father', intones Peter like the Mad Hatter in Lewis Carroll's chilling tea-party. Goneril didn't, of course. She did not even quite send him packing. Lear walked out, of his own volition. As Peter later comments: "He's *influencing* the course of justice." (Again — the Mad Hatter). But Lear, especially this one, can be excused anything. He reaches for the imaginary dogs, "Tray, Blanche, and Sweetheart' to pat them for consolation, and then suddenly mimes their vicious attack on him ... 'See, — they bark at me!' Terror-stricken, he is seemingly in threat (a real, horrible threat) of being devoured. Yet, not so. Peter, brightening, identifies them for us afterwards: "They're *Corgies*, of course," (like those we'd established in the court scene); "Dreadful — they shake before that water-coloured bark — everything runs in one long 'Hoooooooww!' "

Phillips says it's desperately important that the scene must be *dangerous*, too. Lear's response to the escape of the imagined Regan from his crazed trial, 'Stop her there! Arms, arms, sword, fire! Corruption in the place!', suggests how very 'nuts' Lear has become. He presses home the point; if Lear is "simply pixilated, the observers can be reasonably *hopeful*, one can get used to *that*." A very real suffering is needed here. Ustinov totally concurs. It will be only a question of degree, it seems. "A stroke's as far as I'm prepared to go at this time."

McQueen, Barton and Hutt discuss with Robin the question of how awful it is to be asked to participate violently, as Lear demands. What do you do — stamp on those dogs, pursue the escaping, imagined Regan? Barton can do all that, as Edgar/Poor Tom. Hutt and McQueen can only suffer, simply, in how they look on. But Poor Tom, as Ustinov puts it, "sees even more dogs than I do." They are also all as hurt and moved by these daughters who cannot be seen. What's real for Lear becomes real for them.

How relieved they all are to see Gloucester returning with that lamp, if not with the promised vittles. Boy, but the last ten minutes were tough! The danger of what might happen to Lear in all these extremities of threat, images of teeth bared and lips curled, is intensely real. Lear's cry after the departure of the phantom Regan: 'False Justicer, why has't thou let her 'scape!' is what Robin was after; it is absolutely heartbroken.

A small step backwards to an earlier scene, 'Before a Hovel', which we at least *know* is an empty stage (III.iv). The windows in the hall are still open, cicadas silent now. A sudden downpour of rain, beautifully timed, as Lear goes into the prayer to the poor, '. . . naked wretches, whereso-er you are', just as Phillips was about to supply appropriate background effects. Robin is ever-resourceful in sound effects and is ever ready to attempt any one of them. Later, he comments, "How the hell did the Elizabethans cope with all that filthy weather?" (I'm reminded of that prologue scene in Olivier's film of *Henry V* when the groundlings of the Globe ran for cover from a sudden downpour.) Phillips warns Barton that as Poor Tom he is "cutting words." He pauses before adding, "Don't." And it's time for a coffee break.

DRAMATIS PERSONAE

Some additional actors are beginning to filter in, directly from various matinées. Ustinov sits, relaxing. His huge, bearded head is sweat-lathered from the afternoon's work and heat. He's relaxing by sketching Douglas Rain, who is now working with Butch Blake, our 'Old Man' in the play. Butch is a senior Company member of twenty-three successive seasons. We see this drawing later, as Peter trips tentatively to some of us in a sweet parody of an extremely little boy 'showing what he's done to Auntie'. This guileful youthfulness may be his deliberate exercise in relief from Lear's ageful angst. It *is* hard to play a very old man all day.

Robin has begun work on the 'Gloucester and Old Man' scene with Butch (IV.i). He has remained in the hall during the break, sipping coffee, swatting the innumerable flies, jesting casually with those near at hand. Suddenly, now, he departs for a trip to the john, flicking a question to Butch as he goes: "Why . . . why . . . do you think Doug is blind?" "Why???", questions Butch, in amazed high Welch tone, gesturing to the void of the Church hall and the world outside — "Why? Because he's covered in blood, that's why. He's bandaged, isn't he, that's why — hasn't an eye left . . . Why? Because I say here (shaking his script like an irate Merlin) 'I've been his tenant, and his Father's tenant, these fourscore years' — and I can tell you, I've never seen him look this way before!"

Ustinov continues sketching, avidly, delightedly. When Phillips returns he doesn't pursue the issue. Douglas Rain, his eyes bandaged, his lines learned almost since the start of rehearsals, executes his precise judgment of how Gloucester sounds, moves. Butch Blake as the Old Man is simply superb. No other word will do. Bert Carriere, composer, sits, diligently listening. Urjo Kareda arrives delicately, sits, noiselessly. Ustinov still sketches. Douglas cites some background material for his work on Gloucester, which I judge to be personal, and is therefore deleted here. Something of what is heard and seen in rehearsal must remain our special confidence amongst ourselves. Barton, in a less private sense, talks of spending a whole day with a blind man by Lake Huron, which now feeds his work on the scene. Ustinov, watching and listening carefully, continues sketching. It already seems a very long day's work.

After a supper break we're looking at our scene twenty-four, 'A tent in the French Camp' (IV.vii). I've missed an earlier rehearsal. Cordelia is reunited with Kent, in this scene of Lear's awakening into a new sanity. Cordelia (Ingrid Blekys) enters far up-stage, but commandingly, very poised. Slender, taut, with the long neck of an

Mr. Mervyn ("Butch") Blake: Old Man
Mr. Douglas Rain: Gloucester

"I've never seen him look this way before."

27

Audrey Hepburn, her face is entirely her own, with eyes that burn with feeling. The scene is a quiet one, staged with a large group of courtly French Officers who sit in postures of hushed care, Lear sleeping on a down-stage cot.

Phillips stops the scene soon, making minute adjustments to the positions of the officer's chairs, talking quietly to Blekys. He leads her down through the attendants, a long diagonal movement, stepping behind and away from her at moments, seeing her framed past heads and shoulders; he is asking her to think of it as a tracking shot, and it is. This evening he is a camera. "There's a wonderful blue sky out the back there," he reminds me, settling in for another look, humming his seraphic incidental music. He stops to adjust a single attendant's position.

Blekys manages to say so much before she speaks. Her welcome of the "good Kent" grows (from that first try, and a second rehearsal) until it becomes not a handshake but a wonderfully warm embrace. Phillips taps his feet lightly, simulating the otherwise silent entrance of a messenger in sneakers. He then steps to one side and, with a finger gesture, signals a tiny change in an up-stage officer's position. Someone is humming (barely audibly) a high-keyed melody; it's a moment before one recognizes it (I assume, a very temporary choice) as 'Amazing Grace'. Phillips stops again soon, and goes into another quiet chat with Blekys, then returns to his seat as they start once more; the enormous brown eyes, committed to every detail, flick from face to face.

Ustinov is awake, as Lear, yet scarce awake: 'I know not what to say'. Robin, watching every nuance, in Lear and all present, is intently moved by what he sees and hears. 'Let's see: I feel this pin prick', and Lear is kneeling on the floor, in a huddle with Cordelia, sucking on a finger. One remembers that other huddle on the ground with another daughter, but suddenly, now, one feels for him an overwhelming tenderness. Rising, he gestures naïvely to Kent, with many careful looks back to Cordelia: 'Do not laugh at me; / For, as I am a man, I think this lady / To be my child Cordelia'. Then, with nothing as small as the sentimental, but with a serene strength, 'Yes, faith, I pray, weep not.' Most moving of all in this early work is his little turn to the up-stage officers, and his caressingly courteous bow to them before he wanders off.

THE IRISH SCENE

A jump cut, and we are with Edgar, still in the guise of Poor Tom, leading his blind father, Gloucester, to the cliff at Dover (as Gloucester *thinks*; in fact they're a long way from any cliff) (IV.vi). Doug Rain's Gloucester is already physically exhausted; it's been a long journey and he's investing his words with a delicious undertow of familial argumentativeness. It's a touching irony, as he can't know it is his own son leading him and, yet, he is treating the crazed fellow as he might his own son. He's also attuned to the switch in speech from Poor Tom's prose to Edgar's blank verse: 'Methinks thy voice is altered . . .', 'Methinks you're better spoken . . .'

After some time Phillips interrupts. Barton has got to get "back to Edgar"; there's less need here to be so involved in Mad Tom. Phillips "can't hear" effectively. Barton does three quick vocal variations. None satisfies. "It's an *amazing* sight," says Robin, "Try it back from the door; make him believe the distance." Edgar must convince his father that he's on the edge of a precipitous cliff.

Phillips takes a lot of care with Barton. Edgar is acknowledged as one of the most difficult roles in the canon. Starting from the straight young chap, he moves into the pretended lunacy of Poor Tom, in which disguise he encounters Lear on the heath, and later leads his blind father, and is then the peasant who aids the baffled Gloucester, convincing him he's survived the big fall (from this imagined cliff) at Dover. It's a tough role, and the actor playing it needs all the help he can get. Robin is giving some of it now. "Think *distance* — not Edgar, or Poor Tom, or Shakespeare, or anyone." Barton tries it once more and goes on.

Rain, working with consumate, totally consistent reality, already Gloucester in voice and presence, does the fall, almost unconscious on the line, 'If Edgar live, O, bless him.' And Barton, with the calm strength of a male nurse, takes his weight, cradling him, turning many times in a tenderly descending gyre, lays him down caressingly, revives him, convinces him (now in the peasant's role), 'Thy life's a miracle'. It is. It's breathtaking.

The scene moves marvellously, surely on. Ustinov's Lear enters, not yet 'fantastically dressed' but yet fantastic. His route is startlingly simple, with wonderful flexibility of tone and variety in tempo, with an ever-recurrent release of inner gaiety, and it is this which is most affecting. The experience is somehow illumined. I've often wondered what happened to that mouse, having been in the play twice, seen six Lears, read the scene so many times. 'Look, look! a mouse. Peace, peace! This piece of toasted cheese will do it.' And later: 'O! well flown bird!' As Ustinov fashions the moment, we see, we hear the descent of the hawk which snatches it from his gently proffering hand, and we feel the attacking encounter of claw and beak. Lear sucks his finger yet again. He is an herbivore in a world of carnivores. It's worth trying to describe the diverse resonances he achieves when Gloucester asks to kiss his hand. 'Let me wipe it first; it smells of mortality'. He has rubbed it quickly, passing it under his armpit, shaking it quickly, even *as* he says the line. It's a complexity of distaste, unease, guilt mixed with concern (for Gloucester — might *he* not catch the disease?), and practicality: a modest pride in belonging to the human species. Shakespeare offers an actor such chances. This Lear encompasses them all.

Another moment follows near the end of this amazing scene, and no Lear (for me) will ever capture this as completely: 'It were a delicate strategem to shoe / A troop of horse with felt'. Ustinov gallops these silent samurai delicately with undulating hand and fingers, as certainly as any child in a nursery, and completes the image of the resultant carnage as he is 'stol'n upon these son-in-laws'. The 'Kill, kill, kill . . .' is then split in definition, perceived as well as done. It seems that Lear is aware of his obsession, of his own performance.

After the scene, while the set-up happens for the next, Ustinov and Phillips confer. As chance would have it, they are in my immediate earshot. Here's the gist of it. Ustinov: "Terribly difficult one, that!" Phillips: "Until we know just how ga-ga he is at this point." Ustinov: "The recognition of Gloucester seems a landmark, that's why I thought I'd kneel there with him, like a couple of old bookends." Phillips: "There's a lot around there which suggests he's pretty nimble in his head, and yet — " Ustinov: "Yes — trouble is, this scene isn't stretched on any positively dramatic chassis . . . In that way it's the most 'Irish' of these scenes . . ."

This is an interesting moment for me. I'm immediately thinking of O'Casey through Behan to Beckett, the tragi-comedy matrix, laughter and tears inextricably interfused. I hang on, doing my best with modest shorthand.

Ustinov is speaking of "the withering attack on the Rin-Tin-Tin ethic" (the triumph of pure good over pure evil could hardly be better described), "those German Shepherd dogs rushing about saving people ... As if they *could* be saved! And that bit with Gloucester — Yes, I know who you are all right — and don't bother weeping." Phillips also sees the scene as uncompromising in its ingredients but charged with duality, almost as a privy-council. It shows us the way Lear *was* once, in his power; only here, despite the acute perception, there's a "cog out of place." "But *only* just," agrees Ustinov. Lear is mentally sharper here than before in the play, "the intellect slightly out of sync; it's just wasted, doesn't *seem* to go anywhere," concludes Phillips, heavily stressing the word 'seem'. He knows better, as does Ustinov. And so did the man who wrote it. Ustinov is still musing ... "The boots thing, of course, that's a carry-back." Before things all went wrong, he means, when he stuck out his foot to Kent a million scenes ago.

SATURDAY, AUGUST 25TH *continued*

THE BLINDING OF GLOUCESTER

Stage Management, orchestrated by Vince Berns, who is our Stage Manager, has set-up for the 'Blinding of Gloucester' (III.vii). This scene has only been lightly touched on as yet. They play it through. The first thing that registers, terrifying, pathetically touching — is the response of the three servants, up-stage in their final lines. They've been trapped there during the whole action: David Stein, Geordie Johnson, Barrie Wood. And earlier, Patrick Christopher, who (now stabbed and floored) has tried to stop it happening.

Robin muses that he's "not sure about all that butch acting." Gestures of deprecation from servants Stein and Johnson. Not so. Robin means "Regan and her Fella." It's clear we are in for a gruelling session.

"Why do you think they do it?" asks Robin. "Sadism ...?" is suggested, obviously, but this won't be an easy problem. What *motivates* the sadist? Phillips is positive. Fear. Fear here, if you don't do it, what will happen. Fear of the loss of power, so lately gained, so difficult already to retain. Power, and fear of the loss of it, is many-levelled. Robin mentions the notorious 'Moor's Murderers' in the not-so-long-ago north of England: "*rather* terrible; anyone ever hear of 'em?" None had. "All in the living-room ... Chop-chop." Regan, Cornwall, Edmund too, must find out what the fear is that can drive you to do almost anything. Fear of Gloucester's escape ...

The dialogue develops, Robin leading it. Guilt about Dad. What they've *already* done to him. Fear, again, of the consequences. Fear of the French brought in by Cordelia to sort things out and avenge Lear. Fear of the State. Patriotism. Love of Country. *Anything* was possible in the war; you just got through it, did what you had to do. Robin guys the tabloids, the who-dunnit thriller. Fear of Mrs. Bloggs! A shout from Robin: *"Don't* pull those curtains!" His energy level is intense, wringing his hands, face even paler than his wont. "You've seen it all in the movies, but this is the actual thing ... Months after *Psycho* I had to have a bed from which I could see *everything*."

In a silence, as these ingredients of menace are built up, a dog wails obligingly, near the Church Hall. Sadists are people who are trapped into it. A critic once almost nailed Robin to the lobby of the theatre for like work in a previous production: "You've killed a *real* bird!" And, when he was convinced otherwise: "You've no *right* to be that realistic."

Well, we now remind ourselves, there were some pretty horrific things in this period (the Victorian) and Jack the Ripper was the least of them. Ustinov mildly inserts a reminder of civilians on charges of conspiracy strung up on meathooks. Finally, he raises the issue of those who are certain *"We* are on the right side," What you can do if you're on the right side leads us to Belsen, Hiroshima, and the rest depends on your politics. "Bomb a few more to save the cause," says Robin. And now, "Try that first little bit again, and see if you can find the *size* of that anxiety."

What follows is as brutal as an S.S. or Tsarist interrogation, or one by the K.G.B. or F.B.I. For Cornwall and Regan are patriots, too. Phillips, unrelenting, even on that opening little bit (the exit of Edmund and Goneril), wants more contained fear in the farewell: "She's off on a mission; will she get through?" — until she's safely out of the scene. Robin had first said that he "wasn't sure we shouldn't be setting up a frozen panic." And here it is. It's done several times. "Vontz murr, plizz," mimics Robin in a pastiche of milder horrors. Cicadas sing busily from outside in the occasional silences. 'Tick-tick-tick ... ' goes the Phillips clock; he has to contribute something as he watches. Ustinov, back to the wall, watches with us. Bill Webster (Cornwall) who must do the eye-gouging, precisely, technically committed. He's a sensitive actor, a delicately inclined actor, but only the best of actors can play such terror.

Phillips steps in quickly and out again after tiny technical adjustments. He signals to Marti Maraden (Regan) to increase the velocity of her hysteria, and let out to the blinded Gloucester more than she should. During the gouging-out of the eyes, he sits, hands clutching his chair, impaled, twitching, knowing that it looks real. He insists on some vocal points; on the line 'Seek out the traitor, Gloucester', he wants the hysterics of a desperate near-scream. "Good-good-good-good"; he's satisfied. It's much closer. He believes they've been driven to it.

SATURDAY, AUGUST 25TH *concluded*

A LITTLE MORE DRAMATIS PERSONAE

And so, let's have "the last one." They set up for the final scene (V.iii). I take this opportunity to speak to Ustinov as he comes my way, asking him, whatever else he may discard (and he discards as much each day as he discovers), to treasure that bit of the felt-shod galloping troop. He seems pleased, saying "Thank you, Maurice." We hear from Robin in the background that "we can all go early if we concentrate." It is 10:45 and dark, now, outside. The soldiers and guards are chosen for the opposing forces. There is a sensation of bustle and love of work. Frank Maraden (who has played Albany before) is given time to sort out some special concerns. The Company throbs with confident application. They know each other to be gifted and well-chosen. Donna Goodhand will be a tough, calculating, very sexy Goneril; Marti Maraden a tenacious, desperate, very sexy Regan. Monette, as Edmund, is to be bristling with wit, game, certain of the outcome, hoping (he tells me) to be hissed. Douglas Rain is finished for the evening, but still watching, abundantly accomplished. The scene is played lightly, technically; it's early days yet. Phillips is watching all, demanding their best, proud of them all. Ustinov and Ingrid Blekys are curled on the floor before him. 'Do you see this? Look on her . . . Look'; the last words of the dying Lear are unheard, almost, in these almost last breaths of the day's work. Peter falls back on Greg Wanless's shoulder, his arm in its gesture still trembling. Frank Maraden blows out the (imaginary) candles. It's the end of our second week of rehearsal. But there will be four more to come.

"Dramatis Personae"

VIGNETTES

Mondays, as I've mentioned earlier, are the actors' time out from work, and I've been using mine to keep up with my rehearsal notes. With most of the *Lear* cast engaged also in a minimum of three to four shows each, with often two performances on Saturdays *and* Sundays, and with the aid of Peter Ustinov's civilized attachment to time off, there is *some* breathing and thinking space. Of course, I also have to learn the lines. I'm also learning how to make a virtue of necessity. Learning *Lear*, which means effectively re-learning it,

34

watching others do it, and doing my best to describe how they are doing it, are commitments which nourish each other.

For the moment, I'm trying to fabricate a small oasis of calm, before the next deluge of priorities (as a writer as well as an actor) bursts over me. There are always additional and important ingredients in our theatrical stew which are worthwhile blending in, and here's one — with some help from a crumpled but unforgotten note.

One day, Robin was delving into the question of sex in the 'Tom Wood as Oswald and Marti Maraden as Regan scene' (IV.v). The question is if the knowledge or suspicion of promiscuity in either sex is a turn-on for the other. Phillips asks Wood, "Do Fellas like this kind of thing in women?", and asks Marti, "Do women know that Fellas like this kind of thing in *them*?" Richard Monette is listening in. Phillips asks him which of the two, Goneril or Regan, does he think Edmund fancies most. Richard, after a pause for thought (he's an actor who thinks very hard) replies, "I really don't know. There isn't anything I could find in the text to tell us. I don't think he really likes either of them at all. In fact, I don't think he likes himself either, very much." (Pause.) "Or at all."

Later in that session, Phillips asks Marti (and, perforce, Tom Wood must follow) to play the scene Southern, "Georgian Plains." They are asked to think of it as "just post-Dallas"; this suggests a concept of Cornwall, now dead, as a politician (which he is, of course) and Regan as a widowed politician fighting to stay alive. Maraden and Wood, in the new, sedate, measured low-keyed cadence, achieve a quite chilling, very calculative menace. A barely throttled-back hysteria lurks in every syllable.

Another vignette returns to me. Upstairs in the Greenroom at the Festival Theatre, Daphne Dare (Designer) and Berthold Carriere (Composer) are having lunch together. Daphne, who has a dry wit, reveals that she, herself, is accredited with a full 'Score' for *Lear*. Her best melodies, she says, were for Gloucester, and she hums — quite deliciously — "There'll be blue bells over . . . The White Cliffs of Dover," with Bert adding a contrapuntal "Two Lovely Black Eyes . . ." Not to be outdone, Daphne insists her best theme was for Bill Hutt's Fool, "Losing my timing this late — in my career — send in the clowns."

And one more encounter, with Renato La Selva, Men's Tailor in the design department and arbiter of actors' shapes. The costume workshops and the two small fitting rooms are a frenzy (a calm frenzy) of activity. One fitting room has already reverberated to the strains of the Italian Anthem and a Tosca aria, with the raised voices in duet of La Selva and Ustinov. I'm very sorry I missed that. Renato tells me that Peter's rendition of the combined opera orchestra, ("He can do *all* the instruments!"), was enthralling, but that it was "his conducing . . . his *conducting*" which was flawless, as was his command of more than a native range of Italian dialects in his anecdotage.

TUESDAY, AUGUST 28TH   THE AVON THEATRE

DAPHNE DOES IT AGAIN

Some Fall rain and thunder storms erupt over Monday night. There's a full cast for the Company at the Avon Theatre. The entire set for *Lear* is already on the Stage. Daphne Dare has given us a deep, clear space, contained by three austere wall-panels; two diagonals backed by a third, up-stage, in which can be found (only if open) three functional points of entry or escape — one cannot quite call them doors. All three walls in mute, dull wooden tone, are highlighted only by a light definition of horizontal and vertical laths. The effect, for much if not nearly all of the action, whether interior or exterior, is that of a cage. It can be a comfortable cage (set up now with furnishings for Scene One in the court) but it is, at all times, essentially a cage. Even our exteriors, for the storm, or that eventual blue sky, will be only minimally opened up by the back wall panel, when flown out, to expose a small extent of sky. I like this feeling of the cage for *Lear*. Decor could hardly be more pared down than this. The action of our play is essentially in the head; 'Who alone suffers, suffers most i' th' mind . . .' (*Edgar*, III.vi).

The deep space of the stage is steeply raked from the absolute black of the proscenium with only a slightest change of level (two steps) to the upper stage area. It's all very uncompromising. As Phillips says later in this first day on the set, "Daphne has done it again." Certainly, there is no escape in such a space, no excuse for any mere 'acting'. Only the truth could be tolerated here. As Robin comments, "Anything else is disaster."

The cast are already scattered, sitting in various parts of the auditorium. Ustinov arrives, wearing one of his invariable ample alpaca light cotton suits, cigar already lit. "Not many here for the Filibuster," sighs this Southern Senator, settling into a stalls seat.

36

Phillips is already on-stage (I can imagine him being there almost from first light), making minute adjustments of furniture positions. There's a lot: a heavy Victorian chaise, a huge desk (for Lear and Gloucester), high-backed chairs, big bulbous lamps. Robin sits in all the chairs, one by one, posing, calculating all effective actor's options. To watch him is to glean, technically, much of the best of attitudes in any of these positions. Many of the cast are doing just that.

Rehearsal begins gently, lightly, with several looks at technical matters, some entrances and exits, some small linking scenes. The Avon auditorium still reflects, literally, its music-hall and operatic past, with chandeliers set against long wall-mirrors, the largest of these overhead, centre-stage. But the one-time cupids, crimson and gilt, have been banished by the overall black through darkest green in walls and seating. Daphne Dare, who developed the new wide stark proscenium opening which now serves every production, will probably find her green-slime tones in costumes and lighting easy to realize in this atmosphere. Robin himself, on arrival in Stratford six-odd years ago, climbed the highest ladders with others to efface the earlier rococo. In this newer Avon, the eye, as in darkly containing kaleidoscope, can only be led towards the stage.

It is rumoured amongst us that Ustinov insisted on *Lear* at the Avon, as opposed to our main-stage Festival Theatre and its over 2,300 seats. Here, at the Avon, there is even a 'gods', and there are seats for a comfortable eleven hundred, all of them with a perfect view of any actor on stage. Seats for the nineteen performances of *Lear* were completely sold out within days of the announcement of this production.

Ustinov, heaving himself up out of his (for him, none too wide) stalls seat, joins some of the cast on-stage for a look at that opening scene. Actors are, I've long noticed, traditionally weakened on first encounter with the set and trappings of the actual event, and on these occasions rehearse with varying inaudibility. Douglas Rain, as usual, is the first to be truly heard. His infallible pitch (he's never merely loud) is an almost irritating constant.

Phillips is lying down on his side on the black pile carpeting of the forestage, arm and hand supporting his head, dressed mostly in white, a negative image out of Manet (Le Déjeuner sur l'Herbe). Ustinov is ad libbing, now and then, the sense and meaning, if not yet the right words.

SOMETHING'S COMING

A younger Company member, sitting before me about midstalls, turns his head and tells me he's beginning to feel depressed. I understand his misgivings, but refrain from enlightening him. Ustinov's early morning frolics (he's already got the Company on a roar), and deceptive underplaying at this stage can easily disconcert the uninitiated. At times he, too, is seemingly guilty of inaudibility. But wait. Just wait. Years ago I remember like expressions of doubt from new recruits when I was rehearsing with Joan Greenwood in Ibsen, or Elizabeth Bergner in Giradeaux. "Won't be heard beyond the front row," complained some juveniles. But long before the seats are filled, the greater mouths and woices in theatre yaw into effect. I recall the especially large ones of Bergner, Greenwood, McMaster (the Irish actor-manager, last of the dinosaurs, with whom I first did *Lear*), Maggie Smith, Olivier, Peggy Ashcroft, Wolfit, and now here is Peter Ustinov. His mouth is often open, as Lear, and it's a big one in a big head. However gently at times, he is greatly heard, and this morning (I'd take a bet on it), he will open the throttle enough to assure himself, Phillips, and some others who have that special itch behind their ears. I know that any major actor will take a moment, somewhere, on the first day of work in the actual performance space to let the fuller sound go, exploring the acoustic, feeling out the sides of the stalls, and the back wall, and the upper reaches where the cheap seats are.

Work continues, quietly. The opening scenes are tackled again. The main body of the Court, those with few or no lines holding their respectful stance on the steep rake, are locked in the reverential posture of actors in Court scenes, hands joined in front (or behind backs); where else can you put them? The first time on the set, one loses the freedom (for a day, anyway) which has been worked for so long in the previous two weeks' rehearsal.

Things will relax later. The call has been for 'Full Company to Work Through Play'. Work Through Play! That's obviously impossible. But Phillips, on this first day on the set, wants all on hand. From here on, everyone, from Lear to the least of the non-speaking parts, will be making the most of the true space, where it will begin to happen to full seats on October 5th.

38

Donna Goodhand (Goneril), who has missed much earlier rehearsal due to her other performance and rehearsal schedules, is nicely calculating stage space with Marti's Regan (I.i). They rehearse cautiously, testing the distances between chairs, in their minds'-eye allowing scope for the fuller skirts they'll be carrying later. Donna, exceptionally quiet for this while, then stretches her range a little to Lear with 'You strike my people, and your disorder'd rabble / Make servants of their betters!' (I.iv). Miss Goodhand, two years out of her drama courses at the University of Regina, was lucky in one part of her training; she was a protegè of one of the best voice teachers in Canada, the Irish actor and singer Robert Armstrong.

Phillips, working deftly on further Goneril/Regan sequences, runs light-footedly up and down from the stage, back and forth from his varying places in the stalls. And Cordelia (Ingrid Blekys) sits far back in the stalls, arms on the seat before her, calculatingly concentrated. 'He love'd our sister most', we hear from Goneril, and immediately, one can add envy to those many motivations leading to violence explored last week, in the blinding scene, which drive these not yet so wicked sisters.

Phillips continues to manoeuvre his cast delicately, easing them into the set, and the steep raked stage. He sketches in some 'beggars without the gates' at Goneril's household, before the arrival of Lear (I.iv). It's like a small edge in a Brueghel canvas, the tiny group settling down with a handout from a servant within Albany's palace. And Colleen Winton, Pamela Redfern, Janice Greene, and Bob Ouelette receive the same attention from our director as that he gives to an Ustinov.

Peter doesn't know the words too well yet, or as well as he did last week; he, too, is a stranger on the set. He continues to settle for the sense of it, for now. He's jocular about his own maltreatment of the text: "Oh ... This is that *famous* nonsense ... *What* is it? ... Ah — *Yes*, 'Ingratitude, thou marble-hearted fiend, / More hideous, when thou show'st thee in a child, / Than the sea-monster!' Is *that* it?" And, now and then, it *is* it. Robin flits around on-stage (yes, during the action) setting positions of Knights: "Sit here, Sean ... David Holmes — up on the step"; he is motivating everyone, contributing to the asides, while principals continue to work around him. Peter's bold-striped shirts (we enjoy a bolder one each day) emphasize his pot, a small word for such an amplitude.

It is our Scene Five — and Shakespeare's too, for once. The stage is cleared of furniture and actors. The three stark panels remain, and then the middle one flies out. Enter Lear, Kent and Fool. But not before Robin and Peter have a rapid mumble up-stage, and a slight cut is agreed. Two words, 'to Gloucester' are cut to make the speech, from Peter, start 'Go you before — with these letters'. There is a somewhat tortured syntax in this speech (I.v). I know this, as I'm currently trying to learn it myself in an attempt to keep ahead of Peter. (If I fall behind, the danger is I'll have to unlearn much Ustinov.) The small but crucial point here is that there is a difficulty about 'plot' in that speech, and I'm delighted at the change, for entirely personal reasons. Besides, it makes for cleaner story telling. A small cut can keep unopened a can of unnecessary beans.

Peter and Bill play the short scene almost sotto-voce, feeling out the void of the stalls, and each other. Peter gets one line entirely right in response to the Fool's question — 'Because — they are not eight?' He has played it with tentative guile, testing his own, as well as the Fool's, wits. Bill responds approvingly: 'Yes — *indeed*; thou would'st make a good Fool'. They both enjoy a shared congratulatory laugh. Peter then confirms the point with a slight clown's stumble (and instant recovery) on the side of a step, and yet he's on the edge of the poignancy of the lines: 'O! let me not be mad ... I would not be mad!' That's the big trick in a lot of the best acting; to risk a jest on the brink of the profound. They finish, and shuffle off together. "Very nice," concludes Phillips. True. It's been very acutely executed by two actors with their entire wits very much about them. Off-stage one can hear Peter's voice raised in badinage and the accompanying laughter. Robin flicks a switch, touches a dimmer on the stage management console, and the houselights diminish to total darkness.

Phillips exercises this total control of lighting in the auditorium and on-stage at all times. A theatrical Prospero, he flits to and fro from stage to stalls, commanding the ever-boiling, or rather, strongly simmering, ingredients. Next to the actors, it's the light that responds most to his subtle or intricate demand; the special dimmer-board is his conjurer's staff.

On Robin's left, up on the forestage, Bert Carriere, short and muscular, bare legs in shorts, perches at his small upright piano; a one-man orchestra, he ripples a constant flow of improvs, linking scenes or moments, composing as he goes. The theatre is darkened to deepest dark, the only glows those over Bert's keyboard and the Exit signs. We are in the dark because we are having a look at the 'Blinding of Gloucester'. The scene is worked with the usual remorseless detail. The only extraneous sound is the tap of Phillips' shoe leather, coming and going, coming and going from the stage. Ustinov's cigar glows from the stalls. I leave. I don't really want to see this scene again, even in costume, until others in the filled seats can watch it with me.

A FIRST CRY

I return for the next scene called, and am very glad I did. If I hadn't, I'd have missed a reward I'd been expecting for some time. Lear is before Gloucester's castle, enraged on discovering his servant (Kent) has been placed in the stocks (II.iv). Peter is partially back 'on book', his insecurity with lines only mildly baffling. He is talking to Robin of one of those "different colour" objectives, something evidently facitious (there is some laughter); "Would that help?" "No," replies Robin lightly, promptly, positively.

On the next try they move further into the scene, Lear re-entering from the house: 'Deny to speak with me! They are sick! They are weary! / They have travelled all the night!' Lear is firming up. The petulance, the dotage, are still there; humour is suddenly, if not banished, somewhat far from hand. Doug Rain, a very wearied Gloucester, expostulates with him, doing his best to calm him down. He almost succeeds, but it's out of hand again in an instant; Lear, like a Churchill at a too-late-in-the-day cabinet meeting, is taking people to task — and is in danger of going too far: '. . . bid them come forth and hear me, / Or at their chamber-door I'll beat the drum / Til it cry sleep to death.'

It's wonderful. As the voice builds on a rising curve to the line's end, Peter has moved downstage left, brushing followers aside, turning up-stage, back to auditorium, raising both hands, shaking them with crazed vigour, and the last word becomes elongated to an extraordinarily extended sfortzando; '. . . Deaeaeaeaeaeaeaeaeaeaeathh!' Heads are turning, on-stage and off, and eyes are opening more widely, as everyone within earshot pays instant, unqualified attention.

With no comment made, they've begun to run the sequence again. The second time Peter tries it, he has built the effect — in sheer operatic magnitude — to double the original scale, and we wait for it

41

to end: '... Deaeaeaeaeaeaeaeaeaeaeaeaeaeaeaeaeaeaeathh!' An extra-ordinary sound, accompanied by a stamping of the left foot, re-peatedly (to render it 'unheroic'?), an additional percussion. Real, startling, and angry as the sound is, it also manages to be 'Lear Acting' for the benefit of his Knights and, of course, himself. (I mean both Lear and Ustinov.) The long singing shout lasts so long (like an opera star showing off on an extended high C) that Doug Rain as Gloucester (always *as* Gloucester) shrugs his shoulders and walks off without saying his exit line.

In a note-break after, Ustinov, pleased a little with himself, says "I'd really have liked to throw some stones up at that window," he mimes the throw at the non-existent window) "but I'd probably miss" (as Lear, he means, always *as* Lear) "and hit Rex." Rex Southgate, playing the maturest of Lear's Knights, being in fact the maturest of those present, is invariably as close (as dangerously close, I'd have thought) as is Greg Wanless. There's some risk in every-thing.

Robin, remaining on the forestage during the next try, is sig-nalling to Peter to seat himself (on that bench again) as he takes the following line, 'O me! my heart, my rising heart! but, down!', and Peter, getting the line almost right, takes a prompt or so, and is *glad* to sit down. Bill Hutt, following with one of his especially tricky lines, is soon in difficulties also. Hutt: "Having a bit of trouble here myself." Ustinov: "Glad it isn't just me ... Yes, I'd rather *like* to sit down — thought I was sure of *this* bit." The jesting doesn't cloud the delight of the preceding moment. Robin leaves the stage, his Cheshire Cat smile the only clue to the fact that he's hear-ing now, as well as simply knowing, that his Lear can deliver all that the aficionado can hope to expect.

The 'Grovelling-on-Knees' with Regan follows (II.iv). I've missed an intervening rehearsal. Butch Blake, who was there, had told me that they'd introduced some business with a snotty handker-chief. I can now watch it with relish. Marti and Peter, with fussy alternation, are attempting to clean the mucus from Lear's nose and cheeks. The handkerchief passes back and forth, Regan starting it and Lear confiscating it in irritable response; I sense that Peter is recording some of these options for retention in later work, the con-ditional point being that it won't be done to be funny or to raise a laugh, but because it has become part of the dramatic mix. It's what great acting is often about, having the alertness to extend from the imaginaiton of a great dramatist; an Ibsen, an O'Casey, a Shakespeare.

It's a messy business — nobody is pretty when they cry. Laughter is cauterized by pain, when it isn't the other way around. There is one line which I regret is cut from the production (it goes, alas, in proximity to some lesser ones): 'I will die bravely, / Like a smug bridegroom. What! I will be jovial ...' (IV.vi). This Lear, first of all, is the story of a man who has to learn to live bravely. He'll have a better chance if he's also a man who, despite tough odds, can make the decision to be jovial, as he does by the time he gets to Dover.

The scene is worked again, Robin leaping in and out, for each Knight a new position, motivating every presence as the work goes on. He leads a discussion on the difference of focus on this pro-scenium stage. Most of the cast do much of their work on the Festival thrust stage. But here, at the Avon, it's up-stage places (a Phillips style) for onlookers, who accent attention on the speakers down-stage. This demands exhaustive application from those who stand and wait.

We've reached Lear's plea to Regan: '... Tis not in thee — To grudge my pleasures, to cut off my train, to scant my sizes.' The work stops for adjustments and Peter, amiably indulgent, an affable yet plaintive teddy-bear, improvises a playroom tragedy; once a plethora of toys, toys, toys, but now ransacked of trains and all accoutrement: "A One-and-Only level-crossing left."

The day flies on. Peter exercises his voice occasionally, a very loud humming of snatches from 'Il Trovitore'. And his 'Reason not the need' speech is amazingly muted, swept by tears of self-pity, and it works. It will be a while yet before this Lear learns how not to cry. But that's what our second act is made for.

FRIDAY, AUGUST 31ST

A NOURISHING DAY

We're back at the Avon. I've missed two days of rehearsal, my own schedules keeping me away. Robin confides in me that he was almost relieved by my absence. "People have begun to twig what's going on." In fact, I've made no secret of my occasional note-taking, and many of the cast, aware of my first hesitance, have been urging me on. Robin's only fear, and this is what matters to both of us, is that actors may begin to clam up. There is an intrinsic privacy in the rehearsal process. Many sessions are posted on the call-boards in all theatres as "Closed" to all but cast and production staff. This is especially so with Phillips' own productions. Our work is a conspiratorial collaboraiton. Robin and I discuss this. It's agreed that I am my own censor. It's up to me to know what I must leave out. I'm honoured by the trust and the implied confidence invested in me. More significantly, I'm certain that had any one member of the cast expressed any real doubt or unease to Robin, he would not have hesitated for a moment to tell me so. So I'm going on. This, along with learning Lear's lines and (in effect) being prepared to go on for Peter, in performance (or in rehearsal) is my only responsibility. It's enough.

Of course, in a contractual sense, I'm obliged to be present at any rehearsal involving Peter. (Though traditionally, this is seldom so; the Stand-By usually looks in once a week to note moves and business.) And, of course, it's a fact that in standing by for Lear I've been present at as many rehearsals as possible. That covers a large part of the play. But it's also true that I'm here to see a great deal more. In a strictly contractual sense I could have been asked (at least on these occasions) not to have been here at all. But that hasn't happened — so I'm going on. Of course, having gone this far I'd go on anyway. Nobody says me nay, perhaps because nobody *can*: the accoustics and sight-lines are as good in the 'gods' as they are in the stalls.

The work is calm today. But then it is almost always calm, however concentrated. Robin's in white again. Festive. He pulls the loose top of his gym-type slacks (a discreet flash to a delighted Alicia Jefferey) to indicate that all is indeed white. Bert Carriere is enplaced, stage-right at his keyboard, offering up some incidental phrases. Robin is everywhere, about the stage, as people work, lurking like a camera, hardly — or rather seemingly — not watching at times. He leaps back on-stage again to adjust the angle of Monette's head in that first Edmund soliloquy (I.ii). He talks at length on 'Exterior' and 'Interior' components in the speech and how to achieve them. Later, as the tempo of work begins to vibrate with more resonance, he hums (having less to do, less to offer) with a sawing mime of cellos to Bert, who rapidly makes notes on his score-sheet. Bert strums a few bars, signals to Robin, who moves a touch closer, head cocked alertly to hear this new variation (just composed) on a linking phrase.

Remembering, suddenly, that the theatre is still in work lights, Robin flicks a switch, pushes the dimmer lever, and the light changes to dark. Back on-stage a moment later for adjustments, and stepping back briskly over the forestage (silent on the black carpeting), his shoes tap-tapping again on the steps into the stalls, he calls back to Monette: "Must *learn*, Richard, now. Can't do anything while you're fidgeting with that book."

Vince Berns, Stage Manager, as correctly smart as actors once used to be, calls into his mike, and the stage crew, ever alert, fly in the rear wall panel. Some actors, still failing to exit correctly, are going off too close to the proscenium at down-left or right. Robin calls to have the wrong exits taped up.

The lights in the auditorium remain out, the stage working light, always on instant control from Robin's dimmer-board, is never that gloomy movie-cliché of a naked bulb or two, but a powerful combination of strong F.O.H. (from Front of House) spotlights, hitting the actors directly in the eyes — which is just where every actor always wants it. Phillips' rehearsals are far more starkly lit and seen, alas, than any of the ultimate productions. But it's fine to have the light at least for the practice. Rehearsals count to Robin. There are only so many rehearsal days from now to that night in early October when we open and play a mere nineteen performances. For the exact time between now and then I'm already reluctant to be specific.

Those nineteen performances and two previews are long booked out. Only nineteen: I don't know what the logistics of this mystery are; it simply isn't my concern. It's incidental that the name of Alexander Cohen, impressario and Broadway producer, was (still is) bruited about (that is by the Press), and it's a fact that his name is linked with much or even most of the announcements of production. Not one of us seems to know anything of this, and none of us seems to care. Everyone is concerned, simply, that we are doing *King Lear*. When does one ever get the chance to work on this play? Not many times, in a lifetime. For some — never. This is my third time in twenty-eight years, and it's one reason why I accepted this contract. Butch Blake, who is now our 'Old Man' for this show (and has already done Lear, Gloucester, Kent, in other productions), tells me that, at seventy-two, he's still learning how it can be played. I've done only Edgar and Kent, and I am, too. Like me, Butch "never saw that mouse thing ever work that way."

Robin continues his blithe journeying on-stage and off, and on and off again and again. Adjusting, modifying. Consulting, mostly, today, in a low voice. Here and there, he says (very occasionally), "it's possible to do an overlap." Not often. With considerable cutting, especially of the Fool's part, which oddly enough increases the edge and impact of the role for Bill Hutt, the text remains sacrosanct. The show serves the text, bending and swaying with it, marvellously flexible. The words live for all of us, in the action the words release. Phillips continues his leaping about. Back. Up again. Back. I don't know what genius is. Probably nobody does. But I can recognize energy. It's direct. It's infectious. It's self-regenerative. It can always say "Once more."

Work ranges lightly through many shorter sequences to entire scenes. The play has begun to flow. Douglas Rain, with nicely unostentacious mock-modesty, would welcome the attention of *his* attendants. "My lot — my *two*." David Stein and John Wojda are obliged to oblige, and on a later work-through in the day their ranks are swelled by the third presence of Barrie Wood. Robin confides a confidential note to Bill Webster, who then grins conspiratorially. He offers Marti Maraden another clue on Regan's troubles (II.i): "I told you it was more trouble than it was worth . . . I'd rather do *without* the tiara!" Concentration is total. The light taps of Phillips' shoes (on-stage) are the only punctuation between snatches of acting. After a reference to Kent being 'combined' with the riotous Knights, he points to a possible allegation for a real (or alleged) gang-rape. Later, it "should be just possible" for Regan affectionately to touch Gloucester's beard — a grace note rather chilling when one remembers how she will pluck at it so nastily in that later scene.

The opening of the next section is done again after a coffee-break, but this time it's injected with a fierce energy (II.ii). Tom Wood (Oswald) is advised to breathe shallowly, "*Then* you'll get out of breath." It's suggested that McQueen's Kent should give up the chase (of Oswald) at an earlier place. "The spirit is willing, but he's too old for much more than that," says Robin. Gloucester's servants are told they can relax more; it's a domestic, not a military fracas. "You're just Fellas, not guards," says Robin.

Barton's Edgar is suddenly on, for his solo bit, another victim of conspiracy (II.iii). Phillips flicks switches on his dimmer-board, making crude guesses at later lighting (it's a small console and Prospero doesn't, in fact, control *all* circuits yet). But Barton's single figure confronts us disconcertingly in the stranger light. Now he's a silhouette, anonymous, anyone in trouble with authority; he exits, suddenly, running . . . by a wrong exit.

46

A GOOD BLOCK

We move on to the Dover Scene again (IV.vi). Rain, as Gloucester (it's a "blind session" for him again) seems to have his eyes closed all day. Necessities of rehearsal schedule confine him often to blind scenes for the full day's call. He tells me, dryly minimizing what's involved: "It's *easy*, really." He holds back that rare Rain smile. "I never know *where* I am. No moves to worry about. Rodger's got all the blocking. (Pause.) I assume he has, that is. (Pause.) I just never know."

Ustinov gets into the scene, or rather *drifts* into it, in his mad (or not so mad) entrance, not so fantastically dressed, hands often in pockets. 'No ... they cannot touch me for coining: I am the King himself.' He knows the words. In this most difficult of scenes to play, the words are the easiest of all to learn (as I've found), because it's the scene in *Lear* which one so often remembers, if one's seen it, or been in it before. Peter, today, is letting us see everything, as he imagines it; some recruits he is absently inspecting at the Butts in target practice. Anachronistic — or is it? A gentleman's sport, archery, and popular with the ladies also in Victorian parklands. He shows us how to draw a good bow. He salutes that devouring hawk, and shoots at it, successfully; his bow has quickly become an arquebus — for greater accuracy.

In the adultery sequence he takes time for some definitive brushstrokes, some very specific copulations to be seen today: the wren (a flutter of the hand) and the fly (with both hands, and very busy fingers). He assumes the look and sound of the 'yond simp'ring dame', and on 'Down from the waist they are Centaurs' he contrives to do something with his feet that conjurs up whole mythologies. He is simple, too, at all times. (And I think, right in this, always; there isn't any choice, here, for Lear to be otherwise.) The entire exchange with Gloucester is a benediction. After 'When we are born, we cry that we are come / To this great stage of fools.'; he accompanies the following: 'This 's a good block!' with a confident tapping of his leonine head with one finger. It's a wonderful discovery. He congratulates himself (as Lear) that he's not only still all there, but even more so than before his recent rough time out on the heath. He shares this discovery (as Ustinov) with us, too, his eyes seeking out those of us in the gloom of the front stalls, as he adds immediately (was *that* his actual moment of discovery?), "*This 's* a good thought." It certainly is, and it was a good block that thought of it.

There's something extraordinary here. Learned footnotes and learned performers I've seen opt for readings on this as profoundly dull as: bootblock, mounting-block, hat-block, executioner's block, stump of a tree, or the truncated dolmen on which some Lears (Wolfit, for instance, was very 'actorish' here) actually *stood* for the line.

Ustinov has a lot of strength, too. Being largely Russian I'd expected him to know Turgenev's tale of *A Lear of the Steppes* (I asked him but he didn't) in which the hero tears down his ancestral home with his bare hands rather than let it pass to unworthy inheritors. There's nothing so herculean in Ustinov's Lear, but there is always something else, a bonus from that actor's guile (there's some peasantry in all of us) which never quite deserts him. One of Lear's exits, in this scene so close after the sublime, takes a risk on farce, and Peter is not lacking in execution. 'And you get it . . .', says Lear to the French Officers who have found him, (first pointing offstage in the opposite direction), 'You shall get it — running.' As Peter has said, in previous rehearsal, it's an old trick. But the best of the old tricks always work. Peter waits, now, like any old Variety Pro until everyone has turned to look, in the wrong direction, before he gallumphs off. This time he also fabricates an offstage crash. Well — it's rehearsal, and we can all do with another laugh. 'Sa, sa, sa, sa, sa!' he adds, re-appearing, "He probably put that in because it was the only bit of French he knew." (Mr. Ustinov means Mr. Shakespeare.) Robin is pleased, and lets Peter go home early.

We go back to the scene of Edgar's encounter with his blinded father (IV.i). Much work has already been done here, but Robin is in gear for more. First, a few lines from Edgar, solo, before the arrival of Butch Blake leading a slightly irascible Rain. Douglas has been led all day, and in any scene he always starts and remains with the basic reality. His strength is always in unclever acting. Robin interrupts. Rodger was "very good" until 'World, World, O World' on the sight of his father, so 'poorly led'. Actually, Butch is making a good job of it — in so far as he's allowed. The blind, especially the newly blind, as Rain knows and performs it, are very reluctant to be led.

Robin goes into an intensely felt examination of what the scene means to Edgar, what it *does* to him. There is in it "a huge emotion, a desperation of silence, exactly like a strait-jacket," he says. Edgar wants to say something, and can't. Poor Tom *can*. It's the best possible thing that could have happened to Edgar, to have such a role ready-made to play, and, in playing, hide behind it. Half of Edgar's sorrow is what helps him to hurl himself into Poor Tom; otherwise, he'd go directly to Dad (if he were only Edgar). He desperately wants to be able to do something. As Edgar, he can't. Indeed in a plot sense, his disguise must be retained until the play's resolution. But Shakespeare (as Beckett learned from him) respects the plight of the actor, and gives him always a rationale for action. To act means to do. Poor Tom can lead Gloucester. Edgar can't. Edgar must unmask only for the finale when he tackles the baddies, or rather, *the* baddie, his halfbrother Edmund, 'onlie begetter' of so much pain. Edmund does not beget all of it, of course. Lear, like so many of us, sets up his own crucification. But a half-brother is as effective in this as any alter ego.

Every character in the play has his or her shadow. Cordelia has two. And Lear is his own double, as is the case for all the main characters in the play. The darker sides of our natures invest the brighter aspects with further lustre. It takes a lot, including much intelligence, and more than a little toughness, to be good — as Lear and Cordelia and Kent and Gloucester all find out. Not all of these thoughts should be attributed to Robin Phillips (though he may share some with me, such being the osmosis of work in theatre), but I've got to do something while I watch and listen. *Lear* does that sort of thing to all of us.

Robin is still working on the same scene. He's concentrating still on Edgar, on how he is to move, and — more important — when; in sudden spurts, in maimed postures. The rehearsal has thinned out. Douglas, Butch, and Rodger are on-stage, incarcerated in the action. François Regis-Klanfer, Assistant Director, is busily taking notes. Robin deftly orchestrates Rodger's sudden surges and stops of helpless movement, each one triggered in this exercise by an abrupt chord from Bert (back on his piano stool) in response to a flick from Robin's finger. The staccato chords are as stark as something from Stravinski. Robin has become conductor and choreographer. He jabs a finger to his left to Bert, whose dissonant short strums sound the pulse of every move from Edgar/Poor Tom; on his own lines, or even counterpointing syllabic breaks in the words of Gloucester and the Old Man. "Don't move, Rodg — *only* when you hear the piano!" Bert, with one free hand, annotates his score-sheets as he as instantly responds to the tiniest gesture from Robin. And Phillips, his left hand signalling with diminishing frequency, "You see, Rodg," as Edgar's and Gloucester's hands finally touch, "that trembling is now in *your* hands. Douglas thinks he must calm *you*. Everything you do makes him believe you more."

It's been another long day. I'm not sorry I missed the two before; it helps me to find my own perspective. Missing a little seems best. I can judge the jumps in the frames of the pictures on offer. Out into the sunshine from the darkened Avon I walk away in a mood of quiet exhaltation.

SATURDAY, SEPTEMBER 1ST

SOME ARIAS

We're back in the sticky sanctuary of St. John's Church Hall, from which I'll have to leave early to do a show. There's a storm again in the heavy air outside, and we are rehearsing ours. Top of our Part Two: 'Who's there, besides foul weather?' (III.i). Again, Jim McQueen and Patrick Christopher encounter in the gale. Difficult. It's a plot scene, mainly, and on top of its strenuous action, it is crammed with information about the remainder of the play. Kent, seeking the King, encounters an acquaintance, entrusting him with messages for Cordelia, away in France. The speeches, though heavily cut, are still packed with description of the storm as well as plot. All taking place in an open space and in driving wind and rain. Very tricky.

Phillips adds a further conflict, or, as many good modern actors would call it, a resistance. Both men are to be in a desperate hurry, Kent to get to the john, and the Gentleman refusing to stop. Then they try another, in gibberish this time (which tends towards Japanese), but holding to the same content. It's like an encounter of two warriors from an historical Japanese movie, compelling enough for us to abandon any subtitles. But the text seems clear. Ustinov, watching, enjoys the exercise. It's an excellent old trick, I've seen it work not only at Stratford, but also in Joan Littlewood's Company twenty years ago, and with the late Harold Lang, a director who had much in common with Phillips. The scene is played again, 'for real', the storm more convincing, and the news more clear. In fact it all has twice the original velocity. The big trick with quick is to make it also clear. I'd print that as a motto over every theatre dressing-room mirror, after improving it to: "The biggest trick is quick when it is also clear." All our shows would be better and we'd go home sooner.

Next comes 'Blow Winds' (III.ii). Ustinov, knowing Phillips' liking for "Once More" says he'd better "keep a little in reserve for a second time around". Who does he think he's kidding? The best of actors *always* do that — even when they don't have to. He shuffles to the back of the little church hall and erupts into the aria. Robin, just in front of me, hugs himself, savouring the sensation, and I'm delighting, myself, in some very raised eyebrows nearby. Even those somewhat prepared had not expected this. The sound is huge. At last, it's gallery time at La Scala. Being Irish I know that acting must finally get back to singing, sooner or later, if it's to lift the scalp of the customers. Robin might quibble with me on that, but none-the-less, he has joined me on a deep chair next to my couch to distance himself from the sound and relish it the more. Peter doesn't quite yet know the score. He's in difficulties here and there, and a prompt in *Lear* seems as weird as a halt in the surge of 'Boris Godounov'. There are plenty of prompts. And that's part of the joy, too.

He gets the opening section spot on, with much enjoyment in the hissing sibilance of his '. . . *spout* / Till you have drench'd our steeples' . . . 'Singe my white head . . .' / 'Strike flat the thick rotundity 'o the world!' In the second sequence, the 'Rumble thy bellyful' is enormous, led off by a gastric exhalation of rolling R's ('RrrrrUMBle) : but we are in mild trouble on the next line for words. 'Nor *rain* . . .' — "Christ, — it's this *catalogue*, isn't it?", (still holding to his tempo) "Ah, yes! — 'Wind, thunder, fire — are my daughters.' Then, on that third big chunk, holding his own for words until 'close pent-up guilts / Rive . . . ("Oh, God — it's two big Cs, I know"; he's still beating out the tempo with forearm conductor's downbeats — "Ah, yes — that's it") : 'Rive your *Con*cealing *C*ontinents, and cry / These dreadful summoners *grace*.'

He's using a trick of old hams I've known and worked with, who'd yell at a prompter "Give me a *letter*, not a word. No words, dammit! — A Letter, *the* letter!" And his sound on 'grace' eclipses that he'd given on the 'death' of yesterday. It's all perfectly logical and technical, of course; that 'grace', as the text shows, *can* be a cry, indeed, but it takes a certain kind of talent to spot this, as it takes a kind of sound to execute it. It's a comfort to encounter a great voice in theatre. Most actors get by with something much less.

There's a little pause at the end. Peter flaps the loose tails of his broadly striped green and yellow shirt over the excellent belly, upper chest glistening with sweat, his slow ingenuous smile spreading out from the jove-white beard across the wide cheeks. He knows he's done well, like the schoolboy who *did* do his homework. Phillips is smiling, also. He says, "That's fine." What else could he say? "Fine," he says again, gently, "Let's print it." I know how he feels. It could get better. And yet, in a sense, it can get *no* better, as it's already there.

Peter wipes his brow and admits, "Ran out of words half way through." There's a little chat. It's agreed that the words must wait, when necessary, for the biggest cracks in the thunder. There may be an extra-loud one before or after 'I'm a man / More sinn'd against than sinning'. Peter comments, "In the light of the previous scene — more peed against than peeing." Robin has strong certainties on which way the elements will be attacking; the wind veering in gusts from *both* sides, the thunder "right overhead." It seems we're in the exact eye of the storm, the rain a downpour, moderating to squalls. "Thank you very much!" says Peter, "It's terribly difficult to direct traffic if you can't see the cars."

They have another go, Robin sitting far back. On the final exit, Lear joins in Hutt's dance (as the Fool) and for a moment, one can't tell which is Lear and which is Fool. Knowing that the 'Hovel' scene is scheduled to follow, Peter is improvising a little snatch of song, and I catch the end of it: "It's time for Hoveltime." Robin says "It's all right, for the time being. Nice."

They have another little chat, some "connectings" are still to be thought on. "It'll be easier when the words are more settled in your head," says Robin. They'll have to choose the really big bits, and less big bits, "Or you'll never make it through the week." Peter admits that "The Celestials helped a bit; I suppose it's this working in Church." It's suspected that the 'Howl, howl, howl,' of the last scene will be much tinier. Resting a little on mutual laurels, Robin then asks Peter to "Do that Sergeant" (some Ustinov immitation of some previous day), and Peter, for the benefit of those who missed it, gives us a reprise. The sudden stance and barrack-room vocal bludgeoning of this Sergeant (with immense belly growl) beggars description.

They discuss some ingredients of the 'Before a Hovel' scene before going into it: how it is with Lear by this time, his wits astray. A typically rich Ustinovian fantasy develops, as Peter lightly improvises on a Lear now faced with the loss of all knightly comforts, even (a Dickensian ripeness) of those who could *do the howling for him* ... "That *excellent* society of very old women from Hemel

Hempstead; they can make a *dreadful* racket!" Of things neglected, large and small, he adds "Poor Florence Nightingale — should have made her a Dame long ago . . ." And a wider spectrum, convinced now that the 'Prayer' which precedes the entrance of Edgar/Poor Tom into the scene, is a "sociological speech about the dispossessed — and then," adds Peter with delighted certitude, "Promptly enter 'Jockstrap'." An early coffee-break is declared and Ustinov subsides, waving us away to "Hysterica Espresso."

Mr. Rodger Barton: Edgar-Poor Tom

SATURDAY, SEPTEMBER 1ST   *continued*

SERBO-CROAT

Afterwards we take a look at this 'Before a Hovel' scene (III.iv). Peter again struggles with some of the words. Who wouldn't? 'Thou'ldst shun a bear', is followed soon after by 'Thou'ldst meet the bear i' th' mouth!' The second one really trips him. He inter-

53

jects, "Serbo-Croat — that bit!" It would be a mouthful for anyone. I recall one Lear, excellently weathered for the role though he was, who shook his head like a bemused rhino and demanded a three line excision. (This was Anew McMaster, and he cut them only until he'd learned all the rest, which took some doing.)

The scene is brought to a halt a little later. Barton (now Poor Tom) is out of breath. This is not surprising for, from his entry as Poor Tom, stripped for rehearsal to running shorts, he has taken a killing pace and pitch, mostly in total falsetto, while hurling himself about the periphery of St. John's Hall. It's a hellish commitment and as crazed as bedlam. A pause is called while Rodger recovers, and some small points are cleared for Hutt and Ustinov. Rodger, breath returning, says he had to try it all in his top voice. "I don't think," cautions Robin gently, "that your top voice lives in your throat." They return to the scene, this time finishing it. "Very brave, Rodg," says Robin. Barton emphasises that the earliest attempt "was whole hog," and our director concludes that it was "a nice try — and also nice to get it out of the way." Rehearsal is a time to reach for anything. Here, one may sink or swim, without endangering oneself, or others. In rehearsal we do it for ourselves. In learning to fly, as we must for performance, we often risk sinking a little. It's a small price to pay for the chance to make the sea-change into something rich, and often strange. As the thought nudges me, it may have something to do with a little sing-song from Ustinov, in deep bass and hardly in earshot: "Full whole hog my father lies ... of his bones are 'something' made." I don't know what Peter is thinking, but only that his mind seldom (if ever) moves away from his objectives as Lear; the actor lives most acutely in rehearsal. There's more talk on the enormous technical challenge in the role of Edgar. Rodger, lathered in sweat (someone has brought him a towel), is drying off. Phillips thinks that it probably doesn't need to be so loud; that it needs, in fact, to be quiet. There is something, somehow, that manages to calm him down. An initial fear for Edgar is to maintain his disguise as Poor Tom. Kent, the Fool, or Lear would all have known him as Edgar in the court, and later in the scene he must face his father.

Robin says Rodger must give himself time to think. He might, for instance, even smile at what other people won't, "something totally irrational." Marti Maraden offers a discovery she had made while working on Ophelia two seasons past: the desire of Ophelia from within her madness, to still communicate — to the King, to others. How might this be related to one who is pretending madness?

Phillips points out that Poor Tom insists he is being chased by a devil, but is there not perhaps something equivalent to a friendly gesture, of "Don't come near *this* hovel"? Ustinov adds, only half-jesting, "Vacancies for Three — afraid there's no room for Four . . . frightful!"

Robin is still insistent that much of Poor Tom can be played at low level. He asks if Edgars are usually inclined to hysteria in this scene: the question is rhetorical. Douglas Rain, present in this rehearsal, and a previous Edgar at Stratford, remains silent. Having once done Edgar myself, I've a strong compulsion to contribute, but don't want to break my observer's stance. My own ideas (as I've found, again, while remaining mum) are often encapsulated by others. Peter has one: "Edgar talks like a defrocked clergyman." I'm thinking myself of the obsessive sexuality implicit in this scene (almost every allusion from Mad Tom is carnal), as will be the case in so much of Lear's 'madness in sanity' on the heath later. Robin concludes that it is the sexual undertow in the play that releases that engendering of daughters, sons — the perpetration of all the blindings, murders, abandonments. My own conclusion is that Edgar elects to play the sexual game because this is what Lear so evidently wants to hear. The talk goes on, with many agreements. Lear has become a nurse to Edgar, but it's a reciprocal service. Edgar is a protector in the play and serves in that role throughout. He allows his Dad to jump (only when it's *safe*) to prove a point. "It's a play about appearances," says Peter, "What people wear is what they are." Indeed. The naked truth, as it is argued for by Edgar, Kent, Cordelia, is what links them all, and they pay the same price — expulsion and banishment — and are stripped of both clothes and inheritance.

SATURDAY, SEPTEMBER 1ST   *concluded*

MORE EROSION

We are to have another go, Rodger being asked to think of all these things "happening to your loon." Perhaps he should try only a *suggestion* of dialect, with less accent. Afterwards the talk resumes. Robin asks Peter to comment on the words 'When the mind's free, the body's delicate,' which Ustinov does with dazzling articulacy.

55

For Lear, the whole play is a journey to fundamentals. It's a tough trip, but he knows "he will be enriched if he survives." It's a discovery, for Lear, of what is the basic need. The encounter with Poor Tom is a critical step, with this Ghandi taking off his clothes (as Lear assumes) for some psychological reason. It's no wonder that Lear thinks that this creature speaks Greek; he must, with so few clothes on! Peter has invested many of his lines to Poor Tom with a marvellously excessive academic inflection: 'First let me talk to this philosopher!' 'I'll talk a word with this same *learned* Theban.' 'What is your study?' 'Noble philosopher, your company.'

Peter warms to the theme that "because Poor Tom is clearly nuts, Lear isn't scared of him," as both Kent and the Fool are, who try to protect Lear from him. He's no room to hide a gun, this naked creature; where would be put it? Besides, the creature might lead him out of this mess, along the paths of survival, if not righteousness; he seems to have been out on the heath some considerable time. "What do you do," asks Peter, "in your third year out here?" He offers up some thoughts on city derelicts, "as jealous of their space as the prostitutes of their pavement." Robin tries a short exercise. Rodger is to do one of his "straight" Edgar speeches from earlier in the play, but become progressively madder as he hears Robin's hand clap on a copy of the text. He is stopped quite soon with the caution that to go any further "would mean that we wouldn't understand a word you say."

We start on another 'look' *Before the Hovel* again (III.iv). Robin soon stops it, and asks them to start again, but not before he has lugged Lear's huge high-backed chair into the middle of our empty space. "Oh," mutters Peter with sham simplicity, after gazing at it a moment, "that's very convenient. It's just *abandoned* there, is it?" Then he adds, more seriously, "To stop me fidgeting?" He has some reluctance to get into it, and says it's "the most uncomfortable of chairs!" He should know, as he's endured it often enough in that opening scene. It seems he has tremors of that Blinding Scene: "It's just that I'm afraid they may tie me into it." Finally, he sits, agreeing to explore — better — those first big speeches of the sequence which are, indeed, "rather reflective stuff."

The immediate result is more contained, filmic. Phillips has asked him to lock his head as in a tight close-shot. The line 'Seek thine own ease' takes on an extra definition of serenity; it's implication of "I've got my own now — look after yourselves." Robin suggests that Lear, here, "has come to a plateau in feeling." Peter agrees, with minor reservations that, from the 'prayer' on, "there is a new attitude toward man." Lear, after the weeping fit, when he *had* to hit out, still has the will to continue; he doesn't want to lose that anger. Though there are no tears left now, it's because he's too tired. But (and here's the reservation) Peter's "not sure that the prayer is altogether a prayer ... He could be cheating." And more than a little; it's true that Lear seldom does anything by halves. The "post-orgasmic serenity" is there, Peter feels, as a preparation for Poor Tom, but in the 'prayer' Lear may well be twisting the end. "If you're clever enough, you can cheat the heavens." This is close enough to Robin's notion that there is no energy left any longer to say more than "Just go away ... Go find your peace; I've found mine." Calamity hasn't done to Lear what the others imagine. He's even beginning to be more astute (within his crazed boundaries), and could be — as Robin puts it — "halfway to the thing with the flowers" (IV.vi).

Some jesting points are entertained after the next work-through. Peter does an improvisation on Lear's new awareness of waste, the pomp under criticism being nicely Victorian (or closer to our time) as Lear growls out suspicious distaste for showtime excesses, those troopings of the colours. Peter envisages, too, some use for umbrellas in the downpour; Kent's could be forever blown inside out while he is doing his best to shelter Lear. Poor Kent! Lear is driving *him* mad with all that stuff about the daughters. Other troubles also, such as "That thermos, with the rancid beef-tea," and the poor Fool, shaking to death near him. Robin, countering this half-levity, adds, "Moments's too, where something in the wind could be related to Cordelia."

The session is wearing down, yet they try once more. On Barton's entrance as Poor Tom, he is stopped, begins again, and is stopped. Each time Phillips slows him down more. "Ask him again," he says to Ustinov, 'What has't thou been?' 'A serving man, proud in heart and mind', begins Barton, on this aria in prose. Phillips stands just behind him, a breeze of thoughts, blows onto his back, calming him, slowing him down. "Ask him again," says Phillips, a hand on Barton's shoulder, the other holding a quickly-given script from Vince Berns, as he slowly gestures Barton to the floor, crouching him, easing him onto his back. Rodger tries to rise with the words, but his head is put back, firmly but gently: "You're going under anaesthetic ..." Phillips becomes narrator and interrogator. "Imagine it's the Crimean War. You're on a stretcher. Wounded, delirious." The purpose of this exercise is soon clear. It reduces — reduces. "What were you ... ? I see ... " It's a bit of the confessional, too. "Oh, a *real* man I was. So God-fearing, Sir! Brave! Proud! But — I have to admit the seamy side. Used to get pissed, gamble and screw around ... 'Served the lust of my mistress' heart, and did the act of darkness with her.' "So I got turned out, Sir. Things been 'orrible ever since ..." Robin, concluding, says: "There's a whole case history here."

Just so. The week ends as it began. With reductions. A paring down. As the work of rehearsal washes over the characters, the whole play, the whole massive shape of the work, eroded more and more, gives us all back much more to think about, always much more to know.

MILD? — IT'S LETHAL

Back in the Avon this morning, Marti Maraden and Tom Wood are on-stage as Regan and Oswald (IV.v). A heavy desk, square on, down-centre, is pivotal in the spare action. Sparce, strained words. Marti is nice in long brown skirt, tight tank-top sweater; Tom is easy, as always, in jeans. Regan is on the spit, suspicious. *What's* her sister Goneril up to with Edmund? She knows a lot, but not enough: 'I know your lady does not love her husband' ... '*Some* things — I know not what!' ... 'I'll love thee much' ... 'I know you are of her bosom.' Tom Wood, a hugely sympathetic actor, playing a 'nastie' here, but never with the cliché cringing cadences of an easy route to the role, is adamant, tough in his own corner, not giving an inch (in any sense), unflinching even to the pent-up assault of Marti's, 'Y'are! I know't!'

Robin steps in for his first quiet commentary of the day. He has the angle of the desk changed to a diagonal. He stands close to both actors while they do it again, considering (but avidly), his eyes flicking from face to face, picking up options for tiny moves on syllables. Adopting a fencer's stance, he executes very quickly some lithe advances and retreats, giving nothing, neither way, for either of them. They try it a few times, the lunge and riposte of the dualogue sharpened with increased danger to both. Bert Carriere (still in his hacked-off jeans — it's hot outside but cerebrally cold in the Avon) offers up some linking music for the exit of Regan, which they are now practicing. Robin, back to his dimmer-switch, eases down the stage lights as Marti, moving to some lingering ambiguous chords from Bert's piano, "Exits, pursued by the desk." Well, the props have got to get off, too.

A big jump back in our story follows. Play rehearsals — like movie takes — are worked on in any sequence: it's Tom Wood now and Donna Goodhand's Goneril (I.iii). Robin is busied with the manner of their entrance, its exact tempo, timing it with the music (from Bert), manipulating them to hit the stage on a precise phrase. They do it again and again. "Go!" (this for Donna), and "Go!" he calls again (for Tom). He then leads them off-stage, consults, ushers them into it once more. Tom is asked to breathe deeply, and Donna to experiment with a different use of space. The exact rhythm of the entrance will set the tempo for the start of the scene. "Are we in prose?" asks Robin into the dark of the auditorium. We aren't, in fact, but it is something related to a prose feeling he is establishing. He dwells on a topical variant: "Ah . . . Like Eh . . . Ah . . . You know . . . Eh . . . Ah . . . Y'Know . . . Sort of . . ."

Ustinov enters, first cigar lit, greeting all in a momentary break, settling into a stalls seat — note pad on his lap — he starts to sketch rapidly. Robin, calling "Go! — Go!" once again, supplies a full farmyard cacophony: distant chickens, dog, goat. Goneril, in very sour mood, asks: 'Did my father strike my gentleman for chiding of his fool? . . . His knights grow riotous'. Robin reminds Donna that the whole place, now become Lear's new party-room, *her* place, is now in a dreadful mess. (A glance, somewhat later, at Peter's cartoon, shows us a very different interpretation.)

It's time to move on. "Next!" calls Robin briskly, and we're into the Dover scene; Barton and Rain, son and blinded father (IV.vi). Rain is utterly secure (as an actor) in the terrifying insecurities of Gloucester: 'Away, and let me die', is already very moving. Phillips gets Barton to try the cliff speech again. "We'll all close our eyes and tell you if we think we are outdoors." Then Ustinov is on, up-stage, as Lear; plays his long scene, knows it, and gets off — or rather gallumps off: 'Sa-sa-sa-sa-sa.'

Things are getting done with extra speed today. We are on to Cordelia greeting Kent in the French Camp (IV.viii). Attendant officers are on in an instant, standing in a long diagonal corridor from up-right to down-left. Robin orchestrates the entrance of Cordelia; her sudden stop, her long walk down to Kent, momentarily pausing, a sudden right-angle turn and down the steps to face

Mr. Peter Ustinov   Mr. William Hutt   Mr. Jim McQueen
Mr. Rodger Barton   Miss Donna Goodhand   Mr. Tom Wood

"Did my father strike . . . ?"

him. They start this again and again with Bert, still at his piano, playing the bridge into the scene. Robin conducts the precise flow of the movement — or the movement he so precisely wants. Cordelia enters, stopping for two beats, and the fluidity of her long move is suspended in a rhythm reminiscent of the best romantic movies (Natasha — or any princess — arriving at the ball); the move continues, slowly quickening into that final arabesque.

It's pure choreography again. "Once more!", and "Go!", calls Robin for the courtiers, and "Go!" for Cordelia. They prepare once more, Robin pauses, asking: "Anything wrong, Ingrid?" Ingrid ventures that it seems "Odd." "Yes," responds Robins, loping off-stage to his stalls seat. "*Very* odd — it's called art." Settling into his seat he murmurs, "Art as opposed to — naturalistic." Instantly, he leaps back again on-stage for further arrangement of positions — and sounds. Peter is still sketching.

He tells courtiers to inhale together, sharply, as Ingrid enters, and to hold breath during her long walk down, exhaling just as she makes the last turn into Kent. He takes it through meticulously with Ingrid, doing the whole walk with her, "Now, *here* I feel 'Public', and still 'Public', and then, on this last bit . . . 'Private'. This extra move at the end will make me think you've gone past a colonnade." It's tried again, the "Fellahs' inhaling and exhaling — quite a twelve-fold sigh — and the response, from those sitting out front, is rapt. "Now, do it like 'Rose Marie', calls Phillips; and Bert Carriere, responding with alacrity, adapts his music, improvising with abandon. Cordelia and her Fellahs give an immediate evocation of the worst excesses of sentimental nostalgics, and Jim McQueen, as Kent, encouraging Ingrid's lesser bravura, misses the final embrace and clowns a full-length fall. "*Now* do it 'serioso'," calls Robin; and we have it for the last time, on the way to perfection, and it doesn't seem like "art" at all. The customers, when they're here, may even gasp a little, not knowing why. The best of our tricks are always to make it more real for them.

When we get to Lear's entrance, Robin softly calls "Pierre," and Peter eases his way out of the wings and onto his couch (Still IV.viii). He awakens, when his time comes, to 'fair daylight?', which today he invests, not with rapture (he's tried that already), but rather an early morning unease akin to a hangover. On the pricking of his finger he tastes the results as doubtful evidence of life. He ends the scene with simple, uncomplicated candour, with an extra deep bow to the upstage Fellahs who had entertained him (and the rest of us) so well for the previous hour. It's an easy start into the day's work. And it's time for a coffee break.

During the break I encounter Peter backstage, and he tells me he's read the first dozen pages of my journal — I'd given him a copy of the opening section at the end of the previous week. He says he's enjoyed it, and I deprecatingly remark that it's somewhat mild as yet, but that I'm hoping it may become richer as it goes along. "Mild?" he responds with mock ferocity, "It's lethal!" He as quickly assures me that it's a lot of fun, a fair account of proceedings, and thinks it worthwhile that I should continue.

But that's as far as I've time to go today.

TWENTY-THREE EXTRAORDINARY LINES

There is a very new dimension, an added resonance somehow in the theatre this morning. Or perhaps there is more than just one special thing in the atmosphere which intrudes, nudging my consciousness; it's a long time before I recognize or admit it. Berthold Carriere is present, as usual, ensconced in his usual place, down-stage right on the forestage, strumming out early thoughts on his incidental music, his score sheet already heavily annotated. A sprinkling of the cast sits close to the stage along the left aisle, a popular place, being, as it is, close to the back-stage pass-door. The stage is set up for the end scene, with Phillips moving quietly about the stage area, thinking, considering options. It's the usual hush of concentration, of actors sipping coffee, talking in quiet asides. Although it's not yet 11 a.m., the mood, as at any Phillips rehearsal, is deferential, charged with expectancy and challenge. After all, he is one of the masters.

But nothing about this is surprising. The hush attendant on Phillips' working sessions (he is as particularly inconsequential when he's chatting and relaxing) is as absolute as that a major orchestra accords a Beecham or any front rank classical conductor. But all of these are standard ingredients. It is something else in the air which suggests promise.

And then I belatedly notice that the Lighting Designer's place is set up, as is traditional, slightly back from mid-stalls, dead-centre; and there is another off-stage glow from the shaded lamp over the board and lighting charts. Michael J. Whitfield is assisted by Harry Frehner, who designed the lighting for my production of *The Playboy of the Western World* some time ago in Montreal. There is something especially significant about the first appearance of the Lighting Designer at rehearsal, not unlike the point of no return in a long-distance flight, as exact for me as the thrill of a full house theatre, hungry for that sensation we work to achieve. And, yet, the thrill is tempered by the thought that so much of the rehearsal is gone, and only so much of it is now left to go. (With three weeks of rehearsal almost past, there are just more than three weeks of work left in hand.) People will always continue to come and *hear* a play, but they'll hear it better with the right light in the right places. The presences of Michael and Harry signal the start of the technical

62

skills which will be welded to the esoteric extravagances of our actors.

But also, today, there's a further grace-note which lends a certitude of action to our endeavours. Patrick Crean, Fencing Master, veteran of innumerable safe conflicts in some thousands and more plays and films, is here to take note of requirements. Clipboard in hand, painstaking, impeccably de rigueur in blazer and slacks (except for the work-session plimsoles), wonderfully, almost implausibly British as only an Irishman can be, Mr. Crean is Courtesy Attendant on Massacre, redolent of slayings, and all of them safe ones. A rare 'Pro' for the Pros, Paddy is lightly moustached in the tradition of Ronald Colman, or Errol Flynn (who was his close friend), and those romantic good looks of that never-vanished Ruritania. The stage this morning has been set up for the last scene, which will include the sword-fight between Edmund and Edgar (V.iii).

Our final scene will embrace the typically several deaths of Shakespearean tragedy, all but one off-stage, however. In the course of events we'll hear of the deaths of Regan, poisoned by Goneril; Goneril, stabbing herself; both the Fool and Cordelia, hanged off-stage by order of Edmund; and Edmund, mortally wounded by Edgar and borne off-stage to expire, leaving the stage space unsullied for the passing of Lear. However, in our case, we're being loyally Elizabethan and having the bodies of Regan and Goneril brought back on.

The scene is rehearsed up to and including the dialogue covering the fight. Robin, in close conference with Paddy Crean, outlines essentials. There will be lots of Seconds, both Junior and Senior, much flashing of blades, salutes — formal and dangerous. It will be cavalry sabres, with lots of lethal swishing, and cut rather than thrust. On the conclusion, Phillips rehearses a sudden eruption from formal tight-lipped restraint among the courtly group into desperate mayhem as Goneril struggles off-stage. The niceties of all this worked out or, rather, its basic scenario, Paddy Crean can withdraw to his study to envisage and set down in neat type (often with illustrations), his exact choreography. Ustinov arrives, to try the entrance with the dead Cordelia and the 'Howl—howl—howl.' Robin then tries it himself, carying the dead Ingrid, as Peter supplies the words and can better judge little options of when exactly to arrive; when and where, exactly, to set his burden down. It's a nice early-in-the-day gesture from Robin, himself an unfathomed well of stamina; he's a preserver, as well as a nurturer of it in others.

As Peter tries it once more, Robin prowls selective parts of the stalls, checking sight-lines, a protector now of a perfect view of all proceedings for seats extremely left or right. At one point he makes a long walk from the back of the stalls, up onto the stage, and far up-stage, to minutely adjust two soldiers' positions, stopping on his way back to minimally alter an obscuring knee of Rodger Barton beside the dying Lear. Much of the work today will be essentially technical, and it is certainly technical needs which are nudging most elbows. And yet, as in any rehearsal of a great work, there is always the chance of a momentary revelation.

The final set is struck, and we go back to Lear's expulsion before the storm (II.iv). They push on today to include the arrival of Goneril, and Lear's final plea to both sisters, 'Reason not the need'. Anyone familiar with the text, or its performance, will know that this speech is the vocal climax for Lear, before his departure to face the elements. And many will also know that at this point an audience expects, as in the tradition established in Grand Opera and its devotees from Dress Circle to 'gods', that the hero must dazzle with the fullest blast of vocal theatrics. It's odd, I've often thought, that this amazing speech contains one of the greatest potential farce lines in Shakespeare. 'I will have such revenges on you both / That all the world shall — / I will do such things, / What they are, yet I know not, but they shall be / The terrors of the earth.'

Peter Ustinov is a very funny man. His extraordinary gift for humour springs from a rich range of very personal resources, not the least of which is a delightful ingenuousness. The fifty-eight-year-old star actor is (amongst all the other parts of his persona) a six-year-old boy who wants to be an actor. He does nothing to make the above lines funny. But what he achieves with them, in how he sounds and how he looks, is one of the most moving things in acting I've ever known. Not too surprising, perhaps, as Lear, in these particular lines, is nothing if not ingenuous. But the entire speech, in the context of Ustinov's and Phillips' conception, is studded with surprises, all of them startlingly true.

At the moment the speech begins, Lear has been ground down in successive budgetary restraints by Regan and Goneril, from a hundred retainers to fifty, to twenty-five, to 'What need one?' As Ustinov builds the sequence up to here, his loudest explosion has been on 'How came my man i' the stocks!' (or its successive variants in the text which Peter, at this stage, is struggling to untangle). He offers us increasing sforzandos on the recurrent 'Return with *her*! — and fifty men dismissed', a somewhat earlier speech.

Yet now, taking Goneril by the hand, absently (but mixed with guile), he sits with her on that trunk and makes his last bid — managing to disguise the fact that it *is* his last desperate bid — for a decent deal and friendly compromise. The bitterness is there, but held in rein. Lear may be sitting down: what Lear but Ustinov's would dream of that, in this moment, but at least he's not on his knees. Marti Maraden's delivery (as Regan) of 'What need *one*?' is not that old-hat stridency, but almost gentle, cajolatory. And Peter's 'Reason not the *need*' has the throw-away simplicity of a grandfather's "Don't be foolish, little girl."

The slow growth into anguish through the following twenty-three line speech is as startling and miraculous as a birth. Peter even manages to raise a laugh (his own, but one in which we can uneasily join) within the 'Thou art a lady . . .' section. His growing grief is released into self-righteousness and conjunctive self-pity. His increasing loss of all emotional control is counterbalanced (by Robin's staging) with the slow withdrawal of both daughters, first Goneril and then Regan, leaving him isolated on the trunk now, battering it with his heels (we'd seen Robin suggest this), 'Fool me not so much / To bear it tamely!' The appeal to the gods, 'touch me with noble anger', is a cry beyond the frontiers of family into a Pascalian void; and 'let not women's weapons, water-drops / Stain my man's cheeks' is the more overwhelming because, by this time, his face is awash with tears. His closing words are remarkable. 'You think I'll weep: / No, I'll not weep: / I have full cause of weeping, but this heart / Shall break into a hundred thousand flaws / Or ere I'll weep.'

The effect assumes proportions of the heroic all the more as this Lear (where so many Lears decide *not* to cry) has succumbed absolutely to that 'Hysterica passio' he had most feared at the start of the scene. The last six words are unendurable: 'O Fool! I shall go mad.' Without the help of his Fool, here, at last, is a Lear who would never make it off the stage alone. Bill Hutt's quite long move down to take his hand, and their slow shuffle off, becomes, for both of them, an apotheosis of actors; two Lears of our time who can both play a Fool.

And yet, in this quite technical day's work, nothing we do or see each other do in this Company is ever final or self-congratulatory. We are faced with the moment by moment necessity of going on, buttressed by moments such as these. There is always the following scene(for me the next paragraph) to draw us on. It occurred to me often during the day that prompting (and Michael Benoit is doing his best with Peter) is a difficult skill to acquire. Different actors need a different type of prompt. In Peter's case it's problematic knowing when to step in, for he has an alarming capability to invent blank verse when he misses half a line (or more) and substitute his own colloquialism.

Today, Peter graciously acknowledges, "Sorry, I can't quite get this act together." But the words matter less at this time, when it's thoughts that count most. Robin suggests a sudden switch here and there in emphasis or direction. They try the scene again, and some small details are added on the departure of Lear and followers. Elements found today, rejected or retained, for the time being coalesce in the shifting montage of the scene taken again, and again, in whole or in part.

Peter exploits his difficulty in seeing Tom Wood (as Oswald) amongst the throng. "It's quite effective *not* to be able to find him at once." And his '... do not make me mad' to Goneril becomes progressively dismissive, and also larger and louder, but still in the realm of the family squabble, from which there is the sudden pull-back into pathetic regret: 'We'll no more see one another.' It reminds me of the way in which O'Neill's people keep putting the knife in — and as instantly say how sorry they are — in that other great family play, *Long Day's Journey Into Night.* (In fact, it's hoped that Robin will direct it next season, in conjunction with a revival of *King Lear.*) And now, this family row is built, with Phillips ad-libbing for all of them. As a director, he is at his most finely attuned in dealing with the family play, which gives him an extraordinary range of great plays on which he can work. He is now improvising for all of them; Goneril, Regan, Cornwall. "*Not* guilty? ... What d'ye mean! ... For God's sake, the whole bloody family is biting each other's heads off! ... I mean, *you* tell him ... Just you tell him! ... He can stay out! ... His own bloody fault! ... And no good coming back!! ... No spare keys.... The *Elements* can teach 'im!"

I scribbled these bits down, but Robin *acted* them. And acted them well. No actor worth his salt would fail to pay attention to such a bonus from a director — most directors, even some of the best, are not able to act at all. Phillips knows how to give up, in order to move on. Despite his protestations to the contrary, there was once the loss of a real actor when that director was born.

"You're absolutely right, Marti, and another thing I can add — " he is saying, improvising now for Miss Maraden. "There's a tremendous logic to all this," says Peter, very often. How right he is.

They are all back on-stage to do Lear's exit again. 'Horse — to horse!', calls Ustinov from off-stage, changing it to a confused sound because Robin felt there was an effect needed there: "It doesn't *have* to sound like anything." 'Horse', — "Haaheehiihoohuugh," supplies Ustinov. Robin is often getting in close, lying on the fore-stage, a dark silhouette today contrasting with the harsh light in the actors' faces. After Lear's exit, Douglas Rain's re-entrance as Gloucester, 'The King's in high rage,' reminds us that Hutt and Rain are almost nonparticipants in this area of the play; and for Rain, especially, it's been a long wait, watching the steady build-up to disaster for Lear.

The whole group is back again to work on Lear's exit. Robin, suddenly, to release the muscular and mental tensions of the long rehearsal, calls to Bert, "Get 'em to dance . . . Dance!" To the cast he calls out, "Say any one line in Shakespeare, and *dance*! Da da — da da, da — dah!!! Go!" And seventeen actors break into a wide and wild variation of soft-shoe and tap, accompanied by syncopated snatches from seventeen plays. Or perhaps not quite so many because, though Ustinov lifts a game leg (for an instant only), and Hutt, still sitting comfortably, taps a toe, Rain remains imperviously immobile. With tension released (it *does* work), it's back into the scene. Some tighter rhythms are tried, some words are not right; "Don't you make me angry!" from Peter, for 'I prithee, daughter, do not make me mad!': "Ah. There's *another* bit I never get," says Peter, adopting tones of sweet reasonableness, the paterfamilias, a perfect 'Vicar of Wakefield'. And yet we get the violence in Lear, too. Donna and Marti put on more and more pressure. Robin calls for another dance: "Da da — da da — da dah," and thirty (or so) feet pound the stage.

At one point in the day I have a chat with Peter. He reaffirms his blessing on my record of our endeavours, and is very happy to receive a copy of my *John Synge Comes Next* (the book of my one-man show, Oxford University Press, 1973). "I share a birthday with him, you know. With Synge, Chaplin, and Anatole France — quite a combination!" Peter knew Chaplin well, though he never worked with him, it seems, and he tells me the bizarre tale of the black-comedy theft of Chaplin's body by a Pole and a Bulgarian. Peter's own lawyer in Switzerland set up the police-trap. We later talk for a while of our production of *Lear*, and our cast. He's extremely happy with the Company and admires our level of discipline. I'm able to tell him we feel the same way about him. It occurs to me often, when we talk together, that Peter's humour, though a gift, is also a choice; as with Shaw, the laughter is always a part of the mask.

Later, they've set up for the opening scene once more. Robin cautions all the girls, even as they relax before they begin, "Daughters, I don't think you should lean back in your chairs." Obviously, Robin is already thinking forward to costumes. The scene begins, low-keyed, with clinical political edge. Doug Rain and Jim McQueen, adroit as senior civil servants, discuss the bastardy of Edmund almost (in fact deliberately) in his hearing; Monette as Edmund is within spitting distance of both in this terse prologue. Ustinov is soon on as Lear, with cigar, green and yellow shirt, and yellow socks, Churchillian pauses and rhetorical flourishes — and very slow on names. (The hesitancy is Lear's, not Peter's, though one difficulty sometimes leads to the other.) On the conflict with McQueen's Kent, he collapses into that uncomfortable chair, suggesting something close to a further stroke. Lear's rejection of Cordelia, his departure from the room leaning on Burgundy, is silly, foolish, self-indulgent, awful.

The scene runs on into the trio of the sisters, through Cordelia's departure, Goneril's and Regan's calculative coda — very quietly played. Monette's soliloquy follows (I.ii). Edmund stakes out the trap for his Father, Gloucester, and for Edgar, Barton entering 'pat' just when needed, and the whole huge sub-plot is unleashed. Monette, rehearsing with cool, clinical insolence, walks out whistling Mozart. The stage is empty — only for a moment — before Vince Berns calls for a strike and set-up of Albany/Goneril's Courtyard (I.iii).

When I return a little later (I *do* actually walk away from it sometimes), the scene is well advanced. The Knights-Followers are in full laugh at Hutt's and Ustinov's jokes. Donna Goodhand's Goneril is gaining enormous strengths very quickly. With one outburst on the 'not to be endured riots' one can hear that, as with Lear, there's more than a bit of the family energy in her. Robin joins them on-stage to make changes in space and positions. He pays particular attention to Donna, rehearsing her (in her short skirt) as though she already wore her longer dress with its Victorian train. Donna executes a few turns, on her lines, before and after a line, kicking her imagined train behind, always in preparation for her next move. Robin comments, "I love these," and tries a few himself, looking for the best moment for each kick and move. I've a hunch that next time we see Donna she'll be in a longer rehearsal skirt. We've reached Lear's exit: 'Go, go my people'. And we all do, as it's a break at four-thirty. But the day's work isn't over yet. There's a special call tonight for anyone who is available. As I am.

THURSDAY, SEPTEMBER 6TH *concluded*

FRIGHTFUL NEGOTIATIONS

A small group is gathered in the Greenroom at the Festival Theatre. Some uncertainty — a rare thing — there may be a cancellation of rehearsal. With productions at three theatres, the smallest being The Third Stage with 500 seats 'in the round', the call-sheets issued daily assume the complexity of those for a major motion-picture. In our case perhaps more so, with eleven productions still in performance and *Lear* the last of the season in rehearsal. Robin joins us (very relaxed), and tells me Edna O'Brien is in to see *Love's Labour's Lost*, and that Ustinov, last seen in her company, appears to be lost. But Peter arrives not long after. He'd got it wrong and gone first to the Church Hall. "Deserted! Thought I was the first, for once."

We then gather in the rehearsal hall, the little group sitting in a small circle; Rain, Wood, McQueen, Marti Maraden, Barton, Webster, Hutt, Phillips, Ustinov, and Greg Peterson, an assistant director who came for two months in February, and has stayed on. The feeling is so relaxed one wonders what (if anything) can be done. The light-hearted mood has been brought with us from the Greenroom. Robin had told us (before Peter arrived) of Ustinov declining an enormous fee ($120,000) for a commercial for powdered milk. The manufacturers, Peter discovered, were under scrutiny because of its doubtful nutritional value, albeit enormous sales in under-developed countries. He's also told us of Peter's imitations of the Company of a couple of days before, and of their weird accuracy — "But I really couldn't recognize myself at all." (One seldom recognizes a perfect imitation of oneself as others can.) Robin has promised us, downstairs, that the rehearsal will begin with him asking Peter to do Phillips.

True to his word, he now turns to Ustinov, blandly informing him, "Our rehearsal begins with everyone's immitation of me, starting with you, Peter." Ustinov, collecting himself, sensing conspiracy,

69

confines himself to a few basic Phillips traits of vocabulary. "Sorry, but I'm really not prepared for more." The exercise is dropped, much to my disappointment, the better mimics in the Company being present.

Robin decides on a calm, sit-around, D.L.P. (dead letter perfect) run-through of some scenes, starting with 'Before that Hovel' (III.iv). Phillips maintains a gently determined eye on the text, and Peter is in trouble promptly. But only for an instant. He then quickly gets one right, 'Pour on; I will endure', just as the cannons boom behind our backs. "*That's* the penalty!" he cries, "for getting it correct ... Didn't that surprise you!"

As we limp on through the long scene, it seems to me that Robin is taking a rare easy night (Robin resting is a contradiction), but we are all meantime on call to help Ustinov with his lines. 'What is the reason ...' ... "*Cause,*" insists Robin, interrupting, though his eyes are no longer on the book. 'What is the *cause* of thunder' — "It's *my* question, you know!" responds Peter.

His continuing ad libs, sotto voce under the continuing dialogue (when it isn't his turn to speak — in his crazed extempore bit with Poor Tom), have Bill Hutt in something close to hysterics. "*Fright-ful* negotiations, these, outside this hovel," Peter complains, explaining his troubles in getting them right. The scene at last comes to its conclusion, Peter running — almost — out of invention. 'No *words,* no *words,* no *words*' concludes Rain as Gloucester, agonized, giving us the best laugh of the rehearsal in his over-emphatic insistance. "What?" mutters Peter, "Not even Greek!"

"Very good," encourages Robin, "Let's do that much again." "Which much ...?" queries Peter. "*All* this much," insists Robin. Later we do another very long scene, that one at Dover (IV.vi). Rain and Barton are both meticulously correct on lines, and Ustinov, also (but with a little help), in his long mad arias. 'Fie, fie, pah, pah'. He corrects himself (one 'fie' missing), and secures it in his head with a tricky pop syncopation: 'Fie — fie fie! Pa Pah!'

We all go home, earlier than expected. There was a sweetness in the evening. The day's work has marked the exact halfway stage in our rehearsals, and I'm glad, and a little saddened, that my journal, also, could be half way towards its end. (I can add, now, with hindsight, that our rehearsals, and my journal, were merely getting into their stride.)

A TOUCH OF GODOT

The larger part of the cast is assembled in the Avon. It is almost 11 a.m. The stage is empty. The side panels of Daphne's cage contain the space, the up-stage wall flown out and, in the gap, the dimly perceived sky of the cyclorama. The whole is starkly lit by the glare of the Front-of-House spots, diminishing to gloom in the dark sky at back. Into this vacuum materializes, abruptly, the 'Jovial Presence,' garbed this day in bold-striped red and green shirt, cigar glowing. "Blow winds and crack yer Cheeks!" it trumpets gaily, the image as bright as a sunbaked general of the Risorgemento. "Bon Giorno, Pietro," responds Phillips quietly, "But it's the wrong scene." "Sorry I'm late ... Oh — I'm not? Ah, Good! ... I was on the telephone. From Ankara! That's probably a first for Stratford."

Things settle down promptly, Vince Berns calling for the Courtyard scene following Lear's expulsion, or self-expulsion, from Goneril's home (I.v). Lear enters with the Fool and Kent — whom he sends on with letters for Gloucester and/or Regan. It's that tricky bit again, and as complicated to describe as that. Our playwright, here, is clearly setting up all and/or any plot options. To name but two: there's the choice open in the later action that it can be from Gloucester's home (and not Goneril's or Regan's) that Lear is expelled, this making Gloucester dramatically culpable; and, most usefully, that Gloucester must suffer in his own home (the blinding) what — for his character — is the play's catastasis. But suffice it, for this moment in our action, that Kent goes ahead with those letters.

Lear stands, attended by the Fool only. Two potently evocative figures, they both shuffle forward a little; they both have the same walk. Who, I wonder, is watching whom more carefully? They both look out front as absolutely as two competing Variety comics. The dualogue proceeds or, rather, tries to, in the early day uncertainties, the grasping for correct lines attuned to the presence (in both) of the correct thoughts. It's a halting attempt at comfort from a Fool to a Master who has recognized the folly of being comforted. The sense of dereliction and isolation is as absolute as in Vladimir and Estragon; and my conjecture is immobilized as I realize that both actors can clearly encompass the demands of either Beckett role.

71

This is the kind of acting I love: perhaps it's the dimension (most freshly found) that our audiences never witness.

Phillips lies on the forestage, a foreground silhouette as in a landscape separating these two very vulnerable and bravely vertical figures against the dim sky on the bare stage platform. As the scene ends he rises, moving back to get a fresh cigarette: "*Deeply* moving little scene," he says quietly, his stress on the 'deeply' a guide to the depth of his feelings, and the range of ideas it has unleashed in him. It's worth remembering how he remarked (on that second day of rehearsal) that he thought there was "something extraordinary here." There certainly is.

There's time, first, for a brief chat. "Not *quite* right on the lines there — but *almost* right," claims Peter cheekily. He agrees with Robin that Kent's mission should be made to sound a bit like "sending James Bond behind the lines." Bill Hutt, typically, preserves his reserved, smiling silence. He's done Lear twice already, and I often wonder about how many of the lines he still remembers. Possibly more than Peter or I have yet managed to memorize.

They try again. "Stop!" calls Robin, even before McQueen's exit, and then dwells on the difficulties of this departure from "this Beckett-lit platform." Robin and I have shared no exchanges on this, but hearing this warms my conspiratorial heart. He pursues the Beckett resonance for McQueen on Kent's exit, "There's no *definite* route. Find out the terrain. Try to find which way you should go." Robin gestures from the dimly-lit stage into the darkened Avon, "Look at the bloody bog before you." I glow inwardly a little more. That thought, those words, are almost exactly out of 'Godot'. They have another go.

Hutt's Fool attempts his patter of consolation, each of his lines a fresh beginning in distraction, and Lear, embedded in his guilt and unease, is unable — or incapable — of being distracted or consoled. It's very like the discussion of the two Beckett tramps on the theoretic proposition of hanging (as a way out for one of them), which they at last abandon — a technical difficulty — in the absence of reliable props in their almost empty landscape.

It gives me a feeling of interminable sporadic exchanges by two aging brothers from adjoining beds far into the night, on themes worn smooth by variations since they were boys. Ustinov, in the broken, unfinished line 'I did her wrong...' startles me, as I'd always thought that Lear was thinking of Cordelia here; and yet, it could be related to Goneril, or perhaps even his wife — and all we know of her, in the play, is that she is dead. The Fool's line, 'Thou should'st not have been old till thou hads't been wise' is one that Lear does not want to hear, one (the way Bill does it) that we do not want to hear ourselves. We hear it often this morning, as the scene is taken again and again.

Robin steps up, quietly, from the stalls, after pushing his dimmer-switch, taking the stage lights out to total darkness. His cigarette is the only glow in the black. It grows brighter each time he sucks in a thought. "*Outside acting* is very weird," he says, "let's go again in the dark." And the words flutter out to us again; contained, locked forever, each one of them in the passing instant of each word's delivery. Like leaves, they fall as interminably, as inexorably as the cadences of Beckett's tramps, confirming again the genesis, the origin of Sam's so special species.

Phillips pursues a theme to which he so often returns: economy in the voice. In this scene, or any scene, it's always better to use a little than too much. Not that the words must be frozen forever into a murmur, but, rather, that the issue is never to push the sound towards any of those unnecessary extras. "It's astonishing, always, when we have — when we *find* that total confidence in knowing that the voice *will* communicate." In illustration of where the voices go, and how they go, he pitches his words only a tiny fraction more than the lesser murmur of his talk, "Ingrid! — Are you up there?" Ingrid Blekys is, as usual, in her favourite place near the back of the stalls, to glean from the day's endeavours. "Yes," she responds, catching Robin's precise, unexaggerated pitch. "Have you got your ash-try with you?" Robin continues. "Yes," responds Ingrid again, as quietly.

The scene is done again, from the top, once more in the dark, the voices of Hutt and Ustinov finding the words, caressing them, releasing them. And the pauses also assume an equal power with the words. Silence in great dramatic writing is as potent as the sound. The thoughts of Lear and his Fool run on in the silences between them, as absolutely as the music moves on in the rests of Mozart or Beethoven. The scene ends once more; there is a long — thoughtful — pause. The lights come back on.

QUITE A GOOD MOTIVATION

This is a fresh set-up (IIi.). It's the scene in which Edmund persuades his brother to abscond, fakes a struggle, and wounds himself in the arm to lend credence to his plot. Phillips soon interrupts, walking slowly up onto the stage for a long quiet chat with Richard Monnette. As he returns to his seat in the stalls his voice loudens (a typical Robin device for dissemination) to share a summary of what he'd been after. It's again a matter of voice: "The right one is in there, Richard, it's *inside* the voice and body — but you've still a bit of 'convention' hanging about. See if you can throw the convention out." The scene moves on to include the entrance of Barton (as Edgar) and his subsequent flight. Another interruption. There is some confusion: Monnette thinks he is "inside," but Phillips puts the matter right. "No. You are *outside*. There've been endless explanations about this courtyard — Edgar's out there on a fire escape."

"Go!" calls Robin, and they start again. One can feel the night air. Barton, entering, contrives not only to give first the sound of his jump, but has found a device to suggest the zinging of feet off that fire escape. Robin had mentioned it as a good suggestion (for Barton) of athleticism, and this Edgar seizes it. (I check this out by a quick trip to the wings and find there is a perfectly-placed steel ladder a stride or so from Barton's down-right entrance.)

The scene moves on to include the entrance of Gloucester and, later, Regan and Cornwall. Before the next try Robin again joins them on-stage, zeroes in on the action of Edmund wounding his own arm and the issue of this in terms of character. "It's a very weird mentality to use a knife like that ... find out exactly what this is ... The value being that you don't have to do any make-believe ... You've done it — shit! ... Wonderful *not* to have to act anything ... All you *know*, or can say is, 'I'm cut — and it *hurts*.' Gives you a totally new feeling. The sudden amount of blood. Remember what it's like when you do it with a breadknife ... Ahhh, I've done it."

Robin remains, standing, locked in concentration on the idea. His usual style is mobility, but often his stance becomes extraordinarily still, the impeccably neat persona, clinically committed to the thought, the problem in hand. He can stand thus, fingers

74

pressed together, even minute gestures subordinated to the flow of his thought. He is, like Ustinov, exceedingly articulate, and it takes tenacity to convey the essence of his style. Perhaps he has no style. He will abandon any route when he has pushed it to its limits, and as instantly find or invent another. As he put it to the Company on the first day of the season, "We will not *allow* ourselves to say something is impossible. Though you may, *if you have to*, say that something is not possible — *yet*."

Now he is giving something to Marti, to motivate her Regan, "What you've gone through is nothing to what *we've* gone through," that is, herself and Cornwall, as distinct from Gloucester. Then Robin gets back once more to what lies behind Edmund's feelings (after wounding himself): 'No — no — I *don't* want to know who gets the land . . . How do you all think it feels to be attacked, by your own brother?' "It's amazing how quickly one can get caught up in such *real* feelings when you've *real* blood trickling down your arm. Think of what it's like when someone you love says something unkind about your performance, how *that* hurts, much more specifically than criticism from a stranger." He asks Monette to remember that, as Edmund, he is too upset to contribute opinion. To the question, 'Was Edgar in consort with the riotous Knights?', the answer is just there, 'Yes.' As if it mattered. It doesn't matter to Edmund, who doesn't have to be malicious in the context of the scene, but merely matter-of-fact.

The next scene has been called by Vince, and Robin steps down, reluctantly, going towards his seat, but his mind is already flipping back to the previous point of that wounding. He calls lightly to Richard, as he goes, "Try it with a razor on the side of your arm — or somewhere it doesn't matter." Monette demurs. And yet, I've a hunch that Robin quite seriously means it, and that Richard (or Robin) would be capable of considering it. Mixed with the laughs there are some comments of unease from others. "Yes," concludes Robin, settling into his seat: "End of career, but quite a good motivation."

IT'S NOT POSSIBLE — YET

In the following sequence, Jim McQueen's Kent, entering to confront Tom Wood as Oswald, has a fine glint in his eye (II.ii). As he sets about Tommy, chasing him around the stage with good technical menace, Robin watches for a time and then interrupts. He tells Tom, "If you're frightened, the only muscles you have to control are the muscles of control. There's a lie going on if you tremble all over."

Robin pursues this proposition for quite a long time, during which I reflect on the challenge in this casting (as Oswald) for Tom Wood. He's an actor who works out from a basic central charm; he is essentially simpatico. Already, in Oswald, he is investing the role with an insolent sexuality, especially in the exchanges with Goneril and Regan. Robin, concluding his remarks (he's very reluctant to conclude), calls for the scene again, and suggests, "This time, Jim, *really* kill him." He adds, moving down off the stage, "Careful, Tommy." He then adds: "It's your fault if you get hurt." And again, he adds, "You're allowed to hit back."

They try again. Jim, discarding his own personal, quite genteel, mild manner, goes after Tom with added volatility: they are all over the stage, up and down the steps, Tommy at one moment beating frenziedly on the up-stage walls, calling for rescue. Every time the action flags for a half instant, Robin calls, "Go on! Go on! Go on!" On the mass entrance of Edmund, Cornwall, Regan, Gloucester and attendants, which multiplies the tumult, he has leapt onto the stage, repeatedly calling for them all to "Go on! — Go on! — Go on!"

He stops them for a moment, only for further exhortation. "If you can get there — *get there!*" he urges Jim. "Once Richard is on, it's *his* job to protect Tommy — and Bill, too." (Webster as Cornwall.) "Don't worry about Tommy, he'll be alright, he's a funny chap anyway, likes a certain amount of it." The laughter in the Company increases, Tom leading it. "He'll tell you when to stop; there's a certain point when it ceases to be pleasurable."

The scene is taken again, the pace and pressure multiplied, the mass entrance compounding the hurly-burly. "Go on! Go on! Go on!" shouts Robin again, and again, until Jim subsides (luckily, as a break is called), saying that he doesn't have any energy *left* to

76

go on. "Not *now* that is, not *yet* . . . All right — I'll give up cigarettes." "Well, that's about fifty percent of the energy requirement," asserts Robin. "Fifty!" exclaims Jim, though one can tell that he's accepted the challenge to summon up more, if more is needed.

After the short breather the scene is taken again. Phillips stresses that Jim and Tom can be sure they are safe with the same push and pace if they both have confidence in each other. They keep going this time, up to the point of Kent being put in the stocks, and a longer break is called.

FRIDAY, SEPTEMBER 7TH *continued*

A NEW JUVENILE

Some of the Company relax in the coffee shop across the road. There's some talk about Edna O'Brien who, it's hoped, may be writing for a production here next year. "A very good writer," comments Ustinov, who is one such himself, and has in fact started work on a new play, triggered off by his work this season on *Lear*.

Back in the Avon soon after, we start on the scene in Gloucester's Barn (III.vi). Lear (his mouth trembling, open, from the encounter with the elements), the Fool, Kent, Poor Tom, all begrimed, wet and exhausted — which they all manage to look — and led by Gloucester, mime a crouching entrance from the storm outside. But — not quite four: one of the quartet is missing. Bill Hutt, entering from the wrong side, momentarily lost, is apologetic, "Sorry, in my script — I've marked it down — it says 'Enter Stage Left'." Bill Hutt, veteran of over twenty years at Stratford, and far more starring roles, so many of them in the Avon, is delightedly reminded by many of us that 'stage-left' is indeed where the others came on. Just as delightedly, Bill concurs, "Why — so it is!" "Never mind," Robin consoles him, "It happens all the time to the new juveniles." As they move into the darkness of the wings to do the entrance once more, Ustinov can be heard, lightheartedly: "I'll talk a word with this same learned 'Hessian'." He clouts Bill affectionately on his disordered locks. Bill has an academic look — excellent casting for professors. William Hutt would be the last to describe himself as learned, and yet he is so. A quarter-century of grappling (with his intrinsic relaxation) onto major roles equips

77

him beautifully for this Fool. Bill's unique Fool is a powerful cumulative contribution to this show, to be learned from by our juveniles, aged or no. When the quartet is ushered in again by Rain as Gloucester, and left in the centre of the space, they establish, instantly, a picture of dereliction and total exhaustion. Ustinov, benumbed in body and wits as Lear, declares he will take an oath before this 'Distinguished!' ... "No?" ... 'Honourable assembly'. The hushed voices, the destitute figures, their helplessness in the presence of Lear's encroaching hallucinations; it's a breath of Beckett.

Mr. William Hutt: The Fool   Mr. Peter Ustinov: King Lear
Mr. Rodger Barton: Edgar   Mr. Jim McQueen: Kent
Mr. Douglas Rain: Gloucester

"Bring in the evidence."

SOLIDARITY

They're stopped for notes. Robin suggests a subtle change in the voice on Lear's 'bring in the evidence'. He thinks there might almost be the sense of an echo on the word 'evidence'; that, though being in a small place, Lear may imagine himself as being in a larger one. Rodger is reminded of what should be his terror (in Poor Tom) of getting too close to his father, Gloucester, who might conceivably recognize him, even in his stripped-down disguise. Robin suggests that Rain should not come back on too soon on the re-entrance. Peter should let the images of Goneril, the escaping Regan, the dogs, come in at his face, from anywhere, going anywhere. Of Regan, Robin says, "Remember, she can get out, anyway. Try it as if she were coming down a huge flight of stairs, from that exit sign." The imagined dogs could come from any direction, berserk hounds, a hunting scene gone mad. Peter thinks that he might give Rodger an imaginary piece of sugar (real enough to Lear) for his protection from those dogs, in reward for a task well done. Edgar, in his pretended madness is to be the only one to participate with Lear in these imaginings. Kent is helpless and the Fool — on Lear conjuring up Goneril — is cautiously neutral, 'Cry you mercy, I took you for a joint-stool.' Robin says try once more.

And they do. Lear swats a mosquito from Edgar's back, and squashes it with his foot for good measure, before moving across to begin the mock trial. The atmosphere of dereliction increases in the static presences of Kent, Fool and Edgar, trapped by Lear's instructions, helpless and inactive. Faced with Lear's trauma they finally manage to get him to subside. Peter had begun to yawn, suddenly, on his call to 'Anatomize Regan'. He mimes the start of post-mortem cuts with a knife (very keen surgical dispatch), to 'see what breeds about her heart'. But he is overtaken by a yawn, even on his scholastic query, 'Is there any cause in nature that makes these *hard hearts?*' He settles disjointedly into rest, insistent on the closing of the curtains with a querulous exactitude. The action subsides, very absolutely, into a semi-silence punctuated by the breath and mumbling of Lear, a hushing from the Fool, a just-perceptible humming of a lullaby from Kent, the now decreasing shiverings of Poor Tom. Into this extended magical pause, which contains all of human desperation, enters Gloucester with his lantern. Douglas Rain judges perfectly the delay in his return that Robin had requested. The rousing of the half-sleeping Lear, the hushed exit of the tiny group, has the pathos of innumerable refugees, resourceful survivors all, a symbol of human solidarity. Edgar's brief coda to the scene, in soliloquy, confirms this, 'How light and portable *my* pain seems now.'

The rehearsal moves on. Tom and Marti try their scene again (IV.v). Robin joins them for a long session of notes. Then, there's another look at Lear's arrival at Goneril's (I.iv). Phillips stops for small changes of certain actors' positions, nudging Bill Copeland and Rex Southgate, as two of Lear's maturer knights, into more telling areas — capitalizing on their relative maturity. Rex kneads Lear's shoulders, calming him after the dismissive behaviour from Oswald. Keeping close to Lear, as Rex does so consistently, and Greg Wanless also, in the manner of pilot-fish, can prove disconcerting. On a previous rehearsal of that later scene of Lear's row with Gloucester, Rex (placed by Robin so that Lear could brush someone aside on a move downstage during 'Vengeance, Plague, Death, Confusion!') was so absolutely 'brushed' that he disappeared altogether, suddenly and absolutely through the concealed door in the side panel of the set — supposedly inoperative in that spartan court-yard.

In a note session later, Peter tries something new in the first entrance with the returned, disguised Kent. He takes in Kent's response of 'Authority' with a slow, satisfied savouring, checking out the faces of those about him. "Authority — *there*, consolidates my feeling for the men," is what he's after.

FRIDAY, SEPTEMBER 7TH   *continued*

A MIRAGE

We move back to the start of this scene, to Kent's arrival and short soliloquy explaining how (in disguise) he will continue to serve the King (I.iv). "Stop," calls Robin, from way out in the stalls. "Did you see 'Lawrence of Arabia'? Remember, that mirage-like arrival of 'what's his name' (*Omar Sharif*) on a camel — how he wasn't there — and still wasn't there — and suddenly he was?" "Yes," says Jim. "Can you do that for me?" asks Robin. "I can *try*," replies Jim. They rehearse it a few times, Robin back in the darkness of the stalls, making a very weird accompanying background effect. Kent enters, as far up-stage as possible, his presence indeterminate because of the gloom, and those calculated activities of a small group of 'without-the-gates' peasantry. A slow, unostentatious move forward, some quicker steps, and Kent is there, in our laps, telling us his plot.

Robin continues to make refinements, sharpening the device. It's a sleight-of-hand, another of his specialties. They try it again: "Ang-gang-gang-gang-gang . . ." goes Robin, again simulating the soundtrack on Lean's movie. Perhaps Bert Carriere could write in some music here, with the most improbable instruments, but it could never sound so right. Kent is conjured up once more, the Front-of-House spots hitting him in the eyes.

The entire scene proceeds, with the exchanges of Hutt and Ustinov gaining in richness. The laughter, from them both and from the knights, grows, spreading into the scene, everyone savouring each turn and twist of the double-edged badinage. 'And sometimes . . .' (Hutt setting up the joke very archly) . . . 'sometimes I'm whipped for holding my *peace*,' contriving, of course, a piece of ambiguity. Beyond the bellylaughs, the lighter jests, there's a strong hint of danger and unease, especially for Peter: 'A *bitter* Fool', he quite rightly complains. And later, 'When was't thou wont to be so full of songs?' Peter plays this line after a curiously judged pause, telling us here that he's aware that he knows this is a Fool who can dare to *sing* what he does not dare say.

The scene over, Robin, stepping forward, says "Very good. Very nice, Excellent. And — Once More." He steps up on-stage to add something to his mirage effect with Jim, going out of earshot: "Girls, Beggars, Riff-raff!" — and has a long talk with them. They do it all again. "Wonderful," he says. "Next!"

They set up for another section (II.iv). Daphne Dare, notebook in hand, is sitting in on rehearsal all day. Daphne's presence is yet another proof of the advance in the work. Costumes can't be that far away. It almost seems a pity. We've all become so used to the look of these characters in their own work-a-day garb. Peter especially. Lear, for a long time, perhaps forever for me, will be clad in rumpled alpaca (which he's worn for most of the time), open-necked, riotous-coloured shirts, feet forever on the move while he speaks, in squeaking soft rubber moccasins — a bargain in the town square.

It's lights out again and a run of the Lear/Regan scene (II.iv). Marti does a jump cut and Peter says: "I *think* we've cut out a bit — seem to have missed our snotty handkerchief." "Oh — sorry," says Marti, who has invented so richly in her work on this scene, "I shouldn't have forgotten *that*." "Happens to me all the time," replies Peter, "I don't see why it shouldn't be hereditary."

ALL THAT SWEAT

"Have a little break," says Robin, when they finish, "and then we'll have a little talk." When they all return, Robin continues his notes to delicate nuances. Asks Rodger to thing out his route down from that fire escape (II.i). Tells Jim not to get angry too quickly (II.ii). When left in those stocks, he suggests Kent should do something very minimal: "Just go . . . hands opening and closing." And for Rodger, on his soliloquy, 'I heard myself proclaimed . . . ', Robin wants an extra subtle something; "that sense that 'somebody's been here' " (II.iii). It's a wonderfully atmospheric point, as the stage has been recently so full of event, and Kent, at this point incarcerated in the stocks, asleep, is sharing the stage with him. In general, Robin insists that Jim should now consider "being a little more selfish." Describing Jim as a very giving actor, he thinks he should now start "taking more attention for yourself," reminding Jim that "there will be that thousand people out there, watching you take it." Who will *want* to see him taking it, Robin means, concluding that "some self-indulgence is needed here."

He continues to flick lightly through points. Those stocks are to be taken off, most conveniently, at immediate stage-right, and not up-stage centre lugged by attendants in the middle of an important scene. A diffuse note for Monette: "I'm not sure it isn't the old thing of training ourself physically to being as bright as possible, so that our body can respond. It's a question of finding the right *face* for him." He asks Rex Southgate to remember that "you're a brilliant rider, very good at the trot and canter," (he mimes both), "sure as God you didn't walk here."

"*Now*," Robin begins, with that priority inflection he invests for those notes which are to be picked up by all, and not merely an

82

individual, "given all that sweat, start thinking of the costumes." It's clear that he means not only the sweat of Lear's seventeen Knights-Followers, but the collective sweat of the entire cast in Daphne's designs. He reminds the comfortably attired cast how, when they haven't for so long, it "almost hurts to wear a tie." Now, however, everyone will have to be aware of creases. "Oh, the *attention* all that takes." He flicks at his very elegant slacks. "Even a handkerchief has become . . ." (the glance is to Marti, wielder of that snotty one) "so stiff you have to break the starch on it." With all this struggling in corsets "even sitting can be tough." The cast is being asked to think ahead to the time (so soon now) when they'll be encased in costumes. Daphne Dare, still sitting in with us, smokes her umpteenth cigarette. Feet can be relatively free, "feet we've got — that's good." And our girls will have "Huge pulsing hills above top edges of corsets." And the Fellahs: "Everything clear only at the sword area." Boxed in by clothes, as they will be, the cast is asked to think of the wonderful new thrill — in finding that their ribs exist — when they take them off. Robin seems to be stressing that the sensations of how a character feels and thinks with his or her clothes *off* is a part of how they'll all feel with them on.

FRIDAY, SEPTEMBER 7TH *concluded*

STRINDBERG, THIS ONE

A sequence of scenes is set up again. Robin calls out, before they start, "A lot of originality, please. No — *no convention*." The few scenes are run, without interruption of any kind, and I know that the rehearsal of *Lear* has passed another aesthetic milestone. When they're finished Vince Berns says, amazedly, that we're ahead on the day's schedule. "What's next?" asks Robin. "Oh — it's that sexy scene," replies Vince, with relish. (He's seen it and I haven't yet.) We're with Goneril and Edmund, before the following scene with Albany, by now her cuckolded husband (IV.ii).

Robin interrupts quickly and tells Donna to "go for a big run around the stage, or you'll get girlish. I want *vulgarity*." Donna departs, riding crop in one hand, Richard Monette in the other, on a backstage gallop. We can hear the approaching breathlessness. Robin, still unsatisfied with the entrance, which is already marvellously fresh and out-of-doors, joins them and leads them off-stage for more intimate consultation. Returning, he calls back over his shoulder, "And don't come back until you've done *all* that — and more!"

They try again, and Robin adds more vulgar refinements. "Just make the voice more — let it be more darkly 'Huh! — Huh!' It's a much *lower* sound than you think. What you've been doing back there wasn't polite!" Donna starts on her words again, but doesn't get far. "No — don't cover your boobs on the curtsey. And give him hell with your hands. You don't need the crop — we know it's a riding scene." They try again and Robin stops them again. "Don't lose heart." He stays out in the stalls, repeating to Donna, "Don't lose heart. Just after the curtsey, the voice was in a *marvellous* territory, and you started pretending again." He approaches the front of the stage. "You can help her more, Richard, in the wings; let us see that she's removing something from you, on the entrance." They go on with this game of the pursuer and the pursued.

As Robin continues to grind over the section, in a further long chat off-stage, I turn to Ustinov, who has joined me in the near-stage seats, evidently enjoying the scene. I cite the Beckett echoes of earlier work in the day, and he agrees enthusiastically. We find other resonances: "Strindberg, of course. 'Miss Julie', this one!" he chuckles, nodding towards the stage. Peter starts sketching avidly.

Regan and Edmund reappear for another try. Donna and Richard have found the right predatory level; there's quite a bit more of that slapping of that crop against thighs (her own and Richard's) — they've gone far enough in the exercise to know, later, how much they can cut it down. The scene progresses into the following dualogue of Albany and Goneril. 'See theyself, devil ...' Frank Maraden, his exceptional height emphatic on a top step, and with the much shorter Donna reaching up against him, gives us the non-embrace from two people who have rejected each other, typifying a crucial turn in the play: from here on, the role of Albany (as with Edgar) serves the slow but certain movement towards retributions.

The whole day's work begins to merge into other days when the efforts were as difficult, but less rewarding. I can't remember when Robin last pushed his dimmer-switch to plunge us into darkness, as he did for that early scene with Lear and Fool. As he did again today for the trial scene. The darkened auditorium (where it is so often impossible to take any notes) which we inhabit while watching and working, brings the fiercest light of concentration to the stage, where we must make it happen. The work is to find answers, choosing and accepting the disciplines of what will best serve the search. The play is growing and it's almost the end of another week.

Mr. Frank Maraden: Albany   Mr. Richard Monette: Edmund
Miss Donna Goodhand: Goneril

'. . . See thyself, devil! Proper deformity shows not in the fiend so horrid as in woman.'

SATURDAY, SEPTEMBER 8TH

STAGE, FILM, AND RADIO

We are back at St. John's. It's a calm day, at least for me, as I know I'm a cursory visitor, able to watch a short period of rehearsal before leaving for a performance. Some scenes I've not seen in rehearsal for two or three days make startling advances and, sometimes, a calculative retreat. If I miss one day (I seldom miss two in succession), the effect is somewhat like running rushes of a film, and being surprised at the addition of a number of takes. The picture is now ready for a rough-cut, but there are some takes in the progression which — though one hasn't seen them can now be guessed at.

The morning is easy-going. We are having a look at that opening scene of our Second Act, of Kent and Gentleman encountering in the storm (III.i). After a run-through, Greg Wanless, sitting near me, thinks we'll move on. He's been in the Company some years, and should know better. Robin chooses to put McQueen and Christopher through a lengthy exercise. There's some talk first of ingredients; the cold, the fear, and Robin uses a pull-back to when he worked with Tom Wood on the fear in Oswald. Here again "scared is a given," as are the cold, the wet and the wind. Again, the question is not to *try* to be these things, the task is to *be* them, and the route to that objective is to know you *"are* all of these things."

Robin gets Patrick and Jim to play their speeches with their eyes closed, backs to the walls from opposite sides of the room. After a time, he approaches Jim, placing a hand against his throat, the other on his diaphragm. He later crosses to Patrick, placing fingers lightly on the actor's throat and forehead. He seems to be signalling a need for the images to become more interior, to assume more mental shape. It was a reasonable guess. "It's a pity," he says, "we don't have the chance to do more radio." He thinks, before continuing. "Projection, stage-projection, takes a lot of the subtlety of our imaginations away." We should be able to aim for more delicacy again, when that's our objective. And we should (as the radio actor does when he wants to) be able to make it "sound as if you're smiling."

Next, we are to have a little look at 'Blow winds and crack your cheeks' (III.ii). Peter asks if he's to be "discovered" (On-Stage, Peter means, at the start of the scene). "Sort of," replies Robin. Peter has his first try, with Bill in attendance as the Fool and, later, Jim as Kent. Robin supplies effects for some of the storm, confining himself to primary gusts. Bill Hutt gradually makes his way downstage, settling for an attempt at shelter in a crouching huddle, a fetal bundle, absolutely down-centre at Peter's feet. It takes him a while to arrive there during Peter's arias, and he does it with economy, suggesting in his very bent stance the full ferocity of the gale. Jim, entering as Kent, plays his speeches with hands deep in pockets, and one can hear from him, as we do also from Bill's interjections, that, were it not for Lear, nothing in the world would have brought them there. On the exit Peter somewhat pre-empts Bill's dance as the Fool, becoming almost amiable. They sing their way off-stage — accepting the odds against them — as we all choose, often, to sing in adversity. Both clap arms to armpits; Peter cavorts like a Fool, Bill walks like Lear. They have almost switched roles. Peter calls 'Bring us to this ... hovel' without that rising inflection on the last word which Robin likes so much. This time Peter doesn't give it, for once, that small wisp of hope we've heard so often in those two floating vowels.

When they finish, Robin asks right away for the restoration of that upward, singing inflection on 'Hovel'. Peter says, "Didn't I do it? — thought I did!" Not as distinctly as before, explains Robin regretfully, "I missed it." Peter promises never to leave it out again. Robin has some other thoughts to offer, for the next time through. "Oh, I know," suggests Peter, "Lie on the floor with my face down?" Well, he's tried — almost — everything else.

Robin apologizes that he can't, as yet, help much with the *real* shape of the storm. Ustinov agrees that he can't know how much he'll have to *penetrate* the storm, "Until it is a given." We know, by now, that Phillips is contemplating a very sizeable one with a lot of wind and thunder and lightning. But we have yet to hear the full technical effect of this storm in the Avon. Peter emphasizes that either now, in the church hall, or on-stage in performance, it will "always be far easier to *fight* the storm than to feel it." Robin is also calculating from which direction the main force of the wind is coming. Deciding, for the moment, that it will be blowing from down-left, he offers an effect which I can't help feeling he has been considering a long time. As Lear turns on Kent, with the enormous vocal assault of 'Tremble, thou wretch, / That hast within thee undivulged crimes, / Unwhipp'd of Justice ...', Kent will be up-stage of Lear, and it will seem, asserts Robin, that "the strength will be in both you *and* the wind." Peter is delighted, and grateful for this idea of elemental reinforcement. They both agree that Lear should be more still, and even more so (wind allowing) when he can be, in the midst of the incredible din.

They are ready to try again. Robin first has a couple of smaller notes, to assure himself that, in the sway of the bodies in the fierce gale, none of them "Muck up the focus." He settles back to enjoy, and quietly says "Turn Over." Since our arrival at St. John's Hall today we've moved from radio, through stage to film.

Peter comes to the centre of the space, waiting for a break in the imaginary tumult, and gets off his first line. Almost. 'Blow winds and crack your cheeks! rage! blow!' But after 'rage' his huge head is tossed in an imagined gust, his mouth caught open, and the final word 'blow' — though hurled away from us — is caught on the wind, flung back at us, broken into segments, pitted with gaps in its long sound: "BLO-OO-OOHH!" There's a great deal of film, radio, and a lot of stage in that. Robin is hugging himself in satisfaction as I turn to go. What a pity I have a matinée. It's the end, for me, of another week of rehearsal — time for *Lear* is dwindling.

I return later that evening, post-haste from my show, in the hope of catching more. But the People of *Lear* have departed for an early weekend break. There's a hush in the bare space, among the disordered chairs. Some smoke still hangs in the air. I can still hear the sound of that torn 'blow', and see all of that storm in my mind's eye.

TUESDAY, SEPTEMBER 11TH

SNAPSHOTS AND DRUMTAPS

Avon, 7:00 p.m. Tonight there's something special about the feeling here: all our days and nights in the theatre are unique — only some are more unique than others. Perhaps it might have something to do with the presence, again, of Daphne Dare, who sits in, as usual, with clipboard — and a notebook in which she's never seen to inscribe a single jotting — her concentration forever on the acting, which she relishes at all times. Daphne's continued presence with us is hard enough evidence that all must be more than reasonably in charge back stage at the costume department. Those costumes, so many of them (almost fifty with changes), must be ready for the shapes which will soon ache in them. Fittings for the cast are scheduled every day. Daphne's original thirty-five individual designs, most delicately drawn, reminiscent often of Phiz, would fitly accompany any Victorian romance or tragedy.

But, wonder of wonders, most of our actors, whom I've known for two years and some much longer, perennially clad in jeans or cords or washed-out cottons, are arriving now (almost all of them) in jackets, ties, hard shoes, even suits, and trousers with creases. Yes — creases. Collars are appearing too — there is a rash of them tonight. Can this have anything to do with Robin's reminder, towards the end of last week's rehearsal, of the coming strictures of costume? The cast are now responding with this gesture (I believe), personal wardrobe having been ransacked over the weekend for halfway sartorial substitutions towards the final Victorian proprieties.

Robin himself is extraordinarily smart, his usual neatness crowned today by an extra-impeccable jacket, black shoes and tie. There are some exceptions, however. Rain remains rumpled, and Hutt unflappably casual. But, a sad instance, Peter has changed his suit, the alpaca is abandoned, replaced by a mundane light beige, even the shirt subdued into dark blue. In compensation, he remains consolingly creased and open-necked. He also has a sizeable and high quality camera slung over his shoulder, and is taking shots in the wings during his moments off. The camera seems to be of the best quality as he can shoot in any or no light, which is all that Robin allows, and that little of it on-stage, the merest leakage turning to murky chiaroscuro in the wings. (Alack, with the aid of hindsight, I must add that none of Peter's pictures came out.)

But tonight's special feeling has nothing to do with these ingredients. The new concentrated rhythm is positively a response to the Drum. This is, of course, Robin's drum. It is this drum which heralds our further firm steps forward in rehearsal towards the goal of performance. Another of his rehearsal devices, it usually makes its appearance and sound at that point in our work when he feels he has something to drum up — something to drum about.

This drum is a rather large one, capable of good bass tone and lighter staccato, and Robin plays it excellently. It makes its debut in rehearsal when we've begun to take some sections in sequence, with Robin providing each 'bridge' between scenes with lots of variety and ingenuity. It has an incalculable value to the actors as an aid to the overall tempo of a group of scenes, or the specific rhythms of some. And it's an indication, at an early stage, of the incidental music we will have later. Bert Carriere has been absent from his piano stool for some days, and is now hard at work on his score.

Rehearsal proceeds with calm, gathering certainty. We are looking at the arrival of Lear at Regan's (which, of course, in the strategy of the plot, is Gloucester's place) (II.iv). Peter seems to be flagging a bit; it's already been a long day and I missed the afternoon's work. He's his usual best-humoured self, though still groping for lines. It's astonishing how he encompasses the *sense* at all times. Even when he gets the line wrong or, in some instances, leaves out a line or half-line, its *content* will be there, ad libbed, with occasional calls on the Deity. "Oh, God; ... Yes?" ... "Oh, Christ! ... yes?" "*What?* — But I *said* that" — so often when he hadn't, quite. He's still pulling off strange gains and surprises. Entering, he scrapes the dung from a shoe on the double-step of the set. I can, alas, already envisage him in riding-boots. He kicks Kent, lightly; that is, not *really*, but enough to demonstrate his evaporating (or already evaporated) royal prerogative. It is done in the same style as the half-blow delivered to Oswald in the earlier scene, aggression tempered with half apology. His subtext could be suggested by "I'm old, very old, and — a king — so you won't actually retaliate, will you? If you did, what could I *do!*"

That may sound winsome, merely, but it isn't. This disarming ineffectualness is all that remains of Lear's one-time toughness, backed up as it may have been, before, by generations of bully-boys. But it's dangerous now, to Lear. And it's sad, too, because he's clearly very vulnerable. These small faked aggressions have no threat in them. Lear is no longer tough, and worse, it's clear to anyone that he isn't. He was, once, but it's been downhill for the last fifteen years or so. He'll have to relearn how to be hard enough for life.

In the midst of all these things, so many of them physically idiosyncratic (though not necessarily typical of Ustinov — he's invented them for Lear), he is offering up constant vocal surprises. To put it simply, he is loud when one expects Lear to be quiet, and often quiet when one expects something bigger. And I believe this is because he is still delving about for the truth. It's all very odd, as it always is, when watching a great actor work. It never seems perverse or quirky for the mere sake of it; it seems, in fact, simple. And it can't possibly be simple. Taking risks like this, in such a permanent exercise, is very difficult work, and calls for unrelenting concentration. And yet, in all this, Peter seems to be very relaxed. It's impossible: that is, it can't be described. Better sometimes to bow in wonder. I've been lucky, already, to witness some like talents in action, often enough to feel certain (as well as relieved) when the chance comes round once more. Meanwhile, I'm also vibrantly aware that I'm watching an actor who, despite his superabundant gifts, is attuned to the least experienced of those working with him, and has the simple zest for our shared endeavour to carry a camera slung over his shoulder that he may, like any father at the seaside, preserve the foibles of his family.

Everyone loves Lear, and even the youngest of our Company will know that to be a central truth of our play. Lear is all of us. It's an enormous bonus that our Lear is this avuncular and self-delighting presence. But it means that he must carry, as he so absolutely does, an extra responsibility in his application, alertness of mind, and unrelenting zeal for the role. If he fails, we all do. And he's not about to let us down. Nor could we him. But Peter carries the burden. He is the hero, and he has exactly the right set of sinews and muscles for the task. Of course, there is only one protagonist in a play, or, certainly, in a tragedy. And yet, in *Lear*, one of the greatest of plays, it might be said that there *is* yet another protagonist, and his name is Gloucester. The actor in our Company least likely to default in any commitment is Douglas Rain, and the rest of this cast follow hard at his heels.

TUESDAY, SEPTEMBER 11TH   *concluded*

THE MAN IN THE GAP

Rehearsal goes on, and the action moves back to that opening scene with so much challenge, so often returned to, because, so far, it has not been entirely solved (I.i). We've already had the short prologue which sets up the Gloucester/Kent and Gloucester/Edmund relationships. Robin, emergent in his smart ensemble, on-stage into the thick of the Company, wants a special definition on the entrance of Lear. Or, rather, he wants to take any special edge or definition *away* from it. He evidently intends Lear to arrive in the hazy perspective of an after-dinner adjournment. And yet, asking always for something more demanding, he needs our hero to enter the action unheralded; except, that is, for the one line from Gloucester, 'The King is coming', which Rain is delivering almost (though never quite) sotto voce. The aim is for a royal arrival disconcerting in its casualness. "Good Lord!" — the audience shall say, "*That's* him. That's Ustinov — that's Lear!" It's a nice touch of showmanship to make a first night audience (or any) keep on their toes if they want a chance to applaud the entrance. As they will.

Robin is asking Peter to find his own position, where he can, in the desultory arrangements of retainers and attendants. "Find a gap," he says, "before you come on." And Peter, in high spirit though still in his late-in-the-day struggle to retain the text, promises, "Yes — I'll have no difficulty in finding a gap."

Work proceeds in the very dim light, too dim for me to be able to make anything but the most cursory note. Too dim for Peter to take anything but the rarest of photographs in the off-stage blackout. Occasionally, attention is locked into detailed concern for a single line, or — more often now — Vince Berns calls "Stand-By" for three or four scenes in uninterrupted sequence, Robin beating out the linking rhythms on his drum. During the longer sections I often take a back seat in the stalls or try the view from the circle, savouring the sight and sound of a larger reach of the play.

The day diffuses into a hundred moments of achievement, a kaleidoscopic montage of work done, or later comment on it. Butch Blake, sitting near me at one time, remembering other Lears, including both of Bill Hutt's and one of his own, is marvelling in new discoveries. Ustinov, in the big scene with Regan, merely marks that effect on 'Sleep to Death': "I don't want to overdo it — I've a slight cold." Responsibility in the theatre begins with responsibility to oneself. The continuing calls of "Stand-By" come from Vince. Peter enters with increasing palsy, as he deliberately overacts the trembling, piling on the exaggeration for the benefit of the followers. The stage remains murky, but so alive in the presences of the actors. Peter's camera, slung across his back, is incongruous equipment during his plea to the sisters on 'our basest beggars/Are in the poorest thing superfluous'.

There's an interlude in work on the opening scene. Robin leaps on-stage to offer comment on Lear's attitude to the courtiers, "Well — are you all going to *stand* there, you bloody nellies!" And he arrives back on-stage soon after, when Peter has got going full steam into the middle of a big speech. Peter, turning, finds Robin *still* giving notes to nearby actors. "What do *you* want, standing there, you bloody Nellie!" Again, further on in a later scene, (Lear's second 'curse' on Goneril, II.iv), Peter gets it very wrong, and throws in a 'raspberry' — an apt personal vocalization of his own view of his command of the text at that time. All day, or night now, in the semi-dark up-stage, the brighter blaze down-stage, the light strikes the profiles of the actors. Peter offers a huge sudden explosion, a domestic row at its peak, on the line 'I prithee, daughter, do not make me mad'. After more wanderings, hearing and watching from other places, I return to Butch, who is still marvelling. "He's always getting the emotions and thoughts in the right places." I have another little chat with Butch, while it's momentarily quiet during a notes-session onstage. We agree on the importance of saving energy in working on plays as demanding as *Lear*, what you save being always more important than what you use.

Later there's work on the 'Trial Scene' (III.vi). Peter, on that 'Let them anatomise Regan' speech, had begun by miming an incision, and then, wiping hands absent-mindedly on his trousers, had surged into a real carve-up, a Shylock gone mad in quest of the character of that hard heart. Further elements are introduced: his attempt to catch the gown of the escaping Regan — a full fall forward as he does so. There is more talk of the dilemma of Kent and the Fool; how can they protect Lear? The storm is one thing, just get him out of it — but how to cope with these wild hallucinations? Peter plays Lear in the earlier scenes as if he were dreadfully hard of hearing, though that hand so often to his ear suggests he may also be faking. But now, in Gloucester's barn, he hears with a weird, sharp acuteness. Lear compells the others to witness what isn't there, though for him it's real enough. This problem is nicely encapsulated by Bill Hutt, who, ad libbing for the Fool, asserts "If I can't hear it, you can't accuse me of not listening to it." Bill's Fool has already developed an exhausted pessimism which could lead his character to suicide: an actor's objective I had guessed at, before Hutt later confirmed this to a mutual friend, before the play opened.

They take another look at the opening scene where, at least, as Robin says, "Everyone has a legitimate reason for being po-faced." This reminds me of the time when it seemed to me, in the earlier stage of rehearsal, that no one in this scene could do much more than stand and wait. The scene over, Robin does an extended drum-roll, and they start again into a run of the first scene.

Much later, during the final break of the evening, Peter settles into a flight of anecdotage. He vocalizes the opening of an ominously-creaking door, an effect so convicing (he's done it for us a couple of times) that they'd used it on the soundtrack, instead of the 'real thing', of a movie on the last day of his contract. Unfortunately, they later wanted a like-effect of a door *closing* — as ominously as he had already made it open. The film-crew sent a messenger by fastest limousine to collect Peter from the airport, from which he was due to depart. Peter, who is nothing if not obliging, obliged. "So — I got back to the studio: did my . . ." (he does it now, the closing door, a grinding, *entirely* metallic sound, rusted hinges turning on screeching pins). "They got it in one take — I was rushed back to the airport — and missed my plane."

He then launches into some tales of the Hamburg Opera, where he's worked as director. I can only attempt a mild encapsulation of one. It seems that the management, though rigorous on business matters, were indulgent enough to retain (through many disasters) the services of an old and inordinately inefficient stage manager, their motive being "to humanize the institution." On an opening night of *William Tell* (Peter throws in some of the Overture to colour our reception), a packed audience awaited the opening scene, calculated to reveal teutonic excesses of massed Chorus, plus a large crowd of supernumeraries, some reinforcement from the local military, flocks of sheep on distant vistas, and even more. The cast, wondering at the absence of the expected applause on such extravagance, took a long time (a very long time) before realizing that the Stage Manager "had forgotten to take the curtain up."

The real jest for me was that such big-voiced singers might well have been looking, not only for such applause, but for the customary blaze from front-of-house lighting. The best thing about the hypochryphal is that, if it isn't true, it should be. And for Peter's best rendition of like tales, you should consult his autobiography, *Dear Me*, published by Penguin in paperback. I've got my copy, since *Lear* began, and — so far — have had no time to read it.

THURSDAY, SEPTEMBER 13TH

ARM-ACHE

That damn drum is sounding away this morning as the Company gathers, and Robin tries a percussive warm-up. Something else has been added to his box of tricks. Some on-stage overhead spots and floods flick on and off as he manipulates his small dimmer-board. It's soon clear why he's had the extra overhead in-stage lights linked for his control, as he experiments with some crude (quite blinding) lightning flashes. He plays for awhile, flicking the dimmers up and down. We are to begin today with a look at the storm scenes, and we can go no further in St. John's Hall with these.

The scene is called and Peter goes into 'Blow Winds' with fine early-in-the-day aplomb (III.ii). The shirt is again moderate today, but the voice at Force Eight soars into the gale. It does indeed seem a gale, for a new sound and effect is tearing into the scene.

94

We now have a wind-machine off-stage right, or we must have, for I can hear its roar, and Lear and Fool face us with hair and shirt-tails and trousers flapping (Hutt's narrow, Ustinov's ample), streaming in a pure horizontal from stage-right to left. The machine is evidently a big one, sending Peter's loose-cropped greying locks rising straight from his scalp, and Hutt's generous thatch is in untypical disarray. The sound is also formidable, a very high-pitched whine and constant zinging from the blades accompany the rush of wind.

Meanwhile, Robin is not neglecting the visual pyrotechnics. He's still manipulating the sudden glares (from those overhead spots); flashes of crude white light strike into the set from the back cyclorama wall, for each instant showing the stark outline of the bare side panels of Daphne's cage, catching — with a new, surprising definition — the tiny, threatened images of Lear and Fool. Robin is industrious with sound, also, as he mixes in, from his drum, the lower rumblings, and even higher cracks of thunder. He commands lightning and thunder, a perfect back-up to the wind. It's a multi-dextrous achievement.

As Lear and Kent and Fool half-stagger, half-dance off up-left, the lightning flashes revert to deep gloom, the wind-machine coughs out, and Robin's drum is stilled. He's been (sitting?) close behind me. "God," he mutters, "my arm aches!" You can bet it does. He's doing the drum with right arm, dimmer-switches with left hand, one eye on Vince's Prompt-Copy to follow the score, and the other — presumably — on the stage. "Terrific," he pronounces. "Looks terrific." He drops the drumsticks and flicks on a little extra light. Peter, a little subdued, comes back out from the wings, revealing "I was taking it a bit easy . . ." "That's all right," says Robin. "Let's have the wind-machine out front, down-stage centre."

As the stage crew bring it out to this position (it really is quite a monster), Robin gives a few notes for survival against its formidable resistance. "Keep the feet still. Do as little as possible. And don't try to beat it." "What? . . ." queries Peter, still fingering his eardrums. "It's all right!" shouts Robin to him, "I just want to *watch*." "Oh — Good," responds Peter, "Then I'll take it easy again." Robin removes himself to far back in the stalls (where he so seldom goes), concerned for once with how something looks, rather than how it sounds. Well, that's reasonable. It's a storm he's considering. The words will always matter more than the storm, words will always matter more than anything, but the storm is now coming in a close second.

If Shakespeare had enjoyed our superior technical resources, would he have used so many words on descriptions of storms, voyages, journeyings, battles and their aftermaths? It seems, almost, as though he knew the movies were just around the corner. How easily his words float into voice-over in so many instances I remember on film: the drowning of Ophelia, the surge of sea and troops behind the Chorus in *Henry V*, *Antony and Cleopatra* and so many of the others, reading exactly like a screenplay. Customers nowadays, accustomed to storms on film, from Flaherty's 'Man of Aran' to Lean's 'Ryan's Daughter' would enjoy, might even expect one at our Avon. Well, this isn't the movies, but Robin is nonetheless considering all his options. He's a serious director but he's a showman, too.

THURSDAY, SEPTEMBER 13TH *continued*

A BIT OF BONDAGE

They've begun work on the next scene, 'Before a Hovel', the stage still bare except for the wind-swept figures of Lear, Fool, Kent, and Edgar — entering now as 'Poor Tom' (III.iv). The effect is tremendous, even with one machine. When the words are this good, any effect, supporting them properly, further reveals how good they are. Gloucester, joining the quartet (Douglas with lantern in hand) is suggesting his very slow advance through a quagmiee by being barely able to raise his feet. When he joins them the five small vertical images struggle to remain upright.

Peter, in a new sort of trouble with lines, the wind-machine striking him directly in the face, is calling for a prompt now and then. In fact, he seldom asks for a prompt, preferring to get through with a paraphrase, the content and sequence of thoughts being invariably correct, though in Ustinovian rather than Shakespearean blank verse. Now, when he calls over the howling machine (right at his feet) to Michael Benoit in the third row of the stalls, both requests and answers are obliterated in the racket. Seated near the stage, closer than anyone at this point, I can hear and enjoy some of Peter's wilder variations.

McQueen and Hutt both project almost as cleanly as usual over the din, as Barton elects for that earlier choice, perhaps, of giving too much. In this new challenge it's not so surprising. Rodger is stripped to his usual Poor Tom working garb of running shorts, and one of his bare feet is bandaged, occasioning Robin to ask first thing this morning, "What's wrong with your foot, Rodg?" Rodger, it seemed, had himself imposed the stricture, knotted below the instep, to help him suggest a limp.

Robin comes forward at the end of the exercise, thanking them all for the effort. "Very nice — just wanted to see things," adding, immediately, that Rodger was too tense. "Oh, shit!" responds Rodger, regretting, perhaps, the experiment with the bandaged foot. Maybe that's what gives Robin the idea, "Let's tie Rodg's hands behind his back," he says musingly, "and tie his legs together." Ann Stuart of Stage Management departs to improvise some wherewithal for this, returning with a lengthy roll of cloth bindings. "Don't you dare write this down, Maurice," calls Rodger from the stage, a stricture he revoked later, in line with the general concensus that "there's no harm in a little bit of bondage." I'd reached the same conclusion myself — as an aid to acting, especially. I remember an occasion when Wilfred Lawson, one of the greatest of the old (but very modern) English actors, tied himself up several days in succession while rehearsing the role of a paralytic.

Meanwhile, Robin is extending criticism to include all of the quartet. "If *anyone* makes one unnecessary gesture — we'll all start again. And Again! I want very little acting. No gestures. A lot of thought." As Barton is being fitted with the new restraint, Ustinov is checking out his more crucial errors in text. I'm able to set him right on one or two strident and repetitive points of departure as Michael struggles through the Prompt pages, and as Barton is effectively trussed. "Ah! Posing for *The Martyrdom of St. Sebastion* by El Greco," ventures Peter, not unkindly, and they exit (Barton hopping), to prepare for the entrance.

The scene plays through once more, with Lear, Kent, Fool, and later Gloucester, all with their hands in their pockets, no one caught making a gesture, everyone straining every nerve not to twitch any muscle other than those of speech — and even those sparingly. Barton, hopping throughout, taking a minimum of positions, (his options being limited), is agonizingly effective, especially when he subsides into a crouch at Peter's legs. Later, forced into a full fall by the action, he's beyond hope of regaining his feet. As they all finally depart for the relative delights of the hovel, from a space made terrible by wind machine, darkness, lightning flashes and thunderous tumult (Robin ambidextrously at it again), Peter, turning back to the immobilized Rodger (still gamely struggling to rise), says, instead of 'Come, good Athenian' — "Come, my earth-bound Philosopher." As he moves off-stage, he turns once more, adding gently, "Join us when you can." Tenacious always to a jest, he ad libs to Gloucester, "Haven't you got the key to his handcuffs? Ah — left 'em in Folkestone! Thought you were on your way to Dover? Ah — that's another scene? . . . Sorry!" His presence, with those of Kent, Fool and Gloucester, finally fades from the stage.

THURSDAY, SEPTEMBER 13TH *continued*

NO CONVENTIONS, PLEASE

Robin joins them again on-stage for minor comments. "Very good. *Better*." Stage Management is asked to set up for the following scene. "The Farmhouse," announces Robin. "The Hovel," calls Vince Berns. "Ah, the Mock Trial" insists Peter. (III.vi). "And let's see if I can get some real tears from you three — not Douglas," says Robin, meaning Hutt, McQueen and Barton. "And no conventions, please," he continues, "Just a bit of direct communication."

There is a remarkable development from the last rehearsal I'd seen. The Fool, Kent, and Poor Tom, all ignoring the instruction from Lear to sit, remain isolated in upstage positions, evading the bench down-stage on which Lear sits, sometimes, between his increasingly dangerous outbursts, made all the more so as he seems so contained, arguing his crazed hypothesis with childlike assurance. Ustinov achieves some quite weird vocalizations, including an unquestionable singing of some phrases, nightmarishly mock-liturgical. On the speech of the 'anatomized' Regan he suddenly, and very clearly, tears the wall of her cadaverous chest apart, groping in with fierce surgical curiosity, being so perfectly prepared for his absent-minded query to Edgar, (to anyone), 'Is there any cause in nature which breeds these hard hearts?' It's staggering. At this moment, open-mouthed in surprise, I turn to look at Robin, and find in him (I believe) an identical response. The scene has further riches. The desultory humming from Kent after Lear subsides on the cushions is further extended into the long, filled pause. Hutt is using the moment to look more doomed than Lear, his Fool becoming, in facial expression, an evocation of every insomniac's dawn. Barton has even forgotten to shiver, in his helpless and desperate inaction. Hutt's last line has a valedictory cadence, 'And — I'll go to bed at noon', delivered into the half-sleeping face of an old man as vulnerable and important, as the old are so seldom, regrettably, to any of us.

A RISK FOR SOMETHING CRUCIAL

"Can we all come back here," says Robin, and the Company gathers round him — and myself — as this time I'm sitting closer than usual to the stage. "Not bad," says Robin. Placed where I am, this note-session assumes a more immediate nature, as I'm almost enveloped by it, rather than watching it from the outside at a point near or far.

"Careful how you walk over the mattress," Robin is saying to Bill Hutt. (There is an old mattress or bedding behind the bench on which Lear finally subsides.) Bill replies that he was lifting his feet to avoid tripping, as one might, in a strange place. Robin wishes him to preserve the sense and feeling of place, and caution, of the damp and cold, but asks that Bill should realize all of this with less specific movement. That may sound picky but it isn't; not from a director like Phillips to an actor like Hutt. It is as difficult to describe the precise subtlety of these little modulations which Robin asks for, in voice or movement, as it is for the actor to execute them. But it is always clear to the actor exactly what it is that Robin wants. This is a crucial point, and is why I stress it. It is *never* difficult for actors to understand exactly what Robin means or is asking them to do. Which partly explains why he takes such pains, and often such a long time in delivering his notes. It's the doing that is difficult and there is great fascination in that. I'm making this point to counter the allegation, by some, that Robin is a monologuist, my contention being that when he is — as he is so often — it is to this absolute purpose.

Phillips now speaks to Ustinov with that added delicacy and caution he uses when he's after something crucial. He's nailing down extreme advances made in this last rehearsal. I'm glad I've revived a basic, though hardly de-rusted old skill in shorthand. Robin speaks with delicate rapidity, and I confine myself to stabbing at essential elements, scratching away as he talks.

He begins by blending caution with commitment. He's not altogether certain he should make the point at all. "I'm not sure if it is advisable — it may even be arrogant." But he's decided to risk it. "Whenever you reach something marvellous," he is saying to Peter, "it seems that you have a desire to know that *I know*." I'm reminded immediately of the day when Peter tapped himself on the head, again, after doing 'This 's a good block' — repeating it, for himself, for others? Robin is concerned that, "with the extraordinarily varied and brilliant imagination" which Peter so often displays, he may also be inserting an extra element, unconscious or (and this is the crux) conscious, which, in fact, serves to "diminish it down for me." What emerges then is something, possibly, *less* than that which has been conceived in the "white heat of simplicity."

It seems to me, as I listen, that what Robin is asking of Peter is what he so absolutely asks of all of us, an economy of means and content in the actor's objectives. He is aware that he has to risk a calculative and delicate look into the secrecies of a creative process, in this case Ustinov's: he wants Peter to reach into himself for the impossible (the possible, beyond that), not only for himself as Lear, but for all of us, that we may be the gainers, too, in the effort. Robin continues, cautious but determined. He wants Peter to work always towards those moments, "with *all* of your life and experience, where I *know* there are riches . . . when you unleash all those untold brilliant sparks of life, and oddity, and humanity." And it is clear that he wishes Peter to reject — if it's there — any extra edge of technical comment on it. I'm aware, as I listen, that this is a finely wrought assessment of what is at issue, if indeed there is an issue here at all. But the risk has been taken.

Peter, thinking carefully, replies that he really doesn't know; that is, if he is actually doing anything "extra," but that he'll consider it, infuse the thought into his working process. He is sure, however, that it may be because he is "not quite settled . . . I'm still reaching all over." Robin, before relinquishing the question, cements his injunction, "Add nothing to make it clear for me."

He asks everyone in the scene to "try not to tread too much," and I'm reminded that I'd felt, when watching, that all the actors had sustained very static positions. Good though this was, it seems Phillips wants better. Peter offers a summation, his variation on that best of older actor's adage, that there is always a danger that "Sometimes, when everyone is in a state of grace, it's awfully unfair to the *next* rehearsal." There's enough laughter on this to confirm that, with this Company, there's little danger of any self-congratulation.

ZOO TIME

Robin is still questing. "Oh! there's that marvellous thing . . . Anyone remember me talking of it before . . .?" And he's off, full flight, into a tale of a kindergarten drama session. He makes the rapid preface that "it's the unknown" we must always be after. That if any actor wants to reveal what's in his mind on an objective, Phillips will always respond with, "Don't *tell* me. Because then, if they do it or not, I won't know if I really recognized it, because they informed me in advance." It's always a blessing of our work in theatre that nothing worthwhile in techniques need ever be abandoned. Joan Littlewood insisted on a like principle to Robin's, I recalled, at her Theatre Workshop, twenty years ago. She would have warmed to his analogy of what he saw with the kindergarten kids.

"They were all doing a Zoo, and it was wildly energetic. There were lions, giraffes, buffalo, elephants, lots of noise, immense activity. And — there was one little boy, he'd crawled under a piano . . . And he was crouching, all on his own . . . crouching . . ." I turn in my seat to watch Robin. He's adopting this little boy's pose, hands tentatively in front of the face, his own eyes intently glowing. "And then — the whole class became gradually quiet. Began to watch. Perhaps *my* concentration started to capture theirs, I don't know . . . We were all quietly watching this little boy, all on his own, crouched under the piano. And I asked him what he was doing. And he said, (Robin does the tiny voice) 'I'm doing a beetle'." There's a silence, after some chuckles from the cast, as we sit in the quiet of the stalls, each savouring the image. "There was more . . ." says Robin, "more extraordinary *hold* and control in that . . . The face was just — alive! Best acting lesson ever."

The note-session is not yet over, and Robin turns to Barton (long unfettered by now), "Much better Rodg — wasn't it?" Several heads besides Barton's nod in assent. "Much *less*, much better. When you were tied — *remember* that, how much better it was when all you could do was nestle close to Peter. Very cold and wet. We could really feel it, as you clung to Peter's legs." He congratulates Peter on the bit where he rewards 'Poor Tom' with the piece of sugar for helping him fend off the attack of the dogs. "Poor chap," comments Peter, "thought he was eating ants." (This is in reference to their little Lear/Edgar mimed section up-stage during a Gloucester/Kent exchange, when they are both down on their hands and knees together.)

A conversation develops, relaxing into useful generalities. Someone is talking of ant-eaters, another of seeing people eat ants, and I miss the jump to images of dogs copulating. "No expression at *all*," says Peter regretfully, "Except, maybe — any traffic coming? About as much fun as an orgy!" The talk moves on to monkeys — the connection here more obvious — Peter wondering what they might say if they could chat while doing it. "Fuck Darwin!" suggests someone. "Yes," agrees Peter, "but with their minds on something else — that great lack of emphasis ..." The talk extends to people, very old people, who will just sit — and pee; and they talk more of Lear, for he is this, too; really quite old, perhaps about eighty-eight, senile, fighting it off. And, finally, succeeding.

Robin is still unfinished. He'd rather do the storm "without *any* sound effects." He thinks that the size of the play is growing, and showing this, as we work on it. He's confident that though we started with an empty shell, in the past week or so it has begun to integrate. The real size of the play is beginning to assert itself — in bits — here and there. He interrupts himself, checking his train of thought in order to clarify it: "I never ask for anything easy," he says, easily. "I remember one actor finally said to me, 'What you're saying is simply that you want me to act better.' 'Yes,' I replied. And after a long pause the actor said, 'That's terribly hard'." Robin stresses that our work on *Lear* should aim to be "amazingly ordinary."

He assures us that "This great balloon of a play has started to get bigger and bigger." We know, all of us, that it will get bigger yet. His balloon analogy is recurrent. Last season, during rehearsal of one production, he called the entire cast on-stage, and got us all, collectively, to envisage the size of that balloon, to gather round in an enormous circle, some near the centre, most on the outer perimeter, and slowly mime the raising of such an enormous balloon, sending it up, from that deck of the thrust stage in the Festival Theatre, until we had raised it and held it in suspension over our heads. "Now," he had concluded, "Now that you've all put it there;

leave the stage, slowly, start the play, and finish the Act, and *never* let that balloon descend." I've forgotten, now, if we succeeded that day. I know that we tried.

The note-session is slowing down. Peter recalls a discovery of yesterday's rehearsal which is worth recapturing, he says. "Remember, when we all tried to tease Goneril out of her ill-humour — until it gradually got rancid?" Robin, concluding, thinks that it would be a mistake to really compete with the storm. Nature is too *big* to contend with, and this applies to Ustinov as well as to Hutt, Rain, Barton and McQueen. There is something of the tragi-comedy to be found in it, in the face of all that thunder, the thought: 'For God's sake, take your voice down — you'll only lose it.'

Talk still floats on. Some stories creep in about flying — there is much need for flight in the best acting. Ralph Richardson's saying that 'our job is to dream after eight' comes to mind, and we're certainly beginning to fly a bit. There are some conjectures about those who've managed it for a little, in the actual air, from the days of Leonardo to the American who made it over the English channel a few weeks ago. Peter commemoratively muses on those who had tried for so long before they so briefly dropped. "They must all have been *bitterly* disappointed for that last tenth of a second!"

THURSDAY, SEPTEMBER 13TH, 2 P.M.   *concluded*

STILL THRASHING ABOUT

There's been a coffee-break. Most actors prefer the concentrated rehearsal sessions, uninterrupted by a longer indulgence over lunch. Time off is better valued in the evenings, before performance. Our schedule loosely adheres to the practice of the eight hour day, which includes the actor's time in rehearsal as well as performance. This entails a daily demonstration of much ingenuity by the Production and Stage-Management staff, as all of our cast for *Lear*, with the exception of Ustinov, are involved in other productions on our three stages. With my own work in three current shows, attending all possible rehearsals of *Lear*, keeping some notes on proceedings reasonably up-to-date, and — not least — learning the role of Lear, I haven't any of the actor's alleged luxury of free-time. The same can be said of any member of this Company, not excepting Mr. Ustinov.

I've mentioned his new play already, and have since seen in his dressing-room the usual seemingly disordered evidence of a writer at work, in his case a jumble of pages in bold (felt pen) hand. And when Peter isn't rehearsing *Lear* he's kept very busy talking about it, the publicity department sending him on forays to television and radio stations at all points of the compass.

Our rehearsal is back in gear, and Robin is at it again, up on-stage, giving exacting notes (I.i). Peter is under some pressure. He asserts that he is "still thrashing about." As Robin returns to the stalls before they make a new start on that first scene, Peter calls down to us, "I know you Modern People!" He glares with marvellous feigned indignation, "I *know* how you're all expecting me to *crawl* around the theatre three times!" He might, at that, though I'm not sure what the burghers of Stratford would make of it.

The scene proceeds, but not before Robin makes a special plea to Peter to get one line right in that opening speech, asking him to put 'unburthened' before 'crawl', where it should be. Peter, in danger now of learning his mistakes in the text, expresses surprise, but promises to put it right. Again, as we watch and listen, he gives us 'As we crawl, unburthened — towards death'. Robin's sigh blends with those of Stage-Management.

Douglas Rain, upstage left, scratches his head in concern, in a nicely correct gesture as Gloucester, hearing Lear's steady progress to disaster, not least in dividing his kingdom in three, 'That future strife may be prevented *now*'. Any cabinet minister, especially in Home Affairs, which is about Gloucester's niche, would blanch at that, and Douglas already looks the role. I can imagine him in costume. It'll be a pity. I'll miss the typical year-round alternating green shirts and unvarying ubiquitous brown trousers.

Robin reminds the girls (again) not to lean back in their chairs. The approach of costumes is no longer a thought that can be evaded. During a chat with Robin later he confides that he shares my attachment to the look of our actors as they are, and have been since the top of rehearsals. He agrees with Peter Brook and some others who would aim for a radical change in our ideas of design, for something added to our usual working daily look — as was the way for Shakespeare's men — rather than the usual, all-over smothering in head-to-toe. He recalls that everyone always agreed that the most thrilling of all run-throughs at the Royal Shakespeare Company was always the last run in actors' clothes.

The action proceeds, and there are lots of gains. Donna Good-hand's Goneril plays a half-smile at Cordelia's first blunder in replying 'nothing' to Lear's request 'What cans't *thou* say . . . ?', an ambiguous gleam of triumph covered by an inner expression which says "Silly girl — you don't *really* mean that, do you?" Peter has doubled the extent of the already sizeable stroke which catches him after banishing Kent, and also, his increasing impatience with Burgundy on his slowness in understanding the point that Cordelia's price has fallen significantly. And the moment before his departure, on 'Thou hast her, France!', is accompanied now by an extraordinarily petty seizure of rage, eyes glazed with senescent fury, a fearful intake — and exhalation — of breath; it's an excruciatingly embarrassing moment of rash decision from which, of course, there can be no turning back. All of Lear's oncoming agonies are engendered here, every subsequent disaster heralded in his look, in Peter's delivery of '. .. let her be thine, for we/Have no such daughter, nor shall ever see / That face of hers again . . .' It's unendurable. One feels like shouting at him, with the wisdom of any child: "Don't! Stop! Take it all *back!*" In this instant Lear unleashes the whole interior storm of the play. Robin, agreeing with me on this during a later talk, believes that it is all the more effective, coming as it does out of a burst of petulance.

The scene over, Phillips says "Try again." "Why?" queries Peter, who should be attuned by now to the constant call for "Once Again." "For lines," replies Robin, with a game attempt at sternness. "*Lines,*" repeats Peter, savouringly, as if he knew them all quite perfectly. Marti Maraden (before the scene begins) has a problem and comes down-stage, shielding her eyes (they are very commanding eyes) with a palm raised in protection from the glare of the front-of-house spots. "Yes?" offers Robin from mid-stalls, "What is it, darling?", and Marti steps forward to meet him — a movement of surprise at finding he is indeed out there. As if Robin could be anywhere other than the varying positions from which he relentlessly watches the merest vibration on stage. This tiny detail is more evidence that the rehearsal has attained a new peak. It's an odd fact that the actor reaches a point when the director seems less accessible. But not so, in this case, or anyway not yet. Robin and Marti have a quiet consultation.

Then they start again, and Peter gives a much more than usual demonstration of massacre of text. Robin, reaching to his dimmerboard, reduces the light. McQueen's Kent suddenly doubles his speech rhythms (usually fast and giving, with a penchant for back to audience), and makes a more than throwaway exit with his final lines. Robin is bound to ask him to take more time than that. There is a limit to circumspection, and Kent, like Lear, is much loved by audiences. Peter, exiting on the arm of John Wojda's Burgundy, just after the abandonment of Cordelia, is ad libbing something to the effect that, "She'll find someone else," which seems hardly the point, as Ingrid Blekys, cast down just before, has been taken up by the quintessentially romantic presence of Ed Evanko. Still, it's late in the day.

Donna is making very sure strides as Goneril, after those many missed earlier rehearsals, and is catching up nicely on Marti's Regan, Marti being the kind of actress who, in spite of a useful reticence, arrives fast with many certainties. Robin is asking Donna for some special variations in tone. It can be triggered, he thinks, by externals, even by the shape and contents of the room, with which Goneril will have been familiar since she was a little girl. "Decide on moments . . . when you see that *chair* . . . or you could be thinking, 'I'll have that sofa! *And* the chandeliers! And *some* of the pictures — the ones Mother liked'." Such thoughts, says Robin, can slightly change the voice. Also, neither sister should forget "this problem with Dad started fifteen years ago." Robin sniffs his way around the room, still holding Donna by the hand. They survey it together with the same conjecture of distaste, "I never liked *this* chair — should be a bit of brocade." Phillips pauses, looking within the space of the room, to turn a dissatisfied eye towards the outer world of the auditorium, nailing down Goneril's inner unease. Her voice should go from the real to the non-focused, it should aim for a sense of distance, and Donna, who is gifted and level-headed, will seize all these chances to define an early alienation for Goneril. Most actresses are very responsive to Robin, and Marti, Donna and Ingrid typify the domestic accuracies of this production. The family perspective within *Lear* could hardly be more accessible.

The scene over, Phillips calls for "Everybody" back on-stage. He wants people to change from 'mutter' to 'speaking', especially Peter, on the first entrance. *Everyone* must be aware of everything in this room, which they all know so well, including (a glance in my direction down in the stalls) "the chap who is taking historical notes."

Robin has something choreographic to add on the France and Cordelia exchange before their departure from court. He rehearses Evanko and Blekys with very special care, moving them past the enthroned Lear, showing how the "focus" shifts from them, quickly but smoothly panning to Peter's face, this being that moment Peter has worked towards which culminates in that huge petulant outburst. Whenever Phillips uses movie technicalities I feel more convinced that he's reminding himself of everything he learned when working before a camera, and, in passing it on to his actors, he is honing up on the skills he'll require for the time when he'll stand behind the camera, rather than in the stalls, and quietly say "Turnover" instead of "Once More." Despite any expense, he'd continue to say "Once More" with results which could rival those the young Orson Welles achieved when he invaded Hollywood with his Mercury players.

TUESDAY, SEPTEMBER 18TH

A REQUEST

At ten in the morning I arrive outside the Avon in blinding sunlight on a very hot day. My mission is to ask Robin, rather belatedly, for permission to take photographs, or have some taken, of our cast in their basic rehearsal garb. As I pass through the stage door, I realize it's the crunch now, as the entire Company of *Lear* will be incarcerated in costume within a week.

I descend from the glare and warmth of the street into the cool deep dark of the Avon wings, feeling my way through pitch gloom into the pit of the auditorium. I stumble — quite spectacularly — into the void of the stalls, which is in total darkness. The schedule by the stage door has informed me that Robin should be here with the Lighting team for a 'touch-up' session on the lighting plot. Lighting, in the theatre, is invariably decided on in an amazing absence of any.

The very quiet voice of the Master, alert for quieter entrances than mine, lighting being a secretive science, says, "Hello?" and I mutter "Just Maurice," that I may pass. I join Robin, Vince Berns, and Lighting Designers Michael Whitfield and Harry Frehner, lit at a distant remove only by a small shaded bulb at their centre-stalls control board, and make my request to Robin, and permission is granted. I sit in for a moment to watch some of the work.

Sean T. O'Hara, one of the younger Company members, is 'walking' the stage for lighting positions. The small group of technicians has been here since eight this morning and will remain until noon. They were here yesterday, the actors' day off, lighting *Lear* from eight in the morning to midnight. I stay long enough to line up my exit, with a slight beacon now from the dimly-lit stage, and navigate my departure successfully, to buy some film and a camera. But my main concern, for the moment, is to return to the lighting session. Soon afterwards I descend once more to the air-conditioned stalls, as cold as any tomb, missing the last step, a little less absolutely than before. "Hello?" again. I find my way to the group in their near total darkness, and settle down to watch and listen.

MASTER AND MATES

Work is proceeding towards its conclusion in setting the lamps for the final scenes of the play. Four very casual voices interfuse, blended to low-level intimacy. The short collaborative comments are ground down by long hours of conjecture in the dark. It's that curt, blasé, but very accurate exchange of Master and Mates, a tight focus of command on the bridge of a ship finally homing after a long voyage. I love this jargon of Lighting Design: "Pile On . . .", "Goose Up . . .", "Sneakout . . ."

Ann Stuart (Robin's Personal Assistant and General of Everything, including much Stage Management duty) and Sean T. O'Hara stand down-stage with two very red flags. Not enough. Each is equipped with another flag for the other hand. Still not enough (for the 'look' in assessment of lighting), some of the Stage Crew are asked to join them. Obviously non-actorish, these easy figures hold aloft two more flags apiece. Michael Whitfield calls casually into his mouthpiece, adjusting his headphones, one eye on the lighting monitor (indicating a multiude of circuits on tap), for cues 18 and 19 to come down slowly. "Down three-tenths." The stage light fades on the crimson banners. Vince Berns, only a little louder, calls to those back-stage to "Strike flags and set table."

More hieroglyphics bunch up on the monitor as they call the next cue, "85 — Go!" The stage is a little brighter. Just. More is needed. "Something warmer?" asks Robin. Michael, gently, easily murmurs into his mouthpiece, "84, Show me 84, on-stage — no — that's the big one." "I don't think I like that table," muses Robin, thinking about it, then adding after a beat, "I always prefer it if you don't *have to* use anything." The best of direction is a total concern for actors, and then — if they're really essential — the dreaded props.

Sean is asked to sit on the chair up-stage left where Lear sits, with Cordelia crouched beside him. We are looking at the stage as set up for the final long sequence of the play (from the top of Act V, Scene iii to the end). The back panel of wall is flown out by the Stage Crew and in its place is a dark cyclorama sky. The two side-wall panels remain, as always, but now containing a space suggestive of an interior, with access from the exterior at back and, to a lesser extent, down-left. Technically, it represents the British Camp near Dover. The inside look is established by a large number of chairs, arranged in rows on the rear platform, on a pronounced diagonal from up-left to down right. With the addition of the forestage space, this supplies an area of large choices for the action of the concluding scenes. Down-right is the offending table, lit now by two flickering candles.

They begin to light the position for Edgar's final entrance to challenge Edmund, and Sean moves to stand in it, at down-right. Robin will want to see "as little of Rodg as possible." The lighting is called, spots glinting up and down on Sean's frozen figure. "118 at 45 . . . Take 115 out . . ." Robin thinks they might try a touch of blue in the cyc wall. Michael calls up a little. Robin muses, but only momentarily, "I think it's rotten — take it out." Harry Frehner calls the change, and the slightly pretty glow is flushed away. "Much better black," Robin murmurs.

More lights are called. "94 at 40 . . . coming down a point. 83 at 35 . . . down a point." "Very nice" says Robin, easing back in his stalls seat with a sigh. "I love scenes where you can hear but not see. We see far too much in the theatre." He pursues the point, to Vince, of "Hearing the truth of what you hear spoken, uncluttered by the truth of what you can still see . . ."

A moment later he calls to Ann Stuart to "Strike that cross for the one that stands up," and Ann is off and back instantly on-stage with a new cross, a small vertical between the two flickering candles. I'm wondering about the paradox of a cross, even a small one, on Edmund's field-desk, in a play about a pagan world, Victorian Christianity notwithstanding. They're still busy with lights. "24 up another point."

"Those chairs?" queries Robin, "Can you feel you're in a room?" It seems to me, I tell him, that we do. With the two side panels suggesting they are at right angles (though we ourselves know the angle to be widely obtuse), it's the alignment of the chairs themselves, facing diagonally down-right from up-left, which creates the illusion of two sides of a room.

On an impulse, I leave my place and go down the aisle and make the tricky assent to the stage. It's dark on those steps from the stalls. I advance up the two shallow steps onto the higher area and move through the chairs. It reminds me of an actor who refused a part in that play by Ionesco, being under threat from so much furniture. I'm surprised and shocked at the extreme rake of the stage. In spite of the fact that I've often acted (even sung and danced) on steeper-raked stages than this. But it's very uphill from the forestage to the back through Daphne's walls, and I'm better attuned now to the ever-conscious adjustments our whole cast has learned to achieve on this sloping deck. Perhaps, needing to know and feel just that is what brought me here.

I try a quick snap with my camera through the lonely chairs of Sean's lonlier presence, and move for a second shot from behind his shoulder. "Hurry a bit, Maurice," says Robin, from out in the stalls, "as the flash does something to our eyes." As I make my cautious return down from the stage, I'm reminded of shows I've lit myself, and can appreciate Robin's tolerance. It's easy to 'lose your eye' when lighting — and a flash (or two) could be disconcerting. Which reminds me of the mistake (in younger and callower days) when setting lighting levels myself, and looking (once is enough) directly into a spot from on stage. One's focus can be glazed for a long time afterwards. The trick, if you have to focus lights for yourself, is to look just a little to the left or right of each lamp — and you can be sure, later, that the spots are still looking at you.

When I rejoin the team, Robin is calling to Ann to replace the two candles (now also offending) with a lantern. Ann does so. "Looks better," says Robin, considering the new, steadier light in the table area: "It could be coming from Himself with that cross there." Vince reminds us that the sabre-duel contains a detail of passing the blades through the candles' flames (a piece of Paddy Crean ritual). Robin says that the business can be dropped; he doesn't want two distracting glitters of candles, prefers this little glow. "Much better," he says, "to be able to see what you *want* to see than to have to see what doesn't matter."

They are still adjusting nuances of Edgar's light at down-left. They also want the Herald's breastplate to gleam a little. "See the shine from Sean's buckle!" (Sean now standing in for Chris Blake), "that's it!" And then, "Kick in a little more back-lighting there . . . That's better! . . . On the O.P." (Opposite Prompt-Side spots, from stage-left at the Avon) ... "So he's lit sideways! That's it. 20 up a point ... Whoops! Down ... Good." Michael is pleased. The figure gives us a definite sense of the 'outside'.

Now for the middle area, at centre steps, where Lear will finally settle, with the dead Cordelia in his arms, before expiring himself. A little "increase" adjustment is called for in 87. Not enough. Some more is added. And more, "Warm it a bit more." They're working on a bit of a boost here for the dying Lear. "Up to 30 ... 35." Robin, justifying it (as if he needs to), reminds himself that "There'll be *lots* of torches there to give us an excuse." (You can bet there will be!) "Ann, just lie across his knees." Sean is Lear again, sitting, centre, on the steps. "Is there some back-light for here?" asks Robin, knowing there will be. I should explain that if, or rather *when* you bump in a lot of strong Front-of-House Spots on something important, it is less obvious if you compensate with some further lighting, on the same subject, naturally, from the sides or rear. And here it comes. Michael and Harry have calculated the option in advance, and there are two lights set and focused on the exact place, and a *choice*, also, "A 'warm', and a 'cold'," says Michael. "Flash 70, warm first, then the cold."

The lighting intensifies in Lear's death place, Sean and Ann huddling in it. Or, I should say, that the effect *seems* to be less intensive, with the aid of those back spots; though in fact, it is even brighter than before. Very bright. And why not? Great roles require to be generously lit, especially when inhabited by greater talents. The distinction between 'bright' and anything less than bright in Phillips' productions is very sharply defined. Last season in 'As You', coming on for one of those reflective scenes as Duke Senior, immediately following one of Rosalind's exits, I found myself transitorily bathed in that aurelian blaze of lighting reserved for Miss Maggie Smith in romantic high comedy. It proved, alas, to be an evanescent sensation, and the glow expired with disenchanting rapidity as the electricians caught up on a late lighting (or 'unlighting') cue.

Phillips, meantime, continues lighting Lear — and I do mean Lear, which, of necessity incorporates his final prop of the demised Cordelia. "She'll be a bit lower than that," reflects Robin, considering Ingrid's final pose: "Peter lets her fall between his legs, and her head goes further back." Robin calls to Ann to make the adjustment, and approves the result, "That's it ... with her head up — should look quite dead." Still not satisfied, they add more light from the front spots, "A bit more on the front one ... good, read this for Cue 87."

Master and Mates pore over their charts; they've now lit their way almost into port. Again, someone is heard entering our Stygian depths from the pass-door, negotiating those steps with the same difficulty as myself, and Robin, alert for any non bona-fide intrusion, again queries, "Hello?" Again, it's someone with a legitimate purpose, nobody deigning to say them nay, and it reassures me — with a tiny glow — that I have some real business to be here after all.

Vince and Michael are concluding details of the final lighting cue. This will be for the fade-out of all lights, ending — one can be sure — with those on centre stage. It'll be a "wipe to coincide with sound" and will be timed with Bert's music later. I'm not sure who said those words, but the implication can mean only the same thing for us all. I can feel the play begin to escape from us here in the stalls. The light is ready for the cast. The costumes are around the corner. The stage is set for actors, and the play finally belongs to them.

A final grace-note from Vince Berns, confirming this late point in our voyage. "Do you want to set anything (he means light) for the Curtain Call?" he asks, knowing the answer. "No ... no, no ..." says Robin, absently, but absolutely. He never does that until the last possible moments. The play may belong to the actors, but he's not giving it to them quite, just yet. It's a break at noon, and time for me to leave for a matinée.

SPASMS, SABRES, AND SWANSONGS

I'm back at the Avon on this still very hot afternoon, to find the Company at work on-stage. They're rehearsing the section leading up to the duel between Edmund and Edgar (V.iii). Richard Monette, luxuriating in an unshaven two-day's growth, is working so consistently in his darkest baritone, where his voice is at its most expressive, that I'm not so surprised when he tells me he's "playing it butch for the day!" Frank Maraden's Albany has arrived into the action, 'Hear, reason ... I arrest thee, Edmund ...' to lead us to the play's denouement. Frank's high-tension performance can also manage to be extremely relaxed. Marti Maraden's Regan finds that her 'Sickness grows' upon her with a significantly uglier spasm than ever, making Donna's aside as Goneril, 'If not, I'll ne'er trust medicine' seem chilly understatement. It's greatly to Donna's credit that such an absolutely melodramatic, very Victorian line has never yet sounded funny.

Robin steps on-stage to organize increased agonies for the poisoned Regan, and they take the section again. Marti, in a new sudden plunge up-stage, knocks over a couple of those chairs, in a quite spectacular spasm; her retching figure is hurried off-stage by a clutch of soldiers concerned foremost in preserving the immaculate textures of their best on-parade tunics.

The duel proceeds, merely marked in by Barton and Monette, but obviously rehearsed by Mr. Crean in its every nicety. I'm momentarily startled by the insertion of a *new* speech into the text of *Lear*. Christopher Blake, Herald and M.C. for the duel, extols the ritual of this gentlemanly combat. As a curiosity, though not worthy of the best of Mr. Crean's prose style, as exemplified in his autobiography, *More Champagne, Darling?*, it's worth quoting in full. 'The Code Duello has been read . . . There is no reconciliation . . . The affair will proceed . . . I shall speak in English and in French . . . I shall say "Are you ready, Gentlemen?" . . . "Etês-vous prêts, Messieurs?" . . . You will nod if so . . . I shall then say "On Guard! and En Garde!" . . . You will place yourselves in the Guard Position . . . I shall then say "Go!" . . . "Alléz!" . . . If, for any reason I must stop the fight before conclusion, I shall say "Halte!" . . . "Are you ready, Gentlemen?" . . . "Etês-vous prêts, Messieurs?" "On Guard!" "En garde!" "Allez".'

And they're off, with neither gentleman hesitating either way on either language. Paddy's new *Lear* speech doesn't seem at all incongruous, so speedily delivered in this fading nineteenth-century evening. Ustinov sits in the stalls, arms resting on the seat in front, in typical enjoyment. I sometimes wonder, thinking of Ingrid's so similar pose, who is imitating whom. All three daughters bear a useful resemblance to Dad, none more so than Marti as Regan, as a profile picture I've managed to take should show. Peter now makes his way through the pass-door, followed by Ingrid, to stand by for his last entrance. In the post-duel scuffle, before Goneril's struggling exit, the lantern on the table is knocked on the stage floor, and begins to smoke formidably. It's a highly-paced scene and nobody notices; such is the general concentration of all those onstage. Vince dispatches Ann to retrieve it, and Robin leans forward to dim down the lights as Peter enters to 'Howl!, Howl!, Howl!'.

ANOTHER REQUEST

As they finish, Robin goes to join them for a quiet consultation. The atmosphere is suddenly very relaxed, on this exchange of minor points. That 'looking-glass' Lear asks for, as Peter says, need never be proffered, "He'll be so tired — he'll forget he mentioned it." And that feather, which Lear insists is stirring near Cordelia's lips, is totally illusory, unlike the literally glued-on reality insisted on by nineteenth-century tragedians. Robin and Peter exchange some thoughts on the powerful simplicities of Lear's last words. The Company, sprawled about the stage, become reflective, stilled.

Peter, suddenly jocular, recalls Voltaire's last words. "When they brought the candle close to his eyes to see if he was still living, he opened one eye and said 'What? The flames already?' " He then remembers Chekhov's last sentence, "Which could only have been his: 'I think I'll have that glass of champagne, after all'." Monette remembers those last words from Gertrude Stein, 'What was the answer to that question?', and, when nobody knew, 'Then, what was the question?'

Ustinov's thoughts jump from that last moment in the play to his first entrance as Lear. He has, he says, a request for "something which would be *tremendously* helpful." I can hear the change in pulse of some present, not least Robin Phillips. Peter suggests that, in establishing that after-dinner bonhomie, and in addition to that cigar we're now accustomed to, he'd "rather like, also, to be carrying a rather large brandy balloon." Robin, sitting on the forestage, alertly attentive, is silent. And Peter, obliged to continue, continues.

"It really would be awfully helpful, you know . . . I can put it in Gloucester's hand — absently — forgot I still had it with me . . . Shouldn't give to *him*, of course, but it's all part of that stupidity we're doing . . . He doesn't really know who people *are* . . . What their jobs are . . . And it would add to that over-indulged thing . . . One can get very unpleasant when drunk . . . *Not* that he's drunk

114

of course, but *flushed* ... It really would be terribly helpful to me, you know," Peter concludes, an engaging boy cajoling the Master.

Robin finally interposes, "If ..." (a determined pause here before he continues) "*If* you promise not to do anything else, not to change anything else." "No! Absolutely. Not a thing!" confirms Peter, with a suggestion of an unguessable complicity of schoolboy high spirits and responsibility. "I mean, absolutely!" Who could resist him? "In that case ..." concludes Robin, making him wait for it, "permission granted." No camera could fully capture the pleasure in Peter's face. We're halfway through another very technical day.

TUESDAY, SEPTEMBER 18TH *continued*

'VONTZ MURR, PLIZZ'. SCENE CHANGES

"Stand By, and Places, Please," Vince Berns is calling, promptly, at half-past-seven. And "Stand By your piece of furniture," calls Robin. The entire cast is on-stage, as at the end of Scene One, to practice this scene change, and all others throughout the play.

Rehearsals have advanced to the time for a Run-Through for our first half of the show in uninterrupted sequence. In achieving this all scene changes will need to be smoothly integrated. This ante-room at Lear's court is, just now, cluttered with sixteen pieces of furniture, much of it very heavy, including that big desk, and on it, an unwieldy lamp. "Go!" calls Robin, and the stage erupts into action as chairs, chaise, desk and occasional tables are whipped away with barrack-room dispatch. And silence. It's obviously already been much rehearsed. Berthold Carriere, looking more angelic than ever, with his whole score written and by now recorded (he's told me so), is back at his piano, giving the linking music. "How long?" asks Robin, sucking on a cigarette, as the stage is cleared. Vince, checking his stop-watch, announces "Fourteen Seconds." "Very good. But we can do much better," says Robin.

"Crew to set back" is called. Daphne Dare's back panel comes flying in, "Heads Up! Wall Coming Down," calls Vince, as the furniture is being re-set. Again, and once again, we have this trans-formation from Lear's cluttered courtroom to the empty space, bare except for a couple of benches, of Albany's and Goneril's courtyard. With our newer skills in staging, which means doing as few unnecessary set changes as possible, we've run on to Shakespeare's Act I, Scene iii; all the preceding action (Scenes i and ii) having been played in that opening setting. The final visual touch, with all furniture gone, is the presence of those 'beggars without the gates' of Albany's palace. "You lot," Robin confides to them, "can limp on at any time." In effect, this can mean their arrival during the action of the scene change. "You don't have to hurry," he often says, as the rapidity of the changes increases, with the aid of concentrated but relaxed discipline and careful planning. Some people on the technical team must have stayed up late last night for these calculations.

"Vontz murr, plizz," purrs Robin, generalissimo now of the delights of stage logistics. The changes continue, the end of scenes interlocking into the start of others each time. Vince calls the Stand-By for actors with that different resonance, that little 'formality' one associates with performance time: something not quite, any longer, merely rehearsal: "I need Mr. U., Mr. H., Mr. Christopher." When the change is larger in scale and more complicated, involving, as it so often does, the co-ordinated skills of a large number of actors as well as Stage-Staff, Robin calls (enjoying it all), "Troops ready," or its variant, "Stand-By, Troopies!" In the midst of much technical priorities it would be compatible for Peter to carry off something himself, and Robin might suggest it, allowing for the priority of Peter clinging to lines rather than props.

I move into the wings, watching actors and staff in this turmoil of adjustments, alert as athletes watching for the little flashes on the off-stage cue-lights. "Vontz murr, plizz!" is heard once more from out in the stalls, and this prepared readiness flows into action. It's beautiful. These off-stage images in the wings, with glimpses of the stage beyond, have been caught with such accurate definition in paintings of Sickert, Degas, Lautrec, but they remind me most of the special grace and fluidity of those high-angle shots from the flies in Chaplin's *Limelight*. It's the only movie I've seen which was truly evocative of back-stage theatre; it captured what every actor knows, and what I feel here now, the whole Poetry of the Change, blending into the Poetry of the Play.

When I get back to the stalls, Vince is calling, remindingly, for "Quiet Please — More Quiet Back-Stage!" Robin is wrestling with another big item, the scene-change into the 'Blinding of Gloucester', requiring a desk and more heavy pieces. Everybody is reminded that nobody has to hurry. The change accomplished, satisfactorily, after many alterations, with all furniture set, there follows the choreography of its removal at the scene's end. Robin pauses, exhaling smoke, only slightly tiring, "Whoever did — whatever they *did* — getting it all out here — be ready to do the same backwards." He sucks in more smoke, and exhales, adding "Except *you*" (he means Patrick Christopher who, in the scene's action, went down in the struggle from Marti's sword-thrust). "Except you, Patrick, as you're dead."

A small problem. Bert says he's run out of music. He should know, to the last bar, as he's so recently composed it. They'll have to further shorten the scene change. Bert, meanwhile, improvises a little extra something, redolent (once more) of *The Merry Widow*. Robin, glancing in Bert's direction, says, "He's just sort of busking." "Busking? That's not the word I'd use," responds Vince Berns, (who'll have to cut the change by half), and then interrupts himself with a shout of "Heads Up! Wall Coming Down!"

They're ready next for the following change, from the interior (with Marti as Regan and Tom as Oswald) to the exterior at Dover. That big desk is again downstage, and Marti is in position for her near-exit line, but Robin has planned something better than that earlier joke of 'Exit pursued by Desk'. The best device of stage-craft, in acting, directing, (or writing — look into Ibsen's early drafts) is to turn a problem, even a major weakness, into a strength. It's decided that the desk will exit right, with Marti accelerating off-left — splitting among the three actor-scene-changers coming in to deal with these heavy props. Simultaneously, the rear wall panel is flying out to give us a bare stage (I'd love the cry of gulls) for the Dover scene. What makes it all so telling is that Marti's penultimate line is a chilling reference to the now-blinded Gloucester (we've just seen it happen), 'If you should chance to hear of that blind traitor / Preferment falls on him that cuts him off', and, as the rear wall flies up, there he is, against the Dover sky, blindfolded, terribly frail, yet determined at least to reach the cliffs, the immeasurably moving image of Douglas Rain, led by a disguised son with whom he is in deep familial disagreement.

Marti's delivery of the above line is no barn-storming villainy. On the contrary, it's a tortured committal by Regan to that irreversible path for her character, the route through the darkest part of her nature. In this scene-change rehearsal, concentrated as it is only on the tail-to-top of each scene, the truncated shape of a great play reveals the alarming, and sometimes encouraging juxtaposition of good and evil in all of its characters. As light follows the dark, as scenes interfuse, Robin and his cast accept the challenges of this realisation. The scene-change is as absolutely vital to our meaning in the play's final structure, as the highest rhetoric of any moment, just as the smallest silence has become as powerful as any of the words.

Bert's linking chords for this change are blunt and brutal, with a light tail of more gentle notes ascending into the Dover sky. "Bertie, play that piece again," says Robin, many times, holding Marti by the hand, looking for the exact note on which she should turn to go, slowly, and then more quickly, as the scene change occurs. He wants a precise moment on which she'll turn her head, before she moves. They find it, and then quickly combine it with the change. It's so clearly wrought. It's a perfect example of Phillips' painstaking tenacity to small details. Regan's words resonate in the air along with Bert's notes, and there, against the sky, are Gloucester and son, *'When* shall we come to the top of that same hill . . .' Douglas invests the 'When' with an extra pitch of all-patience-spent (it's about the eighth rehearsal of the device), and there is an appreciative laugh from the many sitting out front. Nevertheless, the finished effect is potently touching, and I hear some murmur of approval. Robin, never a victim of self-congratulation, as instantly calls, "O.K. — what next?" Five minutes later, when he's done something less spectacular, but as important to him, I hear him mutter, sotto-voce, to himself, "Perfect."

They move on to the awakening of Lear to the presences of Kent and Cordelia in the French camp (IV.vii). Peter is borne in on a litter (supposedly asleep), and set down. It's the first time with the real prop, which he doesn't greatly relish. Climbing off it he mutters, "A lot of *give,*" (there is a noticeable sag in the middle). "I don't care for this very much." Stretching deliciously, rising to his feet, he adds "Hate these night trains." He's obliged to get back on the litter for another try. As he's lifted again he exclaims with complaint, "If I can sleep through this, it's a miracle!" The litter is raised with added care. "Trying again? *Last* time they started at a hell of a lick." He's comforted by the thought (as Robin reminds him) that he is being borne on-stage but not off. "Yes," he says, settling again on the flimsy hammock, "I walk out — thank God."

In preparation for the last scene change, the chairs are brought out to the stage. There are fourteen of them, and it looks like forty. "This is pure farce," sighs Robin, "everyone who has a *black* uniform come and join me." The group of those who remember they've been fitted thus, assembles downstage. They finally sort it all out. "That was sixteen seconds, Fellahs, and it should be ten."

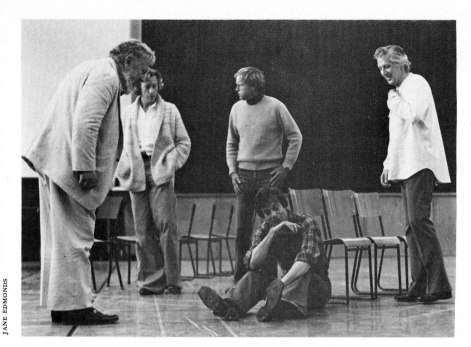

Peter Ustinov, Patrick Christopher, William Copeland, Jim McQueen, William Hutt.

"Mak'st thou this shame thy pastime?"

Robin Phillips, Director, in rehearsal.

Peter Ustinov
"I prithee, daughter, do not make me mad . . ."

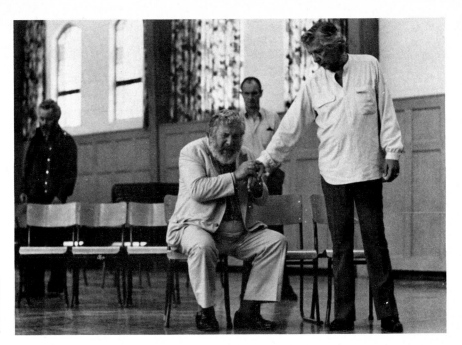

JANE EDMONDS

Douglas Rain, Peter Ustinov, Rex Southgate, William Hutt.
"O Fool, I shall go mad!"

JANE EDMONDS

Jim McQueen and Maurice Good
at rehearsal.

Ingrid Blekys

Make-up call

Richard Monette, William Webster

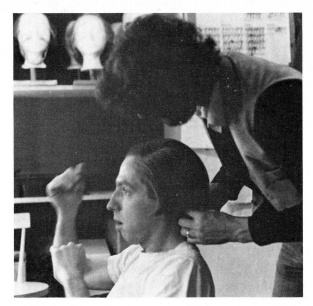

JANE EDMONDS

Tom Wood, Paul Elliot (Wig Master, Avon Theatre)

Wigs and Preparations

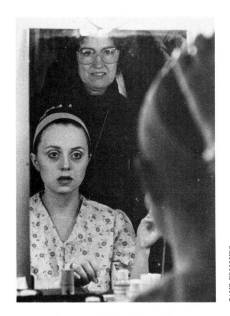

JANE EDMONDS

Donna Goodhand   Marti Maraden

JANE EDMONDS

Peter Ustinov, William Hutt, Rex Southgate, Robin Phillips,
Patrick Christopher, Francois-Regis Klanfer, Vincent Berns.

The day of the Cliche

JANE EDMONDS

Richard Monette, Rodger Barton

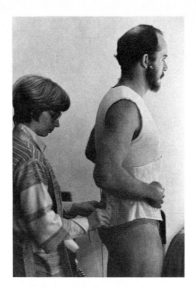

JANE EDMONDS

Dresser and William Webster
Mr. Webster's Corset

JANE EDMONDS

Christopher Blake, David Holmes, John Lambert, Michael Totzke:
Costume call

Bill Hutt, Peter Ustinov, Jim McQueen, Greg Peterson
Another photographer?

Robin Phillips at his Dimmer board.

A FIRST TOUCH OF SURRENDER

Peter joins me where I'm sitting in the stalls, and regales me with some very Irish stories, some of them delivered in impeccable Dublinese, for which I can vouch, being a Dubliner myself. I'll relate one — or some of them — later, whenever it's usefully relevant to the work in hand. But now, everything has been set back to the top of the play, and we're ready for a Run-Through of our Part One.

It all proceeds smoothly, with only one interruption this time, just before that first scene change, when Vince calls a strident "Stop" as Monette takes three steps towards his exit (End of I.ii). Richard remains poised, one foot frozen, lifted and ready for the next step, as Vince continues (a subtle adaptation of Robin's style), "Is *everybody* ready back there for the Change?" Everybody is. Monette lets his foot fall to the floor; he goes, and the act continues with the much laboured-for fluency . . . "Lock door! — Fly wall! Stand by!"

There are things I've grown attached to which are missing, but there are gains also, very often. Webster's menace as Cornwall grows. Bill's found that face he was looking for, ambition engraved by the implacable zeal in masking it. Jim's Kent glides on a non-effort of voice, spreading wings surely within the text.

On a walk backstage, through the wings, I relish the flow of rehearsal, the off-stage energy balancing that on-stage: the diminishing flurry of a dozen voices and running feet in some lower bowel of the theatre continues the burly long after Edgar's flight (II.i). Butch Blake, leaning on the Stage-Management desk (his favourite site), listens to this *Lear*, watching everything, rapt. I'd caught him in a camera-snap, settled there in a break, watching — always learning.

Back out front again, I'm in time to see Kent put into the stocks, the real prop at last, this first edge of physical violence in the play, mild compared to those which will follow. Marti's Regan continues to show that unerring instinct to keep travelling, judging her space, always in a new and often surprising position for the next line. The music from Bert, still at his piano, solders scene to scene, with occasional accompaniments as appropriate as a ballet score.

Suddenly, the act is over. Robin calls them on-stage, says "Thank you very, very much," and sends them home.

The theatre empties with rapidity. It's been a very rich long day, and the many echoes still linger; listening in on that lighting session; the late afternoon rehearsals ending in Peter's request for a brandy-glass; the agonized attention to all those scene-changes; and, now, this completed Run-Through of Part One. A Run-Through of an act must come sometime, of course. And we've just had one, almost without anyone noticing. But there was something missing, in this last part of the day. Robin hasn't said anything. Not a word, not an interruption, not a note.

As I turn to go I look back and see him, for an instant, standing still and alone. The stance is typical, but there's an odd, subtle change. I can identify the sensation, which all directors share: one of the hardest and most difficult tasks they must perform is the conscious surrender of the play to the cast. Robin turns to confer with Michael and Harry. Vince, Ann, and Michael Benoit also join him. It's almost the actors' show. But not just yet.

It's very cold now, outside the Avon. Some of the Company, in short sleeves, thinking of warmer garb, hurry home.

THURSDAY, SEPTEMBER 20TH

ANOTHER LEAR

At noon in the Avon the cast is ready for a Run-Through of Part Two. Vince calls "Places, Please" and they're off (III.i). Jim and Patrick lead, with Peter hot on their heels, to 'Blow Winds' (III.ii). Robin is denuded, today, of his drum. Bert has it by him at the piano to lend moderate percussive drum rolls to his linking score. Phillips, all set to savage his throat if he goes on like this, supplies punctuations of wind, rain and thunder, and occasional fire bolts from the heavens, excelling his usual repertoire, all with one finger and one eye on Vince's prompt-copy.

"Boo-boo-boo-Boomm!" ... "Schchch chhhh ... Spishhhhh ... Pish ... Pizzzzzzzzzzzzzzzz! ... "WhishHHHHHHH!" "CRrrrrrr-RHUMMmmmmmmmPHhhh!" His really big ones are even more impossible to get down in any combination of mere vowel and consonant. Later, he settles for a quieter drip-dripping, accompanied by an almost incessant soughing of wind, or variations of winds (III.iv). It's exhausting just to listen to him. Reduced, as he is, for this while, to a vocal accompaniment, the sheer physical effort (mostly from the back of the throat) increases for those watching and those on-stage, the remorseless demands of the text. Some of the cast seem to be pushing it a bit. Ustinov's hands, which I've so far neglected to emphasize, are as expressive as the far reaches of his voice. A scribbled note in the dark (P's hands — *HANDS*!) reminds me now.

The action of these scenes pulses on, so powerful, and often so simple. The brief fore-stage scene between Gloucester and Edmund advances the sub-plot (III.ii). Sub-Plot! The story of Gloucester and his sons, interwoven with that of Lear and his daughters, is as enormously hewn as the contrapuntal family themes in Tolstoy or Dostoevsky, and Douglas Rain is doing it full justice. If Peter is playing two Lears, in his pact with Phillips and the author to split the man in two and let us see this happen, Douglas is doing the same. There is another Lear on this stage, and his name is Gloucester. Robin, watching the quiet, urgent scene, pushes his lighting switches, and the stage grows darker.

We are on into the 'Before the Hovel' scene, and Lear, raising his face to the palpable rush of rain (Robin is still soaking them), cries out, 'Pour on: I will endure!' (III.iv). It's become one of my favourite moments, especially as he always contrives to look so drenched, so utterly sodden, that one is tempted to shout out "Then get the hell into some cover, you silly old bugger!"

It's a strange Run-Through. It is, after all, the first run of the whole of our second act. And there are (as happened with our Act One) some jolts amid the gains and losses. One of these, in the 'Blinding of Gloucester', is the addition of somebody (from the sound of it) throwing up against the right wall (III.vii). I have to move a few seats, Bert's piano obscuring my view, before I can identify the originator. I'm not surprised to find it is John Wojda, one of the four servants, the one with no lines. I've mentioned earlier the quietly horrified playing of David Stein and Barrie Wood, and Patrick Christopher's gallant 'double' of the servant who tackles Cornwall. Wojda, who starts the play as the Duke of Burgundy, reappears often during the show, doubling with the traditional frequency of the best of younger actors, his final contribution being when he brings the story of the fate of Gloucester to Frank Maraden's Albany (IV.ii). This scene, in the course of this rehearsal, shimmers with the pure certainties both actors bring to it. Both balance each other in a restraint of means. Maraden drags the words up to the surface of expression, 'Where was his son when they did take his eyes?'; nothing added in tonality, it is excruciatingly factual, everyday, humane. It's appropriate that Albany, another herbivore in this world of carnivores, is self-elected for the task of retribution. A great play requires and deserves the best of actors in the relatively minor roles. Many of our younger company actors owe a great deal to the influence and example of Douglas Rain.

This unimpeded rehearsal serves finely in revealing the enormous and sharply executed consistency and restraint in Rain's Gloucester. His performance alone further clarifies the genius of some of the greatest writing in the play. Clarity is never merely a bonus in acting, it is acting's first need. It's in Gloucester's words that we hear the deepest plea for the innocent (IV.i). How strange that it's the crimes against Gloucester, and not those against Lear, which finally turn the tide in this great play. Rain's speeches as Gloucester, blinded, unknowingly accompanied by his banished son (as Poor Tom), reach through the play's action, forward and back, from the sweet memories of an untrammelled past, to the agony of the present, the emergent hope for the future. Before the blinding, encountering Poor Tom on the heath, he kicks him away (III.iv). Later (after the blinding), he recalls, 'I stumbled when I saw' ... '... my son came then into my mind' ... 'As flies to wanton boys, are we to th' Gods; / They kill us for their sport' (IV.i). Rain's lines always tell so very potently because he renews the choice, over and over again in his long, illustrious career, of allowing the lines to speak for themselves. It's no wonder that Poor Tom 'cannot daub it further!' (IV.i). The characters of Gloucester and Albany, as much as those of Kent and Lear, prove an embodiment of the hope that, though 'humanity must prey on itself', humanity may learn, through pain, to do much better.

Rehearsal heads into the home straight. Bert's drum rolls. Robin brings the lights to full — or the fullest we've seen yet. It's suddenly very bright. It's the return of Cordelia into the action in search of Lear, and the words are changing, also, to 'love, dear love ...' (IV.iv). Gloucester and Edgar approach that never-attained cliff at Dover, 'Do you hear the sea?' (IV.vi). And we have the very long, wonderfully believable pause before Douglas, bandaged, grey beard questing says, 'No! — truly!' And, indeed, they're a long way from it. The fall, from the non-existent cliff, is now greatly simplified, with Doug collapsing forward from a kneeling position.

The Gloucester-Lear encounter, soon after, is enriched by Rain's experiment in containing the emotion. His chorus to Peter's Lear, with so little to say, enriches this exchange of a wisdom beyond all tears. In response to Peter's delivery of 'Get thee glass eyes; / And, like a scurvy politician, seem / To see the things thou dost not . . .', Doug offers us a repeated nodding of the head, many times, and even a just perceptible trace of an ironic chuckle.

Luckily, it's a play in which the battle is entirely off-stage, and very quickly over. (Our production expedites this further in cutting the brief Act V. Scene ii, altogether.) Lear, up-stage in a chair with Cordelia by his side, calls some lines in a provocatively mocking shout (both Peter's hands a megaphone) to Edmund at that down-stage table, 'Come! Let's away to prison!' (V.iii). Lear's ascending gaiety of spirits provokes Edmund to battle-wearied and mounting impatience on his order to 'Take them *away*!' On the exit, a typical Peter touch, Lear points skywards to some new-seen delights: the sky, one feels, is filled with the flight of long-absent birds.

The act is just over. And 'The Gods are just'. Goneril's and Regan's bodies are borne in to Albany, and this 'touches us not with pity' (V.iii). Edmund 'pants for life' — a fine last spurt from Monette — in playing the attempt to save the lives of the Fool and Cordelia. Too late, of course, and Peter arrives with Ingrid to 'Howl, Howl, Howl.' The rehearsal is broken, after which there will be notes.

THURSDAY, SEPTEMBER 20TH *continued*

HALF-TIME NOTES — THE VORTEX

This time I'm caught in the heart of the session. During the break I'd sat chatting with a couple of Company members, in the front seats of the left aisle, and Robin now calls the cast to sit close (he's arrived in front of me), hemming me in. I'm torn between a desire to escape to a space which will assure me of at least a minimal out-side perspective (this having been my objective until now) or to accept the chance and challenge of a ringside seat. I've no time, as it happens, to consider options, as Robin is instantly into full spate.

"First," he begins, "it wasn't terribly good . . . We were none of us quite in the right neck of the woods except here and there in smaller bits — not even — hold your breaths — not even for the storm." He is still adamantly talking of where the *voice* is, and, in the day's work, few voices, if any, possessed "the right muscles for the storm." Robin lights a cigarette. "Old Mad Harry," he says, meaning Rodger Barton, "was back to square one; hysterical, rather than cold." He's not sure *anyone* (I'm very close to Peter and Douglas) was in the right territory, vocally, though bits were "O.K. in the pre-hovel bit" (III.iv). In the middle of such a ferocious downpour, says Phillips, it's better to just *stand*, even if it's only to take comfort in this saturation . . . "If you move, you should *know*, you should feel, that you can drown here." Robin insists, further, on this image, referring to the discomfort of the watchers in today's air-conditioned Avon, freezing now, without the body-heat of eleven hundred customers. As he puts it — and I can heartily endorse this — "I didn't *dare* move my hands out from my armpits for fear of losing what little heat I *have*." Can this have something to do, I wonder, with Robin's energetic commitment to drumming, sound effects, constant sprints on and off stage. Maybe. He's had to be very contained during this past Run-Through.

The spate of comments goes on. They are not so much notes as a floodgate to thought. Many directors, including many of the best I've known, have their stuff written down. Robin very seldom has. To remove his remorseless eyes from the stage would risk his missing something good, and — as important — something bad. A lot of it, today, was "still too fast and with too much energy." This, in the light (it's bright enough now, with all of the Avon chandeliers on) of the hard fact that this second part has run well over two hours.

"We haven't sunk *low* enough yet to feel the right energy," Robin is saying. A lot of it should be, he says, closer in energy to where Peter gets on, 'Reason not the need' (II.iv). He dreads to have to accept the term of 'Run-Through' as it so often sends everybody off on a desperate gallop. We all start doing what "we think we're meant to be doing." Nobody seems to be excused. Marti was "caught in the tidal wave." Most had allowed themselves to become "knotted with tension." It's true that a lot of what went wrong sprang from "a wonderful desire to entertain" but, in the process, we'd allowed ourselves "so little time to look back on all our living, all our experience." It's worth remembering how close those words are to something Robin had already said to Peter not so long ago. The 'time' and the 'living' he speaks of very evidently refers, not only to that of the characters being portrayed, but to that of the actors who are portraying them.

Robin drives on. "It's *emptiness* that produces that rush to the temple of the right thought, but never tension, never tension." He insists that it's the same with crying, with any emotional condition. He unhesitatingly exploits (in example) a story of his own illness last season. He had been brought to a condition of absolute exhaustion through overwork. He sketches a bizarre and wonderfully funny little scenario of a Doctor he "couldn't even see" (Dr. Williams, on occasion our Company Doctor, is not especially tall). "Couldn't *see* him, but gradually, I began to *hear* him, saying the same thing over and over: 'Stop panting, and breathe slowly!' " Robin is emphatic that he was "in a desperate state" but "wasn't clutching the bed," and he remembers clearly "that, though I thought I was dying, I was absolutely lucid . . . or I wouldn't have heard his voice from under the bed." The value of how this idea can be harnessed is, for me — to use Phillips' earlier phrase — 'one of the best acting lessons ever.'

He finishes his point. In so far as Robin ever finishes a point. With so many of our emotions — these being the hardest extremes to know in our own lives — it's often best, in the course of our work, to "cling to the funny ones." I'd venture to think that this is one of the constant choices that lies behind the richness of Peter Ustinov's work. The encounter of Phillips and Ustinov could not fail to release the best in each of them. And that's the best of reasons, in our work, to seek out the talents which invigorate and nourish our own.

Some essentially more personal exchanges follow, and my pen rests, as I edit out by relaxing. There are things which I hold back, not only because they are personal, but because they are as uncommunicable as the flotsam every artist sifts through in the endless search of craft. Among actors, these processes are, of necessity, wrenched open by ourselves in communal trust so that we may share our common muse. As Ophelia says: 'We know what we are, but we know not what we may be'. Actors aren't mad; we aim to be and often become hyper-sane. It's our job to know what we *are*, that we may succeed in knowing on-stage, what we *may* be.

Robin's stream of notes surges on. Donna was "very nice at the end!" She is cautioned to trust the action and the text "where you're in the state in which the voice will take on the colour you need." Everyone "got better later." "From the Doctor on, we were nice," Phillips informs us (IV.iv). The "Doctor," not to be confused with Dr. Williams to whom he bears little resemblance other than the possession of as Freudian a beard, is Rod Beattie, who enters the action in the later Cordelia scenes. And Rod, whose work at Stratford spans Robin's entire seven years stay here, is one of those most

Mr. Rod Beattie: French Doctor

finely attuned to the (seeming) non-effort in voice that Phillips strives for in all.

"You (Douglas Rain) were all right," says Robin. And Doug allows the merest half-beat before rejoining, "Helps — when you're blind." Many are reminded that their voices were "in marvellous territory while in the rehearsal hall." I'm reminded so often, while working with Robin, how less talented directors insist so often, with abysmal results for all, on actors raising projection to enormous and vilely unnecessary proportions the moment they move from rehearsal halls to the stage and theatre.

"*You* came into your own at the end," Robin assures Monette. He then reflects for a while on the case of a famous actress whose compulsion it was to take on *all* the scenes, encapsulate every element, play *all* the action. And that can't be done. Far better to settle for one or two or, better, just one objective, which can be felt and played. For instance, we can't play the battle. Shakespeare wisely hasn't made us do so. If they want a battle let them go to the movies. Robin summons up a battle for us now, the one we don't have to do in *Lear*. "Great flanks of people . . . !" He mimes the wild plunging menace in gestures, then sounds the opposing battalions and cavalry companies; he gives us their growing canter, the gallop, the crazy charge. "We don't have to do any of that!"

He pauses, slightly, "What *else* was desperate?" Then, interrupting himself — a calculative interruption — "This is just so you'll believe me, when I tell you later how good — not how bad — you all were." His eye rests on Christopher Blake, Herald and Overseer of the Duel, "*You* were very good, Chris. And you," to Frank Maraden, "you were terribly good until you got tense. Very nice in the earlier scene." He reaches for a Company generalisation, and finds it, "In all of this totally believable humanity, *one degree* of theatrical muscle is — disaster."

Robin stops, thinking. "You know, it's the stillness of the storm, it's *that* that drives one frantic. As I said to Michael — when we were trying to light it, it drove us nuts — now, *that*" (the lighting they finally chose), "*that* has got wind." He pauses slightly, thinking it out, adding, "I *know* where the voice sits in all that rain and wind and slush." He then admits to us that his one-man storm effects had left him in some trouble. "My saliva dried up in my throat. It's *impossible*! My voice box was simply not up to it."

Marti is again reminded that she "allowed herself to get too much involved." It's the old problem of the first Run-Through, 'We'll give him (the director) a Run-Through to remember!' And it won't work that way, yet. Ustinov, silent for so long, arms resting on the seat in front, as gripped in attention as any, interjects "It's easier, it's easier, of course, when we've got the first act behind us."

Phillips talks on, in full, even spate. And it's almost always a matter of voice. This reminds me, so often, of what the great Czech actor Frederick Valk replied when he was asked what the three most important things in acting were. "Voice," he said, "and then — More Voice," he added, "and then More Voice" he concluded. Robin would accept that, with the proviso (I'm sure) that we are not also thinking of merely louder, and louder, and louder. His next contribution is intriguing, and enough to keep one up late into the night. " I get strange echoes, when it's *right*" (and he's talking of the Blinding of Gloucester scene), "I get strange echoes of *The Cherry Orchard. There's* something to think about . . . and I know the scene, too. But I won't tell you which. It would merely confuse you."

While some are dwelling on that, Marti asks if there'll be any "real blood." Yes, there will; some people will have pellets concealed about them. But mostly, it will be a question of "just acting it." And the pain (Robin looks down to Douglas sitting beside him) will be precisely in "those two points at the back of the head." He indicates, and Douglas (has he done some research?) nods his head in accord. Not *much* blood, though, it's agreed. More a sensation of water, Robin wryly ventures, felt in the front rows. He's still very tenacious about the problems of this scene. It's the one that had gone most awry, with far too much "acting" (III.vii). The idea of blinding Gloucester comes "subliminally." It's triggered off by the words laid down in the scene, from Regan, Cornwall, and finally — most of all — by Gloucester himself, springing, as it does, out of that interrogation on why he's sent the King to Dover: 'Because I would not see / Thy cruel nails pluck out his poor old eyes' . . . 'But I shall see / The winged vengeance overtake such children.'

Bill and Marti are both cautioned, "You shouldn't have a muscle in your body thinking 'pluck out his eyes' — don't *try* to get to a cruel stage." The point is that the text will bring them there. "Just think of the terror." This is a very difficult problem for both of them, as Donna's Goneril, in her brief presence at the opening of the scene, has said (however subliminally) 'Pluck out his eyes.' Phillips, significantly, will later expunge this giveaway line by use of an overlap.

Switching to Gloucester and Edgar in their two big difficult scenes, Robin says "It's terribly important that you're both tired, but don't *think* yourself into a state of tiredness . . . Why should you?" And again, for those huge emotional feelings unleashed in Edgar, in the presence of his blinded father, Rodger is asked to remember that emotions "happen at very funny times." He encourages Barton with a note on an earlier rehearsal, "when you did something — perhaps I shouldn't tell you — I won't tell you where, when you did a *wonderful* laugh. Very frail. Lovely." In a slight pause, Peter comments emphatically — an old joke of the actor's alleged computerized emotional resources — "Ah — yes — that would be Number Forty-Three!"

Again, as happens so often, Robin shares with us an extremely bared analysis of what was, for him, an intensely personal emotion. His actual response, as he defines it, was delayed far past the earlier point when he himself would have *expected* it to affect him, or affect him deeply, and then it was triggered off by something quite minimal, very ordinary. In summing it up, he insists that the big emotional feelings are such that, "you can't plot them." He quietly hammers home his message that, where the emotions are really big, there is no time for any pretenses. That old Yorkshire saying of 'When in doubt — do nowt' comes to me. Even 'nowt' can be potent, when nothing, *feeling* almost nothing, is all you can be sure of playing with truth. When we are hit by these biggest emotions, Robin insists, the best objective we can have is what guides us in our everyday lives, to say to ourselves, "I should feel something, but I don't — other than shock."

A lot of the finest actors do just that, which makes us more ready to share with them the precise spasm of emotion, when it comes, because it has been waited for so truly. And I know Robin is right, because I've used the same route myself. 'Bursts into tears' writes Ibsen often (in his stage directions), as he does for Hjalmar in *The Wild Duck*. I thought that was nonsense when I first read the text until, finally, in rehearsal, I got myself on the exact tightrope of feelings which Ibsen had laid down; which was, in fact, mostly a state of waiting — of a postponement of emotion — until the tiny triggers in the writing, which a great dramatist knows how to calculate, are released. And one knows, as I was able to know, performance after performance, what it means to work in a masterpiece built with the massive certainties of the Parthenon.

I've joined my thoughts here to Robin's musings, just where I'd marked in my notes that he's taking one of those long pauses. It is a very long pause. He suggests that tomorrow we may start with "little bits, little sections of scenes, to see if we can scratch a little closer to specifics." His mind flicks back to the problem of how Edgar must make it clear how he feels about his blinded father (IV.i). Gloucester, in asking to be taken to Dover, even offers Edgar money to bring him there. Robin, releasing his banked-down thoughts and feelings, suddenly lets it all go in a very moving half shout: "Lead you? — *Pay me*! I'll *carry* you!"

Another pause, though not so long, before Phillips pursues some conjectures on the difficulties Shakespeare's Company must have had to overcome, their resources for storm effects being so much more limited than ours. There is a full two-thirds of the action from the start of the storm to the end of the play, and I'm thinking of the almost two and a half hours of our second act. The biggest problem for Shakespeare's men would have been, says Robin, "just to produce something for the *ear*." Our duty to the text remains the same, "Just to be able to catch the slightest change of timbre in each others' voices."

He is dwelling again on the storm and its aftermath, and where the voice is to be placed against these sounds. He has (he explains) listened to innumerable recordings of rain and wind and storm, in fullest spate to lulls of diminishment, to a constant dripping. "Rain in a pine-forest" is one he recalls. "Remarkable, how one can hear the odd bird, still singing, in the midst of all this downpour." Robin reflects between each image. "Endless gurglings of water rushing away." He brings it home to the cast, how they must imagine it, feel it, "dripping off your raincoats." In such a state the voice "hardly needs to go anywhere."

Rodger "can help Peter, by being in this weird space, vocally." What is wanted is, "an amazing voice . . . spooky . . . dead." They examine some of Poor Tom's speeches, and Robin finds what he's looking for in Edgar's first words in Gloucester's Barn, '. . . Nero is an angler in the Lake of Darkness' (III.vi). "That's the key," says Robin with certainty, "It's a pool of darkness! And you're setting Lear up in this strange place . . . Smell of all that straw . . . Musty . . . Everything, including yourselves, totally saturated." Which will help to make it understandable that Lear can imagine all those images of Goneril, and Regan, and dogs coming in at him. "I dread to say this" (and Robin says it nevertheless), "but — you can quite realistically think of your voice as being heard *under* water." It's a very difficult acting note, but a staggeringly right one.

Robin still muses on, wonders how loud *anything* has to be. He recalls the story of the little boy concentrating on being a beetle. How quiet that was. "What level do you really say, 'Quick March' . . . I don't know." And then, he mimes a child playing trains, or motorcars, which makes me remember the hills and valleys in the undulations of childhood bedclothes. He does a big-scale noisy boy, lots of sound, lots of movement; and then he suddenly switches to a very quiet child, doing a very quiet, tiny, train. Very little journeys. Very little stations. Tiny whistles. How far is it, Robin asks us, from this minuscule world to "that great universe of the play." I often wonder, when listening to him, how much (or how little) most actors in their lives, in reading, thinking, remembering, manage to bring to a play. Robin now cites 'The little dogs, and all / Tray, Blanche and Sweetheart', as Peter does them, how they erupt suddenly like great Alsatians. "Enough to make you jump out of your skin." Another short pause.

"*You* were wonderful," he tells Bill Hutt. "But not very good yesterday," says Bill. Robin enlightens us. How Hutt (as Lady Bracknell, in the revival of *The Importance of Being Earnest*) "got as far as the 'handbag!' and laughed in the audience's face ... after three years of performances!" Marti Maraden (also in 'Importance' as Cecily), supportive of Bill, tells us that the entire cast was having some trouble with one man in the audience, "Somewhere on the left, making the most amazing sounds, an incredibly snorting laugh." "Like a seal in heat," concludes Hutt. Robin is finally ready to finish. "Apart from not being terribly good, then — fine." A last glance to Monette: "*You* were terribly good."

It's a Company break, until the photo-call, everyone to be in full costume and make-up by eight p.m. Before leaving the theatre I have a chat with Jane Edmonds, whom I have engaged to take photographs, and who has had her camera set up in the other aisle for most of the afternoon. Jane works in the publicity department at the Festival, appeared in *As You Like It* for the two previous seasons, and takes superb pictures. Robin had chanced to see an especially beautiful landscape she'd done, a lush cathedral-grove of trees, and had adopted it for last year's Festival poster. Jane hasn't had too much luck today, as it had been agreed with Robin that she wouldn't shoot towards the stage during the Run-Through, though she has managed, she says, to get quite a lot of cast and crew in Front-of-House shots. We'll try again later, hopefully in the rehearsal room of St. John's Church Hall, where the lighting is more plentiful and consistent.

THURSDAY, SEPTEMBER 20TH   *concluded*

THE PHOTOCALL

I interrupt my notes on the Thursday night, although at first I hadn't meant to, but I'm glad to escape from the demands of this journal, and as glad to get back to the theatre. The Photocall is well advanced. Both stage and stalls are engulfed in activity, the full cast is in costume, already coming and going, coping with all their changes; there's a full back-stage technical crew, entire Stage Management, all costume and wig people, publicity and public relations departments, dressers, photographer, and me. It's like a major sound stage at MGM in the grips of a multi-million dollar movie. Robin, exhaustively himself, is prima donna of it all. He is everywhere.

They are involved now with shots of the opening scene, and the entire stage is wrapped in smoke. Yes — smoke. Stratford production photographs are synonymous with smoke, redolent of the many battles we stage here (including those off-stage administrative ones, whisps of which are eagerly pounced on by the press), and the opening scene of *Lear* is no exception. Technically, the objecitve is to diminish and obscure the out-of-focus externals. From down-stage (in the front row of seats) the smoke-machine emits its dense spurts of smoke, cued by Robin between each set-up, even between individual shots, and the coiling clouds pour out at floor level; he wafts them up-stage with a large wedge of hard-board. He then lurks behind the photographers, spreading smoke on every shot, motioning actors into the centre or the edges of the frame from out of the up-stage swirling murk.

Peter is encased in costume. And it's not a shock at all. He could have been in it all his life. As he later says to me, it's one of those happier occasions when the clothes are immediately acceptable as one's own, especially his second lot of cosy travelling browns, in which he will face the daughters and, later, the storm. He's in his 'at-home' stuff now, in the court, an already much creased black 'dress' tail-coat (it's the tails that are creased), epauletted, brass-buttoned, breached to the knee, silk-hosed to the foot, shoe-buckled. All very formal and black. Between and during shots he is muttering steadily in what sounds suspiciously like Russian.

Douglas Rain, entirely in browns, is an absolute image now of the Victorian politician, hair plastered down into a relentlessly untypical parting. More smoke is needed and Robin waves it up-stage. He gestures — a hand-flick — Monnette in closer to Rain. Clayton Shields, fashioner of wigs, hovers down-stage right, ready for anything awry. The young Fellas are now hirsute in mutton-chops, bearded and greyed into seniority. Lear's Knights-Followers have matured out of juvenile makeup boxes.

The men are, or seem, incredibly tall, and those taller ones (like Maraden) are taller still, all leg and ramrod-spined. I sit in with Renato La Selva, who is comfortably sucking on his pipe, calmly self-congratulatory (as well he should be), and he assures me that *every* man is corsetted, even the many who didn't need it. Everyone, that is, except Peter, Douglas (who's been given a small pot), and Bill Hutt. I'm reminded that Lear, Gloucester, and the Fool are perhaps the only characters in the play who will be *seen* to bend — to grief, to the fates, or to the wind. I don't count Edgar, as he's 'starkers' by the time he says that what makes him bend makes the king bow.) From the look of it (I could almost say the *feel* of it), nobody in these costumes could manage even a basic bend, and *if* they bow — when they must — it'll have to be sharply from the waist, or rather higher. It'll be one bit of acting that won't be necessary. The girls, also, will be contained to the elementary alternatives of the curtsy and the sit, and no sit being possible except with the straightest of backs. I've often argued that the art of acting (when there is any) is simply the art of reducing the odds against you: knowing one's words; accepting the clothes, the direction; finding one's lights. The biggest of these odds, to start with, is often one's costume. Nobody in *Lear* can complain of that. Ingrid Blekys, in her first costume and make-up, golden-wigged, is already releasing the shine in her enormous eyes.

On a quick count, I can number almost eighty people, and more are still arriving. Anyone with any business to be here, is, and perhaps some with none. Most of those present, among the watchers, from the administrative and publicity departments, are palpably agape at the sight of this swirling nineteenth-century court. John Wojda as Burgundy, resplendent in light blue and incredibly gold-braided, looks like Sergius, all set for his cavalry charge in Shaw's *Arms and the Man*, and Edward Evanko as King of France, in darker blues, inordinately high-stocked, looks as though he would send him on one. Bill Webster, Jim McQueen, and Richard Monette are seemingly wired into their coats; they don't carry the costumes, the costumes carry them. But that's true of all the men.

Robin, closely attendant on every shot, ducks in and out under the camera. He sets up some solos for Peter, then Bill. Hutt, with flying iron-grey hair, unkempt in creased greasy green velvet frock-coat, looks as if he's strayed out of a Franz Hals group-portrait, comparatively archaic, a revealed Dorian Grey seemingly saying, "Oh, well — just for you, old friend — I'll try to make an impression."

They've moved into the next set-up, and Peter and Bill, surrounded by their hard-riding gentlemen, swap gags, relaxing from the exigencies of the real (and still often elusive) lines of the text, now try some of their own. "Keep a Seville tongue in your head." "A ha! You fell into that one." "So will you, boy, every night." Robin whips in and out, flagging more smoke. Suddenly he hefts a large trunk, plonking it on Rex Southgate's shoulder, up-stage in the shot.

And now, we've a set-up for the storm scenes. Robin is wetting everyone down with a hand spray. He calls for wind and smoke, and the wind-machine transforms the belching wraiths into an appearance of horizontally driving rain. Loose strips of scarf stream in the gale from Peter's and Bill's shoulders; above the roar of the blades, Peter, now in much broken-down browns, bootless, breaks into snatches of Wagner. He's very much like Ustinov should look in such a role. He's Every Inch a Lear. Robin dodges in and out of smoke and wind to add more spray to Peter's hands, neck, beard, cheeks and glistening brow.

Suddenly, the foreground is galvanized into activity as a score of hands manipulate a huge black plastic covering over the fore-stage, extending to the steps of the upper platform. All seems set for some pièce de résistence. Two large children's wading pools appear from nowhere, one of them weathered, the other brand-new and iridescent with Donald Ducks, Snoopys, Mickey Mouses. The moment gleams with anticipation. "Oh" (from Peter), "for our second childhood!" "There's one for you, too," gloats Hutt as the spanking new one is set down before the steps at Peter's feet. "My turn for the pail!" howls Peter in childhood tantrum. "Now — you're not going to start on that one!" wails Bill with matching belligerence.

And, with that, a six-foot ladder materializes beside the kiddie-pool, and Robin is climbing to its top with a very large — and full — watering can. "Now then, you two!" Everyone crowds forward to the front of the stage, from the wings and the stalls as, with wind-machine roaring, the two eminent and senior Company actors step down for baptism into the bright round bath. "Fine," says Robin, "let's have it from 'Rumble thy bellyful!' ", and starts to pour. Hilarity rises amongst the Company as Peter and Bill are deluged in an unremittent downpour. And Peter's lines are stopped, literally, in the mouth by the channelling streams. "Spout! . . . Rain," he splutters — and he does indeed — "I tax you not, you watering-can, with unkindness . . . Then let fall your horrible 'waters'." He gulps it out — and some of it in — valiantly finishing to a sustained round of applause. As our two distinguished actors stand like especially naughty children, soaked in their Sunday clothes, Robin quickly gets a refill. And more than a dozen actors in turn are urgently insisting to me: "Maurice — you've got to get this one!" Alas, I'm without a camera, though none could do justice to this event. Happily, however, Peter later offers a contribution, a "retrospective cartoon," which may yet celebrate the occasion.

As Robin, replenished, ascends his ladder for the reprise, Peter, always ready with the most apposite quote from *Lear*, calls up to him, "Nature's above Art, in this respect." And we have yet another replay ("Maurice — get this one!"), as Peter and Bill, sodden to their squelching shoes, play the sequence under the renewed shower with delighted abandon. "Oh! Oh, Oh! *'tis* FOUL!" finishes Peter, with an emphasis he'll never dare to forget in performance. The final drops fall from Robin's can. Peter, shuffling with some knee-clutching, asks in a small voice, "Can I go to the toilet now?" And Bill, boldly relaxed, seemingly reluctant to step out, adds "I have." The Photocall continues. But I go. There isn't anything left tonight that can follow that.

FRIDAY, SEPTEMBER 21ST, 11 A.M.   AVON THEATRE

THE JOVIAL PRESENCE

When I arrive this morning, I find Paddy Crean on-stage with Monette and Barton, taking them through the duel (V.iii). "We'll have the whole thing again, Gentlemen, and very slow." Paddy, his fight scenario in his left hand, has a light foil for any cut and parry indication lightly hefted in the right, and his spectacles are pushed back high on his forehead, lodged in the distinguished hair. Paddy's fight scripts, typed always with meticulous scrupulousness, often accompanied with minute illustrations of each single frame of movement, are always open to re-calculation and adjustment, depending on the skills of the combatants. Monette and Barton are well-versed enough, though cavalry sabres are not quite the weapons they are best schooled in — until now. Paddy takes it very easily, making it very safe for both of them and, most important, anybody in striking distance, also making it look extremely dangerous and convincing. "That's a nice little section," he encourages, "Very good, very good indeed." Sabres are returned to their rattling hangers, and the first and second Seconds perform their rituals. Chris Blake, as Herald and MC, contributes the new speech, and the blades flash once more, Paddy standing at a sensible distance from the fray. "Excellent, Gentlemen! Very good indeed," concludes Paddy as they finish. Our Fencing Master then turns a sanguine eye into the stalls.

135

"Let's have a lady now," proposes Mr. Crean, his eye ashine for any lady. It's a fact that Donna Goodhand is to be momentarily involved in the after-fight fracas. Mr. Crean is known for a primordial gallantry in challenging incautious denigrators of the 'gentle' sex to lethal combat, offenders being allowed recourse to absolutely any weapon of their misguided choice. However, at this moment, Vince Berns reminds Paddy that "You've got to kill Tommy, first." Tom Wood is standing by to be dispatched as Oswald, by Barton as Edgar, in their as yet unstaged scuffle. "Well," replies Paddy, with less enthusiasm but as absolute diligence, "can I have these Gentlemen again today?" Paddy is often short-changed on time for his rehearsals, and is ever hopeful for more chances to refine the conflicts, always to make it safer and more lethal still.

I wander out of the theatre and into the Nut Club Coffee House, opposite the stage door, which serves the Avon as a Greenroom. Pictures of some of the more famed of Stratford actors adorn the back wall: Maggie Smith, Brian Bedford, Butch Blake, Martha Henry, Bill Hutt, and many others. Seated to the right of these is the new boy, illustrious enough shortly to join them, now quite dried out; our Jovial Presence is industriously dispatching a large plate of fried eggs and sausages, English style. Peter gestures to me to join him.

After an exchange of breakfast-time pleasantries, he tells me he is hugely enjoying himself with the play, and the Company. Then, very casually, he informs me, with a large chuckle, "Had another call this morning from Cohen's office." (He is speaking of Alexander Cohen, Broadway Producer and Impressario.) "Oh," I respond, with some caution. I've little desire to get involved in any unproductive theatrical hypotheses. "They wanted to know how I was getting on," he adds with further and enlarging chuckles, the generous girth pulsing, as it does in those exchanges of jests with the Fool. "What did you tell them?" I venture, not really wanting to know any more of this alleged involvement of Alexander Cohen in our *Lear* than anyone already knows, which is nothing. "Told 'em I was having a wonderful time," continues Peter, "Absolutely wonderful . . . best Company I've ever worked with." He nods the hoary head, savouring the truth of this. He begins to chuckle more deeply. "They kept insisting. How was it really going . . . And I told them you've got seats; when you come to the opening, you'll find out."

As I watch this cherubic, zestful dispatcher of sausages (any style), I'm reflecting on comments made to me, recently, that our

Stage Management have been zealously guarding the secrecy of his phone number, on any inquiry from Cohen's office, or indeed, anywhere else. Pushing my natural non-inquisitiveness aside, in my new role of recognized, though originally self-appointed chronicler of our endeavours, I venture to ask, "Then, Cohen never had any involvement in our show?" "Absolutely not," replies Peter with Jove-like certainty, adding immediately, with historical relish, that Cohen's only involvement was "to introduce me to Robin." Mopping up some egg on a sausage, he outlines the facts of all that brought us to this adventure at Stratford.

He's been waiting to do Lear since he was sixteen. Cohen wanted him to do it in New York. Peter was reluctant to play Lear in an eight shows-a-week-run. Cohen suggested he might like to try it in Stratford and offered to introduce him to Robin. Peter and Robin met and agreed to do it. Cohen's only contribution was that happy example of the theatrical catalyst, and he's never had any further involvement, despite endless rumours to the contrary still circulating in the press.

I tell Peter of my own imagined scenario of the genesis of this job, which I had attributed to his encounter with Maggie Smith on the Nile. I'd assumed that, during the making of the movie they both did there, Miss Smith would have suggested that Peter and Robin would work well together. "Absolutely right," Peter confirms, settling into another sausage, "but that all came later ... 'Oh, *yes*, you simply MUST do this with Robin!' " he goes on, getting Miss Smith to the very life.

Ann Stuart arrives, interrupting us with a friendly message that Robin is starting work with the full Company (less those still involved in stage fights) in the upstairs Avon Lounge, but that Peter is not to hurry. And I leave as our Jovial Presence settles into the remains of his eggs and sausages. I faintly regret not having recorded the image (my camera being in my pocket) but some things, bathtimes and breakfast included, should be sacrosanct.

FRIDAY, SEPTEMBER 21ST   *continued*

A TWIG

The Chalmers Lounge, a surprisingly dark deep-purple carpeted lounge-bar in the Avon, has an impenetrable gloom about it. Its reputation as a place of assignation in rare, off-work hours, is a foolish exaggeration. The deeply-uncomfortable foam-filled black plastic covered couches, the Stygian tone, are hardly accomplices to communication, even of the more romantic sort.

When I arrive, the entire Company is lying down, splayed out bodily on the purple pile, prone or supine according to preference. From this Bosch-like mass emanates a low variation in whines. There are, as always, some exceptions to this collaboration: Butch Blake (saving himself to watch through a long day), Bill Hutt, and Douglas Rain are seated; as is Robin, in the deepest chair, deeply concentrating. The low whine spreads, strengthening into a weird caccophony, as McQueen and Christopher, making their way through this underworld, try the first scene of our Act Two (III.i). Robin is having yet another experiment with the Storm.

He calls a halt. The lament subsides. He asks the wailers to remember that, though they must be locked in their own sound of wind or rain or whatever part of the elements which disturbs them; they should be aware more of "other spirits floating nearby." To Jim and Patrick he suggests that "Although you are first looking for help, remember, it is futile to try to reach *anyone*." The unearthly background vocalizations from the spread-eagled Company rises again in greater intensity, with Jim and Patrick attempting to dominate the discord.

Peter, replete, avuncular as always, yet also childlike of visage, enters the space with tentative and exaggerated respect, nodding the massive curl-decked and generously white-bearded, orderly head. He soft foots it over towards me, his mouth wide open in attentiveness, and subsides beside me on another acceptable high-backed chair. I welcome him to our adventure, this little touch of Danté in the day. His alertly hooded eyes (which can be as wide-eyed as a Pre-Raphaelite maiden's) flick round the details of the scene. "Hmmm," he conjectures, and confides delightedly, "Not only stocks, but five gallows for Lilliputians." He means the five beer-pump handles on the distant bar-counter which, indeed, have such definition in gloomy silhouette.

The scene is over. Robin asks them for "Exactly the same again, but this time I want to hear the *silence* of eternity, too." They try again. The cacophonous strains are more muted this time, the air-conditioning providing a spinal hum in the occasional whimperings, a tortured music of the spheres in our Pascalian void. Peter joins in the humming.

138

As they finish, there is a very long pause, with Robin sunk in his soft chair. He then says, quietly, "I'm praying for a storm." He means he is (probably, and quite literally) praying for the way to find the sound that a storm is truly happening. We are to move on to 'Blow Winds and crack your cheeks', and Peter eases himself into the now-standing throng (III.ii). They have a little talk about it first. "Shall I do it more . . . slowly?" asks Peter; "It'll give it more . . . *chance*." The talk becomes general as they discuss *The Tempest*, in which many present have already played. Was there something about that production that made the storm easier to play? Peter locates one of the problems in *Lear*: "The voice starts to do the description, and yet it's so damned difficult because he's put description in." It is strange how frequently actors feel this curious empathy with this greatest, and least elusive, of writers. It's often alleged by too many that Mr. Shakespeare was, somehow, remote. He isn't. He's around every corner of any theatre in which his plays are being done well. For me, personally, he's been a companion on city street corners and village crossroads. But he lives most unrelentingly where actors work. He's a challenging and demanding ghost, but supportive too, a finally accessible presence, ironical, and always modern. He's got an amazing, sustaining, repetitive, everyday knack of walking in on our thoughts (when we've tried hard enough), and of always being there when we finally manage to sort it all out.

Ustinov tries the storm through, for the first time amidst the new wailings. And, then, as they finish, Robin is on to something. He wants Peter to "Show us — lead us — bring us there . . . Just *talk* it to me, maybe it isn't the full thing yet, so much, but a giving of orders to say 'I want it to start'." Peter says immediately, in response, "Yes, as if he *remains* in control of it . . . In fact, I tried to introduce an element of that into it this last time."

I have the delighted sensation that comes when I hear or feel clear minds working so closely geared. Phillips, it seems, did pick up that resonance from Peter, as I can still hear the vibration of command in how he'd just done it. They'll try again with this new edge of the imperative. Robin articulates the idea with relish, "Seventy-Fourth Battalion — Blow! Blow, you Fuckers — Blow!" Basking for the moment in the certainty that there is an idea for yet another 'Once More', the talk adjusts into a short relaxation before the oncoming challenge.

Robin regales us with a tale of his technical debacle as an actor in a production of *Cyrano*, when he impulsively discharged his gun (big gun, mercifully blank wad) "right into Peter Wyngarde's face! . . . Swept off my feet by having an actual gun to fire — might have killed him — to this day the memory makes me blush with shame." (His intense, usually pale face does look untypically flushed.) "Well," says Peter consolingly, getting ready to 'Blow' once more, "The elements are more safe; that is, there is no visible opponent."

As Peter draws breath for 'Blow winds', Robin cautions him, in anticipation of several more tries, not to do too much "or you'll fall apart." "No," promises Peter, comfortingly, "maybe I'll even remember it." Which is a bit cheeky, I feel, as he's never got it absolutely right once yet. He is still, essentially, concerned with finding out *how* to do it, and not quiet (as yet) getting all the words in the right order. In fact, this is a very brave thing for any actor to do, especially as consistently as is the case with Ustinov. It could be argued that this is a latitude he has in common with most star actors, but I believe it's guts plus relaxation that turns an actor into a star actor.

Perhaps aware of some conjecture on nearby faces, and still mumbling something to the effect that the new exercise "might even help me to remember it," he catches me directly in the eye, and asserts with some guile, "That's an alternative *not* to be ruled out altogether."

They try again, Peter blasting out his instruction to the elements; a monarch allowed to display his impotence before an impervious Parade Ground Assembly. "Stop!" yells Robin at the end of the second aria, "Did you say 'Battles'?" Peter wasn't *saying* it; he'd just finished *bellowing* the line, 'But yet I call you servile ministers, / That will with two pernicious daughters join / Your high-engen-der'd battles 'gainst a head / So old and white as this . . .'

They stop, briefly, the adrenalin running high. Robin is not only on to it; he's got it with the certitude of Henry Higgins. They quickly consider the words of that second aria, 'Rumble thy belly-ful . . . / Nor rain, wind, thunder, fire, are my daughters . . .', pausing on that list which gives Peter (and myself) so much trouble to remember properly. Robin asks for it once more, this time with Peter directing, *commanding* the elements up to the high point of 'battle', which is, in fact, so close to the end of the second aria, and the highest point in the curve of the whole scene, vocally. Lear's next speech is the two-liner, 'No, I will be the pattern of all patience; / I will say nothing.' Robin decides to divide the Company into four sections to play, respectively, Rain, Wind, Thunder, and Fire. A couple of actors, anticipating that Fire is very difficult to do, change camps.

Peter asks, ingenuously, "Shall I lie on the floor all by myself?" (everybody else being now so alertly on their feet), but Robin is already setting the last details of our confrontation with the heavens. Robin, naturally, casts himself in the role of the gods: "Peter will do everything he can to encourage you lot (he points to all four lots) to attack *me*." Hopefully, what he has in mind is that, when the attack of the elements fails against the gods, it will turn back on Lear himself, a neatly considered bit of mathematics, reminding me of the calculations of a Bach fugue. "Get into formations," calls Robin, insisting on quite military ones, "and remember, *I'm* the object of attack!" He relapses again into his soft deep chair.

Peter begins, facing the four serried battalions; silent, but never really immobile, taking little steps forward until he dares, commands them into action. 'Blow winds, and crack your cheeks' — and ten cheeks crack, blowing still as they crack. 'Rage!', and they rage; 'Blow!', and they blow, with renewed force advancing on Robin ensconced and implacable in his couch. 'You cataracts and hurricanoes, Spout!' and, at Peter's urging, the second group mixes in a primeval deluge (very good for six actors). The 'thought executing fires' (another six or seven) come first at Robin to 'singe' his dark head and impervious eyes; and yet they hesitate, considering the 'white head' behind them. The 'oak-cleaving thunderbolts' (another four actors quickly improvising, as this wind, or is it a brass section? was uncast) race first at Robin, then at Peter. By the time Lear is into the 'all shaking thunder', the entire mass of the several groups has rounded squarely on him, Robin completely forgotten, as they surge round the Jovial Presence in amazing and very real force, threatening to 'strike flat' the Ustinovian rotundity into the carpet of the Chalmers Lounge.

It really works. As Peter repeatedly advances with those small steps, issuing challenge, turning to each collective quartet, extracting, demanding, more commitment, I'm drawn from my chair to circle the encoiled groupings, creating my own tracking-shot, revelling in this immense orchestration, the sheer exhuberance of outrageous talent, great acting worthy of the great support it is being given. It's worth remembering Robin's promise of what Peter could count on from this Company. There are times when Mr. Shakespeare is not merely around the corner, he's in the room with us. It's enormously exciting, and heartening; analogous, for me, to the sensations released in the final movement of Beethoven's 'Ninth';

something so hugely satisfying can only be described in the light of such another master. It's a short scene I feel I want to go on forever. "Stop!" cries Robin, when Peter has reached those 'high engendered battles' once again.

"Very good," he informs us. Peter has obviously enjoyed it also, relishing the amazing sound he has released in himself, and also from our questing quartets. "The whole Seminole Nation was here," he says, sounding so glad he's finally met them. Robin clinches the discovery that it is, indeed, "Director-time in Opera with all those hordes of extras, full chorus, plus the military!" I'm wondering if Shakespeare's men may have howled thus in backing for Burbage from their Tiring-room. Joan Littlewood, who used such back-stage tricks and exercises, often insisted that they did.

Peter and Robin discuss technicalities.

ROBIN: "Those 'blows' are still not quite enough, and yet . . ."

PETER: "Yes, otherwise it's only a cadenza . . ."

ROBIN: "You will be properly exhausted, by trying to get more . . ."

PETER: "Yes — without having to *act* it . . ."

ROBIN: "It's really asking — attempting — the *impossible.*"

The talk loosens into comments on the night before. Peter, relishing the useful lesson of the watering can, nonetheless concedes that his baptism was somewhat moderated, "Really quite warm. It was a tropical storm." Robin reveals that, on waking up this morning, he'd momentarily felt that he had "got up with a *cold,*" but decided as there was *"no way"* he could dare admit that, on this of all days, he'd had to abandon the idea of having a cold altogether.

Smaller points in the scene are discussed. It becomes "more personal" in the storm when Kent arrives. Peter still finds that "all those 'Cs' are very difficult to get out." They touch on options for scale changes, and have some talk about the "mental pace." One can be *too* slow. Some final gear changes are agreed on within 'Art cold? / I am cold myself . . .', near the finish. "Quite clearly a stepping down," says Robin. "And then, at the end — it's a little song!" — from the Fool — 'Though the rain it raineth every day'. (A major casualty of the cuts in this production is the Fool's solo, that final speech which is the actual coda to the scene.) Robin, still sunk in the deep black plastic, reflects on the amazing movement within this really quite short scene; the three brief arias from Lear, the counterpoint from Kent, the final song of the Fool. "It's a *huge* journey," he muses, "from 'Blow' to that little song . . . a lunatic journey." There is another of those very enjoyable long pauses.

"A twig," suggests Peter, brightly. "Perhaps one should have a twig for that conducting." "Yes," concurs Robin, "I was thinking of that myself when you were trying to orchestrate 'Beethoven's Ninth'." (Robin has been ahead of, or with me, yet again.) "Well, I've got myself a brandy glass," Peter is saying, "perhaps I don't deserve a twig." He contrives to make it sound as if he actually doesn't. "Oh, yes," responds Robin immediately, gently, "Oh, yes, you do."

I'm continuing to relish the nourishing new discoveries that can be triggered off by our concentration on one word, the way that image of 'battle' leapt out at us. Everything we do, everything we try to do should be a direct attempt to release and support the text, always the text: and the harder our work on the text, the more simple our acting becomes.

The chat relaxes further, Phillips dwelling on the evident amazement of the many extra people from administration who had come to the photocall last night. And yet, they'd all been well-informed, and they had worked on all publicity, brochures, press-releases, all of which made no secret of the mid-Victorian design. After they'd recovered from their initial incredulity ("Is this the *Lear* rehearsal? *Can't* be!"), one could feel, says Robin, "that collective amazing conviction about the power of the period." This is the seventh *Lear* I've witnessed, and none I've seen has been brought so close to our time, unless Richard Burton decides (as he may) to play it — a red sweater in the opening scene? — in the rehearsal clothes of the eighties.

Phillips is urging this cast, now, to exploit the sensations nurtured by the clothes they'll be wearing, that they shouldn't let up for a second, even in the wings, "Eyeing things — every forbidden territory." He goes into an extended reverie on the rich options presented to our actors from encasement in such clothes. The sense of pleasure should be increased at the very thought of being able to take all that stuff *off* — the release from the restrictions of corsets and stays, tight-buttoned coats and tunics of the men, the resultant response of "going crazy with the added pleasures of all that desire and promise." All the men seemed to have "wonderful legs" and with those high-corseted waists, appeared to be "straight up from ankle to armpit." Sensual potential was wildly increased, reminding us that the Victorian girls had to watch out even for the older chaps. Robin gestures across the room to Douglas Rain, concentratedly removed in a corner in his short, creased, brown patent-leather jacket-top, glasses pushed back into ample locks, a pencil (ready for any note) stroking the grey-out-of ginger beard. "Even 'Old Lurky Drawers' was capable of producing Edmund when well into middle age, and this 'Old Fart' (Robin's eyes flick to the Jovial Presence) produces Cordelia at a time when they're not supposed to be able for it."

The reverie swings back to the costumes, the cunning choices of Daphne Dare. "Very successful — that over-ripe plum, those funny berry blues, that deadly nightshade." Robin's early experience as a designer always nudges him usefully. He asks again, not waiting for any answer — as on that first day in rehearsal — "I'm not alone in this, am I, this feeling of all that passion beating against whalebone to get out . . .? Far better than all that nakedness."

FRIDAY, SEPTEMBER 21ST   *concluded*

AN UNKNOWN LEAR, AND OTHERS

We are waiting for McQueen and Wood, still fighting, down on-stage under the tutelage of Paddy Crean. So, meanwhile, we are to have a little look at 'Before the Hovel' (III.iv). All the Company lie about again, outstretched, supplying the elements. Ustinov, in typical stance, delicate steps (with, in fact, very big feet), is constantly judging his space, his benignly bearded head on the heavy neck and deep chest, most of the weight of the long trunk through the heavy middle is sustained by those ever-alert, short sturdy legs. (It's not too surprising he's a tennis-player.) Shushing the Fool and Kent into silence, he tries the calculative 'prayer', and finishes with a couple of stubby and most eloquent fingers raised in admonishment to the heavens. And then we have the long (very long) scream from Hutt off-stage, from a distant recess of the Chalmers Lounge, and the scurrying eruption of Barton's 'Poor Tom' from his hovel, settling on the carpet-pile near Robin's feet — 'Beware the Foul Fiend!' "Stop!" calls Phillips. And he asks Rodger, "What's the Foul Fiend?"

I lay my jottings aside and, in fact, add nothing extra for forty-five minutes, shortly before the session ends. I'm very interested in the answer to that question.

It's twenty-five years now since I played Edgar myself, and as long since the same question was asked of me. The Lear who asked it was the Irish actor-manager — Anew McMaster, better, I think, than Wolfit (certainly as Lear). Much of what Mac did, in all his roles, would now be judged very 'theatrical', in the fullest sense, but it was also endowed with the kind of power and truth that would be recognized as revolutionary today as it seemed to us back in the early fifties.

Mac's Lear was the crowning role of a long and illustrious career, even exceeding his earlier peak as 'Coriolanus' in Stratford (U.K.). Its ultimate triumph in Dublin was for me something of an anti-climax, but its progress in rehearsals and performance in the small Irish towns for almost a year still hangs in my memory with brighter significance. It's worthwhile and, I'm sure, fertilizing and relevant to take time out, for a spell, from our Stratford *Lear* to dwell on the background of one of the great 'unknown' Lears of our time. My tactic is a deliberate and necessary device to distance us usefully from this Stratford event, evoking another Lear, or Lears, or even a bonus of the 'foul fiend'.

A provincial tour of Ireland with Mac is an epic worthy of a book in itself. I'm steeling myself to dwell on it only as long as is essential. I spent the best part of my first three years in the theatre in what seemed (except for short respites at Christmas and Easter) an Odyssey through small and larger towns, and incessant perform-ances, giving as many as ten shows in seven days, as one old poster I've had for years testifies. For we played on Sundays, also; it was too good a night to lose. Sunday was the climax for towns where Mac's visit was a holiday week. He and his Company were, in truth, as his posters said, 'The Theatrical Event of The Year'. (I might add, the *only* theatrical event of the year!) At the height of the tours we had sometimes fourteen plays (yes, *fourteen*) in the reper-toire: seven or so Shakespeares, three Wildes, at least three service-able thrillers, and, always, our one Sophocles, *Oedipus Rex*. Time was swallowed up in the ceaseless round of matinée and evening shows, unending rehearsals and, for many, the 'Fit-Up', the daily (even thrice daily) striking and setting up of the scenery, sometimes changing over four times in twenty-four hours when we had a school's-special and/or matinée, followed by a different play at night.

Our tours progressed through interminable small towns and vil-lages which were as rudimentary as the three converging roads of our *Oedipus*, where audiences of gentry and peasants on Jaguars and donkeys materialized out of the green wilderness of the Golden Vale to watch a show in the Doric simplicity of a concrete hall. We came to the stages of towns whose lights flickered out when ours went on: with sufficient electricity only for us, perhaps (since the pubs were dark) they *had* to come. From the stages of Theatre Royals, like Waterford, where the boards hadn't been changed since Kean, to others like Cahirsiveen, where we clamped planks across barrels and built our own stages — undreamt of since the Commedia del Arte — anything from twelve square feet to twelve square yards — we acted on them all. We'd got the equipment. Several tons of scenery, actors' baggage and lights, but mostly lights, including every sort of effect spot for moving clouds and lightning flashes. Apart from acting, lighting was Mac's special gift.

We broke our way through the ornate ceilings of stuccoed town halls (unless the holes were there from the last visit) to hang our fifteen battens of drapes and giant spot-bars. Sometimes, on muddy Mondays (the travelling day), there were near mutinies from junior actors faced with the tonnage of hampers and five flights of stairs to the scene dock. From the little places, from Drumcollagher to Castlebar, Skibbereen to Moate, we journeyed to an occasional respite like the Cork Opera House or Gaiety Theatre, Dublin, where resident theatre staffs assumed some of the chores, and watched in awe as our vast trucks disgorged their contents at their stage doors. What, they would think, what in hell does he do with all those lights? What, indeed, as we used everything the biggest theatres had installed, as well as all of our own. Mac's concern for lighting, close to obsession, was also good for business; he used it in support of our classic texts, competing with the cinema across the road (often empty or closed when we came to town), and it was to meet this competition also that he used so much incidental music. In many respects, in terms of pure showmanship, Phillips has a great deal in common with McMaster.

And from the small fields of the West to the rich pastures of the south, the audiences streamed in to see *Lear*. 'Welcome Home McMaster' read the street-banners which we had stretched across the streets, ourselves, in the dawn. Mac had just ended his second Australian tour. 'Anew McMaster and His Celebrated International Company' proclaimed the enormous neon sign we'd just built. Celebrated we weren't, although many young actors from Mac's tours have since had fame enough, and one distinguished playwright of today swapped punches with me during a week of bad digs and overwork. International, though, we undoubtedly were: English, which often meant Welsh or Scottish ("Much better in Shakespeare, if there's a Celt somewhere in the blood" being one of Mac's precepts), Irish, of course, Australian, American.

It was picaresque as well as picturesque, like a touring novel by Smollet or Cervantes. But it was grim, too. To begin with, it was (or seemed to be) always raining. A whole day would be spent just looking for a place to sleep. There were, of course, the lovely places, and we did see the gorse and heather, but they passed in a swirl of dust and travel. For the rest, the brown wet fields encroached interminably, even to the stage door. Dublin, small when one lived in it, seemed as remote and magical as Mecca.

This then, was the backdrop for the first encounters I had with some great plays; with *Othello*, *Oedipus Rex*, with *King Lear*. Towns like Thurles or Tipperary were (and Mac knew it) closer to Thebes than Shaftesbury Avenue; closer too, than Broadway and, indeed, Stratford, Ontario. 'Poor Tom' of Bedlam, the disguise-role Edgar selects to shelter behind in *Lear* still proliferates in the rural parishes of Ireland and England, and from the Yukon through the Ozarks to the Everglades. Or for that matter, at any street corner. Poor Tom, whoever he (or she) may be, is the outcast, excluded from comfort and security, troubled with hunger, with cold, with the deprivations which for so many lead so often to madness.

Poor Tom, in *Lear,* is also much troubled by the Foul Fiend, to which he refers in the text as much as fourteen times. This is a liberal allowance (for any fiend), especially as Edgar/Poor Tom has a mere ten speeches, from his first assay from his hovel, none of which is aided by any footnote in our text or in any schooldays edition that I remember. It is sex, of course, personified as the Foul Fiend, which brings so much trouble to Poor Tom. It's what we all carry in the crotch that gets the blame for the disorders in our heads. Mac, as Lear, was emphatic that the encroaching madness of Lear is best demonstrated by his growing sexual preoccupations, and that Edgar, *acting* his part so well (in a well-educated choice of obsession with the foul fiend), becomes the catalyst who propels Lear into insanity.

This is the objective which links Ustinov to McMaster, though never Wolfit, who was crazed from that first 'Blow' or even before. And, if memory serves me well, it was the same choice for Scofield, Michael Hordern, or Gielgud and Olivier: there simply isn't any other way to play it. This is dependent, always, on Edgar *not* being mad, but clearly pretending (for the audience) to be so, or there can be a clouding of a crucial issue. Lear's lunacy is the only one in the scene. As Mac put it to me so long ago, there must be no doubt, for the audience, that Poor Tom is Edgar, disguised, and the disguise of Edgar lies in the seeming madness of Poor Tom. Mac admitted to me once that it was traditional for Lears of the past to be plagued by confusions in the audience, or even in some critics' notices, with very high praise for the *two* young actors who had achieved such wonders in *both* great roles.

I can add, now, on this occasion in the Chalmers Lounge, that the Foul Fiend (after an exhaustive quest) was finally located and identified. Perhaps not too many of those present were in any real doubt about the matter, but it's as well to be certain. It certainly took quite as long for the exercise (or rather, much more) as I've allowed myself on this brief trip into the past.

As the Stratford cast of *Lear* leaves the Chalmers Lounge and returns to the Avon stage, I decide on a different route, making my way up to the circle, in search of another perspective on the shape and sound of rehearsal. It's all quite startling, from the front edge of the balcony, this sharply defined view of the steep-raked stage, the austerity of the bare platform, sided by two of Daphne's panels (the rear one flown out), and beyond the dark gap of the sky. Here is the space which will serve as the heath at the opening of Part Two. Just now, the house lights are still on, the central chandelier reflected in the wall mirrors of stalls and circle.

Robin is rehearsing McQueen and Christopher in the opening scene of the storm (III.i). The voices project up to me in the sharp acoustic. I already regret not sitting up here more often. Phillips joins both actors on-stage. "There's a huge acting problem with speeches like these . . . The best time you did it was when you were both worrying about getting to the loo." Peter crosses unexpectedly in the dark gap at back, on his way to his entrance position — or somewhere else. He does a momentary half-dance, and a dozen voices in the stalls below me dissolve into laughter.

Shortly afterwards, he is on-stage himself to try a 'Blow winds' and incorporate the earlier discoveries of the day (III.ii). I retreat to the very back row of the upper balcony, sitting in the exact seat I've long booked for the final performance of *Lear* on November 4th. (Which doesn't seem so long away.) Peter is giving his opera director's orders to wind, rain and thunder (it's easy to imagine the lightning, from my seat in the 'gods') with vigorous signals from a riding-crop, standing in for the twig as yet to be found. "It's a twig — not a crop — just a twig," he assures Jim, as it quivers before Kent's startled face. (He slips in the information between two lines of blank verse.) I'm reminded of that wonderful line from *Timon*: 'A twig, a twig, no cedar I.' Peter may not be a cedar but, from up here the voice is still enormous. I have a strange déjà vu, a curiously certain hunch that Burbage looked like this, a burly Lear, an actor with his weight stacked in the right places. He might have had the same generous but orderly beard, the loose, short-cropped curls dominant above a rumpled ruff, perhaps, for that very first 'Blow winds!' And we can be sure that Shakespeare's men didn't waste time on woad. Though I'd like to think that Dick Burbage might have ventured a request for a twig "with absolutely nothing on it," and that the request would have been granted.

As Peter's voice swells up to my seat in the Avon 'gods' and I look down at his small figure and, at his feet, the fetal huddle of Hutt's Fool, I'm thinking forward from the sight of this bare space to that cluttered Victorian interior which will greet the audience's gaze on our first night. I find myself longing for a drop-curtain (which the Avon still houses above its proscenium) that we may husband our surprises. But perhaps the presentation of furnishings, the comfortable upholstery, chaises, deep-padded chairs and desk, lamps and tables, will be something for our audience to conjecture on before the stage becomes filled with the extravagant presence of a full Victorian court.

Phillips, meantime, has joined Ustinov and Hutt on-stage to discuss the niceties of the effect of wind, as distinct from rain or thunder. It's fascinating that though Bill Hutt is so often present during such exchanges, he preserves a stoic and exemplary reticence about the storms he's already faced as Lear himself; his long countenance daily evolving a patina of patience, he's become The Fool I seem to have known all my life. From now on, for my money, the Fool must be older, though perhaps never quite as old as Lear. Bill Hutt, for me, has forever proved that you can't send on a boy in a man's role.

The voices of Robin and Peter carry to me in my new aerie. Robin is saying that one is affected by rain, or wind or thunder, in different ways. "They can come from anywhere." He wants Peter to start the rain, and develop its shifting force, letting it travel. He does his own neat exercise in the use of space, turning on his own axis at centre-stage, pointing with alternating hands as if he were a camera in a panning shot, following the varying direction of the wind and rain. "Try giving us 'building images' instead of 'connected ones'," he suggests to Peter. Their quiet voices rise effortlessly to me. Again I have the odd sensation of being an eavesdropper at the old Globe on Bankside. They mention some "ordinary bits" which Peter is taking very low, " 'Pour on — I will endure,' and all that crap."

Robin asks if Peter can find an up-stage centre-mark (with the later aid of some glow-tape) as he's planning a very extra-special lightning trick. Peter enthusiastically responds "Oh, yes. I can see rather well in the dark!" Robin informs him that he's setting up a particularly violent stabbing shaft of forked lightning "Aimed to hit you right on the head — Very Alarming!" Peter then mutters, "I don't know how I can add to that."

I descend from the 'gods' to the wings at stage-right, and stand there near the off-stage hustle and exceptional quiet of concentration, watching the next work-through of the scene before the hovel (III.iv). Poor Tom, stripped to the usual running-shorts of rehearsals, is offering up something more specifically sexual: there is now a wild simulation of high-pounding masturbatory gestures running through the whole of his longer speech. Immediately after the scene, I rejoin the group in the front stalls to hear Robin, congratulatory but cautioning, advise Rodger that "There is a large difference between being attacked — or pursued — by the Foul Fiend, and actually provoking him." Rodger, acquiescing, insists that he was merely being precise in driving home the big point of the day.

Most of the Company have already been released. The rehearsal winds down. Peter and Rodger, crouched together on the steps mid-stage, wrap up some points with Robin, who joins them. I attempt some photographs. The day is spent, a day of the Foul Fiend, which was a long time coming. Back in the street, outside the stage door, the evening is colder, though still bright, but more leaves are falling as I hurry away to my typewriter.

SATURDAY, SEPTEMBER 22ND

THE CLICHÉ AND THE BELL

I arrive in St. John's Hall for the afternoon rehearsal accompanied again by Jane Edmonds, equipped with her camera to take some pictures. On introducing Peter to Jane (she'd known everyone else present), they are both quickly involved in that photographer's passion for taking pictures of each other taking pictures of each other.

150

There is a general feeling of levity and, returning to the hall with a coffee, I've missed some initial chat on "cliché acting." But I'm in time to hear Hutt claim, "I'm a walking cliché," and Rain, who always sits when he can avoid standing, asserts with like certainty, "And I'm a sitting one." Robin tells us of the day, during rehearsals for 'Importance' when, tiring of the lesser stuff and absolutely insistent for once on the best "at every second," he announced that he'd ring a handbell on hearing, or seeing, any cliché whatsoever. "As I put it to them, you can all *do* it — the correct stuff — you all *know* when you're doing phony acting ... Why should I bother to tell you ... I'll just ring my bell." Apparently, the rehearsal which followed was closely accompanied by frequent and clamorous bell-ringing until it gradually diminished into silence by the end of the day.

Robin's tale reminds me of a favourite device of that wonderful director Harold Lang, with whom I worked in a couple of Ibsens. On a tired day he would state that he'd confine himself to saying "What?" from the back row, if he couldn't hear anything. Harold's subsequent "What?"'s were unrelenting. Driven to final incredulous riposte on one occasion, I shouted back to him "You must have heard *that.*" "Yes," was his impassive reply, "but I didn't quite altogether *understand* it."

In this afternoon's *Lear* work there's a delicate and high-humoured exchange of badinage, a sharply attuned response between Robin and cast. It's been a hard week and by now the techniques of all are subtly rarified. It's that distinct realm of intimacy on objectives which comes to a Company after long, tenacious and high-reaching ambitions in work together. Tom Wood, just finished going through a sequence, admits to having evaded four specific 'clichés' as he went. And I've a thought of a child making his way over a river only by those stepping-stones which he knows, from long experience, are firmly embedded. The trick in that, of course, is that you don't take any of them for granted. Our stepping-stones in acting today may not be as reliable as those that served us yesteday, or the ones we'll be testing, with each breath and risked step, tomorrow.

Peter, on his way up to the top of the hall, in preparation for his entrance to a scene, goes "Ding-a-ling-Ding" to himself, a precautionary advance warning. Facing up-stage to non-existent actors on the tiny stained-glass-lit stage of St. John's hall, he intones gently, "Unclean ... Unclean." It occurs to me that, rehearsing as we are in a United Church building, there could well be a hand-bell nearby. I ask Greg Peterson if he can spare a moment to seek one out, as I'm so reluctant to miss anything. They are rehearsing the final scene of our Part One, up to Lear's departure into the storm (II.iv). Peter, always trying for new things, keeps getting it wrong, especially in places he's usually got it right before. "Oh, shit," he is obliged to say more than once, when groping for lines.

I've at last found time to read Peter's autobiography, which was excellent company for a couple of sleepless nights. *Dear Me* is no answer to insomnia, being essentially a cerebral book, almost constantly funny and often profound, especially in those cantatas in which the author so musically talks to himself. The thought is largely serious, as with Shaw, just as the talk is always fun. It's the talk that matters, the sheer music of conversation, especially as he can argue so beautifully with himself. Out of the quarrel with ourselves we may make poetry, but out of the quarrel with himself Peter makes Ustinov. If he weren't Russian, or Ethiopian, or French, he'd have to be Irish, who are as zestfully convolutionary about where they come from. But wherever Peter comes from and whenever he speaks in English (which he mostly does), it's a sound from the bedrock of British prep and public schools, especially when he uses ruder language.

Alicia Jeffery, understudying Marti's Regan, is so cajoled and affected by Peter's appeal, 'No . . . Regan, *thou* shalt never have my curse . . .' that she dries, herself, even with her book in one hand, "Oh, shit — I'm sorry" she mutters afterwards as Peter waltzes her into a correct position, in the flight of his next speech. Greg Peterson, returning and sitting beside me, shakes his head at the unavailability of hand-bells.

Robin interrupts to explore a way of keeping Peter closer to Rain's Gloucester, before Douglas is sent off to rouse Cornwall and Regan. It becomes a big gain in the curious blend of rage, from Peter — close to farce — and the attempted conciliation from Douglas — rich in pathos — made more potent now, the two grizzled heads so close together, as it's one that they make together; 'Tell the hot Duke that — / *No*, but not yet; may be he is not well.' It's always been a favourite moment of mine in the scene and, I suspect, everyone's. Jane Edmonds is busily clicking away with her camera.

The difficulties are increased, also, for Doug Rain who, as Gloucester, can wish for nothing so much as to escape from this confrontation, which is not of his making. Peter, sharply attuned to every actor's response, in or out of character, says in mock amelioration, "I'd give him another brandy glass — if I had one — so long as it comes free with every eight gallons." (As Lear he could hardly afford a more generous reward, being down, in the text at this stage, to fifty Knights.) He concludes the jest with a little impromptu dance, a dance which could mean anything. The Company dissolves into laughter. And, this time, Robin is the last to recover. And then can't, quite. "You're all· as mad as hatters," he finally says, and has trouble even getting that much out. He continues, with a slight step to composure, "Watching Doug ... I've been watching Doug — until — his face ... is as young as twelve!"

Watching Peter, I'd have put him (as I often do) about six. Robin, trying to conclude, as Ustinov and Hutt stand before him like two very naughty children at the seaside, pleads more to himself than to us, "Musn't get hysetrical ... still got a *week* to go!" We're to have a little break and do it again.

When they start again I'm amazed that no matter how often I watch some scenes, there are always new surprises, new riches in store. And I sometimes wonder if this production is as good, as absolutely good, as I believe. It's a question I often ask myself. And I keep having to answer with a healthy affirmative, while always admitting partiality. We must love what we do, as actors, as directors, to do it well. Though it would be absurd to claim this principle as exclusive to those of us who work in theatre. It's our job, and we do most things best when we work through love. I've found that we have to try hard to cling to that idea. Most actors are in love with their vocation, but it doesn't come as a gift, it has to be worked for and earned. Tougher still, it has to be renewed with fearful frequency. This production of *Lear*, sub-titled *The Education of a King*, becomes the re-education of every actor in it. None of us is altogether happy in the theatre all of the time, but it's to our credit that, having chosen the job, we all struggle to go on loving it. If we didn't try and, so often, succeed, we'd do a lot of bad shows and the audience would desert the box-office. Like Beckett's two heroes in *Godot*, we must at the very least, at all times, be seen to keep our appointments. Vladimir claims, 'How many people can say as much?', and Estragon's immediate reply is 'Billions.' Our curse and blessing as actors is that millions, or even billions, must see and hear us while we try to keep ours. The point was never merely that the show must go on — but that the show must be seen to go on *well*. In art as in life you take big risks if you're after big gains.

The rehearsal resumes with the last long scene of our Act One, Lear's arrival with his train shrunk to so few followers (II.iv). 'How chance the King comes with so small a number?' asks Kent, from the stocks, after Peter struts off (an *attempt* at strut) to rouse his daughter. With much practice in St. John's I've evolved the best position in which to savour proceedings. A little way up the room, sitting against the wall, I have the action of the play before me and to my left, and to my right at the other end sits Robin (when he's sitting), flanked by his Stage Management of Vince Berns, Ann Stuart and Michael Benoit.

The scene under scrutiny is the short exchange between Kent and Fool, with some queries from Patrick Christopher as a Knightly-Gentleman, while the small group awaits the re-entrance of an irate Lear with a mollifying Gloucester. Hutt sets a fine edge of foreboding of worse things yet to come, in the Fool's smartly pragmatic analysis of the decline in his employer's status and prospects. McQueen's Kent and the few others (very few today) stretch this colour of unease and tension. 'Where learn'd you this, Fool?' asks Jim. 'Not i' th' stocks, Fool' responds Bill with bitter certitude. You can tell from such playing that Lear is now definitely in big trouble.

I'm dwelling on moments like these because the time has come when I must fill in some edges. This rehearsal is valuable because it is so sufficiently (indeed, deliberately) relaxed that one can examine the smaller areas of the whole texture, as in looking into any of the Old Masters, we can seek, with every confidence of finding them, acutely urgent truths in every corner of the canvas. One of the things that makes all good acting good is that we don't tolerate anything less than good in seeming less significant places. Everything contributes to the collective power and strength of the whole, just as you'll never find any sloppy execution in a half-inch of a Chardin or a Vermeer.

When Peter re-enters (as Lear), his light jacket is off, and there are big sweat patches above the armpits of the incredibly yellow and orange shirt. Acting the big roles may call for delicacy in detail, but it's also navvy work. On Lear's burst of rage and its attempted control by Gloucester, Doug contributes a perfectly-judged and embarrassed laugh to balance one of Peter's. On Gloucester's exit, Lear *tries* to laugh at the Fool's lamely encouraging joke. These jests that we are all sharing, in watching this build-up to domestic disaster, though wrenched from a total truth in character, today have an extra edge of mischievous definition.

'Who put my man in the stocks?' roars Lear again, and again. '*I* set him there', responds the very lesser shout of Michael Benoit, on book for the absent Cornwall of Bill Webster. '*You*, did you?'

growls Peter, advancing in exactly correct trajectory on the invisible Cornwall, and still advancing through the space usually held by an invincible Webster. '*You, did you!*', Peter is delighted to continue roaring, now directly into Doug Rain's right ear, who is holding his position, as ever, at the top of this long diagonal.

It's vastly amusing, and a fast glance back to Robin shows me he's close again to the edge of hysterics. And Douglas, impervious to the actor's failing of breaking up into laughter, is saved, finally, from capitulation. Peter desists, at last, turns down-stage again, his face embellished with the smug smile of a job-well-done — which is entirely in character. Someone plunges into the next line and the scene goes on. And Douglas Rain, face tense with restraint, relaxes into a pained smile. And that too is entirely in character. The scene goes on into the speeches of Lear's terror and grief. Jane Edmonds is still taking photographs, and I hope she's captured some of the edges of this canvas. Peter, moving for the exit, stiffens his walk, brushing the tears of sorrow (and joy) from his cheeks and forehead. And here's where we stop again.

"Good," comments Robin. Which seems a fair assessment. Peter subsides with the aid of a long cheroot, and confides that "It takes an awfully long time to get warmed up . . . it's because of being so long off the stage." I'm so busy noting the above (with much incredulity) that I miss the introduction of why, now, they are all talking about children's parties. Rain's daughter, Emma (now seven) had hers yesterday. "And I did *all* the hamburgers the night before," claims Douglas, pausing very calculatively before adding, "Cat got most of them."

After the short break we are having a look at the 'Before a Hovel' (III.iv). I'm jotting a note which (as later deciphered) reads simply 'Kent's back'. In fact, there isn't too much back-acting called for on the proscenium stage of the Avon. But a great deal of it is demanded at the larger Festival Theatre of twenty-three hundred seats; a half, or even two-thirds of which are presented so often with the backs of the traditional Stratford actor. The typical Stratford actor evolves or must evolve a species of most eloquent back. As Lear stands alone for the 'prayer' downstage, McQueen waits up-stage centre, just out of earshot, head slumped and hands in pockets from the freezing rain and cold. And there's no cliché in that. But wait . . . Here comes Douglas with a hand-bell.

There's been some nicely-judged acquisitiveness by Mr. Rain. He's managed — *he would* — to scour the back-stage (or back-church) and come up with a sizeable bell with large clapper, its long smooth handle now in his sure fingers, held before him with delicate and certain caution. He has substituted this challenging prop in place of the lantern which he should hold to lead Lear, Edgar, Kent and Fool away to the relatively quiet safety of Gloucester's barn.

I glance at Robin and his Stage Management to assess any complicity, but their delighted anticipation equals my own. This is a scene with a lot of energy and movement. There is now the added by-play and calculation as the bell (for lantern) asserts its challenge. Doug places it on the floor with a delicacy as usual (no more) as that he accords the afore-used lantern. The wary quintet moves within its immediate radius, staggering about (it's a wild night), evading the smallest tinkle of cliché. Doug reclaims his bell and they all make it off-stage to a quiet huddle of jokes and grins — a clutch of conspiratorial children.

Robin, foxing them, calls immediately for the barn scene, and all five troop across the space (with no bell ringing) to the opposite side of the hall to make their entrances over the highly-polished floor. The entrance, with Doug leading, bell held by thumb and index finger, and the subsequent very busy scene, with all its lively choreography, proceeds with Stage Management, Robin and I avidly waiting for the first note from that bell. Doug puts it down once more, picks it up later, passing it to McQueen. Jim puts it down and, again, later, picks it up to guide a reluctant (very arm-waving) Peter to bed. Doug finally retrieves it as they all struggle off-stage with the exhausted but still highly obstreperous and unpredictable Lear. And the bell, despite the many manipulations, hasn't rung.

Robin, quietly considering, preserves a long and thoughtful silence. Doug subsides on a chair, wrapped in concentration (where Jane catches him in beautifully sharp focus). Bill and Jim return to my end of the hall as Stewart Arnott, understudying Barton, finishes the little coda of Edgar's speech. The silence lengthens. Then Peter, from the furthest end of the hall, pussyfoots it back to behind Robin, making the journey with incredibly total silence, except for a tiny give-away squeak of his rubber soles as he finally settles into a chair by the wall.

Still the pause continues. "Good, Good," assents Robin, at last, looking nowhere in particular, and then, very deliberately, he turns his head around to look at Peter. Another pause, before Peter, reaching quietly for a cigar, notices Robin's gaze. "All right?" asks Peter. Robin nods assent once more. Then he launches gently on a wide range of new points, including some thoughts for the absent

Regan and Cornwall. For Peter he suggests that at the height of the mock trial "it's more worrying if you're looking back into the group — through them — at the imagined movements of Regan and Goneril." He likes the way Peter had placed Goneril low, a crawling vision, and Regan high-flying as a bat, in their supposed presences. It's agreed that as the scene draws to its conclusion it moves "irrevocably towards sleep."

The talk veers to children's parties again, that feeling of "Thank God, they've gone off at last" — unless some almighty fire engine goes by! Which is how Kent needs to respond to Gloucester's reappearance at the end of the scene, in case the intrusion might re-awaken Lear.

At this point it's agreed that Douglas be released from rehearsal and he's free to go. Just before he does, however, he stops for a moment to unwind the old handkerchief he had wrapped around the clapper of that bell. Well, he'd certainly fooled some of us. Maybe tomorrow that same grubby handkerchief will be back to its usual place as a blindfold, glued to his head all day, as he says among those lines of his long role, 'I stumbled when I saw'. Even with a stifled bell nobody stumbled here today.

Robin asks, "What *more* can we do?" There's time for a little more work, another look at Lear's arrival at Goneril's. Peter mixes in a sudden extra chill on the exchange with Rex Southgate's Knight, when informed that since Cordelia's departure the Fool 'has much pined away'. When the Fool enters, Bill Hutt's 'cox-comb' (a modern metaphor) has become the pulled-out lining of a long, grimy trouser pocket, and he slaps Peter's hand with some vehemence as Lear reaches for it. Phillips has some notes afterwards for those absent Knights: it'll be all right to laugh when 'Dad' and Fool are 'up', but watch it with any levity when 'Dad' is down. He offers some thoughts on the annoyance of Lear's followers and their disappointment in the level of hospitality. Like actors on tour, at the worst of those 'Beady-Bag' receptions, they are victims of the mean assumption that all they'll need are "good bread sandwiches." Robin builds the vehemence of their reaction. "Good bread-sandwiches . . . Bread-Sandwiches!" he screams — and is immediately launched into a brilliant fantasy of a Stratford Company on a cross-Canada tour spurning the inhospitality of some stingy host. It's a wild extravaganza, richly peopled with Canadian and world theatre notables, quite unprintable and delightfully, beautifully inflated. His concluding parallel for Lear and Knights, and Regan and Goneril, is that both sides are entirely justified in being angry with each other.

"O.K.," he concludes, "çe soir we'll do more." But çe soir I'll be away at the Third Stage for a performance of *The Taming of The Shrew*.

ALACK THE DAY

The high-ceilinged room of St. John's is swathed in smoke as I manage to return by ten-forty p.m. There are enough smokers in the Company to accumulate quite a haze, in which Barton is now doing his solo, 'Welcome then, / Thou unsubstantial air that I embrace . . .' (IV.i). Robin is suggesting that the feeling Rodger needs is that of "Looking out at the blasted ruins of some city." Which seems apt, in this smog-laden end of the day. Turning to Vince he calls "Next!"

It's been a hard evening session, and it shows in the pale faces of the company. Donna, Ingrid and Marti (the latter two wrapped in long raincoats) look especially frail. Scenes are set up, rehearsed briskly, notes given, and they're on directly to whatever's next. Earlier, things had been more indulgent. Patrick Christopher tells me that he and Jim had yet another go at that first storm scene (III.i). Robin had turned out all the lights and they'd worked for forty minutes in the dark. As Patrick put it, "It's quite an honour, but a scary one sometimes, to work through this food-mill of theatre for so long, with an entire company looking on." But things are brisk this evening, however shaken and wan with care the entire cast seems to be. Robin is again calling "Next!"

Here's Goneril's scene with Edmund, with Greg Wanless as the servant who steps in privily to advise us (a divorce detective in shoddy ulster) that husband Albany is very close at hand (IV.ii). Donna's voice is down lower, her breathing heavy; her playing, and that of Monette, is shorn of those wilder lashings of riding crop; from both of them, between breaths, there's the sense of compulsions, hints of sado-masochism. Frank Maraden's Albany is a refined line of judged emotion, his voice held in a surprising, deep timbre. Wojda's servant enters (with the bad news about Gloucester), exhausted by emotion and travel and tells us, horribly, how it was.

Robin calls "Good," stops them for notes, with an exit device for Donna, "No one is listening to you, darling, but she'll say it anyway." And it's "Once More, Please." Doug Rain's handbell is still prominent on the Stage Management desk, and there's now an extra little one at Robin's elbow. The scene plays through. Donna exits from Frank and John, as wrapped in her own objective as they are in theirs: 'I'll read — and answer!' A light touch of Chekhov. "Next!" calls Robin.

'Cordelia and the Dotcor' (IV.iv). Robin stamps a foot, punctuating the start and end of each scene, each exit and entrance, imposing a pulse, a new, faster pace. Stamp! And it's the entrance of another messenger (Geordie Johnson) with more news. They finish. Stamp! "Good girl," says Robin to Ingrid, and there's another rapid sequence of notes. Ingrid is invited to do that "old, friendly, family Doctor bit — even though he's a military chap." Robin takes Ingrid's hand and does it with her in a running entrance. "Very good — Next!"

Stamp! Marti in her desk bit with Oswald (IV.v). Greg Wanless is understudy as Tom is uncalled because of his *Shrew* performance. Robin adds something to Marti's exit, doing it many times. Then, for her entrance, he tells her "Find a *new* tempo for the beginning ... Stop, and establish it, before starting; otherwise their entrance (the scene-changers) and yours will get confused." Quickly, they do the beginning and the exit. Robin calls "Next!"

Stamp! "What's next? Ah, yes, Old Blind Pew and Black Spot" (IV.vi). It's the Dover scene with Rodger and Doug, handkerchief back on. Douglas, halfway into the scene, is slightly irascible to Rodger; "I'm an old, old man, can't you manage without that squeezing my arm, digging my ribs?" I can sympathize with the problem, for both of them. Back at the Old Vic as Anthony I'd given a dead Caesar some bruising treatment on 'Pardon me, thou bleeding piece of earth'. It's the acting difficulty of remembering at all times that your corpse isn't a corpse. Rodger's task will be easier as Gloucester is so palpably alive, though blind. Doug's fall (from the imagined cliff) is such that it takes a determined, and very careful Rodger to finally get him back on his feet. 'Feel you your legs?' asks Edgar/Poor Tom/Passing Peasant. 'Too well. Too well,' complains Gloucester, with all the weariness of one who wishes he didn't.

Peter enters the scene from behind them, for his reason-in-madness piece, draws a good bow, shoots a bull's-eye on the hawk ascending from murder of that mouse. But the bow/arquebus has been transformed for this effect to a shotgun, and he gives us the whooshing sound of the shot, hitting its target, the descent of flesh and feathers. 'Hewgh!!! ...' No Burbage or any later Lear will better that. And on 'Give the word', immediately afterwards, to the spellbound Gloucester and Edgar, Peter swings the imagined shotgun on them with lethal challenge.

On his adultery speech, he offers us, tonight, not one gilded fly, but two in busy action. His advice to Gloucester to 'get thee glass eyes' is built into a shared joke between the two wrecks of shattered humanity. Seated together on the floor of St. John's Church Hall, there doesn't seem much more that could happen to either of them. Gloucester's interjection of 'Alack, alack, the day!' has an appalling commitment to the last word. On that 'day' Douglas Rain releases a poignancy equal to his intensely taut tramp in Beckett's *From An Abandoned Work* of last season, a performance which has so perfectly fed his conception of Gloucester in this *Lear*.

It's the end of our day, too. It was a long tough one. It's the end, also, of another week of rehearsals, and there is only one clear week now left to go. It's cold enough outside to need more than raincoats on the streets of Stratford.

TUESDAY, SEPTEMBER 25TH, 1 : 30 P.M.

THE CUE TO CUE —
ENTER CARRIERE'S CHORDS

The entire cast and Stage Management is gathered near the front of the Avon Stalls. It's to be a week of very long days, largely technical, with much of the time devoted to costumes and lighting. Today it's a full technical dress-rehearsal for clothes and lights, and the Company will be here until eleven-thirty tonight.

Robin, who has been pacing about the stage and its full clutter of furniture for the opening scene, joins us in the front seats and, welcoming us to this last total week of rehearsal, makes a couple of announcements. We are reminded that the Tyrone Guthrie Awards will be presented on-stage at the Festival Theatre the following evening, to which the public, as well as ourselves, are this year invited. "Please," says Robin, "to attend." Also, the entire *Lear* Company is invited to the Church restaurant for "Supper and

Entertainment" (a special performance of 'By Sondheim'), after Thursday's Technical Dress Rehearsal. It's intended to be a chance for some relaxation in the middle of a tough week.

He goes on to assure us that in this very technical phase, "It's not worth getting in a state." Lengthy adjustments of lighting and music, on scene changes, exits and entrances, will be demanding and time consuming. He asks for our patience. "If, after I've got it right, and you've still got a problem, wave your hand." There is a further caution that it will be "Extra dark in the wings," and "quite dark on-stage lots of times!" The cast is urged to "make mental notes" of where they are in the total action, because of the exceptional amount of jumping forward and back as lights and music are being set. Robin casts about for any further useful points. He selects two. As it's to be such a technical day, the Company is "allowed to laugh." They are also warned "You might get sea-sick, especially in the storm bits, as the lights — or a lot of them — move, or seem to."

The Company disperses and Robin retires to a far back position in the left aisle, abreast of the Lighting Design control-boards, and subsides into a deep-recliner black chair brought in for this final stretch, in which, I can be sure, he'll not often recline. "Turn Over," he murmurs (like any movie-director), and two seconds later, "Print." Nothing today is likely to be that speedy.

Everything is at last ready to go and I hear the first notes of Bert's score — a clear solo trumpet — rise into the Avon chasm, still lit by the chandeliers dimmed to half. Lear's three daughters in very full dress enter to their places with much swishing of trains. They are stopped, and try it again and again. And again. Robin finally decides on the option of having all three on-stage in the pre-show black-out and, after further experiment, Kent and Gloucester also. The final selection is made. House lights dim to half, as the trumpet establishes its first notes, then to dark in the theatre, an instant of deep pitch black before the stage lights rise smoothly to show Regan and Goneril arranged right-centre on adjacent chairs, with Cordelia isolated on a seat far up-left against the wall, and Kent and Gloucester strategically placed near the down-left desk to usher in the first lines of dialogue.

The action runs on, but not for long, with stops for a gradual rise in the lighting levels, building to the entrance of Lear, followed by the sizable court. But it's not the stately assurance of the men, embellished by the presence of the few court ladies (it is, after all, an after dinner scene), nor the absolute scale of Lear's brandy glass (as enormous as could be found) that catches and overwhelms the eye.

It's the sudden rich blaze of colour in the dresses of the daughters. Regan is in voluptuous deep plum, Goneril in intensely vibrant green, and Cordelia (newly-placed in the shift of choreography), now down-right on a low pouf, has blossomed into an absolute Dickensian heroine, but no shades of Alice or Dora or little Dorrit, or anyone other than Blekys in shimmering golden copper, with wig to match.

A jump forward is now called to Lear's exit and the next music and lighting cue. After the departure of Lear I've a hunch that a first-night audience, and maybe others that follow, will break into an exit round. They will sometimes applaud, no matter how determined we often are that they should not. Perhaps few, if any, in the audience will be aware of the low-level continuation of the louder exit music into a captivating off-stage tune, a Carriere chamber-music as precise and delicate as a madrigal. It helps to counterpoint the following dualogue of the un-wicked wicked sisters, and tails off into a silence long enough only for the next music-bridge, following the exit of the sisters, and then, precisely before Edmund's entrance, there's an ominous chord in the bass, as befits the best of villains.

But I'm getting ahead too fast. Robin has yet to practice the exit of Lear and Court, again and again, and those of the girls, especially the staggered exits of Goneril and Regan; the former to, 'Do something — and i' the *heat*', and the latter to be sure that it won't be done without her. Monette's first entrance is a real treat for the aficionado, and Richard himself was always that (I.ii). Black from head to toe, including the long coat of many buttons, and top hat to be donned later, in unredeemed shade of ill deeds, relieved only by a slight flash of blue in his cummerbund, Richard is relishing the moment. Especially as the lights are now on in all the right places, (into his eyes), and he can't be faulted, should he glitter.

Even this entrance of such established ingredients needs a lot of practice to make perfect. Robin, on and off-stage in light leopard leaps, conducts it all, with some injustice to Monsieur Carriere's score. "Brump — Bummp, Go Goneril! ... Brummp — Brump!, Go Regan! ... Brump — Brum-Brum, Door *shut*! ... Bamph — Bah-Bam, Go Richard!" Even now, when he has the music, while the tape is run back to the top of the cue, he resorts to imitations to use precious seconds. Stepping down off-stage and passing me, he confides, "They're all just missing each other — as in all good thrillers."

A nest of difficulties is encountered and resolved, with more definitions on Monette's entrance. "Who's on Richard's Door?" Robin means who, off-stage, is the one with the job of shutting it. Ann Stuart presents herself. An elf in corduroy, she seems less authoritative than when she had earlier haunted the stalls. Robin's instructions are specific, "Slowly — very slowly — still slowly — then, Chump!" As he seals these niceties I'm thinking that the effect, to be definitive, would benefit if Peter could be secured to supply an ominous 'creeeeak'.

Richard is restrained from whistling his bit of Mozart on the exit and instructed "You can whistle *three* notes — but they must be unrecognizable." Bert's music for the exit is the start of a bridging link of carefully arranged modulations. Richard is advised to "Hold it — when you get to the door — just push — and they'll know you're there." Stagehands are standing by to serve all such exits, and few need to be smoother than this. Richard learns quickly that the best of villains (circa Phillips, '79) need never stoop to mere door handles. Besides, there *are* no door handles, and hidden panels open only at the pleasure of our off-stage crew.

Against the background of Bert's next music-bridge we move into the big furniture removal change, and previous drilling helps. There are further sophistications. As twenty-odd pieces are hefted away (gossamer-winged to the wings in the dim set-change light), Bert's music goes from urgent forté to a diminishment embellished with a rattlesnake tailpiece from the maracas. The bare space, with the rear panel flown out, becomes the forecourt of Albany's palace, and Tom Wood's Oswald, followed by Donna's Goneril, enters with the rising light to the sibilant sound of the maracas in the final shakes of its hiss.

Or, rather, this is what they are after. "O.K. — sorry . . . Once More," calls Robin. He seldom says he's sorry, but it's a lot of furniture to have to bring back for each new set-up. "We need to get Tommy on, *while* the music is still playing." Tom is asked to hit his spot on the last of the hiss. It's clear from Tom's delighted skip and grin that he's as satisfied with his music as Monette was by his.

But Tom is gone. I'm sometimes slow to take note of a costume, but this transformation is absolute. The be-jeaned, the shock-haired, jaunty, mercurial charming Wood is no more. The Thing in his place is a dark two-legged spider in stovepipe trousers, frock-coat topped by minutest hint of white collar which highlights a lugubrious (yet dangerous) face, topped with a lank smoothed-out wig only a little less dark than the whole ensemble. Clutching a very thin briefcase, he looks like that creature in the Auden poem 'who walks out briskly to infect a city, whose terrible future may have just arrived.' Gone, in *Lear,* is Tom Wood, as enters one Oswald.

The scene change is running again. Someone (there is always someone!) crosses backstage from left to right, a disastrous ripple and shadow behind the backcloth. Vince calls sternly to remind all that the back wall is out; anyone crossing must use the understage route. Robin, feigning anger in an already highly-disciplined day, sighs, "Lordy, Lordy ... Weekly Rep!"

I move away from my close-to-front seat. Vince, into his headset, calls for "An Auto-Follow wanted here," as Robin has changed his mind about the intro for a piece from the horns on the recorded score. "Ba-ba-ba-Bamp," and "Ba-ba-ba-Bamp, Ba Brump!" goes Robin, showing where he wants the change. It'll be hard for him, finally, to surrender these variations. Moving past our lighting designers at their controls, I hear them still calling changes in the plot to the lighting booth aloft: "We'll need a *little* more on Richard's right cheek before he goes ..."

Then I'm looking down from the back of the stalls, as they finish the change into Albany's courtyard (I.iii). It seems they've achieved in the lighting a very perceptible tone of green slime in those two side walls, and I'm sure of it when I see Donna entering in that dress again, an anaconda jungle green side-by-side with Oswald's viper black. How little our audience or critics know of how long and carefully and painstakingly we work on craft, especially at these times, when we can still, for a little longer, operate from both sides of the footlights. Not that we have 'Footlights' any longer, or the 'Lime' Follow-Spot that used to go with them. Hardly appropriate for *Lear*. We'll have to get back to Musicals for that — maybe next year?

Any one part of a Cue-to-Cue Technical Dress Rehearsal will be much like any other. I decide to leave and have a more useful day on these notes as I'd like to be up-to-date for a change. Besides, there are also some of Lear's last scenes for which I've not completely learned the lines. If the rehearsal can't hold me, my typewriter must, and to watch any more just now would be self-indulgence.

A BRAVE SOUND

But I can't keep away. Eight hours later, at ten-thirty p.m., I make my way back to the Avon. Everyone, in full dress, is still hard at it, a busy clutch of actors preparing for an entrance from the wings. Peter, in a blue buttoned-up great-coat, about to be borne on that bier, is the first person I encounter, and is, he says "Getting ready for sleep." I get to a seat in the stalls in time to see Lear carried on, very nicely dressed up in his epauletted military blues. The stage is wonderfully bright at last. Rod Beattie's doctor is as smartly accoutred as are the rest of the French officers, all of them a poem in blue, culminating in the gunmetal variation of Cordelia's dress. The blues are as absolute as everything I've imagined since that first day of rehearsal, hues as calming as those in the paintings of Piero Della Francesca. Peter plays his scene (there's no interruption) beautifully. He also gets every word right. I'm sure of that because I've just finished learning them myself.

The night and the play flow on to the concluding moments. Monette and Barton are stripped to extraordinarily bright red waistcoats above their dark black pants for the duel. No need for Richard to act any blood from that belly cut. And as Lear, finally, on the centre steps, very well lit, is holding his 'dead as earth' and decorous Cordelia, one of her quite high-heeled shoes falls off. The picture is what I've also long imagined. But the sound is beyond my highest hopes.

Before the last words from Edgar, the first notes of Berthold Carriere's concluding coda reach out to us. Solemn, strong, yet never martial, rising in successive repetitions of the same short melodic phrase (as I'd heard in that trumpet solo for the opening at the start of the day); louder, and still louder, it continues over Edgar's final lines and beyond; enormously, wonderfully human, it still climbs to a final upward sweep in the brass. It's among the bravest music I've ever heard in a theatre.

It's soon obvious that Robin is going to play about with this finish for some time. Even as the hair rises on my scalp with the first notes of Bert's final melody, Phillips is turning to Stewart Arnott, in quest of any hands, any presence, to mix in more effects. "Stew-Pot," he's saying, "Go and grab a red flag and find your way in there. Hold it well up. And ask some others," he adds as

Stewart goes. With a few deft signals he catches others' attention and first Stewart's high red banner, followed by two, and then more, erupt into a glow of billowing red in the background of up-stage centre, behind the dead Lear and Cordelia. But this is only a rough first draft. Robin brushes in further strokes, the slow fadeout on Lear, over the last words from Edgar, '... we must obey; / Speak what we feel, not what we ought to say ...' Meanwhile the music rises in volume, phrase by phrase, with Barton responding to the caution, "Have to speak a bit louder, Rodg." It's tried with many banners, with one only, again with three; brilliant red cas-cades against the dark, caught by the sharp shafts of tightly focused in-stage spots. It's very powerful. And they try it again, and once again.

Peter is singing the while, fluctuating from bass to counter-tenor. François tells me that Peter had heard "Otello" the night before and has, in fact, been singing much of the day. Robin, commenting on one banner held a little askew, breathes a mild criticism, "So much for juveniles."

There'll be more time later for final embellishments. But it's almost eleven-thirty and the long day is almost over. "Full Company to Auditorium," calls Vince. And they gather into a tired, quiet group about Robin. "Darlings," he tells them, "*try* to remember all you can from today. Make sure you don't look backwards. It's been very difficult for you all when we're jumping about. Thank you all very much." He adds a final caution. Many had worked at half their usual volume; "very dangerous with this fellow here with the extraordinarily resonant voice." Apart from Peter, only Douglas and "our Doctor friend" (Rod Beattie) managed to hit the right pitch consistently. Everyone is warned in the storm scenes to play for "only a suggestion of the storm. Shakespeare will do all the rest." Finally, the Company is reminded that, in a very technical week, it'll all tend to go slower. "So — go faster."

WEDNESDAY, SEPTEMBER 26TH

'BET YOUR ARSE'

There was a larger Company rehearsing this afternoon, though many were absent, for performances. A lot of us among the small gathering tonight at seven-thirty in St. John's have had a busy day.

There's a light, easy, mood here and also rather spent. A metaphor could be gleaned from mountain climbing. There isn't enough energy to climb higher in these hours, but there's the tenacity to hold on to all gains and not slide back. It's a high-placed bivouac on the route to the summit and, though we're a small advance party lacking the complete skills required for the final assault, the combined strengths of all are soon to be unleashed for the last push to the top.

Even Robin's exhortations are milder. It's not "Once More, Please!" but " 'ave another go." Another, which he reserves as encouragement when people are willing but tiring, and in need of assurance they've not been working to little avail, is "Bet your arse." Douglas can also encourage many with his dry wit, and throws in an occasional "And *that's* true, too," a line from a long-ago cut scene with Edgar which, as Doug says it, is a sublimation of Gloucester's (and Rain's) enchanting fatalism. It's possible to be both, if you are Mr. Rain playing Gloucester.

Meanwhile we're back to the Dover Scene (IV.vi). The end section, that is, where Rain and Barton and Wood are setting up a nasty killing for Oswald. Robin is still looking for fresh things, new insights, insisting to Rain, "There must be *something* in this scene that makes it more dramatic than a death." Douglas is not overly responsive. And Mr. Wood's death is not traditionally dramatic tonight. On being stabbed on his own cane-sword, in a calculatedly awkward scuffle, he seems to find great difficulty in expiring, especially with that very long mouthful of plot he still has to get out. Tom Wood (I can call him so again as he's now shorn of the accoutrements of Uriah Heep) elects to die on his head. An exceedingly difficult thing to do. Not many would try it, but I've a hunch that Tom is thinking of rigor mortis in that position: a curled black spider has the same ultimate pathos as that of any fallen sparrow. I've seen Tom take a very long time to die once before, as one of the best Mercutios I've ever encountered, and that was an ugly death too. On Mr. Wood's dispatch by Mr. Barton, Mr. Rain again treats us to that deliciously unnecessary question, 'What! Is *he* dead too?' In rehearsals Douglas is a master of the 'running' gag.

Once again we're headed into delicate territory. Robin re-choreographs Rodger's defense of Rain from the viperous intents of Oswald, suggesting "It doesn't matter how much you knock him (Douglas!) around, so long as you keep him safe." Indeed ... Douglas, his handkerchief blindfold rising on invisible eyes and eyebrows is invited to "Struggle a bit more ... After all, it's hard to prepare your body for a blow that might come from *any* direction!"

Phillips pursues some examples of what we all do under the pressure of war-time or other emergencies. "We'd fling him away — from any danger — as we would from a bomb about to go off — dive on 'im, smother 'im, but save 'im. Bet your arse!" he concludes. But Douglas is steely (presumably) under his bandage; it comes with his territory, with half of several full weeks of rehearsals without eyes. Robin tries another conclusion: "It's escape time for the two of you . . . just get Douglas down." But the Douglas under that handkerchief and all that beard is as conclusive as Dame Edith Evans saying "What do you mean 'a rehearsal'? *That* was IT!" "That's it," he says now, leaning in his crumpled jacket against the wall. He pushes his blindfold up onto the thick locks; "*Total* exhaustion — last hope gone — the instinct was suicide." Gloucester, as Douglas does it, has just tried to throw himself onto Oswald's sword-point. Mr. Rain's intention, his clear objective as an actor, is always based on such direct absolutes when he's at last found them. When he's done all his homework he's inclined to be right. And he's always done his homework.

And yet I can understand Robin's absorption also. Even on a tired night it's always his basic conviction that, in *any* scene of Shakespeare's, there has got to be "something more." My own feeling is more doubtful. In the early fifties I worked with an old (very Shakespearean) actor, Eugene Wellesley, who had had his first jobs with Martin Harvey, in whose Company there was a very old actor who had, he claimed, worked with Edmund Kean. Eugene often reassured us with the thought that, though Shakespeare wrote so many great plays and so many great parts (including lots of small ones), he also wrote a few less than great plays, and a large number of terrible parts.

There's a point here which I'll hammer out because, amongst other things, it has a great deal to do with our work on *Lear*. I've known many huge talents in theatre, including some who were compulsive assaulters of sacred cows. Joan Littlewood was one. Her delight was to knock Shakespeare in deifying her own "Dear Ben" Jonson. I haven't any sacred cows myself and have argued often enough with those who would make cows (sacred if not sacramental) of O'Casey, Shaw, Wilde, Sheridan, Beckett, Behan, Goldsmith, Yeats, Farquhar, Congreve, Joyce, and so on, if, for no other reason than that they're all Irish. But I've loved Shakespeare all my life, more than all others, because I still regard Shakespeare as the best. Perhaps I belong to the only profession in the world of which it can be said that all of us, actors, directors, designers, anyone who wields a brush or spear, will unanimously acclaim the one man who has given us all our best chances.

I'd cross swords with anyone who asserts, however, that there aren't some bad patches in Shakespeare. I don't think there are any in *Lear,* though there may be a few moments when the writing doesn't rise to the highest intensity of which most of the play is fashioned. There are matters of plot, in some obvious instances, when he settles on devices of brusque expediency; the reading of that boring letter by Edgar, prized from the pocket of the dead Oswald, is a case in point.

There's a lot of Shakespeare that can be cut, and his own Company may have cut more than ourselves, especially if they were to manage that "two hours traffic" on their stage. I'm sure Burbage and Company played at a greater speed than ourselves. There is a lost art of faster acting. In the meantime, we must satisfy ourselves with doing our best to act it clearly, even if, for a time, that means somewhat more slowly. I'll concede that there is every chance that some scenes, originally cut from some prompt-book, may later have been lost. As Robin puts it, about Edgar and his father, "We don't have the bit where he tells you who he is."

Certainly, there is nothing in this long scene which I would wish to have cut. But I can accept, and even approve, the quite extensive but well-judged inter-linear cuts for this scene at Stratford: there are, in fact, lines from Gloucester, Edgar, and even Lear that we can do without, although I mourn the absence of Lear's, '. . . I will die bravely, / Like a smug bridgegroom. What! I will be jovial.' And yet our cuts are moderate compared to those of hoary actor-managers who once axed the scene after Lear's exit. That death of Oswald is important in this play, as is the off-stage demise of Edmund, or Goneril, or Regan. They are all creatures of the dark, perhaps, and yet in the great scope of the play there is pathos also in the fate of villains, preparing us for a deeper sadness in the deaths of the Fool and Cordelia, and that of Lear himself, finally, before our eyes. When Douglas Rain, hearing of the death of Oswald, so very close to him, asks 'What — is *he* dead, too?' we may laugh in rehearsal at the helpless confusion with which Douglas invests the question, but our audience won't.

Robin is still wrestling with the end of this scene. He takes Rodger through the fight sequence, "*You* say the lines — I'll do the moves." Later, he is explicit about the uncertainties that can be presented by that letter, "*Very* confusing . . . Have you finished? . . .

Or is this bit a P.S.?" He concludes that it would be best if Rodger reads the letter as quickly as possible. Well, *speed* is often the only answer to most acting problems. It's a matter of having the confidence of knowing that the audience can always hear much, much faster than we allow them to do most of the time.

After a Run-Through of the final scene of Part One (Before Gloucester's house), Robin gleans further notes (II.iv). Even on a tired night, all options are being evaluated. For Peter, he suggests that after the 'curse' (that first one, on Goneril), he should drive on into this later scene and through it, with a commitment to action (I.iv). He wants Lear to enter into the last scene of our act with a similar energy to that with which he left the previous one, and wants this to flow through the Courtyard scene with the Fool; he wants both Lear and the Fool to "feel that that thread is not broken." It's an excellent judgment, I think, as everything we see of Lear up to the storm is in one style, a man set on burning his bridges.

There's a very definite note for Tom Wood. In snubbing Lear with his short dismissive line 'So please you', he should take care that it really *does* sound and look like a snub (I.iv). "It needs a really snotty gesture," urges Robin. "Really?" asks Tom, who sometimes does it like that, and at other times doesn't. "Bet your arse it does," asserts Robin. He goes on to say that it's the same thing when Oswald encounters Kent. Lear *needs* the rebuttal, and "the snottier the better," just as Kent will need it later.

All acting, I believe, comes down, finally, not only to doing what you must for the needs of your own objectives, but in doing as much in feeding the objectives of others. Peter Ustinov as Lear feeds the needs and objectives of every actor in this production, eye to eye with everyone, even if it means with his back to the audience. I've noticed that many of the younger Company actors (though not Tom Wood) don't seem to realise this.

Robin has gone into a diverting ad lib routine on how Kent responded to *his* snubbing from Oswald (II.ii). ". . . What you did to *'im*!, I 'ave'nt fergotten — I tell yer! An' now yer doin' it ter *me*, an' Oime a repersentative of *'IM*! . . . Bet yer arse!" Kent has every motivation for knocking Oswald all over the place.

Phillips asks Hutt for a blazing clarity on the Fool's metaphor about the wheel going down hill ('Get Off — Get Offf!'), and the wheel going up ('Climb On — Climb On!') (II.iv). This last encapsulation is my own. I'd need a page and more to render Robin's variations, which had quite a lot of "Bet your arse" in it. There's a valuable point here, too. William Hutt, in this Company, is much respected for his great authority on meaning and delivery of text, and for Robin to put this to him is an indication of the larger challenge issued daily to all those junior actors who must learn to rise to like demands. Everyone is advised, after Lear's departure into the storm, that Robin "needs to know it will be chaos in that house." This acrimony should pour out at Douglas, as Gloucester, when he makes his plea for clemency. As Robin insists, thinking now, always, of the audience, "It's a matter of telling us what's going to happen in the next act."

The night draws on, and Phillips asks for a large circle of chairs that all may sit around to run lines. He hums the scene changes himself, with progressively urgent rhythms. Occasionally he exchanges a glance with Vince or Michael, their heads down to the prompt-copy, to check on Peter's lines. Vince shrugs his shoulders occasionally. It's near enough. (Or as near, perhaps, as it's ever likely to be.) Lorne Kennedy reads in for Monette. Many laugh at Doug's over-articulated 'How fell you out — say that!' The blaring strip-lighting glares down on the tired faces, the hazy end-of-day scene. Peter enjoys a long cheroot and, having trouble with a line, requests of Tom Wood, "Don't *smile* at me ... When I actually see that benign face it's very difficult to remember *any* of it." Marti Maraden, pale, concentrating hard, has to jerk herself back into attention. She didn't get her correct cue (she says) from Peter. You can bet your arse she didn't.

In the last mintues of rehearsal I take a long careful look about our Company in the 'Fellowship' Hall of St. John's. Our circle has within it that endemic impermanency brought by all actors to their place of work, abstract and brief chroniclers of time as we are. Some words from J. M. Synge echo those of our bard: 'The thoughts and deeds of a lifetime are impersonal and concrete — might have been done by anyone — while art is the expression of the essential or abstract quality of the person.' I've come to know the qualities of these actors, the character they all release through their craft; not many of them can know this is the last practice they'll have in this space; LeRoy Schulz, Bob Ouellette, Rex Southgate, John Lambert, Michael Totzke, Hank Stinson, Bill Merton Malmo, all of our twenty-four actors present now, none of whom know, in this instant, if they'll be in *Lear* again or for that matter, in anything else produced in Stratford next year. Casual labourers in the arts, as we all are, we're all at constant risk, and none more than the girls, for whom there are never so many roles. Marti Maraden, our lone lady tonight, is greatly outnumbered even in this partial Company call. But then, our actresses are always outnumbered. It's a sad fact, alas, but that's true, too.

THE GUTHRIE AWARDS

I've made my way over to the Festival Theatre. This is the night, following the evening show there, for the Tyrone Guthrie Awards. Almost the entire acting Company of the Festival (somewhat over a hundred actors) is present, and the majority of the combined technical, production and administrative personnel, augmented by many of the audience of tonight's performance. The stage is still furnished with Daphne's set for *Love's Labour's Lost,* dominated by an enormous stylized tree, a silvered weeping willow frozen into an autumnal nostalgia of dried flowers.

To one side Berthold Carriere has assembled a smaller orchestra than he's used for his *Lear* score, with himself on piano, Arthur Lang on Double Bass, and a percussion section in the person of Robert Comber, who will supply suitable drumrolls for each announcement of the Guthrie Prize Winners. The occasion is graced each year with some entertainment and, unlike so many other Awards, with short acceptance speeches, or better, none at all. Robin, correctly smart, but no more so than at the rehearsal from which he's just arrived, stands at a miked podium, before which is a generous display of living flowers. They are there, he is saying (an innovation this year), "because, from the waist up I seem entirely relaxed, but my feet on these momentous occasions are inclined to dance."

I've chosen to sit, removedly, in an extreme back seat as I've submitted a suggestion for some small blessing on my *Lear* Journal. It's the honour I'm after, and, perhaps, a modest cheque to cover some photographic and typists' expenses. I notice Peter arriving and settling into as distant a seat, some sixty-odd yards away, in the vast curve of the enormous twenty-three-hundred-seat theatre. We hear that there is $10,000 to dispense, rather less than half the funds available last year. Five awards have been chosen from thirty-seven applications, with two unsolicited and one special award. 'Financial

Assistance in Writing a Book — $1,000 — to Maurice Good' is the second award to be announced.

It's a hoary cliché that one is overwhelmed by an award from one's peers. And I certainly am. As I make my way quickly (lest they change their minds) down to the stage, past the TV camera from the local station, the only thought in my head is that it's the second award I've ever had in my life, and the other wasn't for acting, either. And that's the only thing I manage to articulate in thanking the Company and Guthrie Committee. It's only when I'm back in my place, applauding the other winners, that I'm aware that I haven't informed the gathering what kind of book it is that I'm writing, but I know now that this is one I'll have no excuse not to finish. The Guthrie Awards are meant less for ourselves than in esteem for that giant of theatre in whose honour they are named. That's the big point for me. I don't like writing. I love acting, as I do directing, or teaching. And I dare to say that because they are all a great deal easier. You don't have to do them on your own.

THURSDAY, SEPTEMBER 27TH

STORYTIME, WITH THE FULL PICTURE: ACT ONE

A Technical Dress Rehearsal is to begin in the Avon at one-thirty. Most of the cast have been here for as much as an hour before, to cope with another full day in costume and make-up. The theatre seems gripped in a Dickensian extravaganza. Stage and stalls are flooded with gentlemen, high-stocked, tightly encased from waists up, uniformly tall. Douglas Rain, with that new small pot, and Jim McQueen are both in honest brown; in Jim's romantically cut tail-coat are hints of deeper glows. Barton is tremendously squeezed-in, another goodie in brown. The baddies, especially Monette, gleam in black. Frank Maraden, in high style (surely *he* isn't corsetted?) is epauletted, dripping in braid, but ambiguous in blue-black, as the late-developing goodie of the play. The uncompromisingly sinister Bill Webster wears dark-wine over black to co-ordinate with his lady's plum.

Onstage, the girls — Marti in the plum, Donna in her green, Ingrid in her copper-gold — try their dresses among the furniture.

Robin joins Ingrid to practice some positions, some rises and sits on that down-stage pouf. He adjusts the angle of her head. The set is cleared and we're ready for a run. Robin takes his soft seat in his aisle recliner. Vince calls for "Positions, Please" from the top with the opening music.

Inevitably, there's a hitch, and they have to set back; lights, music and actors returning to opening readiness. Vince locates the problems. The up-centre doors have to open in the blackout, and the cue-lights on the up-stage entrance were not working, which explains why, on that first attempt, Kent and Cordelia were missing. Also, more urgently (Vince speaking the while into his head-set to the prompt-corner) the whole thing is not to take more than *five* seconds.

We're launched into the opening scene (I.i). Gloucester almost glibly defines to Kent the bastardy of Edmund ('There was good sport at his making, and the whoreson must be acknowledged'), who has made a stealthy entrance to down-right, easily — indeed nonchalantly — within earshot. Lear enters, bearing his large brandy balloon, and I immediately accept Peter in his black court silks as readily as I did, for weeks, in those casual, voluminous, lightly-creased suits. But, those wild and irresponsible grey locks are whitened further, sleeked down now with an exacting parting; some-one — Regan, no doubt — would have seen to that before he went in to dinner. On the exchange with Cordelia, 'Nothing?' ('Nothing.') 'Nothing will come of nothing . . .', Lear's perfectly-judged expulsions of cigar smoke rise as warning eddies in the shafted spotlights.

Robin leaves his seat from time to time to make comments to Michael or Harry at their lighting-console and, as I watch, I can see gradations as they're made in the highlights, always hitting the faces of those in the crowded court. We move on into the Edmund-Gloucester encounter (in this same set), after the departure of Lear's court (I.ii). Monette is in his total black, and Rain, now in his outdoor coat (brown again) with astrakhan collar, carries an attaché case reminiscent of his own, which he daily brings to rehearsals. Reading the alleged note of 'conspiracy', his credulity is as apalling as Lear's earlier petulance. Both old heroes of this play have it coming to them. 'O Villain . . . Villain!', coming from Gloucester in the context of this decor, is as convincing as the best moments in Victorian novels, and his plea that Edgar 'Cannot *be* such a monster' is the more apt, and touching, because of the immediate smooth reply, 'Nor is *not*, sure', which, could Gloucester hear (but he can't, being as out of tune as Lear), might save him from the juggernaut of Edmund's plot. 'Tis Strange', indeed, as Doug says, putting on his top hat as he departs.

Barton, entering so 'pat' on cue (what manipulations of clinical expertise in plot from our author), is homely and jaunty in brown, especially the top hat, a flash of copper (deliberate from Daphne) echoing the tones of Cordelia. It's an encounter again of villainous black and virtuous brown. Tragedy is compounded not merely by the villain being so intelligently manipulaitve, but by the hero being so culpably and, perhaps, unintelligently, accepting. Shortly thereafter, Monette, buttoning up, donning black silk-topper, whistles his exit to a new unrecognizable tune. And, so smoothly now, that scene change flows past and we have Oswald (or is it Uriah Heep?) venomous as his mistress Goneril in green (I.iii). Their exchange assures us that Lear is in for a bad time.

McQueen on, now in frayed homespun (still brown), emanates out from the sky; Kent in wide-brimmed hat like a middle-aged Whitman of the Civil War — both forty-eight exactly — now banished, disguised, looking as lusty and vigorous as the good grey poet of the Civil War years (I.iv). But has he really had time to grow that beard, with grey more than mingled in the younger brown? (In the best of melodramas, perhaps, heroes, like villains, have resource to spirit-gum.) Shakespeare is very loose in his time-scale here. In lesser productions, Kent's disguise is dependent on never looking Lear in the face. Not in ours, however, where we have a Lear played by an actor who starts him off in a swamp of impaired senses, which can make it hard going for him to recognize anybody.

This mass entrance, 'Dinner, Ho! Dinner!' in the courtyard, envelops the stage in the browns and russets of Lear and knights. The Fellas are obstreperous enough to convince us they are accustomed to leaving any party room in a terrible state. Poor Goneril! The scene combines a pastoral glow with more than a hint of the dissolute. All tones suggest the Fall, a gentle visual melancholia in these autumnal shades, the brightest accents located only in that little touch of terracotta in Peter's waistcoat and his socks, revealed as Kent gets him out of boots into cosy slippers. And yet, we've a sensation of something ominous mixed in with the levity and high spirits: Hutt's tatty green velvet helps to dominate, is in keeping with the acid edge of some, or almost all of his his exchanges with Lear. The best of design works with the text in better theatre.

Watching the scene, I suddenly anticipate a difficulty when Peter, calling to a non-existent Rex Southgate (exempted from the day's work) to bring 'that clotpoll back' (the ill-mannered Oswald), is vaguely stumped when the dialogue grinds to a halt. Vince, reassuring from the stalls, says he'll read in the absent knight and Peter, delightedly reprieved, says, "Oh? — Good — Good! I thought I'd dried."

Bill Hutt emerges from the ruck, with that exceptional actor's enormous calculation, for his first line as the Fool: the ruck in this case being not the presence of so many actors, but their loosely varied responses to Lear's as varied vocalizations. Hutt's empty pocket-lining, pulled out in conical equivalence to a coxcomb, has a more than nineteenth-century ambivalence. His and Peter's first salutation with fluttering fingers, a delightful invention, both with their hands raised to the sides of their heads, makes a nice contest each day, to see who'll get what in first. Offering Peter his 'coxcomb', Bill usually slaps Peter's outstretched hand — an over-greedy reach for forbidden candy. But today Peter beats him to it, hand moved deftly out of line, and almost smacking Bill's, which is whipped away in a balancing sharpness of reflex. The Lear-Fool exchange continues its dangerously uncharted course, with seventeen actors side-stepping, in contribution to the day's jokes. There's a Fool, finally, in any court, as there's one in any cabinet, and rather more in parliaments, but our Fool and Shakespeare's is none.

Donna's Goneril is on, harshly glimmering among the homely rusts and browns, accentuating the now perceptible emerald tone in the two courtyard walls, a harmony in lighting and fabric in key with the sour turn in the text. Peter tries to keep the laughs going but is finally forced into that temperamental outburst, 'Ingratitude ... more hideous when thou show'st thee in a child than the seamonster'. Then, after his defence of his knights, 'men of choice and rarest parts! ...' he introduces something new and lovely. He stops, full flight in invective, to pick a minutest speck of offending fluff from Greg Wanless's shoulder, easing himself with faltering steps forward, and, in pausing, finds a wonderful transition into: 'O most small fault, / How ugly didst thou in Cordelia show!' And through all of this, Hutt, strategically placed, has a superb agonized choice on every syllable he hears, or tries not to hear, of his master's advance in folly. After the 'curse' and Lear's departure, Frank's Albany, out in his shirtsleeves, 'Whence comes this?', is sensible and restrained, caring and rational.

An easy scene change now; two benches whipped away give us a bare space (I.v). We can feel, as Peter re-enters in his Pozzo-like cape, with Hutt in his unchanging garb (how long has he lived in that bashed green velvet?), that the period is working so well for the play. Our shift to the middle of the last century is small enough, and with three hundred and sixty years gone since its first performance, the production, for me, has become a *Lear* for our time. Hutt looks up to the stars with the conjecture of a Captain Boyle, and finds there the hard truth he's been looking for: as Bill gives it to us, a throttled-back emotion on his warning to Lear, 'Thou should'st not have been old before thou had'st been wise'.

And now we have that courtyard before Gloucester's palace (II.i). And this staging, for us, with three light changes to mark passages of time, takes us to the end of our first act (II.i to II.iv).

First, that hiss of Bert's maracas serves as intro for the next stage in Edmund's plot. After Edgar's flight, Gloucester has some trouble helping Edmund out of such a tight-fitting coat to staunch that self-inflicted wound. Doug manages with usual conviction. Regan's and Cornwall's prompt arrival demonstrates the alacrity of villains in any melodrama, and supplies a passionate splash of colour in the darkened space, especially Marti's crimson cloak over that earlier plum. Bill, top-hatted and in long black astrakhan, has the hint of plum in his tailcoat. He hardly needs beard or moustache; it's a smooth, wicked baron. The resonance by now is that *some* villainy is afoot, as Marti goes into that weirdly difficult speech, 'Thus out of season, treading dark-eyed night . . .' The syntax may be complex, but the sound releases menace in every sharp clipped consonant. Marti moves across the stage spreading the now unimpeded aggression being churned within her. Villains are never born, they're fearsomely self-made.

There's a light change soon after, before the Kent-Oswald encounter (II.ii). I take a break away to taste proceedings of the following hurly-burly from the circle. The action pulses on into Edgar's solo (II.iii). Barton's beard, for Edgar, is a useful decision, and, when removed, should help his switch into Poor Tom. Bert's music under Rodger's 'on-the-run' speech reminds me that this is the actor's own set-up for his next appearance, and one can't go too far in this preview of 'Poor Turlygod, . . . Edgar I nothing am.'

We're on into Lear's arrival (II.iv). On his entrance, Peter scrapes a boot free from farmyard excrements as he passes a step on his way to far-right and to Kent in those stocks. His reduced retinue of Copeland, Blake, Christopher and Wanless is as travel-wearied as he, and uneasy as Kent in their non-response to Hutt's line, 'Winter's not yet gone, if the wild geese fly that way.'

From upstairs in mid-circle I'm struck by Phillips' constant use of the forestage for the main action, with the dialogue played always as near front as possible, the deeper in-stage area held by those constant witnesses, the non-speakers in each scene. This emphasis, oddly enough, locks in on the words, leaving our eye free to wander, as we select our own 'close-shots' on those never-really-silent, seldom still, small-part actors, so often in what was judged to be star-actors' positions. It's another reason for colossal on-stage concentration. Those up-stage eyes, those faces so well-lit, supply an unrelenting second audience, an opposite view of the proceedings which those in the audience are facing. The device is a weird one, at times, drawing from all on-stage tremendous attention to all that is said and done. Often, in fact, it's the upstage reactions, any small decision by any of those non-speakers, in what they decide to express, to release or repress in their individual response — which heighten the smallest action played out before them.

As Peter, sitting on his trunk, goes into his 'Reason not the need', there's a marked diminishment in the lighting, as absolute as when a deep cloud covers the sun, and we are faintly aware of Bert's off-stage score. One of the things I love about Phillips' work is his unabashed use of music in underscoring the text. It is an important qualification that this music is *never* intrusive, never, in fact, obviously there at all, except — and this is when it soars in the succulent settings of Carriere — in those set-piece songs of the comedies. But in tragedy, also, there is a rationale for an off-stage flautist, or distant strummer of strings, happily unaware of ironic counterpoint. In the great popular success of our last year's *As You Like it*, no critic made any comment on Robin's restoration of a song which is invariably cut, and only one critic took exception to the rich and frequent underscoring. The rest, like our audiences, were awash with response, without ever knowing how well they were being played upon by sounds so deeply attuned to Shakespeare's words.

But Peter is approaching the end of his twenty-three lines about all our needs, and the distant flautist is stilled. Regan has already left him, and Goneril has taken the long walk stage-right to join her. On Lear's final collapse into tears, Chris Blake (a very up-stage Knight) comes down to him, a quick to a delicate slow move, to touch him gently on the shoulder. Hutt's Fool comes to him, last. And, on Lear's slow shuffling exit, we hear the first distant rolls of thunder. After that, there is plenty of evidence of angst and chaos in that household. We've reached our intermission.

A LITTLE NOSTALGIA

I've remained in the theatre for the coffee-break. There's a lot of technical work still going on, and why miss anything! Robin, Michael Whitfield and Harry are busy with lighting adjustments, a little more here and there, I hope, and (I can be sure) a little less in other places. Janice Greene is sitting nearby, 'Lady-in-Waiting' in some scenes, and understudy for Goneril. She already has a deep nostalgia for those early days of rehearsal, and for one night in particular. She remembers it with enthusiasm.

A very small group was on call, and Robin decided to make it story-time. He sat Peter in Lear's big chair, lit a couple of candles, and turned out the lights. He first asked Peter if he knew a certain story of Paul Gallico's. Peter didn't, but he got the idea. He wasn't being asked to be 'funny' but rather to be spellbinding. Which is what all the best story tellers must be. And he did just that, for an hour — or two hours — or less — or more. Nobody seems to remember, exactly . . . One of his tales, which he'd said he was about to write, soon, was a curious parable of a family noted for its formidable noses, a seeming tribe of Cyranos. He'd told tales, too, of his own life, his attempt to glean reminiscences from an aged relative about Chekhov, whom this old man had known. The old man hadn't much to say for this great Russian story teller other than that he didn't like him very much, because of the dramatist's politics, and far preferred to talk about himself. I've often heard of this little candlelit session, from Sean O'Hara and other young actors, who were all aware of how lucky they were to be there. And yet, few of them seemed to remember details of the stories, but rather the style of their telling. They'd all felt enriched and very grateful that they had been present. It was a severely regretful moment when Robin finally snapped the lights back on and the 'rehearsal' was over.

Meanwhile . . . Back in the Avon, now, Robin is bumping-up the lights for Monette's downstage soliloquy. The Company is called onstage. Peter, prepared for any scene, in black dress-top and brown breeches, combines both costumes of the act, "I'm rather absent-minded, as you know." John Wojda, with tunic-top off, reveals the full horror of those straitjacket corsets. The tails of Peter's black epauletted dresscoat are much crushed, askew in every direction, Micawber returned from rumpled retention in chancery. The uniform black of all the 'Fellas' is emblazoned only by very many buttons. LeRoy Schulz has immense mutton-chops. Young Pamela Redfern, grey-wigged, tiny waisted, most ample busted, is a middle-aged Sara Allgood, and young enough never to have heard of Miss Allgood.

Monette's lights are *still* being set right. Richard stands in happy patience, glad they are setting them as right as possible. "Don't take too many out," says Robin, "Right, more — more . . . I *think* that's enough." Richard does also, perhaps, trying his three positions, as precise as a ballet dancer; semi-profile, the head turn; the one step turning the body to open stance, legs apart, eyes aglitter. Vince informs Robin, "You've forty-five minutes — enough for the first act again?" But I doubt that, as they start once more from the top.

I watch a little from the wings on the prompt side, not that any-one out there ever asks for or gets a prompt. One minor distinction between the amateur and the professional is that they get their prompt and we don't. If anyone is in difficulties once the show is on and the Stage Manager has retired to his prompt-corner (for such it is absurdly called), they will have to get out of it themselves. Younger actors here are getting a daily lesson in this from Ustinov. Not many of them will ever learn to paraphrase so skillfully, or acquire the skill for such excellent guesses in blank verse.

McQueen is flying again, showing a fine sweeping style, a nice build of bravura up to his exit. From the total dark of the wings we can see the light glow on all the faces, though it glows most absolutely on Cordelia's skirts. Such are the perks of the heroine. Edward Evanko, a fine singing actor, just manages not to make tunes of his speeches, yet you can tell he's a singer.

Returning to the stalls, I'm in time for Peter's back, with very mangled tails, and all those faces in rich light as he exits up and through them. Listening to our three sisters, then, I notice not for the first time this modulation of voices; Marti's relative soprano flexible enough for deeper things; Donna's newly-found mezzo; and Ingrid's relative contralto. Well, that's how it *should* be: as Lear says, right at the end, 'Her voice was ever soft, / Gentle and low.'

The whole cast is into stride again, the play beginning to sail, Robin merely puffing occasionally into its sails. Monette, entering again to his bass chords, takes his pose for the solos, as static as a French actor in Racine (I.ii). Douglas Rain, heart-smitten with emotion, convinced by Edmund of uncommitted treacheries by Edgar, 'We have seen the best of our times', opens the door to disaster. Later, looking down into the next scene from the back of the circle, it seems that it's Donna's dress itself that makes that light look green. How well those first-day promises for designs have come true. But we're out of time and it's a supper break, at about five-thirty.

STORY TIME, WITH THE BEST OF HAMS: ACT TWO

When I get back to the Avon that night the technical staff are already busied on the mechanics of the storm. Off-stage wind-machines, down-left and down-right, are in full roar. Thin shafts of light from the large array of in-stage spots hit the bare platform, and the light does indeed *seem* to move. Smoke, driven by wind-machines, coils across the space, and the intermittent rolls of thunder reverberate amongst the chandeliers. "A mere *technical* storm we don't need," says Robin to me, "but something with a lot of style — not just realism." Such very considerable technical resources seem hardly 'mere', but I'll concede the priority of 'style'. There's a lot of style here. Robin settles for a moment into his deep aisle couch beside me.

He tells me of a previous storm he'd orchestrated for *The Tempest* at Stratford which the critics (entering from a calm night outside) thought real. Our *Lear* storm will continue to build through intermission for any who care to stay in their seats and listen. Robin is out of his seat again, pacing about, checking further variations of wind and light with his 'Mates'. The ultimate 'Number One', Kent McKay, Technical Director at all three theatres, and master of all such events, has joined Michael and Harry.

Suddenly the elements are stilled and, with a flick of a few switches by Vince and Michael, we go from din to silence, with chandeliers all fully lit, for the set-up for the top of Part Two. "Full cast standing by!" Houselights dim to half, the shriek of the storm rises, the full dark descends. As the stage lights rise, there are Jim and Patrick, struggling successfully to dominate the gale and tell their story (III.i). It occurs to me that all the roles in this play, in this production, are star roles, and Patrick has one of them. Moving down front, near to the stage, I satisfy my guess that there's no lighting from far out-front, and the spots furthest out are those from the bank of lights rigged directly above the proscenium. The music and storm-mix at the end of the first short scene gives a sudden surge.

A more horriffic wind hits as the lights return, first in a blinding flash of sheet lightning, then in vicious variations on Peter Ustinov, smack on his mark, dead-centre (III.ii). He does well, with his twig. There's about eighteen inches of it, with a couple of leaves still clinging to it in the gale. He gets a bit stuck around 'Tremble, thou wretch . . .', advancing on Kent, blown across-stage with all that wind behind him. There's a marvellous pause after, 'I'm a man / More sinn'd against than sinning', with Hutt huddled down-stage, before Jim struggles across the wind to Peter. By the end, as Bill and Peter dance off to the hovel, there's been enough visual wealth for chapters; I give only the gist of it.

The short interior follows (III.iii). Gloucester reveals to Edmund his intent to go to the aid of Lear. It's achieved very economically on the forestage, Doug in his shirtsleeves, holding his lantern. Richard, left on his own after a beat of perfidy, sprints off, and the lights cross-fade to the bare space before the hovel.

The storm is more subdued now (III.iv). But the wind still lifts Peter's curls. We have Bert's music, softly, so distantly it might be in the head, under-pinning Lear's prayer, and there's a subtle light shift, onto Lear, as one has in opera; for an instant I even suspect a follow-spot. Music feeds back later, behind Rain's longer speech, 'I'm almost mad *myself*.' Rodger does very well, bursting from his hovel, wet enough to suggest he's just run from a backstage shower.

Another short interior (III.v). Webster and Monette vying in villainies, seal the carve-up of the kingdom, a nasty bit of politicking. Once again it's achieved with a single lantern and rapid exits into the smog, a left-over seepage from the storm. The following change into Gloucester's Barn causes Robin to hiss "Why did that take so long?" (III.vi). The trial scene has lots of strange new terrors. 'Bring in the evidence . . .' sings Peter, with typical one-arm gesture; tentative, into any space. The acting has reached a point where it finds its own peculiar inner tempo, or rather four tempi, from each of the quartet; the opening and closing movement highpointed by the fifth, those intrusions of Mr. Rain. It's a five-handed scene which admits any variation, including those laughs which most Lears work hard to keep out, and which any audience may need to release.

Following Barton's brief solo and departure to 'lurk — lurk', we're again into a music-bridge, with Bert's notes tailing off into another rattleshake from his maracas, and lots of heavy furniture, wielded in, lock us into the 'Blinding' (III.vii). And I pass on that. There's as quick a clearance of furnishings to a bare space, and Edgar's near-naked presence is assuring us that 'The worst returns to laughter' (IV.i). No pessimism in that. There is enough light and hope often enough in *Lear* to alleviate some of our characters' journeys through the darkness. Rodger, caught in a brief glow from warmer Front-of-House lamps, has to cope then with meeting the blinded Gloucester. He does very well, now, in the excellent company of Rain and Butch Blake.

And it's dark again in Albany's courtyard (IV.ii). The stage is bare again for the protestations of Goneril and Edmund, and Maraden's Albany setting afoot the coming retributions, 'See thyself, devil! / Proper deformity shows not in the fiend / So horrid as in woman.' And then, as suddenly, from these few vicious shafts of very white light, the stage becomes very bright at last as the Front-of-House blaze is released for the returned presence of Cordelia and those nice Frenchmen in blue (IV.iv). (Act IV, Scene iii has been excised from the production in the interest of clarity and momentum.) This play can be as simple as a child's story book, and the illustrations which accompany the words are being opened up very clearly today. Which is just how all the most difficult of plays can become when the work is honestly done.

It's time for a touch from those maracas once again, to lead us to Regan, her desk, and Oswald, as she insists to him that someone take care of that 'blind traitor' (IV.v). The villains will need to keep their chins up if they want the light in their eyes. This Regan and Oswald have no hesitancy in that.

THURSDAY, SEPTEMBER 27TH *continued*

THE BEST OF HAMS

We're at Dover again, or a little way from it; for we, like Gloucester though we can hear gulls, cannot hear the sea (IV.vi). Doug and Rodg, in full make-up at last, as well as costumes, present me with exciting surprises. Doug is obviously very close to sunstroke. It's a

183

perfect decision. It's been a long walk outdoors, hatless, for an elderly gentleman from the foreign office. Douglas, who always considers such things, leaves nothing to go amiss with our imagination. In this year's production of *Henry IV*, during notes after the Dress Rehearsal, our Director, Peter Moss, had to advise the large cast of nobility and rank-and-file that Douglas (windswept and muddied) looked as though he'd fought the battle of Shrewsbury all on his own. Right now, near Dover, he looks as if he hasn't a shred of fair skin left on his face. Barton is paler, wearing, as he does, a very wide-brimmed hat. But Douglas, with his high forehead above the eye bandage, and exposed cheeks above considerable beard, has a very red face.

I'm startled into conjecture again. 'Very red face' is Beckett's absolute stage direction for both Hamm and Clov in *Endgame*. I've played Hamm once, with John Neville as Clov, directed by Robert Armstrong. John was more than reluctant to have a *very* red face, and accused me of rivalling Grock in my own extremely crimson visage. The fascinating point for me now, in watching Gloucester and Edgar, is to see from whence Beckett may have so exactly located his two heroes. Gloucester, like Hamm, is blind, and immobile without the aid of his partner. It's true that he has the use of his legs, which he derides when asked if he can feel them, but they are as useless and as suspect as Hamm's are, trapped in his wheelchair. Clov in *Endgame*, like Edgar/Poor Tom in *Lear*, is the controller of all journeys. Just as Hamm/Gloucester is the instigator of them. The analogies between two great plays, *Lear* feeding *Endgame*, proliferate. Locked in this spare set by Daphne Dare, *Lear* proves itself to be a precursor of Beckett's absolutely caged drama. That stark shelter inhabited by Hamm and Clov, with Hamm's parents (as happens, in a sense, to Lear and Gloucester) both relegated to dustbins, is a mere survival chamber with one wall left standing, and two rear windows looking out into the void. The bare gap between our two containing walls for *Lear* is as empty of hope. In *Endgame* there's no mention of a *roof* in this partial retreat. Perhaps it's the remorseless sun and wind, beating down on Hamm and Clov, as now on Gloucester and Edgar, which gives them all such 'very red' faces.

Another odd little echo occurs to me, triggered off for me by the cry of gulls, while looking at Rodg in that wide-brimmed hat. I've a curious sensation of there being *two* Hams on stage. The other, younger variant suggested by that Ham at Yarmouth in Dickens' *David Copperfield*, that other journeyer in a wide-brimmed hat is, maybe, not too far from Robin's thoughts, having been himself the David in the TV remake of the Victorian epic. He might share my conviction that we're all garnerers of the past, which is part of my objective now.One way to make our work real, for me, is to dwell not only on how it looks and sounds, but also on what it makes one feel. The image of Rain's Gloucester, on every acquaintance, becomes more child-like, more vulnerable and exposed. Like Hamm, he has no choice but to live his story through, while in Shakespeare's play, as in Beckett's, 'something is taking its course.' Peter's mad array is unexaggerated enough to be entirely credible. His shirt hangs out over the trousers, his boots lost long ago in some bog-hole when he was unhorsed during the storm. He doesn't seem too sunburnt: it's enough to be so blasted in the wits, and he's been out on the heath long enough to have weathered into reality. He's as burnt out as Douglas. The sight of them both sitting close together, human wreckage refusing to be wrecked, is one I'll never forget. They pick over the bones of thought together, as two old tramps anywhere today pick over the detritus of the consumer culture in the garbage heaps of our own century.

The scene ends on a light note. And why not? Before Lear's running exit from his French rescuers, I'm aware that Lear is rummaging in a pocket with his upstage hand. 'What's he got there?' I'm asking myself, and I am quickly enlightened. As Peter runs off (after the old trick of pointing the other way — and why not, for that works too), he is dropping little pieces of newsprint, on his way off into the wings of a world elsewhere. If you're going to be caught, and this Lear knows that, you might as well have the fun of a paperchase. Oswald appears for his viperous assault and is dispatched, managing to die once more in a forward roll onto his head. Doug and Rodg depart.

The stage is wrapped in brighter light again, for Cordelia, for the good Kent, for the Doctor and the awaking Lear (IV.vii). Peter's Lear manages, like a tiny child, to make it back onto his feet. And he is, as he says, when fondled off-stage on Cordelia's arm, 'Old — and foolish'. This is as much a part of the grandeur of Lear as all the thunder-bashing.

As a technical footnote to this scene, Robin, sitting near me, mentions the recurrent "Director's Terror — all those 'Fellahs' in their reds (red cap and belt) should be in their black ones." Like Lear, Robin can say 'I lack soldiers', using, as he does, the same 'Fellas' for opposing forces, with the minimal change in accoutrements of Red Cap and Belt to Blue of ditto. It's nice to know that the actual terrors of the director are reduced sometimes to such minimal matters. But by now I'm aware that Robin is letting the play go, giving it to the actors, guiding them away from simpler errors, edging them a little more certainly into the lights.

And we're onto the final change of the play, all those chairs coming on in the half dark (V.i). As the lights feed in from high in-stage spots, ten smart soldiers — English, they must be (*Red Cap and Belt*) — hefting very large bright red banners, parade briskly around and off-stage from up-right in a big circle to down-right. Neat enough; it's a stage montage of the passing off-stage battle. It's very eye-catching. And more than that. I hear Robin (for the second time in six weeks) congratulate himself, telling Rod Beattie that the big trick is to get that down-stage table on, and, more important, Lear (in such bright blue) with Cordelia, into their up-left chairs without an audience noticing (V.iii).

Peter, taking his new-born happy time, a Lear calmly restored, cups hand to mouth in an indomitable shout to the down-stage Edmund (at that table), demanding to be led away to prison. The cage resonance continues. We exchange one for another. Some are just more endurable than others. Lear and Cordelia will sing like two birds in theirs: they'll outlast 'in a wall'd prison' until those 'good years' have devoured the 'pacts and sects of great ones'. In the Arden text from which we've worked, there is no foolish adherence to the 'goodyears' of other editions (one word, supposedly a bird!) which afflicts classrooms and means nothing. After the terror and despair we face throughout *Lear*, there's a necessary hope engendered for some good (perhaps better) years ahead.

We move towards the end. In the power game between Edmund's, Regan's and Albany's forces, there is much sabre rattling from our very disciplined soldiers. Too much, in one case. LeRoy Schulz has much trouble with a belt and hanger; he's probably been in a different army, moments before, and those changes would vex the most soldierly of Fellahs. We arrive at that final music and red banners descending. It's been a full Run-Through with the full look, full sound, and the full story cleanly told. Which is the end of my objective for now. It's time for the coffee break.

NEEDLE-POINT
FROM OLD AND NEW MASTERS

The Company reassembles for notes in the stalls fifteen minutes later. Peter Ustinov, sitting just in front of me, smells like a wrestler or, perhaps, a boxer, as wrestlers are known to cheat more often. Such is the price of playing Lear; the best of acting in the best of parts is a sweaty job. Robin warns that there may have to be cuts "only because of time." They won't be bits and pieces here and there but, rather, "bold, swift amputations." He flicks the pages, moving backwards from the end. There'll be "no swords for Fellas" (of the rank and file, he means), except for Lorne Kennedy and Barrie Wood, who need them. Rodger's positions for his first Mad Tom are still not right (III.iv). Robin jumps on-stage himself, deftly sketching in where they should be, where Barton must be if he wants to be in the light. Peter also had chosen to stay too wide a few times. He's asked to keep wide once (and only once) and otherwise hug the centre.

The 'blinding', Marti is told, was still not right (III.vii). On the first use of the word eyes "it sounded as if you were telling him (Webster's Cornwall) what to do." Robin dwells again on the subliminal territory from which the impulse to pluck out those eyes begins. A small technical point: the second eye should take longer to be gouged out — "Very squishy — just a bit longer." David Stein and John Wojda, as two of the watching servants, are instructed to stay nearer to each other: "Tension is easier to play when you're closer together." Tension, I'm feeling, is a mild description of what those entrapped in such action might be feeling. Robin cites the example of what we experience when looking at those Old Masters, where, in group pictures, heads are so often so near to another. Again, he stresses his favourite point of "that other extra layer of the onion, each one of which manages to tell me more than any one layer on its own."

Butch Blake is asked to get "desperate to help Gloucester, not just *desperate*" (IV.i). Rodger is warned again, "Don't be too emotional . . . Emotions are fine, but when I get too much of them I don't get the text." Robin drives home a crucial point for all, that as the rehearsal moved through the weeks, "All those other things we've begun to be so skillful at are marvellous *supports*, but they are *only* supports to the text." And then he questions "The incredibly late setting of the *Barn* ... I'd visions of 'em trying to find furniture in the wings" (III.vi). He also has a note for the Frenchmen who are sent out on the moors to pick up a king ... "Remember, you don't even know the lingo" (IV.vi). He asks Greg Wanless to "stay back a bit more." They can't know what to expect, "He's as mad as the wind and sea," *she* says, (a glance at Ingrid). He wants the French Officers to *ease* their way in; there could be something "very nasty — lurking under — all that...." He looks towards Peter, cosily slumped nearby, close to sleep, and abandons the point.

Robin says it was "the best yet, for Doug and Rodg." He asks Tom to think of that sword-thrust, "a special noise when that thing goes in — and *out*!" He recalls his own childhood sensation of getting his hand caught in the chain of a bicycle wheel. Hadn't felt much pain, but lots of panic. Until the wheel was wound back to release him, and "*then* it hurt." I often regret the time it takes to get down merely a part of what he says; if I'm busy on one note, I often miss recording or hearing something which immediately follows. It is always, as Peter describes it, "needle-point — very sharp, very rapid, and *very* precise." Indeed.

He's now talking of the 'Good old Kent' section, and tells our French officers "You don't need to take your 'at off, Fellas. Nice thought — but no" (IV.vii). And then he asks "Why, why was Richard undressing?" I remember the moment, quite a stretched-out moment, when Monette, entering in the pre-battle set-up, stopped amongst all those chairs to remove his uniform tunic of violent red lining, revealing an equally vivid red waistcoat (V.i). I'd assumed Richard was enthused by that inner panache of his costume, certainly an example of Renato's best handiwork. However, Robin judges this particular fashion show as extraneous.

Everyone, in every scene, is warned about the need to keep their heads up, and their eyes especially, a great deal more often. With so much in-stage lighting from spots at very steep angles, and the very spare use of lamps from Front-of-House positions, most of the light is hitting from overhead, and there are big problems with shadows for most actors. From what I've seen, there is one very positive exception to this stricture, one person with an unerring sense of where the light is, and where to catch it at any time. That's William Hutt. It helps a lot of text if you seek quite a bit of it in the stars. Experience, so often, finds the technical gleam which helps to illuminate it. Years of conscious calculating grow into unconscious reflex. Quick glances of conjecture (always *towards* the spots) retain a lot of glint, afterwards, in the retina of eyes which may then glance anywhere (even to the stage floor) more effectively. Bill sits now, in very different conjectures than many others, glasses set back into hair as wild as the Hag of Beare.

Robin continues to flick through pages, reminding himself of the course of the whole run. "Not at all bad," he says, almost concluding. The text was one-half to two-thirds of what was needed, and the pitch, from most people, two-thirds of requirement. He sets the over-all goal for everyone: *"Cool and clear is very alarming —the simpler, the stronger it will be."* He pauses to guarantee the maximum stress for an overview for all. "It becomes unique as soon as *you* play it ... Nobody on God's earth can be better than Jim McQueen's Kent, or Ed Evanko's France, or Bill Webster's Cornwall ... Somebody else might *attempt* to do it like you, or you, or you — or any of you — but nobody *can* ... You've got to say, now, that's *my* line of text ... The time has come when you must *say* the bloody stuff with your everything!"

Robin's urgings vibrantly remind me of Harold Lang's final advice to me for my first performance of my solo show 'John Synge Comes Next'. Harold made a tape for me to play before the show in my dressing room, after I'd done my warm-ups and preparation, as he couldn't be with me for the opening. It's of such important value to the actor, any actor, that I'd done a transcript as introduction to my text when the book was published. This is a short extract on this same theme.

'... So, as each of us have a unique face — you, because your experience of the world is unique — different from Shakespeare's — different from Bach's — whether it's as great or not doesn't matter, it is just *different*. Whatever it is you have to express could *not* be expressed *by anybody else in the world*. (Pause.) So, if you don't express it, the world will never have it. As soon as you think of it that way, one ceases to think about: Is Synge as important as the Bible, or is he as great as Yeats, or greater.... The *point* is that what *you* are doing ... is saying that his own particular kind of artistic life, the things that went into the making of him as an artist, are singular, and beautiful, and strange, and rich, and *if we lost them* — if we lost these words — it would be a great pity, because they are of a unique interest'.

Rehearsal of *Lear* is over at the Avon. All may go. Everyone but Peter, that is, as Robin wants him to go through the storm again to set some changes in effects. "Just change your shirt," says Robin, "as we'll need to see you in the dark." I leave them together, calculating nuances, and join Bert Carriere, as I'm curious to learn the range of instruments used in the score. It was, he tells me, two trumpets and one of everything else: "One flute, one oboe, one clarinet, one French-horn, one trombone, one cello, one bass — except for percussion — tympani — four of them, vibraphone, and a variety of marching drums. Oh — and cymbals!" he concludes. I should add those maracas, for all those rattlesnakes, which he's forgotten, and some talent, because that's true, too.

Meanwhile, those wind-machines, the taped full howling gale, and smoke, are all besetting Peter, back again in centre-stage. Robin and Mates check their specifications, back on-board, encased on their bridge. Peter commands his storm, alone, tired, happy at the end of his day, with his wife, Hélène du Lau d'Allemans, waiting for him in the wings, as he gets some lines rather wrong. 'You owe me no ... "Whatever-it-Is" — ', and Robin, twenty yards from him, gently murmurs 'Subscription.' And Peter acknowledges the minute projection, "Thought *you'd* know it" ... 'Then let fall your horrible pleasure . . .'. They work for another five minutes, and stop, at last, for the evening. Peter takes time, with Hélène, to look over the album of pictures of the production, ready now from that Photocall. And I pass them in the wings, stopping for a moment to wish them goodnight, leaving them in happy reveries, as Peter, sweating more heavily still, looks over his drenched visage of those few days before.

This is the night the Company is invited to have supper and entertainment at the Church Restaurant. With few exceptions, the entire cast is there, relaxed, fresh from showers, enjoying the best wine and food the Church has to offer. As an interlude, it serves as nourishing continuation of our adventure together in *Lear*. It's a part of our actors' worth (which is serious play) to indulge in some more ordinary play. It's fifty yards across the windy leaf-swept road to the door of the Church. An icy finger out of the vast Canadian north is already filtering into Stratford, and it's pleasant to join the Company inside. Supper, as well as the show, fulfills our best expectations, and our entertainers, Edda Gaborek, David Dunbar and Maida Rodgerson, are three of the best singers in our Company. A perfect audience basks in the appropriateness of 'Send In The Clowns', 'The Little Things You Do Together', and 'We're Gonna Be All Right'.

I'm sure they will be. Before the first departures (myself being one), Butch Blake rises, replenished, informally and correctly suggesting that our host (for it is, of course, Robin) hears our appreciation in the usual way. The sound of applause lingers for me outside in the street, as I turn up my collar from the sudden cold. The show is almost on.

But there are still five possible days of rehearsal to go.

FRIDAY, SEPTEMBER 28TH

CONJECTURES AND CERTAINTIES

The pavements outside the theatre are slippery with the sodden leaves of the oncoming Fall, and I'm a little late at the Avon. Work is advancing with tremendous speed, as the Company jumps ahead and back to tighten loose ends and confirm certainties. They are into the Lear and Knights encounter with Goneril (I.iv).

Watching again from mid-circle, I'm reminded how reminiscent this staging is of that Phillips used in *As You Like It*. In those court and forest scenes of *As You*, as in the court and courtyard scenes of *Lear*, we have the same rich texture of groupings, the same teeming yet casual combinations of individual energies, this collective pulse of the group. Again and again, the focus of action and dialogue is pushed downstage, with that burning concentration from all up-stage faces feeding it, and everything we see is a richly accompanying backcloth to the text. I'm dwelling once more on Phillips' voluptu-ous visual choreography, not only to stress the enormous contribu-tion it makes to his final style, but because I know it sells seats. So many customers, especially at the Avon, buy cheaper, upstairs seats, because it's the look of things he does that audiences also so much enjoy. You can see it all the better, for less than half the top price, in the back rows of the 'gods'.

The cast are in their own clothes again and without make-up, but now have that extra edge of assurance of all knowing exactly how it feels and looks in full costume. The seventeen Knights are now really a hundred, and all contribute to the continuing laughter as Lear tries to humour Goneril. Donna's back to her own skirts and Bill Hutt, in his favourite striped trousers, is taller and thinner each day. I can sense the presence, already, of an audience in this empty circle, responding not only to the words of the story which were worked on so hard and lovingly, but also to the combined resonance of actors, lighting, sets and costumes, everything, in how it looks and sounds.

Right now, Lear is cursing ('Dry up in her the organs of increase') an already childless Goneril, and it's almost the first time I've thought of that. Goneril and Regan are, for all we know, not only childless but possibly sterile. Or, perhaps, both Cornwall and Albany are. Such options are left open by the best dramatists. Peter, pausing in his doddering invective, interrupts himself for a quick upstage glance at the very upright Albany of Frank Maraden — a very significantly vertical presence — before he delivers the line 'If she *must* teem, / Create her child of spleen . . .'. It's in family plays (as in O'Neill's) that people know best how to put the knives in. There's certainly been very little action in either Regan's or Goneril's marriage beds, or Edmund might not have been so well 'beloved' by both. But I think it's all politics, finally. Cornwall and Albany may or may not be much as lovers, but Cornwall is certainly power-crazy, and Albany's late-arriving ethics may be stirred less by real compassion than by pragmatic nineteenth- or twentieth-century political necessities. Albany waits a long time to do anything. Personally, I've never trusted him. Especially when played with idiosyncratic ambivalence by Mr. Maraden. Frank himself expressed like reservations about Albany at an earlier rehearsal. And Bill Webster, I'm sure, is as glad to be himself again, off-stage. Killers and vacillators are fun to play, but it's a relief to escape from them on leaving the theatre.

Our *Godot* dualogue today, from Bill and Peter, comfortable in their own trews (striped and baggy), has the added familiarity and relief of being out of costume. Basic baddie's black, and goodie's basic brown find easy echoes in our actors' own denim and cord, and how suspicious I am now of that older staging of small-part Fellas condemned to down-left and down-right; so unexpressive, so foolishly wasted, compared to our upstage faces which so continuously burn.

There's another surprise, in a line I've not focused on properly before, from Jim's Kent: 'Sir — I'm too *old* to learn" (II.ii). Like Lear and Gloucester, Kent also learns much during the journey of the play. As Jim learns, also, by *acting* him. (As I did once myself). It's worth remembering something of the end for Kent before we reach it. Jim's final exit, after the death of Lear, 'I have a journey, sir, shortly to go; / My master calls me, I must not say no.', is filled with an everyday, valedictory loveliness (V.iii). After a light kiss of symbolic solidarity on Lear's brow, worthy of the understated gestures of loving brothers, he makes a brisk exit, in evident good-humour with the world. This solo exit for Kent is the perfect departure, and one not often, or ever, countenanced by self-considering and now long-forgotten Lears who've expired awaiting applause they think is entirely their own. Jim believes (he's told me) that Kent is off to die. I don't believe that for an instant. This Kent is off in quest of new frontiers, and maybe a new Lear in need of succour. The lesson Kent learns (true for a very few) is that *he* doesn't need to change. His last lines are as confident as his earlier words after banishment in scene one: 'Thus Kent, O Princes! bids you all adieu; / He'll shape his old course in a country new.'

A lot of learning happens in *Lear*. Peter, who starts out so hard of hearing — very frequent cupping of hand to either ear — is sharply challenging by the time he's made his way to Dover: 'Give the word!' 'Peace, *peace*!' . . . 'Look with thine *ears*!' (IV.vi). It is here, in his 'mad' scene, that Lear responds with instant certainty to Gloucester, 'Ay, every inch a king'. For what that's worth, with everyone in sight, including himself, reduced to tattered certainties. His senses grow up with him. He can recognize Gloucester, as he will Cordelia, and finally Kent, though his eyes are 'not o' the best' (V.iii). He's as sharp and astute as old men I knew in the Dublin mountains who instantly recognized me after twenty years, during which we'd aged together a world apart.

There's another tiny touch, which raises an amused response from watchers gathered in the theatre, on Peter's decision to reconsider Goneril's offer: 'Thy fifty yet doth double five-and-twenty, / And thou art twice *her* love' (II.iv). Lear goes to Goneril, a disarming shuffle and, in a desperate gesture of attempted return to nursery-time familiarity, touches his older daughter playfully with one finger, exactly on the point of her uncompromising nose. It's a startling moment, certain as we are that, as he takes her hand to sit down, he hasn't a chance in hell of reconciliation.

They've reached our intermission, and the storm howls through the stalls, with Robin and crew still working on its escalation, while the Company are on a break. Afterwards, there will be a note session.

On going over to the Nut Club for a coffee, I find Peter and Hélène downing very large milkshakes at the counter stools, like two children at a small-town drugstore. They invite me to sit between them (not much room) and Peter launches into some Dublin jokes in a Dublinese as accurate as the accents of home heard in a foreign street. Sitting on a low swivel-stool, as at a soda fountain so typical of a million others on this continent, I have on my right the ebulliently self-indulgent accuracy of Peter nailing those mores Hibernico of my natal place to the counter (the cross of being Irish being mostly that it's our friends who never let us forget that we *are*); and on my left, Hélène, distinguished as a journalist (among other things) who has just written a centre-spread article for *Figaro* describing us all (in the Company) with enviable accuracy. Urjo Kareda, now a director with us and literary manager, who for so long wrote the best drama reviews in this country, is (writes Hélène) "a reformed critic."

Returning upstairs later to the padded discomfort of the Chalmers lounge, it already seems an age since Lear asked for a twig here, to shake at the thunder. Robin first says that he doesn't intend his notes "to sound like criticism," but rather "hints for improvement." It's more a matter of "tuning up the dial." Marti Maraden, he decides, "needs darker shadows under the eyes." And so does Donna, who is told "Good, Donna, but more."

Phillips is looking with some self-questioning into his own written notes. I know that feeling. Robin, in fact, seldom takes written notes, his style more often is to flick through the total text with dazzling entire recall. He's written some things down at last, I'm sure, because it's getting so close to the end and he doesn't want to risk forgetting anything crucial. "All do *more* on Cordelia's line!" he says, somewhat reluctantly. "No — very dangerous," he adds quickly, "so ignore that one." Nonetheless, he harbours the point. What he doesn't want is a state of animation when Cordelia takes issue with Dad, but a suspension of activities, in movement and speech, from the whole court as a *result* of the confrontation. It's an exquisite ensemble point. It should be Cordelia's challenge of authority which makes people freeze. Some quite extensive animation needs to exist beforehand so that something will be *seen* to have become stilled. Robin puts it all more colloquially than this, with some rude language, and he's prepared to scrap the note altogether if there is any danger that any one member of the Company misunderstood him. There's little chance of that now.

Bill Hutt is then solicited to take Monette through that first soliloquy and, while he's about it, that second one also, as Robin finds both speeches to have "all sorts of intellectual rhythms" (I.ii). He often defers to Bill on matters of delivery, as he will to Douglas Rain on a question of stress or beat in verse. In this instance Mr. Hutt volunteers to take care of Richard's problem, later, "Yes — but not in front of the children." Robin flicks on through notes. Something technical for Vince: "Dogs up one point . . . Horns up half a point . . .". There are lots of farmyard effects, appropriately, in a play which is flooded with animal imagery. Phillips looks at Tom Wood and tells him that, on the supposedly dismissive 'So *please* you!' to Lear, Tom looked "as if he really meant it" (I.iv). Pursuing the simple necessity of Tom being genuinely insulting in that moment (a reference back to the previously given note), Robin comments, "I mean — I know my notes are not very good — but to have one actually thrown back in my face!" Mr. Wood promises to amend.

On Donna's entrance with Richard, Robin would like a more continued levity, and wants Donna to speak with no indulgence in a slow burn (IV.ii). Looking back into his notes, he then enunciates his next entry with some amazement: "Enter two Churches?" After further careful scrutiny, he's able to interpret it as a technical note for Vince, "Another two chicken cues, and turkeys or geese." Robin's personal hieroglyphics are not unlike my own.

He promises us he'll have to scour the text "to find some ways to save precious seconds." He doesn't like lots of small cuts. Few actors or directors do. A couple of bold larger scale amputations are often less of a shock. Cuts have been rumoured for days but, as yet, they haven't materialized.

Robin's notes range back and forth. One scribbled thought suggests many others. Something for Peter, in the first scene. His exaggerated proclamatory 'Hereditory ever!' to Goneril was "good," but the earlier one to Regan, 'be this *perpetual*' was "too religious." I know what is meant. Peter often sings a line he likes. And in singing it he gets to like it more. And sometimes, as he likes it more and more, he sings too much.

Phillips asks Donna and Marti to "smile more, and more" as they hear those words of favouritism from Lear for Cordelia; 'And now, our joy . . .' (I.i). "Oh yes, we all know who he means by that tone of voice." He wants Ingrid to be stronger and quicker in her self-defence, after she's been axed. He asks Bill for a "smaller reach for that crown." The gesture's been bordering on a too obvious avarice. And here and there, in Marti's speeches, "there's too much music and I don't understand it."

He wants Douglas to push a bit harder in the first scene with Richard (I.ii). That alleged letter from Edgar which Edmund gives Gloucester accuses parents of being tyranical, and he'd like Mr. Rain to show more edges of that. And Richard's 'Foppery of the world' was too slow. We're back to those soliloquies again. "Too much music," he's telling Richard, "over-stretched and over-enunciated." Monette concedes that there are "lots of 'ths' in it (tricky for this French Canadian), but I'll work on it." Robin again suggests a consultation with Mr. Hutt.

"You look thirty years younger," says Robin, suddenly, to Peter. "What . . . !, responds Peter, who has just been showing signs of dozing off. "You mean — down there?" (meaning on-stage). "No," replies Robin, "I mean just now. Right here." Then they have a brief chat about the bit where Lear shouts so much at Gloucester (II.iv). It's better, they agree, that Lear stays close in that bit, the feeling being, as Peter puts it, "I've been quite right to shout so much, you know, but you may have a point — I know you may be right, too!"

On Marti's following exchange with Lear, on the 'Pray you take patience', he wants more of the "Don't start *that* . . . We've been here before! . . . Don't give me that *again*!" Chris Blake was a little too early down to touch Lear consolingly on the shoulder. The second thunder cue was OK but the third was too loud. Everyone should respond more (except for Dad) to the lightning when it comes. Rodger still has "lots of tunes," but is not doing badly — "Stretch your legs a bit wider." *Somebody* was too late on for the Trial scene (III.vi). Robin accuses Douglas. Douglas says no, and accuses Bill. Bill responds, "What, Doug? — It was *you*!" They both agree that they are both right, and agree to sort it out.

Robin has a general note for Douglas. After that "extraordinary energy" he puts into that first scene with Richard, it's "worth trying to keep as much of that as you can" (I.ii). He wants Doug to return, continually, "to the urgency of what you're doing." Again, in that later short interior, Doug had "such a powerful intensity with Richard" (III.iii). He wants him to retain "all that danger and threat, taking it on into the heath scenes" in the encounter with the outcasts, where, in one long speech, he dwells on the plot against the life of Lear, and the plot against his own (III.iv). It's always seemed to me that Douglas has brought great strength to this sequence, and yet, here is Robin asking for still more.

Then it's Rodger's turn. With the 'Foul fiend bites my back', he cautions Barton to still do it quickly, but "be subtler on how you draw Lear out of it" (III.vi). And those dogs: "Just fight dogs, and let me see you fighting dogs." And, also: "Don't run away from Doug" — on Gloucester's re-entrance. (A note from Robin can be, as here, a precise reverse of an earlier one.) He also says that Edgar should start the short solo which ends the scene *before* Lear and the others are quite off. Robin is looking for every option to save a few seconds. I'm very sure myself that most audiences, and assuredly our audience for this *Lear,* will want to and will applaud that exit, and no Edgar should or could stop them. Rodger is asked to put the greatest desire and intention into the thought (on his soliloquy) of 'Safe 'scape the king' (III.vi).

There's a wonderful irony in the writing here, I've always felt. Edgar's most heartfelt prayer is for the safety of Lear, who has already suffered most of the worst by now, and yet it is his own father, in the following scene, who is the next victim in the plot, and Edgar's next encounter with him will be when Gloucester is blinded. Edgar's brief soliloquy (unfortunately, in my view, amputated from the first read-through by six lines) contains some of the key words in *Lear:* 'Who alone suffers, suffers most i' th' mind'. Lurking in my memory for years, as the line did, I hawked it around to the better 'text' actors in the Company, hoping for identification. None could place it. And it finally leapt off the page for me on my last reading of the scene.

Meanwhile, Bill Webster is cautioned to "just hit that chair," on realizing he is fatally wounded after the sword scuffle (III.vii). Mr. Webster has been treating us to some wonderfully executed variations of vintage-villains' deaths, including one worthy of Basil Rathbone in a costume thirties' melodrama. We've been given a long slide against and then with a chair, which sound and image informs us that, though some virtues are no longer in, here's one villain who is on his way out. Bill is asked to moderate the device.

"Doug and Butchie are much better," says Robin, "with a lot more urgency" (IV.i). It's instructive, as Mr. Mervyn Blake and Mr. Rain are thus congratulated, that seniority most quickly responds to a director's notes. Frank Maraden is urged to be "More — and Faster" (IV.ii). Frank, in response, reveals that "It's the first time I've gotten that note in five years." Robin gives this a moment's consideration and amends it to "A *bit* more, and louder."

"Flag and Light," then wonder Robin, gazing at his own scrawl, "what's *that* mean?" He discovers it's for Bob Ouellette, carrying a banner, who is asked to "have a look, and get some light sailing through it." The desk was "awfully late." Lorne Kennedy and Barrie Wood have a chat on this — some traffic problem in the wings. Peter Ustinov, who has, as yet, had but the one note, is now comfortably dozing.

Robin tells Barton that he'll look more mysterious if he stands straight on in semi-profile, instead of three-quarters to front, because of that special lighting at the end. Bill Hutt is asked to work with Mr. Monette on Richard's last solo.

"Peter ... Peter ...?" There's a little pause before Peter opens his eyes. He's asked why he was late to 'Howl, Howl, Howl'. It seems that Mr. Ustinov and Miss Blekys couldn't see the cue light or there was "*something* wrong" with the upstage cue light, but, says Peter, "We finally decided, after a long consultation, to go on." They are both requested to have shorter consultations.

Phillips has run out of time. He'll go over further points with the aid of the prompt-copy, next time. And he'll decide on cuts — soon. How soon, I wonder, as the rehearsal is broken. And how much may be cut? There's lots I'd like to hear faster, but nothing at all I'd be happy to see go.

SUNDAY, SEPTEMBER 30TH

RELUCTANT UNCERTAINTIES

Today, the Stratford Festival Company are appearing in a total of five productions on the three stages; two matinées, *Richard II* at the Avon and *Love's Labour's Lost* at the Festival; in the evening, *Happy New Year* at the Avon, *Othello* at the Festival, and *The Shrew* at the Third Stage. Yet the Festival Computer (there *must* be one) has seen to it that the majority of the *Lear* cast is free to be called for a seven-thirty rehearsal. I'm able to join them towards the end of the session, coming straight from the last evening performance of *Shrew*.

It's a reprieve for St. John's Hall, as I'd thought that *Lear* had seen the last of these walls and windows. Cigarette smoke is a little less dense than on earlier days and nights here, but they've only had two hours' start on me. There is a very large circle of chairs, and the cast is sitting, running lines. I'm reminded of the very first day of rehearsal, when they all sat in that first circle clutching texts and uncertainties. Some uncertainties are reluctant to go.

Robin's head is deeply inclined into a text, ticking off small notes, ready to list inaccuracies. There are still plenty. Peter is disconcertingly conservative in sensible dark grey sportscoat and slacks and black, very shined shoes on the large feet, and even a very moderate tie. Rain, rumbled, sits stroking his beard and his lines, getting every syllable right.

198

Phillips flings his tie back out of his book, going "chum-chum-chum-chum," contributing the rhythm of a scene change. We're well into the last stretch of the play. Peter, with additional end-of-the-week abstraction, has almost made it (correctly) to the end of that 'Let's away to prison' speech to Cordelia (V.iii). 'He that parts us, shall bring a brand from heaven, and . . . *smoke* us out . . . !' — "That isn't it! Is it?" 'And *fire* us hence', advises Robin, for perhaps the last time. "Ah — yes — *of course!*" — 'And *fire* us hence like foxes', continues Peter.

There's another Ustinovian variation I'm confident I'll hear again. In a speech so well known and oft quoted there are four words, 'Have I caught thee!' which has made me jerk into abrupt attention when I've heard instead, "Have *you* caught me?" And, now, Peter does it again. There's a perfect logic in this, of course. Cordelia and her French chaps have been out scouring the heath with just that in mind. Cordelia finds him, and Lear, awakening, is happy to be found. But perhaps there's a subconscious awareness in Peter of something else. Just as there is a sense for all of us, as there will certainly be in our audience, that, in the unique emotional pull exerted by such an actor as Peter Ustinov, we will all have caught him, most embracingly, most gladly, by the end of this play.

The line-run over, Robin has plenty of notes on errors. "It's better text, and it can still get better." An inflection note for Rodger; not '*enforce* their charity', for we can lose the word 'charity', but perhaps 'enforce their *charity*'. He has found one word for Douglas, not wrong, but a monosyllable *extra* than is in the line. He has a one-line correction for Richard. And he has quite a few for Peter. 'If I like thee no *worse* after dinner'. And 'O! You sir, come you hither, Sir!' (I.iv). On this last, Peter often manages to gesture Tommy across the stage to him, with a series of fluttering, hilarious gestures, with many side glances to others for a 'set-up', ending in an invitation to Oswald for a *very* intimate exchange, heads close together, followed by a sudden push on the shoulder. And, on occasion, he manages all this with no words whatsoever.

Robin is extending his list. 'Cadent' tears is the adjective Peter is often looking for. And there's a valuable extra 'O, Regan' still left out in that courtyard speech. (II.iv). "Ah!," responds Peter, "I did *four* of those O'Regans once and felt terribly guilty." Robin insists on the value of this particular one. Peter says he'll be glad to put another in, "They can be terribly useful when you don't know what's coming next." It may be late in the day, but, for me, it's beginning to sound like the first day of rehearsal.

Phillips is still tenacious; now into the 'Reason not the need' speech, he wants to be sure Peter doesn't leave out 'You see me here, you Gods', as he is, indeed, wont to do. He also doesn't want Peter to say "else."

PETER: But I *never* say else.

ROBIN: Oh, yes you do.

PETER (after a slight pause): Don't believe it for a minute.

ROBIN: Oh Yes.

PETER: I simply don't believe it.

ROBIN (tapping his script): I've got it here. (taps script again.) Several times.

I used to have it here, myself, as many times, but I gave up such records in the first week, a billion years ago. The great head is shaking again, now. It's clear that he simply does not believe that he's ever said 'else'. Perhaps Peter doesn't like the word. I don't like 'even', but I use it all the time.

Robin's quest isn't over. He's mulling over some of Peter's variations towards the end of that very last speech (V.iii). "Not that it matters tremendously but it's so *very well* known ... Always the chance there's some one of *those* people out there ..." He holds back the conjecture and caution a little longer, and then gives in: "It's just those *last* words; you sometimes get to 'Look, her lips, / Look there, look there!' *just* — a little earlier than Shakespeare." (Pause.) "*Try* not to."

Turning to Rodger, Robin warns of the danger of getting too emotional too quickly on the speech after reading Oswald's letter (IV.vi). Marti is told that she's saying (she's saying it very grandly) 'Witness the world — that I *proclaim* thee here ...' instead of 'that I *create* thee here' (V.iii). "Well," responds Marti with much spirit (it runs in the family, as Peter once said), "That's not a bad substitute." But Robin prefers 'create'. Well, Shakespeare may have thought hard over the choice of word.

The night's work is ending. "All right, troopies — thank you all," says Robin. He has a last point. In the long second act, no one should forget that drumbeat that must run as a mental rhythm under it — most of it is to have that drumbeat pulse. And everyone should hear it, in themselves. Everyone, that is, except Peter. And Douglas, he adds.

In the older days of older theatre conventions, and more recent days with conventional directors, a cast was, and is, enjoined to get on with it, quickly, while the hero takes his time. Well, there is more than one Lear in our *Lear*. They all go home. It's the end of their last full week of rehearsal.

TUESDAY, OCTOBER 2ND

SOME MORE CONJECTURE

It's a Company call for rehearsal from one-thirty to five-thirty, and tonight there is a full Dress Rehearsal, to which a limited one hundred will be admitted by special invitation. The hundred has been confined, theoretically, to only those people who have worked on the *Lear* production. The group will include much of the entire acting company, of whom so many are *not* in *King Lear*. Most of those present will be from general Administration, from Costume, Wigs, Properties, Publicity and Public Relations Departments. Department, as a word, is never so clinically dehumanized as the term 'Physical Plant' which Canadians and Americans apply collectively and individually to that inhuman dislocation of university buildings in vast spaces and, worst of all, to the theatre which one can sometimes, with exceptional diligence and much endurance, find embedded in them. Worse still, such theatres, when at last discovered, are too often a reluctant adjunct of English or French studies, and as often prove to be a square concrete bunker, always as black as pitch, invariably described as "a very exciting space," and as invariably inhabited by small groups in leotards, encircled on the cement floor, deeply intoning some 'Improv.', heads bowed into crotches for enlightenment. There's little growth, I fear, in physical plant.

For the People of *Lear*, our day (this day) begins brightly enough, at the Nut Club coffee house, where many of us often have breakfast, Peter again included, this morning. During our short chat he reminds me, flicking through the paper, that the Pope will be speaking today at the United Nations in New York. It's only after I've collected my coffee-to-go and gone, that I remember Peter has met and talked with him, very probably — both of them being polyglots — in several languages.

Lear opens this week, and Paddy Crean is on first call at the Avon for the duel. Paddy is making the most of his short time on-stage, and Richard and Rodger, with sensible zeal, are making the most of theirs. They both want to look like Errol Flynn, as well as Edmund and Edgar. And they've obviously taken free time of their own to sharpen some edges; they both want to look as good as Monette and Barton both can. More actors should show the same respect for words as they do for swords. Words are as dangerous, and as unconvincing, sometimes, as any cut or parry made without conviction. The parallel is no exaggeration. If one trusts the words, and risks everything on them, the writing will be tough enough to sustain misjudgments, large or small. Paddy's scenarios are such that, if (it's always possible) there *is* any mistake, no one will get hurt and nobody will look foolish. Paddy, master of fence, covers all eventualities, as surely as the best dramatists anticipate the failings as well as the strengths of actors. Richard and Rodger wisely concede any request from the other to make the other look better. In the fence, as in the best of acting, there is no victor and no vanquished: the only conflict is to make it look good, instead of indifferent, for each.

Later this morning, on the Avon stage, Robin puts the ten flag-carriers through their paces. Calling for the music again (and again and again), he joins the lead man, marching with him, looking for the exact tempo of the manoeuvre and exit. There's a definite snag, and Bert Carriere is finally located as culprit, when they trace a small but perceptible change in the time. "So grit your teeth," says Robin, doing just that , "as you march right through it." They beat the big problem and attend to smaller ones. One banner is too sloping, and another too straight. Some of the ten are too close, and others too far apart. It's finally right, and they move on to the red flags for the finish. Sean O'Hara, Stewart Arnott and Bill Malmo are chosen, and their flags dip slowly to the ground, at left and right and centre. Bert's taped music is called for again (and again and again) until at last it's all perfect.

The plan today is to sort out technical difficulties, with only a relaxed look at some scenes or parts of scenes, as a gentle preparation for tonight's Dress Rehearsal. For, despite the presence of the small audience, it will be just that — a full Dress Rehearsal — and in no sense a performance. When the company notice was posted that one hundred would be admitted, the quota was filled within minutes. Meantime, advertisements are appearing daily in the local and Toronto papers from people desperate to get a seat — any seat — for one of the nineteen performances and two previews.

There's a pleasantly casual feeling in the day's preparations. They are having a look at Lear's entrance with Knights, and Robin is adding a small new trick (I.iv). Almost immediately after the mass entrance, Kent, following his brief solo plot speech before they come on, is suddenly caught up by the onrushing influx, and then grabbed and held for scrutiny by butchily-zealous Fellas. Just as this mob enters on Peter's heels, Robin arranges for one of them to throw a bundle across and deep up-stage. The flight of the bundle is an action that catches our eye in the audience and allows Kent to appear in a different position an instant later. In time to be grabbed, that is; it's his second 'materialization' in ten lines of dialogue.

I have time to take a walk to the dark-wrapped steps before the stage to confirm my guess that the lighting in yet another scene is entirely from in-stage, with a few slight beams from the prompt and O. P. Perches banked high above the front right and left edges of the Avon circle. Stage lighting has its mysteries, too. "Stop," calls Robin to Vince, as a horn has gone up too loud when it should not. The horn is muted, and they add a cock-crow. Of such small measures the best off-stage effects are made.

Lear is still carrying on with those Knights and the Fool (I.iv). The Fellas give in to very long laughter after that 'head bit off by its young' jest from Bill. The scene is allowed to run to its end, in Frank Maraden's line, 'Well, well — the event.' Frank infuses the same dramatic impudence in his flat delivery that the author did in writing a line which, among other things, confirms for an audience that they are merely watching a play — and there is much of it yet to come. The sure arrogance of the play's scaffolding is something else which Mr. Beckett and others inherit from its structure.

TUESDAY, OCTOBER 2ND *continued*

CARE FOR WORDS

Robin decides to stop for more notes. He's been up and off the stage with usual frequency. He won't be able to do so tonight, with a kind of audience watching. When the cast settle down in the stalls, Robin says there's too much "mutter" here and there, and wants a shorter laugh from Knights, especially on that 'bit off by it young'. He sets up more moments of increasingly pained uneasiness in the scene. They try it, and "Good: *there's* the value of going absolutely silent," he says.

They return on-stage and try again, and suddenly he's up there with them, joining the Knights in this last closed rehearsal, ad-libbing "Yeah! Saddle the horses! Go, you people — bloody go!" I'm reminded of one of my earliest rehearsals with the Company last year (as the Duke in the revival of *As You*) when, just after becoming aware of *not* having a director out front, and turning to speak to those behind me up-stage I discovered that Robin had joined our Forest Lords, indistinguishably blended in the interested detachment they all shared. "Hold it a sec," he's now saying, "When Peter says go — bloody go! If anybody's in front — bloody shove — but go!" He's looking, I'm sure, for every way to save a few precious seconds. He stops for another point. *Any* speech is better than no speech in making the ad libs work; it's far better to say most of 'To be or not to be' than just any old "rhubarb." Everything is "much better when we *really* talk." But he's stopped this time by Vince, calling for a set-up from the top of scene one, a little look at that having been scheduled. And Robin is instantly back up there again, moving furniture, including Cordelia's down-stage pouf — a touch more to the right — to stop her masking Lear. "Harry, I'm moving this. Make sure it's not *out* of the spot."

Then, in preparation for the scene, he takes Donna on a walk-through of some moves and lines of Goneril. It's a tricky prose bit, in the first dualogue with Regan, 'The best and soundest of his time hath been but rash . . .', concluding at 'unruly waywardness that infirm and choleric years bring with them' (I.i).

It's a fascinating little problem, and Robin worries it over with Donna. He makes the point that our author sometimes changes his mind on the direction of the thought *during* the speech. "Changes his mind 'alf way through," mutters Robin, "There's that some-thing extra — on top — it also disturbs us in our *own* lives . . ." He improvises a little longer, and stops. Finally, it's reduced to a choice of inflection on the last three words. They try them all before accepting any and, at last, settle on one, the *only* one, and Robin, passing me, coming off-stage, murmurs, *"That's* it." Catching my eye, he confirms this, absolutely . . .! "That's *it*." Acting, amongst so many other things, is always care of words.

The first scene begins and once again Robin is up there, in among all the words, making a small change of position for Donna. The long scene flows on. Or tries to. Robin whips in again, up on-stage (while the scene is in full spate) to change Goneril's position, while Lear fulminates down at the desk. Peter, cutting Kent off soon after, allots him five days to shield him 'from disasters of the world!'; the sound is now indistinguishable from the Churchillian. Not that it matters. Churchill was as old and as peremptory. There's another nice new touch from Jim as Kent. As he turns to go Jim reaches confidently for Cornwall's hand in farewell. And doesn't get it. It tells us a lot, as much — almost — as the lines, as Jim clasps hands with Albany only, before a still faster exit.

CURTAIN CALLS

And what next? Robin is back up there again, flagrantly, in the midst of dialogue, changing Bill Webster's position, although Bill's posture (in that strait-jacket corset) remains inviolably erect. Meanwhile Peter is having some trouble with Burgundy, in getting some lines out to him, that is. And who wouldn't with a director popping on and off-stage during the action? Peter is grappling with one of those lists: 'Will you, with those infirmities she owes, unfriended, new adopted to our hate, dowered with our curse, and strangered with our oath . . .' To successive corrective interruptions from the bank of people at the prompt table (Robin's back there again), Peter waves one hand for an instant, and continues to count out his clauses, "It's all right! — I'll get through this one using fingers." And he does. To my entire satisfaction, if to nobody else's.

Anything else? Oh — yes . . . Douglas Rain exits (as he often does) with one finger in one ear. And that's all right, too. It's been a noisy exchange.

And, anything more? Ah, yes, there it is, written in my best scrawl on yellow notepad, yellow being the best colour for the dark. It's time at last to set the Curtain Call. That is, that Robin says simply, flatly, perhaps gladly, "All right Troopies, let's fix the Curtain Call."

And they do. Robin had suggested (when? — yesterday? — the day before?) that I might like to go on in it, for now, or in the last rehearsal, tonight. But I won't. I've got used to watching. Used to looking in this direction. The cast is gathering now, onstage, many with that faintly dismissive, so nonchalantly, self-deprecating, half-falsely calculative reluctance to be there. These, our actors of *Lear*, are taking their prescribed, resigned, disciplined places, to acknowledge the applause of the watchers, and bow, at last, in thanks to themselves. The moment, for me, is quite overwhelming.

It's a very big cast of actors even by Stratford standards. And Robin arranges them in a very carefully considered, casual but solid formation, very informal but formidable in the presentation of all their individual presences. It takes a long time to do it all, to do it all well. But, for once, the details don't matter. They have Bert's music, of course. And every time, it all starts from Edgar's last lines. From that last tableau. The music sweeps up to that last high chord in the brass, as the light dies out, the flags dipping with it into total dark. The drums continue to beat, over the dark.

And then, those drums, which no audience will ever hear under their own applause, accompany the return of the light. The solid mass of the cast is revealed, but yet only darkly silhouetted for a calculated moment, a shadowy phalanx, before the blaze of the Front-of-House light hits the full group, the very still heads of the Company. The stillness is held, for a long moment, before the long slow bow to the count of five. Then comes a second Company bow to the same, slow count. And then Peter's solo amongst them all; reluctant, he sings and dances a little step or two for us now. Another Company bow. And then the dissolution: some gone, more gone. Peter, exiting at last, solo, upstage. Will he return? Not tonight perhaps. But later? Bet your arse.

Oh, there *were* details. There *was* a 'front-line' in the huge clutch with Peter in its middle. Butch Blake, I know, was right in the middle too, up-stage, carefully made visible on a raised step, enfolded by the Company, the oldest actor amongst them, entrusted with one of the smallest of all these great parts.

I managed to take a few snapshots, which may come out, as, for once, there was lots of light. But I stop long enough to stand and applaud the final Curtail Call on my own. Well, not quite; Robin and Vince and some others are also applauding, somewhere nearby. After the calls, Robin goes onstage to join them and to say, "Very, very good." And I join them all myself, before they leave, for a rare look out into the stalls, to the chandeliers, to the 'gods'. Peter has carried his camera, slung about his thick neck, to record some of these last events. I unpocket mine and take a quick snap at the void.

Neither this, nor my others, nor Peter's in the wings, ever came out, but no matter.

There was, of course, a coda. Before they left (could they leave otherwise?) Robin had three things to say about the night's coming Dress Rehearsal, with that invited hundred. "Don't rise to the occasion. A nice clean text. And in the Second Act, I should hear drums."

TUESDAY, OCTOBER 2ND   *concluded*

THE ANTI-CLIMAX

The anti-climax is one of the best tools of our craft. A last Dress Rehearsal is the best time to have one. The seats are not yet filled with paying customers. It's the last chance for the cast to take into account their personal and collective insecurities. They are still doing it only for themselves, and the many individual and shared doubts are still useful, helpful, productive. The occasion belongs to the Company as a last judgment in objectives. It's the perfect time to consider, for the last time, imperfect options, before final commitment to the whole matrix of rehearsals.

I didn't hear drums (with my inner ear) during that Second Act, and it was still easily possible to hear drums over the curtain call applause; the hundred or so were not *that* vociferous. But, the text was neat and clean for most of the time, and nobody made the mistake of rising to the non-occasion. Peter, in fact, was very very nervous, which surprised me, and scared the hell out of me. But only in the very opening. He got a good deal of it wrong, especially in his very first speech, when he dropped five lines of text, and also plot, about those sons-in-law. His nerves, understandably, affected his voice, reducing his amazing range for a time by half. And yet, confronting his difficulty, he set about working and discovering. I was proud of him and I knew the cast was.

Lots of things went very wrong, technically. Lights in, or out, too soon. Much of the acting was under the usual high definition of the best of the previous week's work. But I could hear the cast making mental notes, remembering what they'd already done, knowing they were not doing it, and knowing they would, the next time, and the next. Acting on the stage is a very hard job, because you have to do it right, in one way or another, *every* time. But, fortunately, because that's the way we plan it, the Dress Rehearsal is still a time in which we can be wrong. Margot Fonteyn, for her warm-up, is reputed to dance her entire role imperfectly, or as badly as is possible for her, before going on in performance with that ultimate perfection.

It was a very good rehearsal of *Lear*. The hundred or so watchers were there. About two-thirds of them were production people, and the rest were actors. Most of them enjoyed it. Some didn't. All of them, I know, were very very surprised. Many adjourned to talk afterwards. Most of our cast went home to sleep. I was glad to leave, myself.

WEDNESDAY, OCTOBER 3RD

THE FIRST PREVIEW

It's a very strange day for everyone working on *Lear*, for no work is really possible at all. Almost the entire cast is involved in matinées elsewhere, as I am myself. The few who are free may meet in the afternoon with Robin at St. John's, and I hurry over there following my own show at the Festival Theatre. But the hall is empty. I try the Avon, where Vince tells me that the small group of those available, Peter included, had left only ten minutes before, after a short chat with Robin. My next possible appointment with *Lear* is with a full audience for the booked-out Preview at the Avon tonight.

I'm early. As are most of the audience. Every seat having been sold so long ago, people stand about clutching their tickets in relief or disbelief; there are already about two hundred other people present, hopeful in the absence of much hope, of returned seats. One of the comforting things about a preview audience is the pleasantly conspiratorial certainty that everyone is in for a reduced price. And it's certainly true, especially when it comes to the upper seats in the balcony, that there are many customers who love *Lear* and might not have been able to come without the bargain. It won't matter to anyone that what we're to see is still, technically, a rehearsal; though for me, personally, once seats are paid for, this is performance.

With a completely full house, I am accorded the special company-member privilege of being accommodated on the step at the left-stalls emergency exit. This is by special arrangement with Barry MacGregor, Actor, Company Manager, and (on this occasion) House-Manager for the night; very tailored, never too effusive, and yet never less effusive than is necessary for such occasions; in a job which requires a gentleman, Barry MacGregor is one.

Feeling nothing if not partisan, I make my way through the throng and take my place in the packed theatre. I am vibrantly certain of how much everyone wants to be here. And I'm in an excellent position to assess the pulse of the stalls audience, placed, as I am, so nearly where I'd watched most rehearsals. I know they'll like it a lot. Just as I know they'd know nothing of the long routes taken by our cast to bring that play out, living, onto the stage. They expect that the Company will do well; it is, after all, one of the best of Companies.

It is the confidence in the audience which finally ignites the confidence of those onstage. It's something I've learned, finally, in being an actor on any stage: you don't have to have confidence in yourself; yes, you *don't* have to have confidence in yourself. That is, of course, if, in preparation, you've already done the very best you can, and if, *if* you have complete confidence in the text, in the writer who gave it to you, and in every actor onstage who shares that trust with you. You don't even have to be nervous. Especially when, in the best of plays, the power shared by any cast is such a great and wonderful power. It is the very *ignorance* of the audience, even the best informed of them who have, perhaps, read the play the night before, which grants the actor his deepest power. At the most modest, as well as the most complex level, the actor possesses the information about his or her own character, about the whole play, which *no* audience, even collectively, can ever have brought to the theatre with them. The actor is the story teller, and is uniquely irreplaceable, or we would'nt have two-hundred extra customers hungry for seats.

How many of our audience, on October 3rd, know much about *Lear*? Some, very probably, know a lot, others a little or less, and others, perhaps, nothing at all. But I'm aware that all of our cast backstage have come to know the characters they're all playing, and those characters with whom they'll be in confrontation. At the very least, they all know the story of this play.

The House-Lights go down to the sound of Bert's solo trumpet, and that story begins. The audience has time to assimilate all that Victorian furniture, and I can now feel the intensity of their curiosity in watching the presences which spill out onto the stage. They could not know how nervous Peter is, again, in the opening, restoring the lines he'd cut the night before, and (that was the price) cutting another six lines of plot elsewhere. My heart stops beating for a moment with him. But the play flows on, potent, enthralling.

A little way into the Gloucester/Edmund scene, I become increasingly aware of a dangerously untheatrical 'resistance', a considerable and rising altercation of voices in dispute outside the theatre, in the alley outside the emergency stalls exit. Dammit. Sensing potential interference with the concentration of the customers around me, I leave my place and soft-foot it out to the vestibule to inform Barry MacGregor, who departs forthwith to remove the culprits. Once out of the auditorium, of course, I realize I'll have to wait for 'late-admissions' to return. I'd forgotten, for the moment, that it's no longer rehearsal inside. But it's nice, at last, to be useful.

Back in the theatre, later, I find the audience as rapt as before. And the applause after the first act is very sustained. There was very considerable applause on the exits of Lear and the Fool, and in fact both of them had been accorded entrance rounds. The feeling at the interval in the bar is consolidatory, and it's a relief to have a beer in the Chalmers Lounge surrounded by people enjoying *Lear* unknowing of the twig which had first been envisaged there, and which they will soon see raised against any wrath from the 'gods'.

The long second act gets off to a perfect start. Jim and Patrick get an exit round at the end of their first storm sequence. McQueen and Christopher must have basked in that, after all their struggling in these last weeks. Lear and his Fool draw very loud applause on their way off to their hovel. The response continues to be generous, for all of the storm, with very loud applause after the blinding of Gloucester. I'd always been certain of that! Cheering breaks out as the final lights go down, with the flags, drowning even the biggest blast in the brass of Bert's final trumpets. Applause and cheering rises to an ovation on the curtain calls. Not bad for a rehearsal. I'm happy to leave, having enjoyed it all so much, and knowing that the audience has enjoyed it even more than I did mself.

But it will be pleasant to get back to an ordinary rehearsal tomorrow. For there is to be one. I'll be able to be there for some of it, before leaving for a matinée. The downtown streets are full of people, like me, who have just seen *Lear*. An odd sensation. It's late, really late, after a very long show, but I'd heard no complaints of that. A few blocks further away, encountering only the occasional car at wind-swept intersections, I'm almost fully restored to my own special sense of loss and possession.

THE LAST NOTES

Our cast is gathered with Robin for notes at noon. And I'll stay as long as I can; I've a half-hour call for a show at one-thirty. The mood of the Company is relaxed, very personal; the show belongs to them now.

"Everyone in scene one," Robin begins, "can you all move much more, after Peter gets into 'Mysteries of Hecate and the night'?" He also wants "much more background dialogue." With Lear launching into the speech which cuts Cordelia off, the hubbub should convey many concerns, including, he suggests, looking directly at me, "Someone go and get the Press-Secretary!" This effort should continue until Lear shouts 'Peace, Kent — come not between the dragon and his wrath!' Robin asks them to practice it now, and they do so. Peter finishes it all with "Peace, Kent, come not between the Prompter and his Prompt!" Which illustrates nicely that at extreme down-left, as he is at this point, he could not possibly be further from a prompt, if he got one, which he couldn't.

Robin is talking of the "nerves" sometimes in evidence last night for the preview, which was "not the nervousness of courtiers, but the nerves of actors." He would prefer to have a "bold and totally committed actor, hopefully making the right choices." Which seems a fair enough description of Peter, last night or at any time, nervous or not.

"World-wearied ... Contemplative ... Inspired ... Determined ... Arrogant ...," says Robin, stretching the words, or, rather, the intervals between them, as he epitomises all of them himself, while looking directly at Donna. He often starts a note, not by speaking the actor's name, in person or character (as most directors will) but simply by catching his or her eye. Sometimes, if I miss his trajectory, I'm at a loss as to whom he is speaking, until I recognize something in the context. But nobody could be in any doubt for long, as his so absolutely committed eyes soon fix on and never stray from his communicant. His point to Donna is that Goneril could, and should be — "*all* of those things." Though at times, says Robin, Donna "merely gives me bad temper — but all of those things are in there." He says that she *can* supply all these different values. It's all those "other qualities which give different rays of projection."

Robin expands into more general application as he looks among the Company. He's talking about "having the confidence to take your time." And by that he doesn't mean "getting naturalistic." He's usually very wary of the word naturalistic, he says, as one needs to be sure what *he* means by it. I feel that he means spreading, extending, having the conviction to push through, which can best be achieved by finding a 'resistance', and there are plenty to choose from; even the ignorance of an audience can become a useful resistance. "It could," says Robin, "sound a bit like taking things up a little in tempo, but that's not it." He points out that Donna *has* it in the scene with Tommy, "where she has a need to know something" (I.iii). For Goneril to achieve what she wants, all the time, there is a huge list of irritants: "those hounds all over the place, dog-shit under the table, bed-wetting" all of this can be blended into her confrontation with her father. Yes, he *was* talking of resistances ... Phillips' direction devices incorporate much of the best tricks I've encountered everywhere in thirty years. He's fundamentally a teaching director.

"I don't get forty-eight," he's saying, not looking at Jim, who is a long way from him — but I know the line well enough (I.iv). "Very young, really ... ,' adds Robin, but it turns out it's a later bit that bothers him — Kent's speech about women. Jim tries it a few times, Robin remaining unresponsive. Bill Hutt, just in front of me, shakes his head repeatedly. An actor in this Company finds his own inflection; nobody is expected to find it *for* him. Jim tries again ... "Is *that* closer?" Robin is impassive. Hutt shakes his head. It all hangs, says Robin, "on that interesting difference between the words 'love' and 'dote'." The question remains unresolved. It's a change to find something (as Joyce said of one major work) that is actually abandoned.

"I don't believe the pushing." Robin is looking at Marti, then Peter. The difficulty is that Regan's line about 'unsightly tricks' may get confused with the pushing (II.iv). It's Lear's kneeling down in front of everyone, hamming it up, that's 'unsightly'. Robin wants to hear 'unsightly tricks' *before* he sees the push. Better still, Marti promises, she'll recover from the first push and try again. Settling for this, Robin asks her to "*Really* get at that nose." He has a conjectural and not unaffectionate look at the nose in question before adding, "How *can* you tidy it!" Peter, from the moment of this mention of that proboscis, has contrived, in instant miniscule pantomime, to suggest that it's a nose both unmentionably untidy and quite impossible to get at. For a passing instant he looks like an irascible Doc in *Snow White*.

But Phillips is on to the next thing. "Don't make Mad Tom tearful," he's saying to Rodger. This, he insists, can only make things harder for Barton later, when he's in a *real* emotional state with his father — when he can't be tearful either. (Barton, it seems, must steer away from tears at all times.) "Don't try to be sinister," Bill Webster is told, "the text is quite sinister enough." This applies to the short dialogue before Gloucester is dragged on for the blinding scene (III.vii). After Regan 'escapes' from that mock trial, Phillips wants Peter "to cry *more*" (III.vi). The more exhausted Lear seems to be the better; it's exhaustion which finally gets him to sleep. Peter accepts this, but is a little worried about getting back to the little dogs in time, this being his next line. It's agreed, however, that Tray, Blanch, and Sweetheart are well-enough trained to stay until called. Douglas is asked to come past the stool — more centre — on his re-entrance.

Webster was "too quick" with the eyes, getting the second one out still too fast (III.vii). Robin takes Bill and Marti by the hands, runs up onstage with them, and does some quick variations of Cornwall's final exit. They'll have plenty from which to choose. Returning, Robin tells Butch that he was "very very clear" in his secne with Gloucester, "much, much better, and very, very interesting" (IV.i). Butch has learned, and demonstrates daily, how exactly to take a director's note. You do it. Mr. Blake acquired that little skill from his fifty years' continuous work in the theatre.

Robin is up, again, running back on-stage to show how he wants Rodger to contain his use of space, in the Dover scene (IV.vi). I should add, *near* Dover, as there's no proof in the text that anyone gets to the sea's edge. Robin reduces the Edgar moves, pretending he's moved far off, 'throwing' his voice, skirting the body of the (imagined) Gloucester: he uses the very small-scale calculated movement techniques of the radio actor, leaning away (as from a mike) within his own vertical, or soft-footing it a mere step or two to suggest, and call back from, an inaccessible distance. The play may belong to its actors but the teacher won't go home. Watching him, I feel I'm back with many old radio-pals at the BBC in Portland Place.

Returning to join us in the stalls, he concedes that "it's terribly hard when you have to do double images." He pauses a second before adding, looking directly at Rodger, "Half the people last night thought Douglas *was* on the edge of a cliff." Rodger gasps, not in disbelief, but possibly self-criticism. Someone suggests that the sensation of immediate proximity with the sea (and a cliff) is compounded by the sound of gulls that we now hear (I got my wish there) at the start of the scene. But Robin is adamant. "Gulls *don't* necessarily mean sea," he insists, as most, if not all English and certainly Irish people know. There has been a very big storm in the second half of our play, and Robin relishes the point; "Gulls don't stay at sea; when there's a storm, they shoot inland." As an islander myself, this problem was as acute for me, once, when rehearsing *Lear* on tour or later in Dublin. Few people in Ireland live more than fifty miles from the sea, and a cliff like the one Gloucester asks to be led to is alarmingly accessible. Robin is reminding the Company of the hundreds of gulls we've all seen, even at Stratford, after the recent hurricane along the east coast of the States. Besides, he says, the sound of gulls is something that can help Edgar in convincing his dad that they're on the brink of an imagined cliff.

"Using only your voice, you are painting a picture for him," says Robin, "*then* I'll know you're lying." By which he means that our audience will know it also. The success of acting is measured by the degree to which the actor makes the audience know what he wants them to know. "It's a pure bit of Brecht," he continues. "Think of all the care with which you have to concentrate on that farewell . . . 'Farewell . . . !' Think Radio. You don't have to *do* anything. You've got the perfect audience: he wanted this cliff, you invent it for him, "way down there . . . all those chuffs and gulls."

He interrupts himself to reflect on the powerful values of Radio. Radio for the old, for the blind. "If it hadn't been invented — for all those hours of our mothers at their ironing-boards . . ." He pauses, a little, and returns to the matter of Rodger's choice of an 'Irish' voice for Edgar's second disguise-role, the peasant who 'finds' Gloucester after the imagined fall. "Your Irishman should be full of fairy-tale smoothness. All balm, soothing, caring." He warns against the danger of characterising 'Irish' by strange faces and jerky rhythms. How glad I am to hear that: when directing non-Irish actors in Irish plays, as I've loved doing, most of the time goes into removing accent or carricature, and nurturing smooth, very smooth rhythms and never those jerky ones. This much can be acquired, though the accent is illusive and not worth pursuit. Robin, concluding, wants Rodger's Irishman to let his words come down like feathers, "very strange — almost exactly like physiotherapy after an accident — start to imagine pictures — and he'll get it from you. And believe it."

Phillips pauses slightly, before launching into more general notes. "The 'French' Army Chaps will carry torches, not lanterns, so that when they go, you two (Douglas and Rodger) will have more dark" (IV.vi). "Lorne, if you have your coat open you're an English soldier." Presumably, Lorne had a 'red' belt on underneath, and he gives us some back-stage jests on these confusions. To the repeated off-stage query "Are you English or are you French?", there's only one answer — "Both" — as our armies (always the same army) hustle for room on every entrance. (Wing-space at stage-left in the Avon is especially limited, with enough room for only one Fellah passing in single file.) A little point for Frank Maraden. In the Edmund-exchange after the battle, and the other with Goneril and Regan before it, a certain extra edge "would give us that special family relaitonship" (V.i and V.iii). This can be a useful echo of that family row at the end of our Act One.

Chris Blake is asked, as Herald for the duel, to say it all in English and French but not *explain* that he'll do so (V.iii). This will reduce Paddy Crean's new speech by a mere eight words, but Robin is still, as yet, saving only seconds. I'm sure, by now, that those bigger amputations will never happen. Ed Evanko is asked if he has a pocket in his waistcoat and, if so, to put his thumb in it. Rodger is asked to speak louder on the last lines of the play. Everyone is urged to move in closer on Peter when he almost has that heart attack on 'Hear me, recreant!' — "He's even trying to pull out that silly sword, so he might well poke someone with it, so get off your arses and move." These last rapid notes have ranged over the full length of the show. But Phillips is far from finished yet. He's looking straight at Richard.

"It's called a 'ladder'," he says, and then explains deftly that he's talking about that second soliloquy, 'This is the excellent foppery of the world', and that the speech is fashioned like a ladder, just as some others of the big speeches and soliloquys in Shakespeare are "arranged like paving stones" (I.ii). What's especially difficult, says Robin, is when a speech incorporates both the ladder *and* the paving stones trick in the journey of the thought. Robin often speaks of Shakespeare's writing with a writer's intimacy of the craft. I've been painstaking, during these weeks, in setting down what he says as exactly as I can. Which has meant, largely, confining myself to short quotation most of the time. I never attempt to report *all* he says, which would defeat the best efforts of a Hansard recorder, and would treble the length of my journal. Interpretation of what he *means* is, at any time, a matter of my own best guess. As he said himself, when he read some of my earliest pages, "It's *your* point of view."

He's still talking about the 'Foppery' speech, and the 'ladder' trick. "He uses 'em when he wants to do something cocky, when he wants a *result* at the end of it. And there's a big difficulty in attacking a *structure* when it's actually a *result*." He pauses, a moment, to consider Richard's problem as if it were his own. "This is what makes it hard," he says to Richard, looking him right in the eye, "*if* you want humour at the end — which I suspect you do."

Then, with no seeming need or any time for preparation, Robin launches into a brilliant paraphrase of the entire speech, encapsulating its entire ingredients, right down to that 'Fut . . .' — "stains of copulation everywhere!" Greg Wanless catches my attention, signalling to ask if I'm getting it all down. I wave my hands at the impossibility. Shorthand might get most of the words (and even that is doubtful), but you'd need a camera running to capture the animation of hands, face, eyes. Watching Phillips work, day after day, convinces me more and more of what is the most important thing for any actor — after voice but before everything else — it's the eyes that count. It's the eyes, always the eyes that are constantly *telling* us something.

Robin's looking back into the text to pick out something for Donna, to give her "a little extra muscle" on 'I'll not endure it!' (I.iii). "It's as simple and firm as that" — meaning it's *that*, and nothing more than that. His eyes seek out the distant McQueen. On that 'Now, banished Kent', the 'mirage' entrance, he wonders if Jim might consider starting his new accent (to go with the bearded disguise) within that short speech to the audience (I.iv). Jim wonders a bit about it. Doesn't see how he can. Asks if Robin would prefer that? "No," replies Robin, "just a thought." For once, finally, I can't resist it, and offer one thought I've harboured for some time. I suggest that in this very short soliloquy it's Kent's only chance to make it clear to the audience that he *is* the disguised Kent, and that Jim would be wise to give the full four lines, from 'Now banish'd Kent . . .' as directly to the audience as possible. As it is, he's been on the move through this, and only in profile. The point is accepted.

Phillips' notes start to contract into smaller specifics. That brief burst of "dog-yapping" from Chris Blake (as one of Lear's Knights), when they're in that trouble with Goneril, was "good" (I.iv). It had been a longer more extravagant dog before, and Robin had suggested curtailment. All Knights are asked to be sure they get off-stage before Lear's 'curse': "Sexy Rexy" (Rex Southgate), says Robin, is in danger of not quite getting off. It was "nice, that scene with Kent, Lear, and Fool" last night (I.v). And the next stuff (he's flipping over pages briskly) and all the fighting (the Kent-Oswald fracas). Vince is told that there's something not quite right on one bit of thunder. On that departure of Lear's trunk, after Peter goes, we had "an overloud sound of thunder which sounded like the movement of an overloud trunk."

It was all a "very nice — very nice run-through rehearsal." A little pause. "You and Jim did a lovely tango," Patrick Christopher is informed. At the end of their first storm bit, Jim and Patrick had indeed developed the original handshake to a full embrace, two chaps off on desperate missions (III.i). Last night it was a bit baroque on that clinch. Patrick confesses that he and Jim had worked on their end bit quite a bit, downstairs in the dressing-rooms. For last night's preview it necessitated them both travelling across to extreme stage-left like two pine-cones swept away by the gale. Robin thinks it was a bit indulgent: "Like a tango in a fish-tank," and says they should settle on something more moderate, centre-stage.

"Pour," says Robin. And then, "Pure." And then "Poor." And some others I didn't write down. He had trouble, he says, being sure he'd heard Rodger's Edgar say 'Poor Tom . . . Poor Turlygod' in that short solo. Robin wonders if it may sound clearer to a Canadian or American than it does to him. It's a point in usage, on how best some vowel sound should go for maximum clarity to an audience. The matter is thrown open to general discussion. The consensus is that 'poor' here need not be so emphatic as is the case in the U.K., certainly not so entirely polite as the dehydrated version the best BBC voices make of it. Phillips lets the question rest; in these instances he's mildly democratic.

He dwells again on the entrance of Gloucester and Edgar near Dover, the one with those gulls (IV.vi). "It's an *enormous* relief if you and Doug allow yourselves to go for humour." The look is to Doug. "*All* that stuff about what you can hear and can't hear makes us relax." Earlier I noted how Douglas gives us that marvellous irascibility and (very curious, this, and touching) almost a sub-conscious feeling in Gloucester that he's beginning to recognize his own son, under the profusion of disguises. Robin muses on "the clever old fucker . . . " — Shakespeare, of course, about whom he's always thus familiar, who so often writes "stuff like this, in which one can hear the oddest little conflicts going on, as it does here between these two."

He then asks Rodger to be very simple with that letter. "It's *hard* to say a letter well when it's been memorized" says Rodger. Robin is off again into an enlightening diatribe on actor's difficulties with letters and, even worse, with telephone calls. So very few actors know how to act answering the telephone. I can think, myself, of a couple of wonderful exceptions. One was Audrey Hepburn, who answered the phone in her first picture, as a then nobody, with such insoucient guile she was instantly promoted to stardom. The other was Louise Rainer, who answered her phone at some critical moment in some movie with such agonized truthfulness that it still makes me shiver with associations.

Phillips tells us of a workshop he did once on the subject, which evoked the "most extraordinary" subtle variations on even the basic word 'Yes'. How many, from an amplitude of possibilities, do we use in a standard Stage-Telephone scene? He does three cliché ones, (imagine your own), and the cast responds with huge laughter at the so obvious inflections, with that contradictory gleam of mockery in his eyes. "So *crude* compared to . . ." and he tries some *real* ones, not too many, before concluding that "they're *frightfully* difficult to act." He pauses, trying to move on from the point, but he doesn't make it. He recalls his intense curiosity when people answer when he phones . . . "What are you *doing*?" he wants to know. "In the middle of dinner?" "No?" "Well — *eating*, anyway?" "No?" "Impossible!" is his conclusion, really concluding. But not quite — yet.

"Barbara Stewart, don't answer — but *who* is . . . Wait! — I'll find it," he has to add, flipping through his text. He gets it. "Da-la-di-da-da-dah!" He's obviously imitating *someone* in the cast. There's a conjectural pause. Not too long. There's no time left to waste, this last day. It's obvious that nobody knows, except Barbara Stewart. Such is just one of the gifts of Barbara Stewart, Understudy for Cordelia, Company member for three years, authoritative on text, and fluent in Russian. Robin is looking, after his pause, most directly at Richard. "You usually have three in every show," says Robin, "it's how you sound when you're dealing with what you think is a subsidiary clause."

It's a brilliant note. Not that I'm concerned with Richard's penchant for subsidiary clauses; I used to have quite a taste for them myself in roles that require some display of intellect, but I haven't acted anything mildly cerebral for some time. Robin nails down this

218

little delight very firmly. It's just another of those little bits of acting which are quite unnecessary. Why twist ourselves, as actors, into a writer's parenthesis? To act, finally, is to do. It doesn't mean that to do we need not think at all. But many of us often fail to do enough and, alas, think (often disastrously) far too much. As actors, that is. I ran away from writing thirty years ago to escape the thoughts provoked by writing (or trying to write), glad to embrace the seemingly easier discipline of learning and acting the words of others. But acting's just as difficult. Every word is there only because it has a purpose. And, as Robin puts it, "in a good text, any one bit is as motivated as all the rest."

"Darling," Robin is saying to Jim McQueen, "don't wait for the second body." Kent's final entrance in the play, in the last scene, coincides with the arrival on-stage of the two biers bearing the stately dead presences of Goneril and Regan. Admittedly, they don't all come on side-by-side. Jim wanders in from far up-right, the biers from down-left — with some help from handlers. The audience is assisted in identifying Kent by that wonderful line 'Here's Kent!' Which sounds to me, in any production, like an ad lib the original Kent may have solicited from a fellow-actor to reassure the audience of the reappearance of a leading player after so long an absence from the action.

Jim's first line, as Kent, confronting the evidence of carnage is a tentative 'Why thus?'. It's a tricky moment, and Robin informs us it was "quite dangerous last night." It's agreed that Jim should get in a little quicker with his line, without waiting for "that second body" which allows us "to do nothing but look at one body while waiting for the other." Well, perhaps in being so purist, so Elizabethan, in bringing those bodies on, we may encounter like chances of being 'sent-up', as were Shakespeare's men.

Richard is also concerned that, even with this adjustment, "It might still easily get a hoot yet — things were really about to *go* last night." He's afraid he might have "a *very* tricky transition" before he goes into that last speech of reformation, 'Some good I mean to do / Despite of mine own nature'. Robin warns him "be careful you don't get too emotional on that."

Then: "Good-O," concludes Robin, really, finally concluding. They are about to rehearse some special bits, but I have to go, as it's almost one-twenty-five, and I'm almost due at my theatre for the half-hour call. It's been a worthwhile ninety minutes. The last ninety minutes of rehearsal. I'm just on my way when Peter rouses himself (it's been an easy session for him), and launches into a reprise of a story I'd heard from him before. It seems both yesterday and, yet, a lifetime past, when we sat together in an unbusy moment for both of us, and he claimed my allegience forever with a few tales with that old glow of home.

"All that talk of 'poor' and 'pure' " he says, "reminds me — I've told this one to Maurice already . . ." I still have half a minute, and stay to hear it again.

Peter has recently been doing some filming in Dublin, and is sharing a taxi with the actor Jack Watson. The taxi driver is a typical talkative man, with authoritative comment on passing points of interest. Peter asks his opinion of one hotel as they drive by. "Ah, that's a pooer wan, you wouldn't want to go in there — the service there's very pooer." To the outsider's ear, 'poor' in Dublinese does sound like 'pure', or rather 'poower'. Peter, wanting to hear the same vowels in another variation, asks the taxi-man what he would call a native of Morocco: hoping, that is, to hear 'Moor'. After a pause from the taxi-driver, comes the edged reply, "I'd call him a Moroccan." Peter gets out of the taxi shortly afterwards, and the taxi man turns to Jack Watson, and he says "The bastard! He was trying to get me to say 'wog', but I wouldn't, not with *you* in the car." It's been worth thirty seconds to hear that one again.

THURSDAY, OCTOBER 4TH *concluded*

THE LAST PREVIEW

The second and last of the *Lear* previews is crammed to the rafters and, once again, hopeful customers who can't get in, crowd the windy pavement outside or the stalls lobby of the Avon. It's a busy vestibule tonight, as bookstalls, generously weighted, vie in sales with count-down judgments from the box-office. Barry MacGregor, as in a teeming Bourse, dispenses the rare 'return' of tickets among the too numerous V.I.P.'s who have arrived too late. The lucky ones claim their tickets with the triumphant relish of winners at the racetrack. Tonight, the Stratford Festival welcomes those whose perspicacity urged them to think so sensibly ahead. There's a glint of achievement in many eyes.

I've chosen a seat in mid-circle, a little way behind the lighting and technical team, in their roped-off front balcony places. (I'd exchanged for that earlier booked back seat to better savour audience sensations.) Bert Carriere, steadfastly bejeaned, is a late arrival, slipping into his place beside his head-phone equipped colleagues, Michael Whitfield and Harry Frehner, just as our house lights fade into dark, and then the clean note of the opening trumpet sounds. The stage light rises smoothly revealing the tableau figures; the Earls of Kent and Gloucester, the poised, very wide-skirted presences of the three daughters of Lear. "How *do* they *do* that?" whispers one awed customer to her companion just in front of me, amazed at these so silently and so exactly achieved positions in the total dark. Already, the first words from Jim and Douglas are rising, effortlessly, with perfect pitch. Rain's delicate nuance produces a slight prelude to a chuckle on his second line (which I've been confidently expecting from that first hour of rehearsal), and his third speech claims a full ribald laugh from an audience glad to show us it is glad to be there. The audience senses that, if they're to get a laugh or two from *Lear*, sooner is more likely than later in the evening, even allowing for the promise of a Ustinov. The magic of theatre already floats in the air, the give and take, the balancing. The watching listeners support the actors, our players glide on the attention so long worked for and now so fully given. The air is promise-crammed. As I listen, the first tricks of the evening are being taken, as all the tricks, all the haunts, in all great plays, are always ours. Actors fly as well as dream by night. And we have a million tricks to follow.

But my self-congratulatory feelings of conspiratorial acquaintance with the whole of our theatrical calculations, already now being unleashed on our audience, are diminished by the sheer scale of the event. Until now we've always done the play for ourselves, with always an audience in the mind's eye, and now, the readiness is all. This is a play (I think, perhaps, the greatest of all tragedies) which was once supposed (and is still often alleged) to be unplayable, by many scholars and academics. But our Company is playing it now with a massive certitude. Even Coleridge or Charles Lamb would recognize that. It really *is* quite simple, or appears to be. And yet the experience, the performance itself tonight, in any of its separate elements, remains unguessable, intrinsically contained within the whole; unknown, mysterious. As the play unfolds, the story so accessible, second after second, moment by moment, I discover with mounting astonishment more and more surprises at every turn in the road of this already (for us) so well-trodden narrative. The amazement, doubt, belief and disbelief of the audience escalates my own. I hear with each watcher, see with each listener: the audience combines its collective consciousness with mine. At last I can hold my breath with *them* now — rather than on my own.

The story of *Lear* flexes, inexorably, accommodating the strangest varieties of feelings, of thoughts. Again, as I did once at a lighting-rehearsal, I'm acutely aware that I'm celebrating, in the instant, the fact that I'm an actor (or writer) in the humble vineyards of the arts. I've mentioned the seeming 'cage' within which (for me) these actions are being played. Yet Daphne expressed surprise at my choice of image. The constant containment, within these three walls, or most often within two, leading the eye to that lost space deep back-stage, was never quite a cage to her: 'I'd say ... more like a funnel ... perhaps,' she had ventured. And, that's true too. For each of us there remains our own personally selective point of view. Cage or funnel serve alike, as Shakespeare's astonishing structure draws us in, contracting and expanding, breathing its own life, an alternating pulse of conjecture and demonstration, a journey into the womb, an adventure forth from it. The play is the story of all our lives. With all the complexities of that immense undertow of intellect shown in the writing of *Lear*, there is always, finally, a great simplicity. Any child can follow this plot. And a lot of children could (and would, if adults were more venturesome in bringing them) enrich our responses on these occasions, and deserve their places in the theatre. (I've watched kids and their responses at *The Bacchae* and *Hamlet* as well as *My Fair Lady* or *Camelot*.)

Here, any child can say, is an old man. Indeed very old, foolish, angry, nice enough but impatient, and about (it seems very likely) to make some very big mistake. Any child can watch him, hear him, as we all do now, as he makes that mistake, and then willfully — oh so willfully — decides to follow one dangerous idea with another. What a long journey Lear makes before he's ready, finally, with Cordelia, to 'sing like birds i' th' cage', and, accompanied only by her (his Fool, the last distraction, being long gone), be prepared at last to 'wear out, / In a wall'd prison, pacts and sects of great ones / That ebb and flow by the moon.'

The cyclic flow throughout *Lear* tugs us back from its end to its beginning. The re-awakening to the love of Cordelia, and Lear's abjuration to himself (to all of us) to 'forget and forgive', could only have followed on his encounter with Gloucester near the sea; with whom, in the journey's great climactic wilderness, Lear finally

222

withers into reality. Any child, as surely as the child in all of us, watching Lear in his first scene, surrounded by flunkies, the court toadies, the family sycophants, can recognize and isolate the threat from those who are silent and inactive, as instinctively as mourning the banishment of Kent and Cordelia — Good Fairy and Guardian Angel.

For six weeks now I've been constantly reminded that, on that first day of rehearsal, Peter said that the play is about senility. He wasn't joking. *Lear* is about many things, about all of our lives, all stages of the trip from uterus to grave, but (despite the complexities of the whole) at its centre stands a hero more in trouble with himself than with the world. Death is certain, but old age isn't. Nor is senility. But it comes, too often, to cripple the old. As it is known, clinically, to palsy sometimes even the very young. To grow old with ripening faculties and sometimes increased productivity (as did Shaw and some great conductors) is the lucky chance of many. To become senile is the greatest calamity of the living. There is a Lear in every old person's nursing home. Many of us have sent our own Lears there, as many of us may be sent there also in our time. But such places are Elysium compared to those abysses of institutions which house the demented of all our cities, in any country: and there isn't often a Dean Swift to bequeath a fortress of respite as the Dean did for Dublin's poor. God help the poor when they are also Lear.

This Lear is a brave performance, and an important achievement in the theatre for our time. Ustinov's Lear is a strategic and very intelligent blow struck challengingly by a remarkable man and actor in the forgotten name of the old. Not all of the old become senile, or are threatened by it, but many, too often, are. As Peter said himself: "The terrible thing about senility is that it's not consistent. One can break out into lucidity, and then just run out of steam." Any of us who have seen this ourselves, in those we know so well, in those we so much love, have experienced the depth of helplessness this can make us feel. It's wonderful to watch those vocational few who, helping, *can* help; nurses, doctors, or someone who may, suddenly perhaps, sing a song among the beds and high cradles in bareboarded wards, who come with fruit or flowers, or merely something good to hold. As it is wonderful, also, to watch an actor who can act very old age and, in doing so, bestow hope and dignity upon the old, senile or not, upon the old many of us one day may be. Peter, approaching a mere sixty himself with daily relish, rejoices already in anticipation of his older years ahead, without recourse to the so many successful actors' evasions of dyed hair, recurrent face-lifts, perpetual sun-tan; that disguised senescence which afflicts, even degrades, so many reluctantly aging personas in television serials and Californian movies. Peter enjoys the old he's prepared so effectively and actively to join. His personal feelings, as with his acting, display a healthy corrective to anything sentimental: "Having seen dying people, one is terribly conscious of *their* sense of social obligation. They're being terribly tactful, making light of their condition, to make other people less uncomfortable."

Peter, I expect, may make some of his critics, and perhaps many of his public, feel uncomfortable. It's been one of the joys of my life to watch him preparing for this work, with this attendant risk, and to witness him doing it tonight. If you want any of that merely 'tragic' acting, any of the pyrotechnics of established bravuras, don't come to this *Lear*. The real panache in this one is closer to the glow which dwells in the heart of Cyrano: an uncompromising committal to face and tolerate only the truth, be it as ridiculous as excess of nose or belly, folly-decked egotism, or tonight, in this Lear, doddering ineffectualness struggling towards a new sense of life, a new-born determination to grasp it. For me, it's as moving as the image of Henrik Ibsen, almost inert after successive strokes, setting out within hours of his death to relearn his alphabet. As Lear, for us tonight, takes on the battle for his own mind, and succeeds, or almost succeeds. This can happen on-stage, in this play, in the way it can happen also in life.

There's a lot of fun in it all, too. Here is a Lear not prepared to avoid the occasional trip-wires for laughter the writer has cunningly placed, at the oddest moments, to alleviate (at least for the audience) the harshest rigours of the thought. We need a really grown-up man to play Lear. Ustinov's autobiography is proof enough of a man who is nightly growing, always a little more, every day. We can always do with a few more laughs, and Ustinov gives us a lot we need: "I've got three daughters, which is a more thorough rehearsal for the part than anything Stanislavsky ever suggested."

Tonight's Preview is drawing to its close. Lear plays through his long scene with the blinded Gloucester, sane again in his madness, reclaimed for all of us, exuberant, adventurous, one of those two "old book-ends" Peter conjured up for us in rehearsal, many weeks ago. 'Get thee glass eyes; / And, like a scurvy politician, seem / To see the things thou dost not.' It seems to me as if *all* the audience is laughing, however moderately, or cynically, or affectionately, at that. We all know something about scurvy politics. There were many more such moments as remarkable. As there will be on other nights. At the end there is another ovation, and many of the audience are reluctant to go.

FRIDAY, OCTOBER 5TH

THE HALF HOUR CALL

There is no rehearsal today. And no notes. Tonight, at seven-thirty, is the opening night of *King Lear*. Many of the cast are busy during the day, with a matinée at the Festival, and another at the Avon. But even if most of the *Lear* company had been available, it's doubtful if there would have been any calls. It's not the Phillips style to trouble actors who are ready and primed. Last year, on the opening day of *As You Like It*, Robin talked briefly and let us wander away, suggesting we might like to go and "look at a few trees."

The entire Company are already present at the Avon when I wander down, about six-thirty. Many of them are already half-way into costume and make-up. In fact, the majority of the cast have been in the theatre for the thirty minutes' physical Warm-Up with movement coach Jeffrey Guyton, followed by thirty minutes' Warm-Up with voice coach Lloy Coutts. Such appointments are usual every day, before either rehearsal or performance. The ritual of the Warm-Up, before performance especially, is a standard discipline with the Stratford Festival Company, though never, seemingly, obligatory or contractual.

Making my way through back-stage to all the dressing rooms to wish the cast good luck, I encounter Robin several times on the same pilgrimage. In his shirt-sleeves, without the jacket of his dress suit, extra-exceedingly impeccable, he has the lithe grace and shape of a Spanish dancer. I almost wonder if he's in a corset too. In fact, he looks as poised as any of the Victorian bucks that surround us, poised enough to go on-stage with them and look entirely in place. He also contrives to seem entirely relaxed, and his certitude is reflected in every member of the Company. Their confidence in him, in themselves, in the play, emanates from every pore.

I've said my good-byes to them all. Dressing rooms finally become sacrosanct. Peter's had looked as though it was his birthday, festooned with gifts, including the ones he is even now packaging and handing out; and in truth, for Peter and the Company, it is, indeed, a birthday.

Following the performance, the cast is to be presented to the Lieutenant-Governor, Pauline McGibbon, on-stage, in the presence of the audience, after the final applause. Robin McKenzie, our youngest Company member, after a like encounter last season (then aged seven) had much relished his meeting with, "The Left-Handed Governor" . . . though I understand she isn't.

A little time before seven tonight, and the Half-Hour-Call, the Company will gather on-stage to hear the arrangements for this presentation, and (perhaps) a last few words from Robin. I make my way up on-stage, just that little earlier and, standing on the stage, alone for a moment in the unlit set, look out into the empty auditorium.

The theatre is still empty, except for Barry MacGregor, dress-jacket on, coming in to be sure the theatre is as empty as it should be. The theatre, before the customers come, is a very private place. I hear the announcement for "Cast On-Stage" and promptly, very promptly, the Company assembles, in or out of makeup, many already into, or half-into, costumes. Most of them cluster stage-right near the wings, like a very large family on a Christmas morning. They are all trying, like myself, to grow up into artists. Some sit. Butch Blake and Douglas Rain. Most of them stand, including William Hutt, in a tired actor's robe, a most untiring actor with the very long, very pale, wonderfully alive face of Lear's Fool. Peter, still in his street-trousers, is one of the first to shuffle, happily, out from the wings.

I'm thinking, not for the last time, of what Yeats meant when he said that Hamlet and Lear are gay. In the last lines of *Lapis Lazuli*, looking on those "chinamen" on their way up their mountain, he had seen that, in defiance of everything that lay ahead, in the unique solitude and solidarity they all shared, that 'Their eyes, their eyes, their ancient glittering eyes are gay.'

Robin, characteristically, on such occasions, has little to say. There'll be a "little extra music before the start tonight." A few bars of 'O, Canada', a few bars of 'The Queen'. Anyone who needs to remain in their own special imaginations, he suggests, can close their ears, if they need. At the end of the show, the Lieutenant-Governor, Pauline McGibbon, "a very nice lady," will be introduced to the front row. "You call her 'Your Honour'," says Robin.

Other than wishing them all to have a good show, he has only one thing to add.

"Please, to remember, in all your care of Peter, as in Peter's care of all of you, *all* that you said, all that you thought, on that first day of rehearsal."

There is applause from the stage of the silent theatre, before the Company return to the dressing rooms. I may return to the wings tonight, much later, to hear the applause from out there in the audience. But this is the moment I've chosen to go.

As I walk from the theatre, one of my friends (coming to see the show) who had urged me to write all of this, seeing me go, concluded, being as Irish as myself, that I'd kept the appointment. It was a good guess. The job is done.

END PAGES

A wholly untraditional *Lear,* but one that fulfils the expectations of the traditional reading — and then some. The production owes its originality and power to Peter Ustinov as Lear. — FRANK LIPSIUS, *Finanical Times,* LONDON, ENGLAND

Peter Ustinov's performance is a spectacle of greatness reduced to very little ... He is as believable as next year's tax increase, but not nearly so tragic. His Lear lacks point ... the message, whatever it is, gets scrambled in the transmission. — DOUG BALE, *London Free Press,* ONTARIO, CANADA

He still surprises me ... He is one of the funniest Lears I have ever seen — and, moreover, he meant to be funny. Ustinov consistently provides a tragic edge of unlocated loss to his clowning ... He really is fantastic. I did not like his Lear as a whole, but I loved some aspects of it, and I would never have missed it ... Emotionally outrageous, intellectually persuasive, and providing an unanswerable answer to the conundrum of Lear ... It is claimed that every ticket until the end of the season is sold. Personally I never believe such claims, but here it seems terribly likely ... The play has been placed, most awkwardly, in mid-Victorian times, a vain conceit if ever there was one because instead of making Lear universal it ties the play down to most unlikely circumstances. — CLIVE BARNES, *New York Post*

Ustinov was uneasy ... Where his preview performance had been letter-perfect and had come off without hesitation, on opening night he kept losing his lines and at times he was even paraphrasing his speeches. It is a measure of his commitment to the theatre that a man of his experience and renown should have been that nervous about his performance, ... The music of Berthold Carriere attracts attention to itself needlessly; the mid-nineteenth-century setting by Daphne Dare adds surprisingly little to one's awareness of the text; the lighting of Michael J. Whitfield is erratic. A Production which will bring many new to Shakespeare into the theatre. As such it must be welcomed. As an interpretation of Shakespeare's greatest tragedy, however, it leaves many of the depths of the play untouched. — JACOB SISKIND, *Ottawa Journal*

Ustinov is marvellous ... This *King Lear* is credible, audible and human. ... — ARNOLD EDINBOROUGH

Not the tragic Lear we want to relate to ... Daphne Dare's nineteenth-century costumes confuse and tend to dilute the play's classical nature. ... — MARTIN STONE, *Canadian Tribune*

The final preview, which I attended, was greeted with an ovation. The opening night was a little more blasé ... but of Ustinov's survival there is no doubt ... You'll never see a Lear like this again ... Yet Ustinov never surrenders his carefully constructed Lear to the madness of Shakespeare's poetry. He's always chopping the anarchic images to size. — GINA MALLET, *Toronto Star*

An honest Lear, but, I fear, too light, too naturalistic, not nearly massive, resonant or archetypal enough ... On balance, I find this Victorian *Lear* cripplingly superficial. — JAY CARR, *Detroit News*

On balance, this is a Lear which takes life from its star, but which loses much of its cohesion as a play on that same account. The King Lear created by Peter Ustinov and Robin Phillips ... is a continual thrusting up of new images — often moving, often gratifying, and sometimes failed and tedious. — RAY CONOLOGUE, *The Globe and Mail*, TORONTO

One of the best, if not the best production ever seen at Stratford. Ustinov is seen in a luminous performance. By lifting the actors out of the customary skins of the Dark Ages and putting them into the costumes of the mid-nineteenth century Phillips has sharpened the visual focus for modern audiences and clarified the intellectual force of the play. — MAC KENZIE PORTER, *Toronto Sun*

Stratford's shrewd Artistic Director, Robin Phillips, who is as calculating as they come, has calculated strangely with his first Canadian *Lear*. Defying custom, he has updated the tragedy of the ancient king of Britain into a Continental 1860. The production is a prisoner of Robin Phillips. His updating — by an incredible 2,600 years — confines *Lear* to literalness. Ultimately, Stratford's and Ustinov's *King Lear* is a boulevard tragedy done popular-style, with a great deal of directorial and ensemble artistry, as if it were best O'Neill, or second best Molner. — LAWRENCE DE VINE, *Detroit Free Press*

A production of remarkable narrative clarity. The ensemble qualities of the production are always satisfactory, sometimes outstanding in their ritualistic power. Phillips has disdained the customary procedure of distancing us from it by placing it in primitive times, and instead has transferred it into a sombre, nineteenth century — his favourite setting when he wishes to rethink one of Shakespeare's more troublesome plays and give it more focus. Ustinov has ensured that his conception is both fascinating and provocative ... this is a Lear which sees the moral universe as some sort of grotesque joke. — JAMIE PORTMAN, *Canadian Press*

For playgoers who expected Ustinov to meet the challenge of Lear, the production was anticlimactic. Ustinov's portrayal of the mighty ruler stopped short of the grand, larger-than-life and timeless proportions intended by Shakesepare. A further obstacle was the nineteenth-century Victorian setting chosen by Phillips ... While the debate continues over Ustinov's Lear, the misfortune has to be a loss to U.S. theatregoers. If there is anyone who can make Shakespeare commercially and mass appealing, it has to be Ustinov, especially in the context of Phillips' alterations, yet Stratford officials firmly denied any commitments to send it to New York City ... Certainly, Ustinov is the attraction ... It is unquestionably a theatrical treat. — *Saginaw News*, MICHIGAN

Ustinov and Phillips are shedding a luminous new light on *The Tragedy of King Lear* ... The unconventionality of Ustinov's Lear is upsetting the critics who have come to Stratford laden with the baggage of their preconceptions about the play. Reviewers from Detroit missed what they conceive to be Lear's "nobility," and were affronted by Ustinov's "doddering old man." In the text, Lear is in his eighties, a time when a man might be forgiven for doddering physically, surely. Ustinov's Lear IS distinguished by great nobility — but in the middle and later passages of the play ... There have been some objections, too, to director Phillips having changed the period of the play from Shakespeare's prehistoric, tribal England to the purportedly more civilized Victorian England of 1860, with visual reference in the uniforms, at least, to the Crimean War. I thought it suited the timeless play extraordinarilly well ... certainly more interesting to look at than the fake stone decor and hide-and-fur costumes of more conventional productions. Further, setting the play in a period known for its political and social politesse adds a deepening perspective as it probes down to the bone of human behaviour. Ustinov rises movingly to the play's great passages ... as powerful as Scofield, and twice as human. — EDWIN HOWARD, *Memphis Press-Scimitar*

Jim McQueen, Kent; William Hutt, Fool; Peter Ustinov, Lear and L. to R. as Lear's Knights: Patrick Christopher, John Lambert, Hank Stinson, Stewart Arnott, Geordie Johnson, Christopher Blake, LeRoy Schulz, Sean T. O'Hara, William Copeland, David Stein, Rex Southgate, David Holmes, Michael Totzke, William Merton Malmo. Seated: Lorne Kennedy and Gregory Wanless.

Richard Monette, Edmund;
Rodger Barton, Edgar.

L. to R. seated: Marti Maraden, Regan; Peter Ustinov, Lear; Donna Goodhand, Goneril.

L. to R. standing: Christopher Blake, Patrick Christopher, Rex Southgate as
Lear's Knights.

William Hutt as The Fool.

Richard Monette, Edmund;
Douglas Rain, Gloucester.

L. to R.: Marti Maraden, Regan; Donna Goodhand, Goneril; Barbara Stewart, Lady-in-Waiting; Ingrid Blekys, Cordelia and Edward Evanko, King of France.

Peter Ustinov, Lear and William Hutt, Fool.

Douglas Rain, Gloucester; Jim McQueen, Kent; William Hutt, Fool; Peter Ustinov, Lear and Rodger Barton, Edgar.

Frank Maraden, Albany and
Donna Goodhand, Goneril.

William Webster, Cornwall and Marti Maraden, Regan.

Foreground, L. to R.: John Wojda, Burgundy; Peter Ustinov, Lear; Edward Evanko, King of France.

Background, L. to R.: Frank Maraden, Albany; Douglas Rain, Gloucester.

Peter Ustinov, King Lear.

Robin Phillips, Director.

L. to R., foreground: Marti Maraden (seated), Regan; Ingrid Blekys, Cordelia; Peter Ustinov, Lear; Douglas Rain, Gloucester; Frank Maraden, Albany; Donna Goodhand, Goneril.

L. to R., background: William Merton Malmo, Gregory Wanless, Patrick Christopher, Alicia Jeffery, William Copeland.

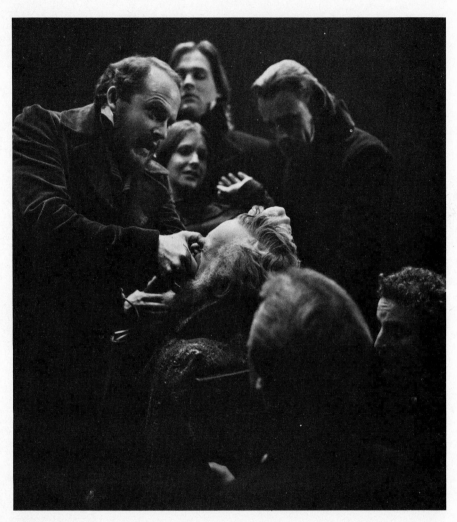

William Webster, Cornwall and Douglas Rain, Gloucester with (L. to R.) Marti Maraden, John Wojda, Patrick Christopher, Stewart Arnott and Christopher Blake.

Ingrid Blekys, Cordelia; Peter Ustinov, Lear; Richard Monette, Edmund.

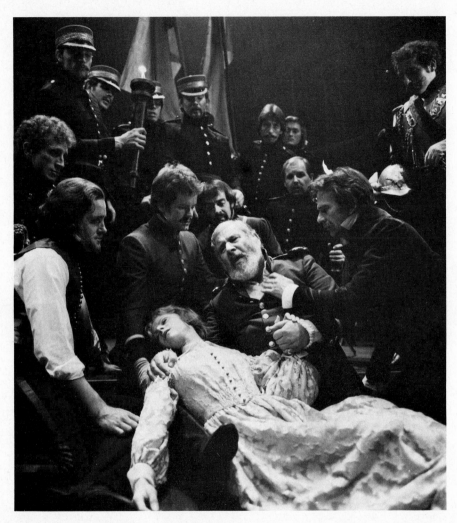

Peter Ustinov, Lear and Ingrid Blekys, Cordelia attended by Frank Maraden, Albany; Rodger Barton, Edgar; Gregory Wanless, French Officer; Rod Beattie, Doctor; Jim McQueen, Kent.

Background: William Merton Malmo, Michael Totzke, Lorne Kennedy, Sean T. O'Hara, Bob Ouelette, Geordie Johnson, John Lambert, and Christopher Blake.